Marcela Breton is a Colombian-born jazz and literary critic. She is the editor of *Hot and Cool: Jazz Short Stories* (Plume), and a regular contributor to *Jazz Times* and other publications. She lives in Danbury, Connecticut.

Rhythm
&
REVOLT

Tales of the Antilles

EDITED BY

MARCELA BRETON

A PLUME BOOK

PLUME
Published by the Penguin Group
Penguin Books USA Inc., 375 Hudson Street,
New York, New York 10014, U.S.A.
Penguin Books Ltd, 27 Wrights Lane, London W8 5TZ, England
Penguin Books Australia Ltd, Ringwood, Victoria, Australia
Penguin Books Canada Ltd, 10 Alcorn Avenue,
Toronto, Ontario, Canada M4V 3B2
Penguin Books (N.Z.) Ltd, 182–190 Wairau Road, Auckland 10, New Zealand

Penguin Books Ltd, Registered Offices:
Harmondsworth, Middlesex, England

First published by Plume, an imprint of Dutton Signet,
a division of Penguin Books USA Inc.

First Printing, July, 1995

10 9 8 7 6 5 4 3 2 1

 REGISTERED TRADEMARK—MARCA REGISTRADA

LIBRARY OF CONGRESS CATALOGING-IN-PUBLICATION DATA:
Rhythm and revolt : tales of the Antilles / edited by Marcela Breton.
      p.   cm.
   ISBN 0-452-27178-9
   1. Short stories, Caribbean.   2. Caribbean fiction—20th century.
3. Caribbean Area—Fiction.   I. Breton, Marcela.
PN849.C32R49   1995
808.83'1089729—dc20   94-47254
                                                          CIP

Printed in the United States of America
Set in New Baskerville
Designed by Eve L. Kirch

PUBLISHER'S NOTE
These stories are works of fiction. Names, characters, places, and incidents
either are the product of the authors' imagination or are used fictitiously,
and any resemblance to actual persons, living or dead, events, or locales is
entirely coincidental.

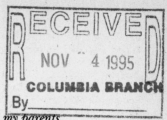
This book is dedicated to my parents,
John Jenkins and Lyll Becerra de Jenkins,
with love and gratitude.

CONTENTS

Contents

See it advance rising and falling on the pulverized wave
see it dance the sacred dance before the greyness of the village
see it trumpet from a vertiginous conch

Aimé Césaire
"Notebook of a Return to the Native Land"

The atmospheric or rather historic pressure
even if it makes certain of my words sumptuous
immeasurably increases my plight.

Aimé Césaire
"Lagoonal Calendar"

INTRODUCTION

I.

Rhythm and revolt are the two sides of the Antillean coin. The lulling waters of the Caribbean sea, the speech cadences of a storyteller, an Afro-Antillean griot, retelling myths and legends, the *bata* drums and chants of ritual and release in Santeria and voodoo, the *tambores* and trumpets of son and salsa, the tin pans of the steel band, the satirical songs of calypso, the lilt of creole and the cacophonous multilingualism of a region where native and tourist are in a constant state of flux; these are the exuberant, enigmatic strains of Antillean life. Slavery and indenture, their attendant revolts, independence from colonial domination, the rejection of bourgeois mores, the incendiary radical, the refugee fleeing political oppression, the insecurity and alienation resulting from a creole identity, the struggle against penury; this is the painful and compacted historical reality of the Antilles.

A tale conveys tradition and history while embracing a wide variety of literary expression including oral and written, extensive or brief. A tale offers a flexibility, an amplitude not found in the term *short story*. The word *tale* links us to the earliest narrative forms, where the teller entertains *and* bequeaths. What these tales bequeath are fragments of the Antillean experience. The most traditional of these tales is Seepersad Naipaul's "The Gratuity," with its simple, straightforward style. The least traditional is Reinaldo Arenas's hallucinatory "The Parade Ends." Lydia Cabrera's "The Hill of Mambiala" is the transcription of an oral tale from a time when the storyteller predominated, while Magali García Ramis's episodic "The Sign of Winter," with its use of taped testimony, signals the collapse of an authoritative narrative voice. Luis Rafael Sánchez's "Etc." denies its status from the first line. "Here it goes: a tale that's no tale because it just happened. . . ." A tale can be a capsule, Ana Lydia Vega's "Cloud Cover Caribbean," or a convolution, Fanny Buitrago's "Caribbean Siren." It is especially suited to stories from a region (W. H. Hudson's *Tales of the Pampas* are a good example). A tale evokes the folklore, history, and cultural stamp of a region or country.

The etymology of *Antilles* is ancient and shrouded in mystery. Aristotle referred to a great island of the Atlantic that the Carthaginians designated as Antilia. This mythical island figured in sea charts as early as 1424. The Florentine cartographer Paolo Toscanelli assigned the name Antille to a large island on a theoretical map in 1474, and in 1493 the name Antilia was applied to the West Indies by Pietro Martire d'Anghiera. It is believed that the Antilles are the emergent portions of an underwater mountain range. The name Antilles provokes thoughts of a submerged past, of dim origins, a place at once imaginary and real.

Caribbean is the colonizers' nomenclature. The Caribbean was named for the Carib Indians, who, along with the Arawaks, inhabited the Antilles at the time of the Spanish conquest. The original name for the Caribs was Galibi. This became corrupted by the Spanish to Canibal and gave rise to the English word *cannibal*. The terms Caribs and Canibals became interchangeable when referring to the native population. Caribbean smacks of the travel brochure, the tourist who cares only for sun and sea and remains ignorant of the cultural, social, and political realities of the islands.

To say "I am Antillean" communicates a state of mind, the recovery of a self-determined historical identity. Like the term African American, Antillean echoes pride and nationalism. It acknowledges the diversity of these island nations but also their link to one another. The Cuban singer Celia Cruz sings, *"soy An-*

tillana, no puede haber definición, no puede haber separación." She declares her singularity as a Cuban *and* her solidarity with those who come from other Antillean islands. To be Antillean is to participate in a shared consciousness. Derek Walcott has written that "Antillean art is the restoration of our shattered histories, our shards of vocabulary, our archipelago becoming a synonym for pieces broken off from the original continent."[1]

The Antilles comprise the Greater Antilles (Cuba, Jamaica, Haiti, the Dominican Republic, and Puerto Rico), the lesser Antilles (Leeward Islands, Windward Islands, Trinidad and Tobago, Barbados), the Netherlands Antilles, the French West Indies, made up of Guadeloupe and dependencies, and Martinique. The South American countries of Guyana and Suriname are culturally connected to the Caribbean, as are coastal Colombia and Venezuela and their dependent islands.

The following islands and nations figure in the present anthology: Cuba, Puerto Rico, Haiti, the Dominican Republic, Jamaica, Trinidad, Martinique, Guyana, Antigua, Dominica, Colombia, and Suriname. Every anthology is selective and personal. When confronted with an area as scattered, various, and linguistically complex as the Caribbean, selectivity is by definition more rigorous.

While these islands and nations differ from one another in historical, linguistic, and cultural elements, they nevertheless share points of reference, converging destinies, and common difficulties that embolden the anthologist to compile a collection of Antillean short stories. The themes that occupy Antillean fiction include: the dominance of sugarcane as a cash crop; slavery and indenture, including the migration of East Indian, Chinese, and Lebanese laborers; colonialism; the persistence of African rituals and rhythms; creole or patois; the indigenist and negritude movements; isolation and alienation; humor; poverty; political instability and revolution; tourism; emigration and exile, including the significance of such major cities as London, Paris, Madrid, Toronto, Montreal, New York, and Miami.

II.

Puerto Rican Luis Rafael Sánchez, author of *La Guaracha del Macho Camacho* [Macho Camacho's Beat], has written that "music, blackness, and wandering define the Caribbean."[2] To these I would add humor and what Milan Kundera has termed the "mediating context" of the Caribbean. Writing of Martinique, he refers to "three mediating contexts: the French, or French-speaking, context; the contexts of African and worldwide negritude; and the Caribbean, Latin American, and American contexts."[3] This multiplicity of identities holds for all Caribbean countries, serving to enrich and complicate the sensibility of the Antillean storyteller.

Music is as central to these stories as is the backdrop of the Caribbean Sea. In Guillermo Cabrera Infante's "At the Great Ecbo," a young couple engage in Hemingwayesque dialogue and then find themselves divided upon witnessing an elaborate Santería ritual in praise of the Orishan god, Obbatala. The drum rhythms, chanting, and swaying threaten to intoxicate the young woman while the young man feels superior to what he terms a primitive rite.

"Black Sun" is Bernabé Quirindongo, a gifted drummer who pounds any surface he can find in search of the sounds he hears inside his head. Díaz Valcárcel's language mimics the sonorities of bongos and congas and brings to mind the rhythmic poetry of the Cuban Nicolás Guillén in poems such as "La Canción del Bongo" and "Canto Negro."

In "Hallelujah for a Woman-Garden," Haitian René Depestre's narrator sings the praises of his seductive Aunt Zaza in sections titled "cantos." His is a paean to youthful eroticism.

"The Singing Turtle" by the Marcelin Brothers is a Haitian folktale about a turtle that sings and, "picking up two iron rods, begins striking them against each other," a reference to the clave rhythm present in a number of Caribbean musical genres.

Samuel Selvon's "Calypsonian" offers an intimate, comic portrait of Razor Blade, a Trinidadian calypso singer down on his luck and living off the memories of former glory days when he was in constant demand during carnival.

Puerto Rican Ana Lydia Vega's "Cloud Cover Caribbean" uses humor, wordplay, and musical metaphor to describe the cross-purposes, antagonisms, and shared destiny of a Haitian, a Dominican, and a Cuban, adrift at sea on an ill-fated voyage to Miami. The native humor captured so well by Vega is a feature of

Luis Rafael Sánchez's "Etc.," Juan Bosch's "The Beautiful Soul of Don Damián," Lydia Cabrera's "The Hill of Mambiala," Lino Novás Calvo's "The Cow on the Rooftop," and Fanny Buitrago's "Caribbean Siren."

III.

Flight, exile, return, Sánchez's "wandering," are insistent realities in the Caribbean. The diaspora—European, African, Indian, Chinese, and Lebanese—that shaped Caribbean society threatens to dissolve it as its people flee poverty, political repression, and cultural apathy, settling in the large cities of the world in search of what they perceive is lacking on their island nations. For the Antillean writer, exile is less a choice than a destiny. Writing and emigration are indissolubly linked in the Caribbean. The writer settles abroad to avoid cheap editions and poor distribution, to enlarge the circle of readership, to participate in a community of artists similarly engaged, a community no longer isolated by geography and indifference, and to have his or her work validated by the larger world beyond the islands.

All of the writers included here have spent a significant portion of their lives in exile. The exceptions are Seepersad Naipaul and Fanny Buitrago. For the English-speaking West Indian, London has been the obvious choice. In the mid-sixties, London was the West Indian literary capital, home to such writers as Jean Rhys, Samuel Selvon, Michael Anthony, and V. S. Naipaul. The French and Spanish Caribbean writer has frequently looked to Paris and Madrid. This has been the case with Lydia Cabrera, René Depestre, Patrick Chamoiseau, and Guillermo Cabrera Infante. Miami has been home to Lino Novás Calvo and Reinaldo Arenas; Toronto to Dionne Brand; New York to Claude McKay, Jamaica Kincaid, Edwidge Danticat, and, naturally, all the Puerto Rican writers; Amsterdam to Thea Doelwijt. Some writers (Lydia Cabrera, Reinaldo Arenas, and Samuel Selvon) are exiles several times over: Cabrera in Paris, Madrid, and Miami, Selvon in London and Toronto, Arenas in Miami and New York. To speak of the Caribbean writer is to speak of a writer in exile.

In "Caribbean Siren," Leandro Palma's twin obsessions compel him to an "absurd untiring wandering around different

18f 304xt12ion,

Caribbean islands and coastal regions." Jean Rhys's "Pioneers, Oh Pioneers" looks at the culture shock experienced by an early settler in the Caribbean.

Jamaica Kincaid's "A Walk to the Jetty" addresses the ambivalent state of mind of a young girl as she prepares to leave her island for America.

"From the Ocean Floor," by the young Haitian writer Edwidge Danticat, uses an epistolary form to describe a harrowing voyage across the sea and the brutal political regime that compels such a journey.

Those who emigrate are separated from family and friends, and the effect of this separation is the subject of Lino Novás Calvo's "The Cow on the Rooftop." A Cuban actress, Rita, writes to her lover Chucho Moquenque, who fled thirteen years before. Her letters describe ration lines, informers, denunciations, reprisals. Her tone is ironic and recriminating. Novás Calvo weaves a masterly tale of suspense and humor.

The baroque and surreal "The Parade Ends" is a fictional account of the storming of the Peruvian embassy in Havana by Cubans seeking asylum, resulting in the Mariel boat lift. Reinaldo Arenas was a "Marielito," and this was his first story written in exile. The 1994 occupation of the Belgian embassy in Havana by over 100 Cubans hoping for political asylum makes this story particularly resonant.

Dionne Brand's "Sketches in Transit" explores the conflicting emotions of a group of islanders aboard a flight from Canada taking them home to attend carnival.

Thea Doelwijt's story "In Foreign Parts" describes the dislocation of a European couple who find themselves in a "foreign, sunny country" where the people speak their same language yet the flora and fauna assume Kafkaesque dimensions.

IV.

Slavery and indenture are the twin brutalities of the Antillean experience. The transport of African slaves and indentured laborers to the Caribbean to harvest sugarcane and do the work of the colonists was bitter and protracted. The aftermath of slavery and indenture has been not only poverty, racism, and a crushing inferiority complex but also an extraordinary linguistic and cultural syncretism, the African mixing with the European, Indian, and Asiatic. Slavery resulted in a diffusion of the African throughout the Caribbean, the blackness referred to by Luis Rafael Sánchez.

In Lydia Cabrera's "The Hill of Mambiala" we return to the roots of that syncretism in a legend of Afro-Cuban folklore. The mythology of the Lucumí, the name given to the largest group of slaves brought to Cuba, is the basis for the story, yet, as Fernando Ortiz, the great Cuban scholar has written, we must remember that these tales are the result of a collaboration between African folklore and its white translator. Cabrera's story reads as if it were spoken, echoing a time when narrative was oral.

Santeria and voodoo are the blending of African and Christian religious elements. One finds this blending throughout the Caribbean. Cabrera Infante's "At the Great Ecbo" offers a dramatic reenactment of a Santeria ceremony. Eric Walrond's "The Wharf Rats" is full of references to the "obeah man," or witch doctor, of Ashanti origin. The story serves as a microcosm of the Caribbean melting pot, peopled with an entire cross section of types; from Maura, of the Bantu tribe, to San Tie, a Chinese "half-breed." In V. S. Naipaul's "My Aunt Gold Teeth," it is the Hindu and Christian elements that are intermingled.

The Indo-Caribbean experience is further explored in Michael Anthony's charming and tender "Enchanted Alley," and Seepersad Naipaul's "The Gratuity."

The multiple identities that seduce the native of the Antilles make for a struggle toward self-definition that has universal relevance. The Caribbean is the meeting ground for the European, African, and Asiatic influences. The blending of these cultural threads has produced the quintessential hybrid, mestizo, creole, or mulatto identity. To be creole is to be invigorated by this complex and various heritage. It is also to be marked by a sense of alienation, self-consciousness, and inferiority, the anxiety of the outsider, or, as George Lamming has written, "To be colonial is to be in a state of exile." Magali García Ramis's "The Sign of Winter" explores this alienation in the character of Professor Antón Orlandi. The journey toward self-discovery, an understanding of one's roots and place in the world, is a fundamental human preoccupation. The Antillean experience, obsessed as it is with ori-

gins and place as signposts of identity, is a mirror of the universal
longing to comprehend who we are by establishing where we
come from.

V.

Caribbean literature is a twentieth-century literature. Before
an autochthonous literature could develop, the Caribbean writer
had to free himself of the cultural models imposed by the colonial powers, whether Spanish, French, English or Dutch. While
there are examples of an indigenous literature prior to the twentieth century (for example, the Cuban Cirilo Villaverde's 1882
novel *Cecilia Valdes,* and, in general, Cuba represents a divergent
case), the emergence of a native literature follows the emancipa-
tion of the slave, independence from the motherland, and wide-
spread education, leading to the appearance of a middle class,
which, in turn, produces an intellectual class. Jamaican H. G. de
Lisser's *Jane's Career* (1913) is frequently cited as the first West Indian novel where the main character is black. The Antillean
writer had to learn to locate literary inspiration in his native land
and people while also developing a means of expression appropriate to a description of this reality. "To write for the West Indies is to be forced to find an appropriate voice . . . and that such
a voice should be a voice from Here rather than an appropriated
voice from Elsewhere goes without saying."[4] The use of creole
serves to forge a "language that goes beyond mimicry and has the
force of revelation."[5] It is not a question of artificially injecting dialect for the sake of local color. Creole, like music, blackness,
and exile, is woven into the fabric of Antillean life, and its literary
use reflects this blending.

With the exception of "Calypsonian," written entirely in cre-
ole, the stories included here exhibit traces and echoes of creole
mixed with standard usage. This is the case with Claude McKay's
"The Strange Burial of Sue," Eric Walrond's "The Wharf Rats,"
Dionne Brand's "Sketches in Transit," Ana Lydia Vega's "Cloud
Cover Caribbean," and Patrick Chamoiseau's "Red Hot Peppers."
Virtually all of these tales contain elements of creole.

The development of the Antillean short story is inextricably
tied to the small magazines of the region, *Revue Indigene* (1927)

from Haiti, *The Beacon* (1931) from Trinidad, *Bim* (1942) from Barbados, *Caribbean Quarterly* (1949) from Jamaica, *Verbum* and *Origenes* (1944) in Cuba, and *Asomante* (1955) in Puerto Rico are a few of these. They provided an outlet for aspiring writers in a region where publishers were few, the activity of publishing fitful, poorly funded and equipped, and distribution non-existent.

For writers from the English-speaking Caribbean, the BBC radio program *Caribbean Voices,* which initiated broadcast in 1946, served to introduce listeners to the first great wave of West Indian writers, including Samuel Selvon and V. S. Naipaul.

VI.

In this anthology, I have sought to offer a panoramic sampling of Caribbean short fiction, with Eric Walrond's "The Wharf Rats" (1923) the earliest story and Edwidge Danticat's "From the Ocean Floor" (1993) the most recent. In arranging these stories, I have followed chronological, thematic, and stylistic exigencies. The stories lead into and out of one another and are clustered according to whether they were written in the same period in the history of Caribbean literature, are linked by similar themes, or share a narrative tone or point of view. In all cases the arrangement is not so much imposed as revealed.

These stories express specific island realities. They fulfill Gerald Guinness's mandate that Antillean fiction reflect local conditions. "I would rather have a talented writer tell me what it's like being a taxi driver in San Juan, or a dockworker, or a Dominican immigrant, or for that matter a present-day jíbaro, but one who buys his food with food stamps and visits his son in New Jersey twice yearly. . . ."[6] Magali García Ramis's "The Sign of Winter" explores the intrigues, betrayals, and disillusionments that permeate the academic community at the University of Puerto Rico, Edwidge Danticat writes of a Haiti awaiting the return of Aristide, and J. M. Sanz Lajara offers a satiric, mocking look at the Dominican military under the Trujillo dictatorship.

While many of the writers included here have established reputations—Jean Rhys, Claude McKay, Lydia Cabrera, Juan Bosch, Samuel Selvon, Guillermo Cabrera Infante, V. S. Naipaul,

Reinaldo Arenas, Jamaica Kincaid—others are new to American
readers—Seepersad Naipaul, Fanny Buitrago, Edwidge Danticat,
Thea Doelwijt, and J. M. Sanz Lajara.

A vexing challenge was locating translated works by writers
from the Dominican Republic, Haiti and the French Caribbean,
and the Dutch Caribbean. Although the Martinican Aimé Césaire was the first to use the term *negritude* in his monumental
poem "Cahier d'un retour au pays natal" [Notebook of a return
to the native land], Haiti was in fact the cradle of negritude. It
boasts an important literary tradition with such distinguished
names as Jacques Roumain, Jean Price-Mars, the brothers
Marcelin, Jacques Stephen Alexis, and René Depestre. Haiti's
writers have long been torn between writing in French for an
elite, primarily foreign, audience or in creole for a home market.
Haiti's status as the poorest country in the Western Hemisphere
with a literacy rate of 53 percent (contrast this with a 97 percent
rate in Trinidad and Tobago) further darkens the picture for
Haitian authors.

The Dominican Republic shares the island of Hispaniola with
Haiti. The severe constraints associated with publishing in the
D. R. make the prospect of wider distribution and translation for
markets abroad an idle, luxurious afterthought. Even in the case
of Juan Bosch, a prolific and internationally known short story
writer from the Dominican Republic, the number of his translated stories is few.

In the Dutch Caribbean the situation for writers is comparable
to that in Haiti. In Suriname, the literacy rate is 65 percent and
writers debate using Dutch or the creole Sranan-Tongo. In the
Netherlands Antilles, it is Papiamento that competes with Dutch.

Writing and publishing in these countries is fraught with
obstacles. In the light of these circumstances, one's admiration
for these writers increases. So, too, the hope that conditions
will improve and that a fostering context for literary efforts will
evolve.

These stories offer a particular perspective on life in the
Caribbean. They impress through local detail, language, and
landscape. Yet the particular is a route to the universal. The characters in these stories express universal longings, motivations,
and frustrations, grounded though they are in the specific reali-

ties of Antillean life. Readers will encounter the strange and recognize the familiar in these tales of the Antilles.

VII.

I wish to thank the following individuals for their generous assistance: Samuel Bandara of the Library of the University of the West Indies, Jo Derkx of the Royal Institute of Linguistics and Anthropology in the Netherlands, and Kal Wagenheim. I would like to express particular thanks to Nancy Griffin for her untiring support and counsel.

Works Cited

1. Derek Walcott, "The Antilles: Fragments of Epic Memory" (Nobel Lecture 1992), in *Dictionary of Literary Biography Yearbook 1992,* edited by James W. Hipp. Detroit: Gale Research, 1993.

2. Luis Rafael Sánchez, "Voyage to Caribbean Identity," *Review: Latin American Literature and Arts* 47 (Fall 1993): 20–22.

3. Milan Kundera, "The Umbrella, the Night World, and the Lonely Moon," *The New York Review of Books,* December 19, 1991, 46ff.

4. Gerald Guinness, "Here and Elsewhere II: Derek Walcott," in *Here and Elsewhere: Essays on Caribbean Literature* (Rio Piedras, Puerto Rico: Editorial de la Universidad de Puerto Rico, 1993).

5. Derek Walcott, "What the Twilight Says: An Overture," in *Dream on Monkey Mountain and Other Plays* (New York: Farrar, Straus & Giroux, 1970).

6. Gerald Guinness, "Contemporary Puerto Rican Fiction: An Outsider's View," in *Here and Elsewhere: Essays on Caribbean Literature* (Rio Piedras, Puerto Rico: Editorial de la Universidad de Puerto Rico, 1993).

Cloud Cover Caribbean

Ana Lydia Vega

September, agent provocateur of hurricanes, signals for war, filling the seas with urchins and rays. Suspicious breezes swell the guayabera, makeshift sail for a makeshift vessel. The sky is a conga drum stretched tight for a *bembé* of the gods.

An ugly thing, this meaty arm of sea separating Antenor from the pursuit of happiness. The sharks don't amount to a pimple on a mosquito's ass beside the real dangers lurking. But he must muscle through. This is his second day amidst monotonous waves that seem to roll off of the clouds. Since leaving Haiti he has not sighted so much as a fishing boat. It is like playing discoverer while secretly wondering if the world is legitimately round. Any minute now he might confront the edge and drop into the fabled abyss.

The putrid mangos, emblems of diarrhea and famine, the war cries of the macoutes, the fear, the drought—it's all behind him now. Nausea and the threat of thirst once the meager water supply runs out—this is the here and now. For all its menace, this miserable adventure at sea is like a pleasure cruise compared to his memories of the island.

Antenor settled in beneath the broiling cauldron of sky. Between the boat's rocking merengue and his own weary body he could have sunk into slumber like an island village, and would have, had it not been for the Dominican shouting for help. You didn't have to know Spanish to understand that the man was shipwrecked and wanted a lift. Antenor helped him aboard as best he could. In that instant there came upon the little skiff a mocking, derisive spirit of the sort that inhabit the Caribbean tradewinds. So violent was its arrival that it nearly capsized the boat. At last they managed to quell it.

"Thanks, brother," said the man from the Dominican Republic, with a sigh of relief that moved the sail to pity.

The Haitian passed him the canteen, then almost had to tear it from his hands to keep him from drinking it all down. After some long exchanges of looks, mutually impermeable words and exhausting gestures, they reached the cheerful conclusion that Miami couldn't be far away. And each told the other, without either understanding, what he was leaving behind—which was very little—and what he was seeking. Then and there was spoken the royal pain of being black, Caribbean, and poor; deaths by the score were retold: clergy, military, and civilians were roundly cursed; an international brotherhood of hunger and solidarity of dreams was established. And as Antenor and the Dominican—his name was Diogenes, a neoclassical baptismal flourish—reached the very thick of their bilingual ceremony, new calls were heard to reverberate under the forbidding vault of the heavens.

The two of them raised their eyes to the waves and described the kinky hair of a Cuban bobbing along, hanging on to the proverbial plank of the shipwrecked sailor.

"A house full of screaming kids and grandma just had a baby," said Diogenes, frowning. The Haitian understood almost as if he had grown up on the Dominican side of the island. Another passenger, another soul, another stomach, to be exact.

But the Cuban howled so mightily, and with such undeniably Santiagan overtones, that at last they yielded and pulled him aboard with a quintessentially Caribbean "what the fuck," as the boat began to rumba.

Despite the urgency of the situation, the Cuban had the good sense to ask, "You people going to Miami?" before taking hold of the Dominican's indecisive hand.

Again the quarreling picked up steam. Diogenes and Carmelo, which was the restless Cuban's Christian name, raised an unearthly ruckus. Antenor intervened from time to time with a meek "Mais oui" or a "C'est ça," when the fury of the moment called for it. But he did not for a minute enjoy the Spanish language monopoly on a vessel which, whether destined for exile or not, was sailing after all under Haitian colors.

With Diogenes carrying counterpoint, and with a discreet touch of Haitian maracas for backup, Carmelo related the misadventures which had driven him from the shores of the Greater Antilles.

"I'm telling you, my friend, it was work, work, work day and night, no matter where you turned your head . . ."

"Hey, in Santo Domingo there wasn't any work to be had . . ."

"It was cut that cane, boy, day in, day out."

"Hey, man, where I'm from they bring in all the madamos from Haiti to do the cutting. The rest of us can lie there and rot for all they care."

The Haitian twitched. The Dominican had mentioned his half of the island, albeit at supersonic speed. He said nothing. Better not rock the boat any further; it was already giddy with the slaphappy rocking of the waves.

"I'll tell you, boy, there is always a stirfry of trouble somewhere," said the Cuban, initiating with this unhappy choice of words a search for food.

In a shoebox inherited from a trashbasket in a rich neighborhood, Antenor had put some cassava bread, two or three ears of corn, a pack of tobacco and a bottle of rum, staples which he had gathered for the voyage with the greatest of difficulty. Lest one charitable act overshadow another, he had taken the precaution of sitting on the box. But a major in black marketeering had given the Cuban a keenly developed sense of smell.

"Nigger, come up off that box," he said, eschewing formality and eyeballing the shoebox as if it were the very Ark of the Covenant.

Antenor pretended not to hear, though Carmelo's intentions were plainly polyglot.

"Get out of there, madamo, 'cuz it stinks of rum and tobacco," Diogenes translated, quickly forgetting the vows of mutual aid spoken with his fellow islander prior to the Cuban's arrival.

Still Antenor played dumb. Our undisputed world record illiteracy rate might pay off here, he thought, assuming the most vacant attitude possible in the face of his brother's demands.

Their impatience growing and their indignation rising at Antenor's passive resistance, they at length administered him one tremendous shove, which nearly sent him overboard on an underwater voyage. And they fell upon the box as if here, indeed, were the celebrated Horn of Plenty.

After eating the cassava bread and the corn, the two rogues renewed their comparative socio-economic analysis of the Caribbean nations. Carmelo chewed while Diogenes cocked an elbow, relishing the rum as though ogling the Statue of Liberty's charms under her threadbare tunic.

"I plan to go into business in Miami," said Carmelo. "I have a cousin who started out as a lowly pimp and now has his own, well, dating service."

"The land of opportunity," the Dominican concurred, his rum-fogged breath hot in the Haitian's face.

Antenor had not let out a peep since they had put him in quarantine. But his eyes were two black dolls pierced through by enormous needles.

"In Cuba," Carmelo went on, "dating services are banned, you know. Now, tell me, how is a person supposed to live with all that restriction?"

"Hey, in the Dominican Republic there's so many whores that we have to export them," rejoined Diogenes with a guffaw of such explosive resonance that it scared a shark that was trailing fuse-like behind the boat.

"Tout Dominiken se pit," grumbled Antenor from his little Fort Allen, which remark Diogenes, fortunately, did not hear, immersed as he was in more ponderous concerns.

"The problem," Carmelo said, digging deeper, "is that in Cuba the women think they are equal to the men and, you know, they don't want to get out and work the streets."

"That may be true now, but the Cuban women used to put out with the best of them," said his friend, recalling the internationally renowned rear ends of Cuban women.

The nostalgic allusion to the Batista era was none to the liking of Carmelo, and the Dominican's line of conversation was getting under his skin. Thus out of nowhere he parried, "Anyway, how is Santo Domingo looking since the hurricane? People who know the city say you can't tell the difference." He capped his dubious joke with a laugh that could be heard back in Guantanamo.

The Dominican went pale—no small accomplishment—but chose to contain his wrath in deference to the Cuban passenger's formidable biceps, the fruit, no doubt, of the accursed cane cutting.

Masking his change of mind, he searched for the canteen. The sea was in open revolt and the boat was rocking like a mambo's hips in Dambala worship. The canteen rolled to Antenor's inconvenient feet. The Dominican challenged. Antenor grappled with him. The Cuban smiled, following the struggle with the benign condescendence of an adult watching children quarrel.

Just then it began to drizzle. The wind, the waves and the great Antillean brawl conspired in that ill-fated boat to rekindle the hopes of the shark. They might as well have been going to China.

The Haitian threw the canteen into the water. Better to die than to quench the thirst of a Dominican cur. Diogenes bolted up, aghast. That's to remind you that we invaded you three times, Antenor thought as he bared his teeth to his countryman.

"Trujillo was right," the Dominican lowed, charging the Haitian's belly like a raging bull.

The boat looked like a patron saint's day float on the loose. Carmelo at last emerged from his indifference and gave notice, "Easy does it, gentlemen, c'mon goddamnit, we're going to capsize the boat."

And capsize it they did, quite as the future Miami businessman had prophesied. Capsized and rained on, with wind and thunder for background music and the wholesome enthusiasm of the sharks.

But in the precise instant in which our heroic emigrees might have succumbed to the perils of the Bermuda Triangle, there came the deep raw droning sound of a horn, like the chant of a priest at a politician's requiem.

"A boat!" cried Carmelo, waving his arm wildly about like a sadist with a cattle prodder.

The three unfortunates united their voices in a long, shrill, hopeful cry for help.

Sometime later—and don't ask me how the hell they kept the

sharks at bay; clearly it was a joint miracle involving the Virgin of Altagracia, the Caridad del Cobre and the Seven African Powers—they lay rescued, tired but content, on the deck of the boat. On the deck, that is, of the American boat.

The captain, an Aryan and Appolinean sea dog of ruddy complexion, golden hair and very blue eyes, drew near for a quick verification of the disaster and said, "Get those niggers down there and let the spikes take care of 'em." Words which our untutored heroes did not understand as well as our more literate readers will. Whereupon the Antilleans were taken, sans tender loving care, into the ship's hold, in which, amidst wooden crates and moldy trunks, they exchanged their first post-wreck glances: a blend of relief and fright, sauteed in some lightly browned hopes.

Moments later the Dominican and the Cuban had the pleasure of hearing their mother tongue spoken. A little fractured, but unmistakable. Even the Haitian welcomed the sound. He seemed to recall it from his tenderest childhood memories and was beginning to suspect he would hear it for the rest of his life. The parched lips of each man in the trio were bending northward into a smile when a Puerto Rican voice grumbled through the semi-darkness.

"If you want to feed your belly here, you're going to have to work and I mean work hard. A gringo don't give anything away. Not to his own mother."

And he handed them dry clothes on the end of his black arm.

TRANSLATED BY MARK MCCAFFREY

The Singing Turtle

*Philippe Thoby-Marcelin
and Pierre Marcelin*

On the bank of the river where he lived, a turtle was quietly warming himself in the sun, when a flock of birds flew overhead.

"Where are you going?" asked the turtle.

"Over to Tonton Jean's garden to harvest the millet," the birds boldly replied.

And they invited the turtle to go along on the expedition.

"I would very much like to join you," he said, sighing, "but, alas, I have no wings! If Tonton Jean should catch us in his garden, you'll get away without any trouble, but I . . ."

"We'll give you wings," said the birds.

They all pulled a few of their feathers and gave them to the turtle, who fastened them to his shoulders with mud and took flight along with them. Finally they reached Tonton Jean's garden and began to fill their bags with millet. The turtle, who was a good musician, made up a very entertaining song to encourage his comrades in their work:

> *"Tonton Jean planted millet,*
> *So the birds could eat it,*
> *Waya, waya!*
> *Tonton Jean planted millet,*
> *So the birds could eat it,*
> *Waya, waya . . ."*

After a while the turtle took off his wings because they hindered his movements and he lay them on a stone so that, in case of danger, he could easily get them again. Then, picking up two iron rods, he began striking them against each other:

> *"Ting ti-ting ting,*
> *Ting ti-ting ting,*
> *Ting ti-ting ting . . ."*

And the birds joined in the song with him:

> *"Tonton Jean planted millet*
> *So the birds could eat,*
> *Waya, waya . . ."*

The harvesting was going along very well and their bags were three-quarters full when one of the robbers who was on the lookout sounded the alarm: "Here comes Tonton Jean: let's fly away, quick, my friends!"

All the birds flew away with their bags, while the turtle, who went to get his wings to fasten them on his shoulders again, was horrified to see that the sun had dried the mud. He tried to get away on foot. Alas! he had gone only a little way when Tonton Jean caught up with him. But, being clever, he began singing a very sad ballad:

> *"Colico, Tonton Jean, oh!*
> *If I still had wings,*
> *I would have flown away.*
> *It is really a shame,*
> *I no longer have them!*
> *The pigeon gave me feathers,*
> *The guinea hen gave me feathers,*
> *The duck gave me feathers,*
> *And the hen gave me some, too!*
> *Colico, Tonton Jean, oh!*
> *If I still had wings,*
> *I would have flown away.*
> *It is really a shame,*
> *I no longer have them!"*

Tonton Jean could not believe his ears. To make sure he had not been tricked, he asked the turtle to sing his song once more. You may be sure the turtle was glad to oblige. And when he finished singing, Tonton Jean took him home and carefully put him in a big earthenware jar. Then he went to the marketplace of the nearby town, where he publicly boasted about his great discovery. Everyone took Tonton Jean for a liar, but that was exactly what he expected.

"Who wants to bet that I don't have a singing turtle?" he asked in a provocative way.

At that very moment the king happened to pass by. He ordered his carriage stopped and asked the crowd what was going on. They explained that Tonton Jean claimed he had a turtle that could sing and was challenging all who did not believe him to bet he was not telling the truth.

"This man is an impostor," said the king to the dignitaries accompanying him.

Then, addressing Tonton Jean, "I bet two hundred dollars that you are lying."

"I am only a poor peasant," said Tonton Jean. "How can I bet such a big sum of money?"

"It doesn't matter," replied the king. "If you lose, I'll have you thrown in the river with a stone around your neck."

Meantime, Sor Mise—that was the name of Tonton Jean's wife—hearing that her husband had found a singing turtle, ran home as fast as she could. She uncovered the jar and asked the turtle to sing something for her.

"I can sing only on the riverbank," replied the turtle.

"Very well!" said Sor Mise.

And she took him to the riverbank.

"You'll have to wet my feet," said the turtle.

"Very well!" said Sor Mise.

And she leaned over the water to wet the turtle's feet. But the animal slipped out of her hands and plunged into the river, where he disappeared like lightning.

At that very moment, paf! a silly toad fell to the ground a few feet away from Sor Mise, who, in her disarray, asked him: "Can you sing?"

"Yes," answered the toad, puffing out his chest.

"Then sing something for me," said Sor Mise sweetly.

And our toad started in with his lips all puckered up:

> "*Ah!... Oh!... Oh!... Of!...*
> *Ah!... Oh!... Oh!... Of!...*"

"Sing something else for me," begged Sor Mise. "A real song, a very, very pretty one!"

But the toad, imperturbable, started up again:

> "*Ah!... Oh!... Oh!... Of!...*
> *Ah!... Oh!... Oh!... Of!...*"

"Brother," said Sor Mise, despairing, "your song is absolutely worthless!"

However, since she just had to have an animal that could sing, she caught hold of the toad, took it home, and simply put it in the jar, hoping that when her husband got back she would come out all right by pretending she did not know anything.

But when the king arrived, followed by Tonton Jean, the dignitaries, and the whole crowd of the curious, Sor Mise, imagining the fatal consequences of her foolish action, fell face down in a faint. No one paid attention to her, not even her husband, who walked over to the jar in smiles.

"Brother turtle, my little treasure," he said gently, "sing something for our king."

And the little treasure self-confidently started right up:

> "*Ah!... Oh!... Oh!... Of!...*
> *Ah!... Oh!... Oh!... Of!...*"

"Get hold of that impostor!" said the king coldly, pointing to Tonton Jean, "and throw him into the river with a stone around his neck!"

It so happened that the turtle had a kind heart. When he realized he would be to blame if they drowned Tonton Jean, he came up out of the water and spoke to the crowd of people gathered around.

"Don't kill my poor master!" he said. "He did not tell a lie."

And since the king was wide-eyed with astonishment, he added: "The proof is, ladies and gentlemen, that I am going to sing you a little song of my own."

Striking the little rods against each other,

> *"Ting ti-ting ting,*
> *Ting ti-ting ting,*
> *Ting ti-ting ting"*

he sang:

> *"Colico, Tonton Jean, oh!*
> *If I still had wings,*
> *I would have flown away.*
> *It is really a shame,*
> *I no longer have them!*
> *The pigeon gave me feathers,*
> *The guinea hen gave me feathers,*
> *The duck gave me feathers,*
> *And the hen gave me some, too . . ."*

The king, marveling, listened to the song till the end. Then, apologizing to Tonton Jean, he counted out the two hundred dollars of the bet. But it was the last time anyone heard of a turtle singing.

TRANSLATED BY EVA THOBY-MARCELIN

The Hill of Mambiala

Lydia Cabrera

It was no secret in the village that El Negro Serapio Trebejos would do anything except work for a living.

He never ran out of excuses, reasons for following this calling. And since he had charm, a gift of the gab, and the guitar, it was hard in the end not just giving him what he asked for: especially since it seemed he asked for nothing. Small change for cheap tobacco and liquor, any leftover food and, once in a while, some old, worn-out clothes—as it was no longer possible to go simply naked.

The shack he lived in with his family had neither owner nor bill collector and, hesitating about collapsing once and for all when a strong wind blew or a storm picked up speed, was held in suspense. (There among palm trees, in front of the little hill of Mambiala, where the road twists in leaving the village and lowers like a reptile to the coast.)

Not complicating his life with anything beyond begging, there was food on the table regularly enough, praise the Lord, for him, his wife, and their children: two potbellied black girls, with their kinky hair tangled and full of lice—dirty, shiftless, forever sprawled out on a wobbly cot, already at an age to be earning their keep: and two long-legged black boys, ragged, troublemakers—without work, worth, or good intentions. In other words, the kind of people you could not count on to be up to any good.

But there came a time, a bad time, very bad—as never before imagined—and food was scarce for everyone . . .

No one came to the rescue of El Negro Serapio . . .

No one ever remembered seeing him cut sugarcane, hoe a piece of earth—or even plant a yam. In vain he now went about playing the guitar, improvising verses, holding out his hat that had been drilled by cockroaches . . .

"Why don't you go to work? There's no soup left and no more guarachas to dance. Lazybones!"

And the good housewives, lovers of justice:

"Tell El Negro—at the gate—don't let him in!—that today's leftovers are for the hens."

"Sorry, brother, come back another day."

Which is how he and his offspring began to feel the pain of hunger.

The little hill of Mambiala, which rose up not far in the distance—a light green, plush and round like an orange—was covered with pumpkin vines at the top. It was a pumpkin patch without pumpkins, and everyone knew that it bore no fruit.

For several days El Negro and his family had gone to sleep without a bite to eat, and one morning, a Palm Sunday, Serapio awoke dreaming that he had been placed inside of a pumpkin, as lucky as an unborn baby in its mother's womb; and with all his teeth intact, he bit down on the pulp, and the pumpkin started to jump and run, bouncing and screaming: "Help! Police!"—something was tickling her and it was driving her crazy . . .

"Could this be a sign from heaven?" El Negro asked, crossing himself. "What if I find Señora Pumpkin on Mambiala today!"

And after telling the dream to his family—feeling greatly comforted—he climbed to the top of the hill and spent a long, hard time searching eagerly. Leaves and stalks and more leaves! In all of that bushy, tangled, overgrown pumpkin patch there was not one miserable pumpkin; and there was no place left to search. He looked and looked until about twelve o'clock in the afternoon—the hour when other men were sitting down for lunch.

Serapio cried, begging to God and Mambiala. He went back patiently to explore the pumpkin patch from one end to the other, leaf by leaf, plant by plant.

"Give it to me Mambiala, Mambiala,
Oh, God, Mambiala!
Poor man that I am, Mambiala
Oh, God, Mambiala!"

"I'm dying of hunger, Mambiala, Mambiala!"

He was completely worn out, but before giving up he knelt down and, in one last effort, raised his arms to the sky. Remembering a picture that recounted a miracle, he started to cry it out to the heavens.

Heaven paid him not the least bit of attention. Not one pumpkin rained down on his head. At the height of his suffering, he dropped flat down on his face. When, after crying to the ground all the tears from his eyes, he picked himself up to leave, Serapio saw, there next to him, a little clay pot, on whose edges the sun reflected like damp gold. The most youthful and gracious ever to leave a potter's hands. So attractive that he felt happy and wanted to caress it . . . He spoke to the pot as if it were the most natural thing in the world that it understood him, and even more natural that it should be able to comfort him.

"Oh, how pretty, and round, and new you are! Who brought you up here? Some poor soul like me looking for a pumpkin?" Then he asked it, sighing, "What's your name, my little fat Negrita?"

The pot, moving its hips flirtatiously, answered:

"Me name is Dishy Good Cooking."

"Is hunger making me hear things?" thought Serapio. "Are you the one talking or am I two people, one sane and the other crazy, and both of us hungry? What did you say your name was?"

"Dishy Good Cooking."

"Well, then, cook for me."

The pot shot up in the air. It spread out the whitest of tablecloths on the grass, and with fine plates and silverware served a delicious lunch to the poor man who did not know how to use utensils other than his fingers; but he ate until he could no more and drank until he felt the hill of Mambiala sway . . .

And the hill became detached from the earth; it was a globe that was bounding up in gentle tumbles, through the deep azure,

higher each time, when El Negro, clinging to some foliage so as
not to fall, fell asleep . . .

When the sun began to lose its strength, Serapio put the pot
under his arm and went home.

His starving family was waiting. As soon as they spotted him,
they started to scream: "The pumpkin! The pumpkin!" But he
made a strange gesture to them, a gesture that none of them recognized—and what's more was difficult to interpret—which by
the time El Negro joined them, turned out to be negative. Dismay was painted on the faces of the luckless who had spent one
more day on sugar and water, trusting in the miracle of Mambiala; and they turned against Serapio, accusing him of eating it
by himself. Up there alone, taking advantage of the fact that no
one could see him!

Only the mother, a shriveled-up old woman who was indifferent to everything, did not move or get excited. She remained
nailed to her stool. Either hunger had turned her into a stick, or
she was made of wood. She was a long, hard stick, La Mama
Tecla. She never spoke. In a kind of confused way, she perhaps
grumbled to herself, or gave curt, unintelligible answers to someone whom only she could see, and who seemed to be bothering
her with useless questions. Even so, they basically must have
agreed with each other, as probably what Mama Tecla spluttered
out, looking impatiently out of the corner of her eye and moving
slightly her lower lip where an extinguished butt of tobacco
hung, was:

"You don't have to tell me anything: I know, I know."

Most of the time the old woman, so stiff and silent in her corner of misery, was only there like an object, expressing in its ab-
straction, intensely . . . nothing.

And no one paid attention to her; already it was asking a lot to
give her what was left—if anything remained—from a hodge-
podge of leftovers. The long, dry fingers of Má Tecla rolled
around the scraps, gave them the shape of a ball, and she swallowed mechanically, not bothering to taste or chew, with an indifference that reached the perfection of scorn.

"Go invite the neighbors—si, señor—to eat their fill with us tonight," ordered El Negro, showing them the pot with pride; but one of his daughters, the one who looked like she had the mumps, replied:

"Eat their fill of what? Rats? This was the last thing we needed. Have you heard? My father has gone crazy!"

And not one of his children obeyed him. Serapio had to go himself to invite the black folks of the village and get, where and how he could, some planks of wood and two sawhorses.

Some came to laugh, others out of curiosity; the guests did not keep their host waiting. In fact, many of them—people of good faith—who saw the table set up across the road with a clean, tiny, empty pot in the middle without a speck of food declared it an insult and wanted to leave without accepting an explanation.

It took a lot of effort for Serapio to gather everyone together . . .

"Chameleon's Banquet," said the limping Cesáreo Bonachea, who used to carry vats of food and was always in a good mood. "Open your mouth and flies enter!"

But then Serapio signaled the little clay pot with a "mofori-vale,"* and in a tender voice asked:

"What's your name?"

"Dishy Good Cooking."

"Well, then, cook for these people like you know how, you pretty thing, you."

And before anyone could recover from astonishment, the clay pot had covered the table with the most succulent and appetizing of dishes. Such chickens, stuffed turkeys and pâté! And what roasted hams, sausages, suckling piglets, vegetables, fruit, and all kinds of sweets. A never-ending supply of everything, and it was all excellent. The entire village ate, and there was no one who did not get drunk on the delicious wine that flowed incessantly from a tiny source at the bottom of each glass.

Dancing all night was inevitable; and the entire next day with its night.

One feast followed another, with the same lavish splendor at all hours. And so Serapio, from a beggar, was transformed into the beloved benefactor of the region. Even those closest to him

*Sign of respect that the blacks of the Lucumi sect address to their *aylochas* and *babaloas*—their priests and sorcerers.

now called him "Don" Serapio without realizing it. Together with the "Don"—and also along with his belly that was growing (worthy of a gold watch chain with a diamond stud)—the black man felt something new entering his soul and speaking to him in a language that was as obscure to him as the brief mutterings of Mama Tecla, who, by the way, remained nailed to her stool in the same silence, looking at them all with the same eyes—fixed, impassive, and hard.

Finally the affair caused such a stir that it became known throughout the five corners of the world. The newspapers spoke about it, and before the evidence of the miracle, the Pope made haste to send an encyclical to the pumpkins, prohibiting that they perform another one without his consent.

While at Mambiala, the little hill was left bald from all the pilgrims.

But the luck that suddenly comes to the humble man rarely does not go hand in hand with his downfall.

The very wealthy went to dine with Serapio, and at dessert one of them said—one whose beard was blackened with varnish like shoes:

"I'll give you one hundred and forty good hectares already sown with sugarcane for your clay pot."

"No, señor," answered Serapio. "With her I have more than enough sugarcane, and brown sugar, and cane syrup and everything sweet . . ."

"I," said another gentleman, belching with elegance, "would give you one of my coffee plantations."

"I," said the owner of the Company of Navigation, a very honorable slave trader, "would give you my schooner *Seagull*. There's not a more beautiful ship sailing the seas with an ebony cargo . . ."

And among the rich and ostentatious there was a millionaire—very much a usurer—a certain Don Cayetano, Marquis of Zarralarraga, who, so as not to lose an opportunity to make money, sold the hair, teeth, flesh, and bones of his dead relatives. In his head of rock, he was making calculations, adding and subtracting while he was eating . . .

"I," said Zarralarraga, dreaming to himself about having a monopoly on world food, "offer you . . . one million pesos for the Good Cooking pot, and not another centavo!"

When El Negro heard "one million pesos," he left running to find a notary public whom, in a short while, he had dragged back by his shirttails. There and then the sales contract was drawn up. At the bottom of a sheet of paper, with a sun that looked like a fried egg, stamped and then crossed by a ribbon, Zarralarraga wrote his illustrious signature—thick letters ending in a point and a triple flourish locked in a belt of ink.

"Sign here, Don Serapio."

"The only problem is, I don't know how to write," said the black man, noticing this for the first time in his life. "And now that I think about it, I can't read either."

"It's not necessary. We're among gentlemen!"

And there you have it: the document was null and void. The Marquis of Zarralarraga, that same night, getting out of his coach, slipped on a mango peel and broke the pot; El Negro Serapio—who already envisioned himself surrounded by pomp and riches, in a three-piece suit, diamonds on every finger and all his teeth in gold, dashing off in a car by day, and at night sleeping on a feather mattress—was left as miserable as the day he was born.

In the course of the days that followed, bitter ones, as the memory of the good so badly lost was still fresh, Serapio looked back one morning at the little hill of Mambiala. His stomach had shrunk to the eye of a needle.

"Who knows," said Serapio to his daughters (the daughters who could have been dressed in silk and instead were barefoot in rags that unavoidably displayed their rear ends), "maybe Mambiala feels sorry for us and will do another little miracle! If I don't find a clay pot, maybe I'll find a pumpkin."

He climbed up the hill. By now there was no pumpkin patch. Just some poor blades of grass between the rocks.

> *"Oh, God, Mambiala!*
> *Mambiala, leave it for me, Mambiala.*
> *Poor man that I am, Mambiala*
> *Oh, God, Mambiala!"*

"I'm dying of hunger, Mambiala, Mambiala!" And he repeated his request, wailing, without expecting anything, when his big toe on his right foot tripped over a staff. A staff made from manatee, the skin of a sea cow.

"What's your name?" he immediately asked, pouncing on it, radiant with joy.

"Mistah Manatee, Good Distribution!" answered the staff in the gruff voice of a man with few friends . . .

"Well, then, come and distribute with me, Mr. Manatee."

Manatee instantly slipped out of his hands, and executing his duty with jealous zeal—Zúava! Zúava! Zúava!—gave him a beating . . . and would have finished him off if the poor black, after going down half of Mambiala under a hail of unerring blows, had not said to him between whacks, spitting out a piece of tongue, two molars and an eyetooth:

"All right, Mr. Manatee, that's e-nough!"

El Manatee stopped suddenly in midair and, calming down, stationed himself next to Serapio, motionless, awaiting orders.

"What will I do?" El Negro asked himself, perplexed, counting the lumps he had on his forehead. "I don't know if it's a good idea to introduce this Mr. Manatee to the family . . . (Yet, it would serve them right!) When I took Good Cooking home, everyone ate their fill and fattened up: neither I nor she skimped on anything for anyone. Isn't it fair that they also share in the beating?"

Down on the main road, the family was waiting impatiently.

They had warned the friends and neighbors. They were very sure, they felt it in their bones, that their father would not come back empty-handed!

"The pot, the pot!" they screamed, seeing that he moved toward them in a strange way that they did not recognize.

"Are we having guests over to eat?"

"Some."

"Go and tell the Mayor, the Judge, the Priest, the Notary Public: all of the authorities! That Mr. Zarralarraga who broke the pot. Don't leave anyone out, there will be enough for everyone; oh, and one more thing . . . tell the doctor and the owner of the funeral parlor!"

It was immediately known that Serapio had come back with another marvel from Mambiala, which gloriously demonstrated how God will protect a bum two times and that there is no reason to get discouraged, but follow the example and wait.

They got everything ready, just as he ordered, a long table in the road, while a crowd flocked in, anxious to witness Serapio's latest discovery.

The rich and ostentatious and all the leading citizens were the first to appear. Green with envy, they took their places, Zarralarraga in the seat of honor.

The rest of the riffraff circled the table, overjoyed, promising each other a banquet and then dancing. Serapio went back to hearing himself called Don Serapio, a garden wall of flattery and smiles.

("But it's not a pot . . . hmmm. They say that it's a staff," insisted an old woman; and wrapped in a cloak, she went back to her fleabag shack, remembering that she had left some beans on the stove that might burn.)

"Attention," Serapio cried out at last, placing El Manatee in the middle of the table. "Don't anyone move."

"Papa, I want ham!"

"Papa, some chicken!" asked the girls.

A wide-eyed hush, as everyone held their breath.

Serapio got as far away as he could.

He climbed up a tree. But no one could move away from the eyes of the staff. Hid among the branches, Serapio said, not without a slight tremor in his voice:

"You there, on the table . . . What is your name?"

"Mistah Manatee, Good Distribution."

"Well, then, distribute fairly, Mr. Manatee."

Pakata! Pakata! Pakata! Pakata!

The thrashing began. Zumba! Tumba! El Manatee beat and struck . . . Pakata! Pakata! was the only thing heard, quick and dry, everywhere and at the same time; stars of fire instantly broke out over the surprised heads. In less than a second, a whirlwind of blows had swept the crowd that escaped tooth and nail, carrying off their share of the feast by the barrelful.

The harshest blows rained on the ribs of the leading citizens; no sooner had the staff turned against whoever was closest than it had attacked someone far away trying to escape with their life on all fours . . . They fell in bunches, one on top of the other, bones broken and flesh opened like ripe pomegranates. And Serapio, up in the tree, shaking the branches with glee like his monkey forefather, was goading the staff on . . .

"Let the Mayor have it, Mr. Manatee, for all the fines he imposes! Hard, even harder; knock the block off the usurer! And the Civil Guard . . . right in the kisser!"

With the Authorities splayed out, their feet in the air and letting out their last groans, El Manatee went into Serapio's shack, where his children were hiding, crouched up in a ball around the imperturbable Mama Tecla. With each strike that Mistah Manatee landed, Mama Tecla said to the other—to her invisible friend—widening a little more her terrible white eyes:

"I know that already! I know it!"

The shack understood that that was the precise moment to collapse.

When Serapio saw everyone lifeless—the Marquis of Zarralarraga, with his mouth monstrously diagonal, his nose like an eggplant, one eye hanging like a tear, his head of rock a scramble of brains and chips . . . his four children in pieces, his old lady dead, sitting on her stool, erect among the debris—and still the glug glug of the blood that the earth kept sucking—he picked up his staff and walked away from the village . . .

"Don't you think we got a little carried away, Mr. Manatee!"

He wandered aimlessly all night long, leaning on his staff, led by his staff.

"Ay, Mambiala, some wonderful gift you gave me! I didn't ask for much, Mambiala, Mambiala! A poor man like me who never wanted to hurt anybody . . . making his way, just going down the road of hard knocks. What's left for me now? Send me . . . But not one of those parasites left to support . . ."

At dawn, the birds broke into song in the morning light of the trees. Serapio found himself seated on the edge of a well that exhaled its protected freshness, its smell of deeply hidden water, of damp stone untouched by the sun. He looked inside and the water signaled him.

"Yes," said Serapio, "it's better to rest!"

He let the staff drop inside the well, and threw himself after it.

This is the Well of Yaguajay.

The black women knew the story. They told it to their children who, enchanted by fear, went to throw stones into the silence at the bottom. With faces hanging inside, they spit in the water. Looking inside, looking, they would never tire of looking into the Soul of the well; at the Drowned One, whom they could not see, but who saw them, sinking ever deeper.

At night, the well would wake them; it was the Drowned One, who made the frogs sing in the hollow sockets of their eyes: and they would return to their dream body, attracted to the intense mystery—to the delight of fear—to look at him, to break, with another throw of a stone, the black sunken mirror, the pupil of his eye round like a plate. To spit, leaning dangerously over its darkness, into the calm, irresistible presence. The Well of Yaguajay at night! Then the Drowned One rose up in the still water; from the deep, the silent, he scaled the silence.

A deaf splashing that dissolved the fallen stars, and the Drowned One came back whole, two open and desperate hands, climbing up on the smell of mint leaves. The black women, who after dark did not go near the well, had seen it. Too late to save themselves, too late for their cries to be heard, alone in their dream at the well, the hands that appeared over the edge seized them, cold and hard like stone, and plunged them to the terrifying bottom of unspeakable secrets.

TRANSLATED BY LISA WYANT

Pioneers, Oh Pioneers

Jean Rhys

As the two girls were walking up yellow-hot Market Street, Irene nudged her sister and said: "Look at her!"

They were not far from the market, they could still smell the fish.

When Rosalie turned her head the few white women she saw carried parasols. The black women were barefooted, wore gaily striped turbans and highwaisted dresses. It was still the nineteenth century, November 1899.

"There she goes," said Irene.

And there was Mrs. Menzies, riding up to her house on the Morne for a cool weekend.

"Good morning," Rosalie said, but Mrs. Menzies did not answer. She rode past, clip-clop, clip-clop, in her thick, dark riding habit brought from England ten years before, balancing a large dripping parcel wrapped in flannel on her knee.

"It's ice. She wants her drinks cold," said Rosalie.

"Why can't she have it sent up like everybody else? The black people laugh at her. She ought to be ashamed of herself."

"I don't see why," Rosalie said obstinately.

"Oh, you," Irene jeered. "You like crazy people. You like Jimmy Longa and you like old maman Menzies. You liked Ramage, nasty beastly horrible Ramage."

Rosalie said: "You cried about him yesterday."

"Yesterday doesn't count. Mother says we were all hysterical yesterday."

By this time they were nearly home so Rosalie said nothing. But she put her tongue out as they went up the steps into the long, cool gallery.

Their father, Dr. Cox, was sitting in an armchair with a three-legged table by his side.

On the table was his pipe, his tin of tobacco and his glasses. Also *The Times* weekly edition, the *Cornhill Magazine,* the *Lancet* and a West Indian newspaper, the *Dominica Herald and Leeward Islands Gazette.*

He was not to be spoken to, as they saw at once though one was only eleven and the other nine.

"Dead as a door nail," he muttered as they went past him into the next room so comfortably full of rocking chairs, a mahogany table, palm leaf fans, a tigerskin rug, family photographs, views of Bettws-y-Coed and a large picture of wounded soldiers in the snow, Napoleon's Retreat from Moscow.

The doctor had not noticed his daughters, for he too was thinking about Mr. Ramage. He had liked the man, stuck up for him, laughed off his obvious eccentricities, denied point blank that he was certifiable. All wrong. Ramage, probably a lunatic, was now as dead as a door nail. Nothing to be done.

Ramage had first arrived in the island two years before, a handsome man in tropical kit, white suit, red cummerbund, solar topee. After he grew tired of being followed about by an admiring crowd of little Negro boys he stopped wearing the red sash and the solar topee but he clung to his white suits though most of the men wore dark trousers even when the temperature was ninety in the shade.

Miss Lambton, who had been a fellow passenger from Barbados, reported that he was certainly a gentleman and also a king among men when it came to looks. But he was very unsociable. He ignored all invitations to dances, tennis parties and moonlight picnics. He never went to church and was not to be seen at the club. He seemed to like Dr. Cox, however, and dined with him one evening. And Rosalie, then aged seven, fell in love.

After dinner, though the children were not supposed to talk much when guests were there, and were usually not allowed downstairs at all, she edged up to him and said: "Sing something." (People who came to dinner often sang afterwards, as she well knew.)

said Ramage.

." Her mother's disapproving expression made
.ore. "You can. You can."

and hoisted her on to his knee. With her head
est she listened while he rumbled gently: "Baa baa
have you any wool? Yes sir, yes sir, three bags full."

gun at the fort fired for nine o'clock and the girls,
ir stiff white dresses, had to say good-night nicely and
to bed.

perfunctory rubber of whist with a dummy, Mrs. Cox
rted. Over his whisky and soda Ramage explained that
ne to the island with the intention of buying an estate.
and as remote as possible."

at won't be difficult here."

I heard," said Ramage.

ried any of the other islands?"

went to Barbados first."

Little England," the doctor said. "Well?"

"I was told that there were several places going along this new
perial Road you've got here."

"Won't last," Dr. Cox said. "Nothing lasts in this island. Nothing will come of it. You'll see."

Ramage looked puzzled.

"It's all a matter of what you want the place for," the doctor
said without explaining himself. "Are you after a good interest on
your capital or what?"

"Peace," Ramage said. "Peace, that's what I'm after."

"You'll have to pay for that," the doctor said.

"What's the price?" said Ramage, smiling. He put one leg over
the other. His bare ankle was hairy and thin, his hands long and
slender for such a big man.

"You'll be very much alone."

"That will suit me," Ramage said.

"And if you're far along the road, you'll have to cut the trees
down, burn the stumps and start from scratch."

"Isn't there a half-way house?" Ramage said.

The doctor answered rather vaguely: "You might be able to get
hold of one of the older places."

He was thinking of young Errington, of young Kellaway, who

had both bought estates along the Imperial Road and wor
hard. But they had given up after a year or two, sold their la
cheap and gone back to England. They could not stand the lo
liness and melancholy of the forest.

A fortnight afterwards Miss Lambton told Mrs. Cox that M
Ramage had bought Spanish Castle, the last but one of the old
properties. It was beautiful but not prosperous—some said ba
luck, others bad management. His nearest neighbor was M
Eliot, who owned *Malgré Tout*. Now called Twickenham.

For several months after this Rampage disappeared and one
afternoon at croquet Mrs. Cox asked Miss Lambton if she had
any news of him.

"A strange man," she said, "very reserved."

"Not so reserved as all that," said Miss Lambton. "He got married
several weeks ago. He told me that he didn't want it talked about."

"No!" said Mrs. Cox. "Who to?"

Then it all came out. Ramage had married a colored girl who
called herself Isla Harrison, though she had no right to the name
of Harrison. Her mother was dead and she'd been brought up by
her godmother, old Miss Myra, according to local custom. Miss
Myra kept a sweet shop in Bay Street and Isla was very well known
in the town—too well known.

"He took her to Trinidad," said Miss Lambton mournfully,
"and when they came back they were married. They went down
to Spanish Castle and I've heard nothing about them since."

"It's not as though she was a nice colored girl," everybody
said.

So the Ramages were lost to white society. Lost to everyone but
Dr. Cox. Spanish Castle estate was in a district which he visited
every month, and one afternoon as he was driving past he saw Ramage standing near his letter box which was nailed to a tree visible from the road. He waved. Ramage waved back and beckoned.

While they were drinking punch on the verandah, Mrs. Ramage came in. She was dressed up to the nines, smelt very strongly
of cheap scent and talked loudly in an aggressive voice. No, she
certainly wasn't a nice colored girl.

The doctor tried—too hard perhaps—for the next time he

called at Spanish Castle a door banged loudly inside the house and a grinning boy told him that Mr. Ramage was out.

"And Mrs. Ramage?"

"The mistress is not at home."

At the end of the path the doctor looked back and saw her at a window peering at him.

He shook his head, but he never went there again, and the Ramage couple sank out of sight, out of mind.

It was Mr. Eliot, the owner of Twickenham, who started the trouble. He was out with his wife, he related, looking at some young nutmeg trees near the boundary. They had a boy with them who had lighted a fire and put on water for tea. They looked up and saw Ramage coming out from under the trees. He was burnt a deep brown, his hair fell to his shoulders, his beard to his chest. He was wearing sandals and a leather belt, on one side of which hung a cutlass, on the other a large pouch. Nothing else.

"If," said Mr. Eliot, "the man had apologized to my wife, if he'd shown the slightest consciousness of the fact that he was stark naked, I would have overlooked the whole thing. God knows one learns to be tolerant in this wretched place. But not a bit of it. He stared hard at her and came out with: 'What an uncomfortable dress—and how ugly!' My wife got very red. Then she said: 'Mr. Ramage, the kettle is just boiling. Will you have some tea?' "

"Good for her," said the doctor. "What did he say to that?"

"Well, he seemed rather confused. He bowed from the waist, exactly as if he had clothes on, and explained that he never drank tea. 'I have a stupid habit of talking to myself. I beg your pardon,' he said, and off he went. We got home and my wife locked herself in the bedroom. When she came out she wouldn't speak to me at first, then she said that he was quite right, I didn't care what she looked like, so now she didn't either. She called me a mean man. A mean man. I won't have it," said Mr. Eliot indignantly. "He's mad, walking about with a cutlass. He's dangerous."

"Oh, I don't think so," said Dr. Cox. "He'd probably left his clothes round the corner and didn't know how to explain. Perhaps we do cover ourselves up too much. The sun can be good for you. The best thing in the world. If you'd seen as I have. . . ."

Mr. Eliot interrupted at once. He knew that when the doctor started talking about his unorthodox methods he went on for a long time.

"I don't know about all that. But I may as well tell you that I dislike the idea of a naked man with a cutlass wandering about near my place. I dislike it very much indeed. I've got to consider my wife and my daughter. Something ought to be done."

Eliot told his story to everyone who'd listen and the Ramages became the chief topic of conversation.

"It seems," Mrs. Cox told her husband, "that he does wear a pair of trousers as a rule and even an old coat when it rains, but several people have watched him lying in a hammock on the verandah naked. You ought to call there and speak to him. They say," she added, "that the two of them fight like Kilkenny cats. He's making himself very unpopular."

So the next time he visited the district Dr. Cox stopped near Spanish Castle. As he went up the garden path he noticed how unkempt and deserted the place looked. The grass on the lawn had grown very high and the verandah hadn't been swept for days.

The doctor paused uncertainly, then tapped on the sitting-room door, which was open. "Hallo," called Ramage from inside the house, and he appeared, smiling. He was wearing one of his linen suits, clean and pressed, and his hair and beard were trimmed.

"You're looking very well," the doctor said.

"Oh, yes, I feel splendid. Sit down and I'll get you a drink."

There seemed to be no one else in the house.

"The servants have all walked out," Ramage explained when he appeared with the punch.

"Good Lord, have they?"

"Yes, but I think I've found an old woman in the village who'll come up and cook."

"And how is Mrs. Ramage?"

At this moment there was a heavy thud on the side of the house, then another, then another.

"What was that?" asked Dr. Cox.

"Somebody throwing stones. They do sometimes."

"Why, in heaven's name?"

"I don't know. Ask them."

Then the doctor repeated Eliot's story, but in spite of himself it came out as trivial, even jocular.

"Yes, I was very sorry about that," Ramage answered casually. "They startled me as much as I startled them. I wasn't expecting to see anyone. It was a bit of bad luck but it won't happen again."

"It was bad luck meeting Eliot," the doctor said.

And that was the end of it. When he got up to go, no advice, no warning had been given.

"You're sure you're all right here?"

"Yes, of course," said Ramage.

"It's all rubbish," the doctor told his wife that evening. "The man's as fit as a fiddle, nothing wrong with him at all."

"Was Mrs. Ramage there?"

"No, thank God. She was out."

"I heard this morning," said Mrs. Cox, "that she's disappeared. Hasn't been seen for weeks."

The doctor laughed heartily. "Why can't they leave those two alone? What rubbish!"

"Well," said Mrs. Cox without smiling, "it's odd, isn't it?"

"Rubbish," the doctor said again some days later, for, spurred on by Mr. Eliot, people were talking venomously and he could not stop them. Mrs. Ramage was not at Spanish Castle, she was not in town. Where was she?

Old Myra was questioned. She said that she had not seen her god-daughter and had not heard from her "since long time." The Inspector of Police had two anonymous letters—the first writer claimed to know "all what happen at Spanish Castle one night:" the other said that witnesses were frightened to come forward and speak against a white man.

The *Gazette* published a fiery article:

"The so-called 'Imperial Road' was meant to attract young Englishmen with capital who would buy and develop properties in the interior. This costly experiment has not been a success, and one of the last of these gentlemen planters has seen himself as the king of the cannibal islands ever since he landed. We have it, on the best authority, that his very eccentric behavior has been the greatest possible annoyance to his neighbor. Now the whole thing has become much more serious. . . ."

It ended: "Black people bear much; must they also bear beastly murder and nothing done about it?"

"You don't suppose that I believe all these lies, do you?" Dr. Cox told Mr. Eliot, and Mr. Eliot answered: "Then I'll make it my business to find out the truth. That man is a menace, as I said from the first, and he should be dealt with."

"Dear Ramage," Dr. Cox wrote. "I'm sorry to tell you that stupid and harmful rumors are being spread about your wife and yourself. I need hardly say that no one with a grain of sense takes them seriously, but people here are excitable and very ready to believe mischiefmakers, so I strongly advise you to put a stop to the talk at once and to take legal action if necessary."

But the doctor got no answer to this letter, for in the morning news reached the town of a riot at Spanish Castle the night before.

A crowd of young men and boys, and a few women, had gone up to Ramage's house to throw stones. It was a bright moonlight night. He had come on to the verandah and stood there facing them. He was dressed in white and looked very tall, they said, like a zombi. He said something that nobody heard, a man had shouted "white zombi" and thrown a stone which hit him. He went into the house and came out with a shotgun. Then stories differed wildly. He had fired and hit a woman in the front of the crowd . . . No, he'd hit a little boy at the back . . . He hadn't fired at all, but had threatened them. It was agreed that in the rush to get away people had been knocked down and hurt, one woman seriously.

It was also rumored that men and boys from the village planned to burn down Spanish Castle house, if possible with Ramage inside. After this there was no more hesitation. The next day a procession walked up the garden path to the house—the Inspector of Police, three policemen and Dr. Cox.

"He must give some explanation of all this," said the Inspector.

The doors and windows were all open, and they found Ramage and the shotgun, but they got no explanation. He had been dead for some hours.

His funeral was an impressive sight. A good many came out of curiosity, a good many because, though his death was said to be "an accident," they felt guilty. For behind the coffin walked Mrs.

Ramage, sent for post-haste by old Myra. She'd been staying with relatives in Guadeloupe. When asked why she had left so secretly—she had taken a fishing boat from the other side of the island—she answered sullenly that she didn't want anyone to know her business, she knew how people talked. No, she'd heard no rumors about her husband, and the *Gazette*—a paper written in English—was not read in Guadeloupe.

"Eh-eh," echoed Myra. "Since when the girl obliged to tell everybody where she go and what she do chapter and verse...."

It was lovely weather, and on their way to the Anglican cemetery many had tears in their eyes.

But already public opinion was turning against Ramage.

"His death was really a blessing in disguise," said one lady. "He was evidently mad, poor man—sitting in the sun with no clothes on—much worse might have happened."

"This is All Souls Day," Rosalie thought, standing at her bedroom window before going to sleep. She was wishing that Mr. Ramage could have been buried in the Catholic cemetery, where all day the candles burn almost invisible in the sunlight. When night came they twinkled like fireflies. The graves were covered with flowers—some real, some red or yellow paper or little gold cutouts. Sometimes there was a letter weighted by a stone and the black people said that next morning the letters had gone. And where? Who would steal letters on the night of the dead? But the letters had gone.

The Anglican cemetery, which was not very far away, down the hill, was deserted and silent. Protestants believed that when you were dead, you were dead.

If he had a letter ... she thought.

"My dear darling Mr. Ramage," she wrote, then felt so sad that she began to cry.

Two hours later Mrs. Cox came into the room and found her daughter in bed and asleep; on the table by her side was the unfinished letter. Mrs. Cox read it, frowned, pressed her lips together, then crumpled it up and threw it out of the window.

There was a stiff breeze and she watched it bouncing purposefully down the street. As if it knew exactly where it was going.

The Strange Burial of Sue

Claude McKay

"She's the biggest bitch in the banana walk, begawd she is," said young Burskin as he tossed down his three ha'pennys' worth of rum and set the glass down on the counter for another. "Sue Turner is worser than a bitch, I say, and says it to the wul'."

There were seven black and brown men in the grogshop, barefooted, with pantaloons rolled up over their knees and their broad gleaming machetes in their hands. All morning they had been chopping down bananas and wrapping them in the dried leaves, fine long bunches to be shipped abroad. And finished now, with money in their pockets, they were come to the grogshop for a drink before going to eat.

The young man who was vilifying Sue was a very freckled, foolish-faced mulatto, thick and able-bodied. He let flow his stream of vilification as if he were telling it to the hills and ravines, for the men in the place were clearly unsympathetic to him by their sullen silence.

Everybody in the village knew that Sue was free-loving. And there had never been any local resentment against her. She was remarkably friendly with all the confirmed concubines and the few married women, and she was a picturesque church member.

Customers drifted in and out of the grogshop, men dropping in for the midday swig, and even school children for a pint bottle for their parents and biscuits. And Burskin, like a mad red mule, kept on gnashing his teeth and telling all the intimate things that had passed between him and Sue.

Peasant matrons stopped to listen, and passed on, ashamed and afraid for themselves. Only the children found it funny. Burskin was really alone in carrying on that way.

Sue's house was not very far away down the hill on a slope of fat banana land running down to the gully. And at last the news reached her of what was going on up at the grogshop. Sue was a notoriously strong brown woman. She had wrestled with many of the men and pretty often came off victor. Only the dwarfish baker Patton had really put her down beaten with the jiu-jitsu tricks he brought back from Colon.

She tore up the hill to the grogshop; raging and jumping upon Burskin like a mad beast, she bore him to the ground and mauled him. Burskin was a strong-set fellow, but he was no match for Sue. And all the time she was mauling him he never said a thing. It was as if something in him was appeased by Sue's beating. When the grogshop-keeper and a couple of drinkers got her up his face was bloody, but his expression was contented and he went quickly on home.

The grogshop-keeper demonstrated his appreciation of Sue by setting up a round of drinks for all the people in the shop. Among them was Mrs. Sam Bryan, who congratulated Sue for giving Burskin sweet hell. The first and only child that Sue had, now a big girl, was for Mrs. Sam's husband. But that had not troubled Mrs. Sam nor the other children that Sam had outside besides the four with his wife. Mrs. Sam was famous in the village for having said she didn't mind what virtue her husband found in other women; he always had to come back under his own roof. And she and Sue were the friendliest of neighbors. Sue's girl lived sometimes with her mother, sometimes with her father, and was equally at home in both families.

According to the peasant-folk idea of goodness Sue was a good woman. Which means she was kind. Sue's mother used to be a "market woman." That is, she used to tramp to Gingertown twice a week on Wednesday and Saturday, the big market days, to buy provisions for the better-off peasant women who were pregnant or had young children or were otherwise incapacitated or did not care to go marketing. Sometimes she toted the goods in a large basket on her head, and when there were plenty she rode a hampered donkey. And from her various patrons she received enough for her own provisioning.

When Sue was born people called her the "market baby," be-

cause, they said, she was begotten on the market route and nobody, not even her mother, knew who was her father. As a little
girl Sue trotted along to market in the footsteps of her mother.
And when she grew up she did the same work. She even went farther than her mother—to the city market on drays which involved two to three days' going.

Sue was buxom and stout, and there was keen rivalry between
the draymen as to which would have her go in his dray. Besides
her market work she was good at nursing in time of illness, and
became the most favored nurse of the mountain region. Nearly
everybody who was sick wanted Sue as nurse, and she didn't
make any difference between those who could give her something and those who hadn't anything to give. It was while she was
nursing Mrs. Sam Bryan through a childbirth illness that she con-
ceived for Sam. But that and her notorious free-loving ways, especially with adolescents, had never diminished her popularity
among the peasant women nor made her any less wanted.

But it was a wonder, though, when Nat Turner married Sue. He
was a good-tempered quadroon and had never been reckless about
love or liquor or anything except perhaps hard and steady work. It
was his mother who courted his first wife for him and married them.

When the smallpox epidemic broke out in the village it laid
low Turner's mother and wife and little son. It was Sue who
nursed them while her own mother was also down. In those days
the peasants trooped to the town to get the medicine from the
distributing center, but they also wrapped the smallpox victims in
long broad cool banana leaves, waiting nine days for the change
in the crisis for better or worse.

There were many deaths in those close-linked mountain villages. Every day for three harrowing weeks there was a death, and
one day there were as many as five. Sue's mother went under, also
Turner's wife and his mother, but his little son came through.
And toward the end of her long nursing, after the death and burial of Turner's mother, Sue also became ill in his house, but it was
a slight attack that did not spoil her happy face, and when she became well the marks it left were just like friendly freckles.

She stayed on in Turner's house after the epidemic had
passed over, and after some months he married her, although
she would have lived with him all the same without privilege of

ceremony. But Turner was indeed a steady man, steadiest of the older young men of the mountain land, apparently undemonstrative and unemotional, and, knowing who Sue was, he must have badly wanted to hold her steadily by him so that she might not lightly quit one day for somebody else.

About as different as a teal from a lamb was Sue to the first Mrs. Turner. For his first wife Turner had seemed incapable of great emotion, but he became blindly attached to Sue. And there was no doubt that Sue was attached to her husband, too, for his fine husbandly qualities and the security she derived therefrom, his simple fidelity and the freedom with which she could carry on as before. And she didn't change, either, in her ways toward the village women. Her good-heartedness was now strengthened by material power. Turner had a dray and a hired drayman that went to the far markets with the peasants' provisions. And now when Sue went along she could afford to bring back her neighbors' provisions without charging anything. She still helped to nurse when she was needed, and many were the very poor village girls who got from her the rags to wrap their little bastards in.

The village bucks swapped rakish tales about Sue, withal they had a real regard for her. There was no malice in their gossip, as there was when the subject was the runted "free-for-all" black cat whom they also dubbed "Stinky-sweety."

One day an indiscreet relative was trying to broad-hint Turner about Sue's doings, and Turner remarked that he felt proud having a wife that was admired of other men. That remark provoked a great deal of peasant thinking and comment, and the folk were divided as to whether Turner was wise or foolish.

Burskin was not like the village bucks who ganged and played together and exchanged their adolescent experiences. He was a freckled, chestnut-skinned boy and was raised by his wrinkledblack grandmother. His brown mother had died before he could remember her.

He was never a playful boy, and was always sort of tongue-tied and comically grave. When he arrived at the age to leave elementary school he had made just half the classes that the average boy usually made. His father was ambitious for him and paid for a year of further study. But Burskin's head couldn't stand it. So his father took him to Gingertown, where he was apprenticed to a cooper's trade.

But after two years at it the master cooper said that Burskin would never learn the trade and he sent him home. Burskin returned to work with his father in the field. He was born for that. Heavy, patient, plodding, perfect for digging and planting in the soil. He was expert at clearing the land and limbing the trees.

Two years in the town had not drawn Burskin even a little out of himself. He was still the same. The lads used to tease him about his lack of interest in girls.

"Why no get you one stucky?"* he was asked. "Even Stinky-sweety. If you no know how, she wi' show you."

Burskin's father's sugar-cane field adjoined Turner's sugar-mill, and it was natural that Sue should notice her young neighbor when he returned from Gingertown. He was just at that curious age.

The Burskins had no sugar-mill, and always did their sugar-making in Turner's sugar-house. And it was while Burskin was engaged in this work that Sue grew interested in him, so withdrawn and heavy with his adolescent load.

Sue came down one day to supervise the sugar-mill and the house while her husband was occupied at home getting banana suckers to plant a field. Burskin's father was attending to the boiling down of the liquor into sugar, a hired woman was feeding the canes to the mule-drawn mill and young Burskin was bringing them in on a donkey.

Sue chatted a little with Burskin while he unloaded the canes in the mill-bed. Burskin had carried a bundle of the canes on his head, and Sue twitted him that it was a poor bundle and that she could tote one three times as heavy. And she offered to carry a few bundles for Burskin.

So when Burskin returned for another load, driving the donkey before him, Sue went along, following him down the foot-track leading to the Burskin field, half hidden by the long leaves of the cane growing on either side.

They reached the clearing where there was a heap of cane. Fat juicy lengths cut short for the mill. Canes of all colors: ribbon cane, black cane, governor cane, white cane, sukee cane. It was fine cane land, dark, loamy earth.

The cane-cutters, two of them, had piled up a splendid heap

*Sweetheart.

and were now cutting on the other side of the little brook that
sounded through the field. Sue and Burskin could not see them
over the tall canes, but the agitation of the long leaves as the machetes were laid to their roots indicated where they were. They
were singing in the island dialect:

> "Chop the sugar-cane, boy, O chop the sugar-cane,
> Chop it down, chop it down, chop it down.
> Sugar cake an' rum foh them people in a town,
> Gingertown, Gingertown, Gingertown.
>
> "Cockish liquor* sweet, boy, O chop the sugar-cane.
> Drink it down, drink it down, drink it down.
> Sugar cake an' rum foh them people in a town
> Gingertown, Gingertown, Gingertown."

The cutters made up new verses as they sang and from the
neighboring fields other voices came joining theirs.

Sue sprawled on the warm leaves swinged by the sun and chatted
with Burskin, while the donkey cropped the young cane shoots. She
was the kind of woman that could make a lad tell her everything
about himself without being self-conscious of doing it. Burskin told
Sue he hadn't seen a girl yet he wanted for a stucky and that he had
never been with one.

"Not even when you was at Gingertown?"

Burskin said no.

Their conversation lapsed awkwardly. Then Burskin remarked
that they had stayed overlong, and began loading the donkey. As
he loaded he exclaimed over a fine piece of black cane, saying it
was just what he wanted for his granny. For she had no teeth and
that piece of cane was soft and full of rich juice and could easily
be masticated by her gums.

"Gimme it!" Sue said.

"No, it' granny's. You got good teeth foh bite any kind of cane."

Sue sprang up, threatening to wrest the cane from the husky
Burskin. She grabbed at it and they closed and struggled to-

*A strong drink the peasants make from fermenting the juice of the
cane.

gether, Burskin warming joyously to it and making a low, cackling sound. Then Sue tossed him, and they rolled and rolled over
and over in the rustling cane leaves. And during a queerly quiet
moment their mouths came together and he felt a strange sweet
quivering awakening him to a new experience.

That week of sugar-making was the most delicious in Burskin's
life. The smell of the white cane liquor bubbling into hot brown
sugar in the huge boilers was sweeter to his nostrils than at any
other time. And he worked with a new zest, scooping up the
warm sugar out of the wide wooden cooler and ladling it into the
tins for the market. His grandmother felt a different sounding to
his walk in the house, remarked the changed expression of his
features, and knew that something had happened to him.

Soon Burskin became a constant visitor to the Turner home.
And besides his intimacy with Sue, Turner showed him every
friendly consideration. Turner habitually accepted any person
whom Sue liked. And as Burskin was quiet and hard-working after the manner of Turner, the men had much in common.

They went fishing and bird-shooting together. And every Sunday Burskin partook of the Turner family dinner. Sunday was the
great guest day of the village. And invitation to a good dinner was
much looked forward to from those who went to the weekend far
market and brought special edibles such as ham, cheeses, and
tinned things from the town.

From the beginning of his friendship with the family, whenever Burskin had to go to the far market with sugar or yams, he
went by the Turner dray. Sue went often with the dray instead of
her husband. And Burskin went as often as she did and he could
find stuff to sell. Sometimes it was very little that could have been
disposed of in the local market. But naturally Burskin preferred
to go to the far market always while Sue was going. Thus they often had the weekend off away by themselves, for the drays left the
mountain country for the town markets on Friday afternoon and
returned before dawn on Sunday. It needed an extra day when
they went to the city market.

More than any of Sue's other admirers Burskin was liked by
Turner, who treated him like a brother. Each helped in the other's
field work. Friendly peasants had a custom of lending days to one
another. And Burskin would lend Turner a day, cutting bananas

or planting yams, which Turner would return with his hired man when Burskin was clearing corn land or engaged in sugar-making. It was even Turner who suggested to Sue that she should sometime take a meal of home-cooked food to Burskin as a change from the rough field-cooked food, as his grandmother was too old to do it.

Turner never tired of Burskin and his constant visits, but they began to irk on Sue after a time. The close friendship lasted from the end of the October rainy season until Easter, when Burskin met a rival in the tall and shiny black Johnny Cross, who had arrived from Panama with eye-catching American-style suits and a gold watch and chain and rings of Spanish gold.

Johnny Cross was welcomed by many of the village families with fiddling and feasting. It was the night of one of the Easter-time tea-meetings in the village that Sue got off with him. It was a big admittance-free tea-meeting (so the village yard dances are called) and the revenue came from the sale of fancy cakes put up at auction and bought chiefly by the bucks for their sweethearts. At these meetings there were two special cakes, one formed like a crown and the other like a gate, symbolizing the crown and the gate of the village. The leading youths of a village always banded together to prevent an outsider getting away with the gate and the crown.

But Johnny Cross was fixed with more money than the village bucks could muster for a year. He bought the crown cake and gave it to the queen of the palm-booth as a gesture of courtesy, and he bought the gate and gave it to Sue. And that night he danced with Sue nearly all the time, and most of all the mountain jig. She was a strong wild dancer, and she flashed some bold movements as they jig-a-jigged around the stout bamboo pole in the center of the barbecue supporting the palm booth. . . .

Sue was obviously worried by Burskin's first-love importunacy. Burskin would show up at the most embarrassing moments when she was with Cross: down at the bridge at nightfall when she was coming from shopping, or in the shadow of the great cotton tree in the late evening when she was going home from the field. Clearly Burskin was watching them. Besides, he was insolent when he visited her house and saw Johnny Cross there.

To the neutral Turner, Johnny Cross was quite as welcome as Burskin had been and all the previous friends of the family.

Sue decided to shake Burskin off and began with tricks. She

would announce that she was going to the far market, and
Burskin would gather together the best stuff of his field to go,
too. But when the dray was all loaded to start she pretended to be
unwell and her husband had to go instead. Three times she
turned that trick. And the fourth time Burskin amazed all the
market folk at the loading-place by pulling out of going to market at the last moment and asking Turner to dispose of his stuff.

Late that night, raving with jealousy, Burskin went to Sue's
house and almost beat through her front door with his fist, hoping to find Johnny Cross there. But only the two frightened children appeared, for Sue had gone to a dance at another village
with Johnny Cross. Burskin could not sleep that night, but
prowled like a mad beast up and down the village.

By morning he had calmed down and decided to go and beg
Sue to be good to him again, as in the old days. But the children
had told Sue what had happened, when she came home a little
before daybreak on Saturday morning and that just turned her
completely mad against Burskin. And when he went to her house
that forenoon Sue drove him away like a dog. Burskin attempted
to plead with her, but Sue picked up the wash-clothes bat and
threatened to beat his brains out if he didn't quit her place.

Burskin quit Sue's place for the grogshop, where he drank
himself drunk and exploded.

When Turner came home that Sunday morning and heard what
had happened, his wrath was a terrible thing. More terrible because
he could not express it like Sue. He had accepted Burskin on the
level, as a friend of Sue and the family and had never shown that he
knew of any irregular relations between him and his wife, and it
seemed incredible that the boy should take such a low advantage of
his hospitality by proclaiming the intimacies between him and Sue
in public. The silver pieces he had brought back from the market
for Burskin were like burning metal in his hand. He took them
down to the grogshop and left them in the care of the keeper. The
men of the village noted the silent change in Turner, his profound
anger, and could not say a decent word to him about the matter.
They were ashamed, thinking of it. Turner was determined to
"bring Burskin before the judge." He said as much as that.

Burskin retaliated by bringing a counter-suit against Sue for assaulting and wounding him. Thereby he hoped that Turner

would retire his plaint, for in his heart he did not nourish any real anger against Sue, although he was bruised badly. But her angry hand laid upon his body seemed to have cooled and cured him of his trouble and he went around now in a hang-dog manner.

Sue was a member of the village church. After her marriage to Turner she was baptized in the Cane River and received into the church. But the little brown parson had never approved of her. He was hard on the sin of fornication. He couldn't preach a sermon in which fornicators were not dragged in. Once he had preached a sermon naming poor old Ma Jubba, who lived in a one-roomed dirt hut with her two sons and their concubines. The parson said he had heard that Ma Jubba slept in the same bed with her elder son and his woman and apparently took an unholy pleasure in her son's sin.

Ma Jubba was so old and gray and toothless and bent over on her shiny bamboo staff that it had never entered the common mind of the village that there could be anything wrong about her sleeping on the same banana-rush bed with her son and his concubine.

It took the young brown graduate of the Baptist college to think and say so publicly. His grandfather had slept like that on the old slave plantation. And it may be that he was so hard on fornication because everybody knew he was a child of it, as the son of the black servant and the quadroon busha of the Cane Valley estate. He was quite a boy when his mother became respectable by marrying a peasant shopkeeper of Gingertown.

The young parson was not so much liked as the white man before him. The country people said he was too much of a self-righteous busybody and that he was shrewd and practical and full of holy tricks. There was a story of how, his horse having eaten of the nightshade, he gave him stimulants and hastily rode to the horse-market, nine miles away, to swap him. He swapped the horse for another, and that same night it died on the hands of the new owner.

The parson thought it was his business to read Sue out of church membership. And did, publicly. He never made it quite clear whether it was because Sue had beaten Burskin or Burskin had slandered Sue. Burskin was not a member of the flock and could not be dealt with. Turner was very wroth and said he would never put foot in the church again.

Because of her husband Sue felt a little troubled. He was such a sure prop to her. Surely she would never dream of comparing much less measuring him with any of the bucks with whom she dallied. Who else on that mountain top would have given her the solid security and freedom that Turner did? She knew the history of her mother and of her own girlhood. Turner had taken her child by Sam Bryan as his own. He was going to educate her a little, and how proud she would be to see her daughter become a postmistress or a schoolmistress. And as Turner never reproached her, she felt sometimes, as a wave of feeling swept her, how good it would have been if her will had been as strong as her body to save him all that pain and shame. And in those moments she would experience a deep and deadly hate for Burskin.

As for him, whenever he spied Sue or her husband any place, he hastily disappeared to avoid them. Not that he was so afraid of physical violence, but he was now thoroughly ashamed of his crazy acting. He tried through go-betweens to get Turner to compromise, but Turner replied that Burskin had gone beyond the point where any man could compromise with him. As Burskin had apparently felt that proclaiming Sue in public only could assuage his hurt vanity, so Turner must have had a vague feeling that the decision of the law courts and the spending of money would wipe out the disgrace. He had already paid five guineas for lawyer's fee, and he had mentioned having a barrister down from the city, but Sue had opposed that.

During the interval before the time fixed for the hearing of the case Sue was strangely restless. She developed a mania for toting heavy loads on her head, although there were Turner's mules and horses to do that, and a girl who stayed and worked with them for her keep. She would bring in heavy logs of firewood from the forest and insist on chopping and splitting them herself. She heaved upon her head baskets of yams and bunches of bananas as if they were the weight of a feather pillow. She rode the vicious kicking mule down and over the hills from the local market until he sweated white. She worked in the fields as never before, digging and planting like a farm-loving man. Sue used to place bets sometimes to demonstrate that she could equal or even surpass a man's work, but the way she carried on now seemed a little mad. As if she wanted to burn up all her splendid strength.

One midday she was coming up the hill from the river with a back-breaking tub of wet clothes, and a terrible pain seized her coming up the hill. She could barely reach the barbecue, and then she could not lift the tub down. She flung it from her head, breaking it. When Turner and his hired black came home from the banana-field, and the two children from school to lunch, they found no food, but dead ashes in the fireplace, and Sue moaning in bed with a killing pain in the pit of her belly.

They got some medicine from the local pharmacist and sent for a doctor in Gingertown. Gingertown was thirteen miles away. The messenger came back to say the doctor was called away from home and probably could not come to see Sue until the next morning.

All that afternoon the village matrons and concubines and maidens streamed down to Sue's house to offer advice and help. And as the news spread more came from neighboring villages. The leaders of the church came also to watch and to pray. The pain never eased, nor Sue's moaning, and sometimes it thrust sharply deeper into her and she cried out fearfully.

Night came, and in the midst of her suffering the folk began to gossip that Burskin might have set the obeah magic upon Sue. But Sue heard and whispered that it was a natural illness. The woman who held her in her arms said she had said something about a miscarriage. And the women began speculating in undertones if Sue had not been making a baby for Burskin and gotten rid of it because of her hatred for him.

Around midnight Sue beckoned Turner to the bed and tried to embrace him. The women laughed and cried "Shame!" at Sue and Sue made a wry grin and died in the midst of the laughter.

The doctor drove up in his buggy in the morning only to give permission to bury. The rural constable had suggested a post-mortem, but Turner said he did not want his dead wife to be butchered and quartered, and the doctor considerately gave his permission for interment. But most of the village murmured against that, being in favor of a post-mortem, so that they might know exactly what had been wrong with Sue. She was always so vital and vigorous yet had died that way. There was something of a mystery in her death and it was haunting.

The sickness and death of Sue gave the opportunity for a great tribute to her popularity. The whole mountain range turned out to assist at the burial. On foot, muleback, and horseback. There were carpenters and grave-diggers enough to make and dig half a dozen coffins and graves. Prosperous peasants brought hampers of foodstuffs on donkeys. Pigs and goats were killed. Mrs. Sam Bryan, as boss of the culinary department, helped by many women, prepared great boilers of food and roasting pigs and salted fish. And the crowd was fed in a booth over the barbecue.

It was taken as a token by the peasants that Sue's burial took place on the same day the court trial should have been held. Some persons had suggested a church service. The crowd was so huge it would have overflowed the church and made a splendid parade.

But the little brown parson was awfully solemn and quietly refused a church service, and Turner, remembering that Sue had recently been read out of church membership, did not urge it. All he wanted was a decent burial.

The service was to be held over the grave, and the grave was dug right next to Sue's flower garden. But instead of the soothing funeral hymns, such as "Crossing Jordan," "At the Pearly Gates," and "The Angels Are Waiting to Receive You," the parson chose such hell-fire ones as "Too late, Too late," "Backsliders, Repent," and "That Lost Soul."

The crowd felt strange singing the hymns, and a feeling of impending woe ran communicating through it. For his text the parson took, The Barren Fig Tree. But before he began the sermon he began swaying and clapping his hands and led off for them better than they could have themselves.

And the hell-fire panic loosed its grip on the crowd. And there was singing of soothing hymns, hopeful hymns, and mingling of farewell tears.

The coffin was put in the hole and Turner threw in the first handful of earth saying, "Ashes to ashes and dust to dust." And he was conscious of Burskin beside him, blubbering like a baby. And he felt compassionate toward him.

The earth was shoveled in and Turner felt the first shovelful falling on the box like a heavy sounding in his heart. But he stood through it dry-eyed until the grave was filled and piled into shape and banked with flowers and two flaming dragon-bloods planted at the head and the foot. Then he spread out his hands and said, "Lord, letteth now thy servant depart in peace."

The Gratuity

Seepersad Naipaul

I

Sanyasi wanted his gratuity. The last few weeks he had been thinking of it more and more; and these last few days he could hardly think of anything else. The thing, in fact, invaded his mind with a strange persistence; it gathered a force and momentum over which he lost all control.

Sanyasi was a road-mender. It was not that he felt too tired from age, or could not carry on because of ill-health. He could hardly have been more than fifty-five; and though he often boasted he was sixty-five (or more!) it was only to show how strong and capable he was in spite of his age. No, Sanyasi felt neither ill nor weary. It was simply that he had convinced himself that he had qualified. "Qualified" was a word that he often used these days.

He would say he had qualified for a gratuity from the government and he would maintain that it was just right and lawful that he should get it. And he was eager to show a good many people in the road-gang itself that he could and would get the gratuity. He wanted it established that he was no fool; that he knew the ropes, while others merely talked.

But he hoped, too, that the gratuity would put an end to his many difficulties. For one thing, he would pay off Sam Lookin, the Chinese provision shopkeeper and retail spirit-dealer, who was becoming distressingly insistent; for another, he would knock down the crude and crooked grass-and-tapia hut that had been housing him, his wife and their two small sons for the last twelve years, and put up a new house—raised off the ground this time—with neat tapia walls and with a roof of galvanized iron. No more grass!

Sanyasi coughed. He sat on a rickety settee in the gallery, thoughtfully smoking a cigarette, and the smoke suddenly rasped his throat. So he coughed, and the cough sent him into a short convulsion, which communicated itself to the settee, which creaked and leaned awry against the half-wall.

Sanyasi, steadying himself, muttered, "You bitch!" But whether the expletive was directed to the cough, or to the settee, or to the cigarette, no one will know.

He uncrossed his legs (he had been sitting yogi-manner), broke off the burning end of the cigarette, blew on his thumb and forefinger, blew on the salvaged piece of cigarette itself, then carefully put the butt with the matches in the matchbox. "You stay dey," he said, addressing the half-smoked cigarette.

Then Sanyasi brought both heels right up on the settee, so that his knees nearly touched his chin; leant back against the wall and, encircling his knees with his hands, fixed a meditative gaze on a single blade of grass that hung loose from the thatch.

Then he began to talk—talking not to Dharnee, who sat near by, nipping *bhaji* in a tin basin—but talking to the hanging blade of grass.

"Must get it," he said. "Bound to get it. Don' tell me I kian't!" He paused in his soliloquy, and then added: "Some one t'ousand dollars. Kiant' be less ... Set meself up in business. Mule and cart. Trafficking. Ground provision, banana, breadfruit. Be me own boss. Hm!"

On a sudden Dharnee shoved the tin basin from in front of her. "Eh, eh!" she exclaimed. "But what happen? You going crazy or what? Talking to you'self?"

He said: "Crazy? Who crazy? I ain't crazy. This gratuity business now ..."

"Oh, that!" Dharnee was suddenly full of contempt. "You will get what you lookin' for," she said, and did not give Sanyasi another look. She tried to appear as though she had clean forgotten Sanyasi and his talk of the gratuity, but in truth she could not. She had heard him talk of the gratuity too often, but she had never liked it.

"All the same," Sanyasi said, disregarding his wife's pessimism, "t'ink I will send in me application."

He stood up and cast his eye on the thatch, spotted the grass-knife sticking in the grass and took it. "Goin' for me grass now," he said to Dharnee. "You bring in the cow."

He limped away.

Sanyasi was a joke in the village. Because he was tall and limped badly in one foot, children and even grown-ups teasingly called him Lang Tam Crab-Ketcher; because he had a thick black-and-grey moustache that went up in loops at the ends, many people, but more so the youngsters, facetiously called him *Moach*. As though the man was all moustache and nothing else. But even Dharnee—when she was annoyed at Sanyasi (which was often)—found the moustache quite aggravated her annoyance. The thing seemed to her to embody all the man's pomposity. It certainly imparted to Sanyasi a look of an aggressive quality, that in contrast made the other fellows in the village look tame.

When Sanyasi was not in the company of the elders, say on occasions such as weddings or panchayats, he did not much mind being called Moach or Lang Tam Crab-Ketcher. In fact, he sometimes enjoyed the fun with the hecklers. But when he happened to be with the elders—and he was an elder himself—he took serious umbrage at the bestowers of these epithets. His personality was hurt.

And once or twice he had even been known to hurl stones and bottles as well as abuse—unprintable abuse—at his tormentors.

And his tormentors would simply guffaw and jump about in mad delight.

And Sanyasi would leave the elders and take after the boys, and when he was sure the elders could not hear him, he would say to the youngsters: "You dogs! You sons of bitches! Who is Moach? Who is Lang Tam? Who is Crab-Ketcher?" And with every question he would shoot a missile, asking: "Moach is your mother man? Lang Tam is your mother man? Crab-Ketcher is your mother man?"

And the boys would once more jump about in a boisterous harlequinade, keeping at a safe distance from Sanyasi, expertly dodging his missiles—lengths of wood, bottles, stones.

Discomfited, all his missiles going wide of their targets, Sanyasi, shining with sweat and breathing hard, would return to the elders in the cow-pen or in the thatched open hut, or under the mango tree, and would say—the words coming out in pieces—he didn't know what the world was coming to; that the young people were going to the dogs, utterly without respect for their elders.

And the elders would shake their heads to agree with Sanyasi, and one of the company would observe it was all due to lack of training and to *kusanghat*—bad companionship—and all the others would say, yes, it was all due to *kusanghat*.

How or why Sanyasi came to be called Sanyasi, probably he himself could not say. For a *sanyasi* was a holy man, a sadhu, one who eschewed fish and flesh food and intoxicating drinks of all kinds; one, moreover, who usually wore under his *koortah* or merino a bead of the sacred *tulsi* wood. Sanyasi wore no bead of the sacred *tulsi*. He wouldn't think of it. And, far from eschewing flesh and fish, he would make a long and noisy row with Dharnee if a pay-day passed without at least crab or cascadura as part of the evening meal. On the other hand, not only was Sanyasi no teetotaller, but he took more rum than was good for him. If, at the same pay-day meal, Dharnee should hint to Sanyasi that he had already had enough rum for one man, Sanyasi would stop eating and glare at Dharnee and ask what the hell she meant by suggesting that he should have just dry hash. And there would almost always be a long and noisy row; when, to end it, Dharnee would push her things into the old and sagging cardboard box and, weeping copiously, would say she was going—going anywhere—rather than stay with a disgusting sot like Sanyasi.

And Sanyasi, without a look at her, would emit a sonorous *choops* and say: "To hell wid you. Tom drunk, but Tom ain' no fool!"

Sometimes the row would take place because Sanyasi would come home quite late after pay, hardly able to walk or talk straight, a cloth bundle hanging from one hand, weighting him down, the bundle containing cascadura or crab or fish among other items of the fortnightly ration—everything hopelessly mixed up: cascadura with flour, sugar with salt; kerosene in everything.

Seeing Sanyasi's top-heavy state, seeing most of the foodstuff irreclaimably spoilt, Dharnee for the first minute or two would be dumb with chagrin. Then she would erupt on Sanyasi: "But look at this puncheon! Look at this ol' soak, this sponge, this . . ."

Sanyasi's defense would be he couldn't help it. He couldn't have made himself less than a man. The fellows at the rumshop had stood one another drinks. If he didn't stand his hand when his turn came, he would have been called a nail. It was true he had got himself a little sweet, but it was only because he had to keep his self-respect.

And so it remains a mystery to this day why Sanyasi came to be called Sanyasi. His real name was Jagat-Guru, which meant World Teacher. But only the elders addressed him by it.

And the application for the gratuity was written; and it was Motee, the lawyer's clerk, who was looked upon verily as a lawyer in the village, who wrote it, charging Sanyasi five shillings to do it.

And truly, just as Motee had guaranteed, within a fortnight Sanyasi received a long envelope. It bore on one side the words: *On His Majesty's Service*. Sanyasi, who could read a little, read the superscription and knew at once the communication was for him from the Colonial Secretary. The letter in the long envelope told him that his application for a gratuity had been received and that the matter was under consideration.

Sanyasi jumped with delight.

Another fortnight passed and another letter came to Sanyasi, and this requested him to present himself to the District Medical Officer for a medical examination and report. Sanyasi complied. Amid heavy groans and sighs he told the D.M.O. that he was done for; his back ached so much . . . his belly . . . his . . .

"All right," said the D.M.O., indicating a cubicle. "Go in there and take off your shirt."

A couple of weeks later Sanyasi got a third communication.

This requested him to call at Head Office in Port of Spain, in order to receive his gratuity. The letter contained no hint as to the
sum involved.

"See!" Sanyasi told Dharnee. "What I tell you? They callin' me
for me gratuity. No mo' hard work, thank God."

Dharnee made no comment.

The whole village knew Sanyasi was getting a gratuity. Sanyasi
had seen to that. He had been going about with the letters sticking conspicuously out of his shirt pocket, so that everybody
should see that he was no ordinary fellow. Yes! And the Colonial
Secretary addressed him as "Sir" and signed himself as his—
Sanyasi's—"obedient servant."

"You don' believe it?" he would say, even though nobody was
doubting him. "Look! See for you'self!" And he would promptly
open one or more of the letters, and begin to read.

And the people—young and old—began to show him respect.
And Sanyasi wanted them to respect him. It appeared to him that
even some of the wicked youngsters had stopped calling him
names. At last he was proving it to everybody that he was not one
to be trifled with.

Sanyasi went to town.

A Mr. Butter took him to the Treasury. Sanyasi was seeing the
buildings for the first time, and he was awed. This was a thing to
talk about when he returned to his village.

Only at the counter did Sanyasi learn that the gratuity
amounted to exactly one hundred and thirty-seven dollars.

"Sign here," said Mr. Butter, placing the voucher open before
Sanyasi and pointing to the dotted line.

Suddenly Sanyasi was quite mortified, quite nonplussed, quite
shattered. "B-but, Mr. Butter . . ."

"Shut up, man," counseled Mr. Butter. "Don't make a fuss."

"B-but I work mor'an fifteen years."

"Yes," said Mr. Butter. "But mostly tasks. Task is contract. Contract doesn't count . . ."

"But Mr. Motee say . . . And besides, this kian't buy a mule. Is
trafficking I plan to do. Bananas, ground prov . . ."

"All right," said Mr. Butter. "Take it or leave it."

"I goin' take it," said Sanyasi, not knowing how to back out. "But mind," he warned, "I going back to work—and I going write the Governor."

That afternoon Sanyasi travelled in three stages, patronizing a rumshop at each stop. In the first place, he drank in Port of Spain, stopping at "The Standard." Then he hopped off the bus at San Juan. Then, not minding how or when he reached home, he gaily broke off journey at Curepe. He thought he was particularly lucky, for he met friends and acquaintances everywhere he stopped. Most of them he had neither seen nor remembered for years; and on any other day Sanyasi would probably have gone his way without noticing any of them, or at most with no more than a shake of the head or a wave of the hand, to acknowledge mere recognition and to show sense of manners. But that day was no ordinary day. It was indeed a red-letter day. The world seemed to diffuse a wondrous enchantment in which everybody lived, moved and had his being. It was a world that radiated sweet fellowship and unalloyed happiness. And he, Sanyasi, was the center and source of that happiness, so that everybody he met became hail-fellow-well-met.

He treated them all at the rumshops; called for a quart at the least hint and, pulling out banknotes from all his pockets, repeatedly let everybody know that "money was no object," and that if Tom was drunk, Tom was still not a fool.

If anyone thought he was a *makhichus*—a miser—he would show him he was not. If anyone thought that his finances were controlled by his wife he would show him he was wrong ... Sanyasi trod on air; he felt he could almost fly ... such was his frenzy.

Reaching home at last, he continued the spree far into the night. And the next day, after an hour or two of respite, he called his friends and started the spree afresh. Money? He would sway and stagger and thrust his hands into his pockets ... He had money. Observing that rum went better "with a feed," he killed many head of the precious poultry that Dharnee reared; had chicken fried and chicken in curry; paratha, dahlpuri—and rum.

Dharnee sweated at the *chulha*. She was compelled to. The two boys ran to and from the rumshop, bringing and going back for more rum.

No sooner had Dharnee finished the cooking than the men began to eat.

Motee ate sitting on a soap-box. Sanyasi sat on his hams on the bare earthen floor, legs drawn up, back to wall. Nanda and Gokool, Sanyasi's road-gang mates, sat astride at either end of a bench, their plates between them. Juman, the village barber, squatted on his heels.

In the middle of the eaters, within arm's reach, stood the rum bottle; and about the bottle, glasses.

They ate fast and ate with relish; ate with heads down; ate with bare hands; until the hot food broke sweat on their faces.

Sanyasi said, *"Chuts!"* and slackened his belt. Gokool did likewise. Motee belched. Nanda threw back his head and blew through his lips till they rolled like drum-sticks on a drum. "Kian't eat no mo'," he said, truthfully.

"Open you's belt, man," said Sanyasi. "Do like me. Make room for more."

"Don't leh the glass get cold, man!"

"That's right, man!"

"Good rum, man!"

"Goin' down like oil, man!"

By midday bottles littered the mud floor. The small boy at length gathered them and put them in a corner, saying he would sell them to Lookin and with the money they fetched he would buy a packet of starlights for Christmas.

The eaters praised their host. They praised him in loud, fulsome talk, punctuated with bursts of rum-sodden, tuneless and crooked songs. Sanyasi had indeed qualities of generosity that few equalled. They had always known Sanyasi was a man like that, though they had never said it before. Sanyasi was this, Sanyasi was that. Sanyasi was "a damn good man."

And Sanyasi made Nanda and Gokool promise that they would never again call him Moach or Crab-Ketcher or Lang Tam. And Nanda and Gokool struck their chests and said not only would they never call him Moach but they vowed they would do for the man—whoever he might be—who dared to call Sanyasi Moach or Crab-Ketcher or Lang Tam.

And for the moment it seemed they meant every word, and no doubt they did. And because they seemed so earnest, Sanyasi gave them more rum, more chicken, more dahl-puri; said they were good boys, after all.

On the third day of the spree Dharnee fled.

"Let 'er go," said Sanyasi. "Tom drunk, but Tom ain' no fool."

A week later Sanyasi returned to the work gang. He had scarcely been spreading asphalt for three minutes when a messenger from the chief overseer informed him he was not to work.

"What!" exclaimed Sanyasi. Then: "Why not?"

" 'Cause you get gratuity," said the messenger. "And 'cause you medically unfit."

"But Mr. Motee . . . Mr. Motee say . . ."

Disgust spread on the messenger's face. "Work then, but work without pay."

Sanyasi tossed away the raker.

"Orright then," he said, "but I will write the Governor."

II

Everybody in the village knew that Sanyasi had got a gratuity and that he had gone and spent a lot of the money on sprees. They knew, too, that when he returned to the road-gang the overseer informed him he could no longer be employed: he had retired on a gratuity on grounds of ill-health. Sanyasi, returning home, told his wife that he was so "cut-up" that he just had to drown his worries in more rum. Which he did.

By evening he was prostrate. He lay flat on the earthen floor, writhing as in the agony of death. He said he was sure he was dying, and asked everybody's forgiveness for whatever wrongs he might have done, knowingly or unknowingly. He beckoned his two small sons, Rekha and Lekha, and when they came he gave them his blessings with a frothing mouth and counseled them to take care of Dharnee when he was gone.

A lot of people gathered round Sanyasi. One of them began to fan him with a felt hat. Another quickly fetched a green lime, cut it in two and briskly began rubbing one half of the lime on

Sanyasi's soles. Dharnee fetched the small bottle that contained *achar* and begged Sanyasi to chew and swallow a piece of the hot mango stuff.

"Open your mouth, man," she urged. "Only one piece . . . It is *achar;* it will cut away the rum."

Sanyasi flung a drunken hand at her.

"Orright, you bitch," said Dharnee, "remain there and dead."

But Sanyasi didn't die. Next morning he staggered up for the tin can on the small shelf against the wall in his room. The tin can, which once contained condensed milk, was Sanyasi's bank. Whether he had money in it or no, a cowrie always reposed at the bottom of the can. The cowrie was for luck; it was also a symbol for cash.

Squatting on his heels, Sanyasi emptied the contents of the can on the floor—some crumpled banknotes, some silver pieces, some coppers. Slowly, almost painfully, he began to count. He counted the money once, he counted it a second time, repeated the process a third time. Each time he made the total a different amount. His head ached and swirled, and when he belched he still belched rum.

Dharnee, seeing him counting and re-counting the money, said: "Eh, eh! But you still drunk, nuh?"

"Drunk? I done with that," he said. "No mo' rum." He shoved the money to her. "Heh," he said. "You count it. Me head swimmin'."

Dharnee quailed. This was no easy matter for her. She had never handled so much money and, even more handicapping, she could count only from one to twenty. Beyond twenty she used grains of corn, or paddy, or peas, or match sticks, whichever were nearest to hand. But counting banknotes was not in her line. Counting banknotes was not the same thing as counting five-cent heaps of mangoes or ochroes or melongenes. You didn't have to know the value of mangoes or ochroes or melongenes by their color. But it was just this mystery with banknotes. You had to know their color, and certain marks, to know what they were worth.

A five-dollar banknote was greenish. Sanyasi sometimes brought one or two of these on a pay-day—if he didn't go and get drunk first. There was a figure on it that resembled her grass-knife. Sanyasi had told her that that was a five. A two-dollar banknote was blue, with a mark that had a curl in it like Sanyasi's moustache. A pink paper was one dollar. Sanyasi brought more of these than any of the others. They were the easiest to recognize: they carried a mark that was like the mile-pole before Jankee's house side of the Main Road.

But just how a five-dollar note was different from a twenty-dollar one, Dharnee couldn't say. Sanyasi had spoken of those but had never brought one for her . . . Suppose he had one or two of these today . . .

She backed away from the money. "Not me, papa!" she said. "Is how you expect me to count so much money all by meself? Them pink notes now . . . with the mark like you . . ."

Sanyasi called for a drink of water, and when it was brought him drank a cupful—to steady himself; then he moistened his thumb and forefinger, just as he had seen the paymaster do when paying on pay-days. Then he set to rechecking the money in a most determined way. He counted it twice.

"Sixty-t'ree dollars and one cent," he said. "That is all."

"The balance gone in spree," said Dharnee. "Is a hundred and thirty-seven dollars you did get for your gratuity . . . Fifteen years' work. Now what you goin' do? Sit down and scratch?"

Sanyasi's forehead creased in thought. "Well," he said, "I kian't buy a mule, and I kian't buy a horse. Well, is a donkey I have to buy. Is traffickin' I have to do . . . Bananas, ground provision . . . Besides," he broke off, "I must show something for me gratuity . . . Oh, me head! I giddy, giddy!"

"Sure!" said Dharnee, sarcastically.

And a donkey Sanyasi did buy. Away in Tobago he went to get it. The creature was at large in a field of scrubby needle-grass. Sanyasi saw it from a distance and at first mistook it for a goat. The owner, a rugged Barbadian who seemed to have been born with a mellow clay pipe sticking out of a corner of his mouth, didn't seem keen on selling the animal.

"Wot? Sell? Hwoy, I doan't care to sell um," he said. "Too young. It ain't finish growing."

Sanyasi said that it was precisely a young donkey that he wanted. Sanyasi grew persuasive and at length the Barbadian parted with the donkey. He made it clear, though, that he had done Sanyasi an uncommon favor.

"T'ank you!" said Sanyasi, and led away the donkey by one ear till he reached the first shop and bought a length of rope.

One afternoon as Sanyasi stood on the roadside watching the donkey crop the green grass, Motee the law clerk (Sanyasi's best friend) came along. He stopped and leaned on the handlebar of his bicycle and gave the donkey a quick, quizzical look.

"So this is the donkey?"

Motee's question sounded as though he was not sure that that was the donkey. Indeed, he sounded as though he was not sure that that was a donkey at all.

"Yes," said Sanyasi, smiling. "This is the donkey. Come from way up in Tobago."

Motee half closed one eye and gave the animal a searching, thoughtful look. "Too small," he commented, "and half starved."

Indeed the creature was small. A midget of a donkey it was—only slightly bigger than a big goat. It was in truth the smallest donkey one had ever seen in the village. And not only small, but pathetically and ridiculously emaciated. It stood on spindly legs that looked like props. Its mouse-gray belly bulged and hung earthward, as though gravitation was too much for it. The animal's long, broad ears seemed much too long and broad for the rest of its body. Altogether, its ascetic emaciation, bulging belly, spindly legs and enormous ears made it look like a caricature come alive. It looked a freak that had somehow survived.

"What you going to do with it?" Motee asked.

"Traffickin' . . . Be me own boss," Sanyasi said.

"How much?" asked Motee, jerking his chin toward the donkey. It was as though he expected Sanyasi to say he had paid ten cents for the animal.

"Forty dollars," said Sanyasi.

Motee clucked his tongue.

This defied interpretation, so Sanyasi asked:

"What you mean?"

"Too old," Motee said.

"Not old," countered Sanyasi. "Young. He young-young!"

Sanyasi gave a low chuckle, as much as to say it was fun how some people, such as Motee, though otherwise quite intelligent, could not tell a young donkey from an old one.

"Come and see," he said. "He front teeth still have to come." And Sanyasi went to the jackass and promptly forced open its mouth with both hands. "See," he said, keeping the creature's mouth agape.

Motee put down the bicycle and went and peeped into the donkey's cavernous mouth. He had a satisfying look; then straightened up and wiped his face and neck with a broad handkerchief.

"It ain't that the donkey so young that all of his teeth ain't grow," Motee said. "The fact is, the donkey so old that some of his teeth drop a'ready." Motee gave Sanyasi a pathetic look and asked, "Where you buy him?"

Sanyasi said: "I tell you a'ready—in Tobago. Way up in a place call Canaan. Man who sell it said he was young."

"What you call it?"

Sanyasi was taken aback. Having never given this aspect of the business a thought, he was suddenly quite puzzled, almost ashamed.

"Oh, nothing," he said. "Just Donkey. We call it Donkey."

"Call 'im Canaan," suggested Motee, and rode off.

So Sanyasi, patting the donkey on the vertebrae, gurgled, "Canaan, Canaan, Canaan," as though murmuring a mantra or incantation, and played his tongue about his lips, as though to get the full taste of the name, and evidently liking it, led the jackass home and told his wife and sons that henceforth they must call the donkey Canaan.

Dharnee thought the name had reference to sugar-cane, but Sanyasi told her she was too stupid, and that the donkey was named Canaan because it had come from a place way up in Tobago called Canaan.

"Oho, *achha!*" said Dharnee, in conciliatory mood, and returned to her *chulha,* mumbling, "Canaan, Canaan," so as to get accustomed to the strange name.

Sanyasi had neither a cart nor a single item of harness, but he was eager to try out Canaan. So he borrowed his neighbor Ramu's cart and harness. Of course everything was twice over-size for Canaan, so that the little donkey seemed overburdened with just the harness, leave alone the cart.

"Jooi!" shouted Sanyasi, standing in the middle of the cart, reins in hand, a whip slung from one shoulder. "Hi, you!" But the donkey seemed rooted to the earth, its legs planted well apart. It seemed determined not to move.

Then, recollecting that the donkey's name was Canaan, Sanyasi gave a jerk to the reins and cried with great gusto, "Hi, Canaan! Canaan, you bitch!" As the donkey still didn't move, Sanyasi yelled, "Canaan, you mother-ass!"

Canaan went forward a step or two, then stopped.

Sanyasi had given much time to the making of the whip—a whip which carried a handle of poui wood. Now he slashed Canaan with it.

"Get on, Canaan! Hi, Canaan!"

The donkey broke into a surprisingly brisk walk for about six yards, then put on brakes, then stopped.

"Ha-ya-yai!" groaned Sanyasi, sweating profusely, shaking his head from left to right and then from right to left, as much as to say that he was damned—that he didn't know what to say or what to do.

It being a "try-out," half the village had turned out to witness the event. Sanyasi felt quite disgraced by Canaan. He had expected the animal to show some mettle. Instead . . .

"Hi, Canaan!"

Four fellows jumped upon the cart. Sanyasi cast a sour look at them, but much as he wanted to tell them to get to hell, he was secretly afraid to do so, lest they tell him to his face what they thought of the donkey.

"Hi, boy!"

But now the donkey positively could not or would not move. Sanyasi began to belabor Canaan with the stout end of the whipstick. The creature came very much to life and broke into a pretty trot; but the moment Sanyasi stopped beating him, that moment he slowed down, staggered and stopped.

"Hi, Canaan!"

Suddenly to Sanyasi's cry of "Hi, Canaan!" someone shouted, "Hi, Grats!"

Sanyasi quailed. He knew "Grats" was short for gratuity. He knew some wit was poking fun at him because the donkey represented the gratuity he had received. Now, not daring to call out,

"Hi, Canaan!" he simply wiped the sweat off his face, jerked the reins and shouted, "Hi, Donkey!"

Half a dozen fellows shouted back, "Hi, Grats!"

The fellows who had jumped on the cart jumped out and began to shout "Hi, Grats!" too.

Sanyasi got off the cart, took hold of one of the shafts, and turned donkey-and-cart homeward.

On the way he met Motee.

"Well, and how is Canaan doin'?" asked Motee.

Sanyasi let go the shaft and the donkey came to a dead stop. Gasping for breath, his face and neck shining with sweat, Sanyasi said: "Canaan? Who Canaan? Is not Canaan. Is me pullin'. Canaan me eye!"

Calypsonian

Samuel Selvon

It had a time when things was really brown in Trinidad, and Razor Blade couldn't make a note nohow, no matter what he do, everywhere he turn, people telling him they ain't have work. It look like if work scarce like gold, and is six months now he ain't working.

Besides that, Razor Blade owe Chin parlor about five dollars, and the last time he went in for a sandwich and a sweet drink, Chin tell him no more trusting until he pay all he owe. Chin have his name in a copybook under the counter.

"Wait until the calypso season start," he tell Chin, "and I go be reaping a harvest. You remember last year how much money I had?"

But though Chin remember last year, that still ain't make him soften up, and it reach a position where he hungry, clothes dirty, and he see nothing at all to come, and this time so, the calypso season about three, four months off.

On top of all that, rain falling nearly every day, and the shoes he have on have big hole in them, like if they laughing.

Was the rain what cause him to t'ief a pair of shoes from by a shoemaker shop in Park Street. Is the first time he ever t'ief, and it take him a long time to make up his mind. He stand up there on the pavement by this shoemaker shop, and he thinking things like, Oh God when I tell you I hungry, and all the shoes around the table, on the ground, some capsize, some old and some new, some getting halfsole and some getting new heel.

It have a pair just like the one he have on.

The table cut up for so, as if the shoemaker blind and cutting the wood instead of the leather, and it have a broken calabash shell with some boil starch in it. The starch look like pap; he so hungry he feel he could eat it.

Well, the shoemaker in the back of the shop, and it only have few people sheltering rain on the pavement. It look so easy for him to put down the old pair and take up another pair—this time so, he done have his eye fix on a pair that look like Technic, and just his size, too, besides.

Razor Blade remember how last year he was sitting pretty—two-tone Technic, gabardeen suit, hot tie. Now that he catching his royal, every time he only making comparison with last year, thinking in his mind how them was the good old days, and wondering if they go ever come back again.

And it look to him as if t'iefing could be easy, because plenty time people does leave things alone and go away, like how now the shoemaker in the back of the shop, and all he have to do is take up a pair of shoes and walk off in cool blood.

Well, it don't take plenty to make a t'ief. All you have to do is have a fellar catching his royal, and can't get a work noway, and bam! By the time he make two, three rounds he bounce something somewhere, an orange from a tray, or he snatch a bread in a parlor, or something.

Like how he bounce the shoes.

So though he frighten like hell and part of him going like a pliers, Razor Blade playing victor brave boy and whistling as he go down the road.

The only thing now is that he hungry.

Right there by Queen Street, in front a Chinee restaurant, he get an idea. Not an idea in truth; all he did think was: In for a shilling in for a pound. But when he think that, is as if he begin to realize that if he going to get stick for the shoes, he might as well start t'iefing black is white.

So he open now to anything: all you need is a start, all you need is a crank up, and it come easy after that.

What you think he planning to do? He planning to walk in the

Chinee restaurant and sit down and eat a major meal, and then out off without paying. It look so easy, he wonder why he never think of it before.

The waitress come up while he looking at the menu. She stand up there, with a pencil stick up on she ears like a real test, and when he take a pin-t at she he realize that this restaurant work only part-time as far as she concern, because she look as if she sleepy, she body bend up like a piece of copper wire.

What you go do? She must be only getting a few dollars from the Chinee man, and she can't live on that.

He realize suddenly that he bothering about the woman when he himself catching his tail, so he shake his head and watch down at the menu.

He mad to order a portion of everything—fry rice, chicken chop-suey, roast pork, chicken chow-min, birdnest soup, chicken broth, and one of them big salad with big slice of tomato and onion.

He begin to think again about the last calypso season, when he was holding big, and uses to go up by the high-class Chinee restaurant in St. Vincent Street. He think how is a funny thing how sometimes you does have so much food that you eat till you sick, and another time you can't even see you way to hustle a rock and mauby.

It should have some way that when you have the chance you could eat enough to last you for a week or a month, and he make a plan right there, that the next time he have money (oh, God) he go make a big deposit in a restaurant, so that all he have to do is walk in and eat like stupidness.

But the woman getting impatient. She say: "You taking a long time to make up you mind, like you never eat in restaurant before."

And he think about the time when he had money, how no frowsy woman could have talk to him so. He remember how them waitresses used to hustle to serve him, and one night the talk get around that Razor Blade, the calypsonian, was in the place, and they insist that he give them a number. Which one it was again? The one about Home and the Bachelor.

"Come, come, make up you mind, mister, I have work to do."

So he order plain boil rice and chicken stew, because the way how he feeling, all them fancy Chinee dish is only joke, he feel as if he want something like roast breadfruit and saltfish, something solid so when it go down in you belly you could feel it there.

And he tell the woman to bring a drink of Barbados rum first thing, because he know how long they does take to bring food in them restaurant, and he could coast with the rum in the meantime.

By the time the food come he feeling so hungry he could hardly wait, he fall down on the plate of rice and chicken as if is the first time he see food, and in three minute everything finish.

And is just as if he seeing the world for the first time, he feel like a million, he feel like a lord; he give a loud belch and bring up some of the chicken and rice to his throat; when he swallow it back down it taste sour.

He thinking how it had a time a American fellar hear a calypso in Trinidad and he went back to the States and he get it set up to music and thing, and he get the Andrews Sisters to sing it, and the song make money like hell, it was on Hit Parade and all; wherever you turn, you could hear people singing that calypso. This time so, the poor calypsonian who really write the song catching hell in Trinidad; it was only when some smart lawyer friend tell him about copyright and that sort of business that he wake up. He went to America; and how you don't know he get a lot of money after the case did fix up in New York?

Razor Blade know the story good; whenever he write a calypso, he always praying that some big-shot from America would hear it and like it, and want to set it up good. The Blade uses to go in Frederick Street and Marine Square by the one-two music shops, and look at all the popular songs, set up in notes and words, with the name of the fellar who write it big on the front, and sometimes his photograph too. And Razor Blade uses to think: But why I can't write song like that too, and have my name all over the place?

And when things was good with him, he went inside now and then, and tell the clerks and them that he does write calypsoes. But they only laugh at him, because they does think that calypso is no song at all, that what is song is numbers like "I've Got You Under my Skin" and "Sentimental Journey," what real American composers write.

And the Blade uses to argue that every dog has his day, and that a time would come when people singing calypso all over the world like stupidness.

He thinking about all that as he lean back there in the Chinee man restaurant.

Is to peel off now without paying!

The best way is to play brassface, do as if you own the damn restaurant, and walk out cool.

So he get up and he notice the waitress not around (she must be serving somebody else) and he take time and walk out, passing by the cashier who writing something in a book.

But all this time, no matter how boldface you try to be, you can't stop part of you from going like a pliers, clip clip, and he feel as if he want to draw his legs together and walk with two foot as one.

When the waitress find out Razor Blade gone without paying, she start to make one set of noise, and a Chinee man from the kitchen dash outside to see if he could see him, but this time so Razor Blade making races down Frederick Street.

The owner of the restaurant tell the woman she have to pay for the food that Razor Blade eat, that was she fault, and she begin to cry big water, because is a lot of food that Razor Blade put away, and she know that that mean two, three dollars from she salary.

This time so, Razor Blade laughing like hell; he quite down by the Railway Station, and he know nobody could catch him now.

One set of rain start to fall suddenly; Razor Blade walking like a king in his new shoes, and no water getting up his foot this time, so he ain't even bothering to shelter.

And he don't know why, but same time he get a sharp idea for a calypso. About how a man does catch his royal when he can't get a work noway. The calypso would say about how he see some real hard days; he start to think up words right away as he walking in the rain:

> *It had a time in this colony*
> *When everybody have money excepting me*
> *I can't get a work no matter how I try*
> *It look as if good times pass me by.*

He start to hum it to the tune of an old calypso (Man Centipede Bad Too Bad) just to see how it shaping up.

And he think about One Foot Harper, the one man who could help him out with a tune.

It had a big joke with One Foot one time. Somebody t'ief One Foot crutch one day when he was catching a sleep under a weeping willow tree in Woodford Square, and One Foot had to stay in the square for a whole day and night. You could imagine how he curse stink; everybody only standing up and laughing like hell; nobody won't lend a hand, and if wasn't for Razor Blade, now so One Foot might still be waiting under the weeping willow tree for somebody to get a crutch for him.

But the old Blade help out the situation, and since that time, the both of them good friends.

So Razor Blade start making a tack for the tailor shop which part One Foot does always be hanging out, because One Foot ain't working noway, and every day he there by the tailor shop, sitting down on a soapbox and talking whole day.

But don't fret you head, One Foot ain't no fool; it had a time in the old days when they uses to call him King of Calypso, and he was really good. If he did have money, or education business, is a sure thing he would have been up the ladder, because he was the first man who ever had the idea that calypsonians should go away and sing in America and England. But people only laugh at One Foot when he say that.

Razor Blade meet One Foot in a big old talk about the time when the Town Hall burn down (One Foot saying he know the fellar who start the fire). When One Foot see him, he stop arguing right away and he say:

"What happening paleets, long time no see."

Razor Blade say: "Look man, I have a sharp idea for a calypso. Let we go in the back of the shop and work it out."

But One Foot feeling comfortable on the soapbox. He say: "Take ease, don't rush me. What about the shilling you have for me, that you borrow last week?"

The Blade turn his pockets inside out, and a pair of dice roll out, and a penknife fall on the ground.

"Boy, I ain't have a cent. I broken. I bawling. If you stick me with a pin you won't draw blood."

"Don't worry with that kind of talk, is so with all you fellars, you does borrow a man money and then forget his address."

"I telling you, man," Razor Blade talk as if he in a hurry, but is only to get away from the topic, "you don't believe me?"

But the Foot cagey. He say, "All right, all right, but I telling you in front that if you want money borrow again, you come to the wrong man. I ain't lending you a nail till you pay me back that shilling that you have for me." The Foot move off the soap-box, and stand up balancing on the crutch.

"Come, man, do quick," Razor Blade make as if to go behind the shop in the back room. Same time he see Rahamut, the Indian tailor.

"What happening Indian, things looking good with you."

Rahamut stop stitching a khaki pants and look at the Blade.

"You and One Foot always writing calypso in this shop, all-you will have to give me a commission."

"Well, you know how it is, sometimes you up, sometimes you down. Right now I so down that bottom and I same thing."

"Well, old man, is a funny thing but I never see you when you up."

"Ah, but wait till the calypso season start."

"Then you won't come round here at all. Then you is big shot, you forget small fry like Rahamut."

Well, Razor Blade don't know what again to tell Rahamut, because is really true all what the Indian saying about he and One Foot hanging out behind the shop. And he think about these days when anybody tell him anything, all he could say is: "Wait till the calypso season start up," as if when the calypso season start up God go come to earth, and make everybody happy.

So what he do is he laugh kiff-kiff and give Rahamut a pat on the back, like they is good friends.

Same time One Foot come up, so they went and sit down by a break-up table.

Razor Blade say: "Listen to these words old man, you never hear calypso like this in you born days," and he start to give the Foot the words.

But from the time he start, One Foot chock his fingers in his ears and bawl out: "Oh, God, old man, you can't think up something new, is the same old words every year."

"But how you mean, man," the Blade say, "this is calypso father. Wait until you hear the whole thing."

They begin to work on the song, and One Foot so good that in two twos he fix up a tune. So Razor Blade pick up a empty bottle and a piece of stick, and One Foot start beating the table, and is so they getting on, singing this new calypso that they invent.

Well, Rahamut and other Indian fellar who does help him out with the sewing come up and listen.

"What you think of this new number, papa?" the Blade ask Rahamut.

Rahamut scratch his head and say: "Let me get that tune again."

So they begin again, beating on the table and the bottle, and Razor Blade imagine that he singing to a big audience in the Calypso Tent, so he putting all he have in it.

When they finished the fellar who does help Rahamut say: "That is hearts."

But Rahamut say: "Why you don't shut you mouth? What all-you Indian know about calypso?"

And that cause a big laugh, everybody begin to laugh kya-kya, because Rahamut himself is a Indian.

One Foot turn to Razor Blade and say: "Listen to them two Indian how they arguing about we Creole calypso. I never see that in my born days!"

Rahamut say: "Man, I is a Creolise Trinidadian, *oui.*"

Razor Blade say: "All right, joke is joke, but all-you think it good? It really good?"

Rahamut want to say yes, it good, but he beating about the bush, he hemming and hawing, he saying: "Well, it so-so," and "it not so bad," and "I hear a lot of worse ones."

But the fellar who does help Rahamut, he getting on as if he mad, he only hitting Razor Blade and One Foot on the shoulder and saying how he never hear a calypso like that, how it sure to be the Road March for next year Carnival. He swinging his hands all about in the air while he talking, and his hand hit Rahamut hand and Rahamut get a chook in his finger with a needle he was holding.

Well, Rahamut put the finger in his mouth and start to suck it, and he turn round and start to abuse the other tailor fellar, saying why you don't keep you tail quiet, look you make me chook my hand with the blasted needle?

"Well, what happen for that? You go dead because a needle chook you?" the fellar say.

Big argument start up; they forget all about Razor Blade calypso and start to talk about how people does get blood poison from pin and needle chook.

Well, it don't have anything to write down as far as the calypso concern. Razor Blade memorize the words and tune, and that is the case. Is so a calypso born, cool cool, without any fuss. Is so all them big numbers like "Yes, I Catch Him Last Night," and "That Is a Thing I Can Do Anytime Anywhere," and "Old Lady Your Bloomers Falling Down," born right there behind Rahamut tailor shop.

After the big talk about pin and needle Rahamut and the fellar who does assist him went back to finish off a zootsuit that a fellar was going to call for in the evening.

Now Razor Blade want to ask One Foot to borrow him a shilling, but he don't know how to start, especially as he owe him already. So he begin to talk sweet, praising up the tune that One Foot invent for the calypso, saying he never hear a tune so sweet, that the melody smooth like sweetoil.

But as soon as he start to come like that, the old Foot begin to get cagey, and say, "Oh, God, old man, don't mamaguile me."

The Blade not so very fussy, because a solid meal in his belly. But same time he trying to guile One Foot into lending him a little thing, he get an idea.

He begin to tell One Foot how he spend the morning, how he ups the shoes from the shoemaker shop in Park Street, and how he eat big for nothing.

One Foot say: "I bet you get in trouble, all-you fellars does take some brave risk, *oui*."

Razor say: "Man, it easy as kissing hand, is only because you have one foot and can't run fast, that's why you talking so."

Foot say: "No jokes about my one foot."

Razor say: "But listen, man, you too stupid again! You and me could work up a good scheme to get some money. If you t'iefing, you might as well t'ief big."

"Is you is the t'ief, not me."

"But listen, man, Foot," the Blade gone down low in voice, "I go do everything, all I want you to do is to keep watchman for me, to see if anybody coming."

"What is the scheme you have?"

To tell truth, the old Blade ain't have nothing cut and dry in the old brain; all he thinking is that he go make a big t'ief somewhere where have money. He scratch his head and pull his ears like he did see Spencer Tracy do in a picture, and he say: "What about the Roxy Theater down St. James?"

Same time he talking, he feeling excitement in his body, like if waves going up and coming down and he hold on to One Foot hand.

The Foot say: "Well, yes, the day reach when you really catching you royal. I never thought I would see the time when my good friend Razor Blade turn t'ief. Man, you sure to get catch. Why you don't try for a work somewhere until the calypso season start up?"

"I tired try to get work. It ain't have work noway."

"Well, you ain't no t'ief. You sure to get catch, I tell you."

"But, man, look how I get away with the shoes and the meal! I tell you all you have to do is play boldface and you could commit murder and get away free."

The Foot start to hum a old calypso:

> If a man have money today . . .
> He could commit murder and get away free
> And live in the Governor's company. . . .

The Blade begin to get vex. "So you don't like the idea? You think I can't get away with it?"

"You ain't have no practice. You is a novice. Crime does not pay."

"You is a damn coward!"

"Us calypsonians have to keep we dignity."

"You go to hell! If you won't help me I go do it by myself, you go see! And I not t'iefing small, I t'iefing big! If I going down the river, I making sure is for plenty money, and not for no small-time job."

"Well, papa, don't say I ain't tell you you looking for trouble."

"Man, Foot, the trouble with you is you only have one foot so you can't think like me."

The Foot get hot. He say: "Listen, I tell you already no jokes about my one foot, you hear? I ain't taking no jokes about that. Curse my mother, curse my father, but don't tell me nothing about my foot."

The Blade relent. "I sorry, Foot, I know you don't like nobody to give you jokes."

Same time Rahamut call out and ask why they keeping so much noise, if they think they in the fish market.

So they finish the talk. Razor Blade tell One Foot he would see him later, and One Foot say: "Righto, boy, don't forget the words for the song. And I warning you for the last time to keep out of trouble."

But the minute he leave the tailor shop Razor Blade only thinking how easy it go be to pull off this big deal. He alone would do it, without any gun, too, besides.

Imagine the Foot saying he is a novice! All you need is brass-face; play brazen; do as if you is a saint, as if you still have you mother innocent features, and if anybody ask you anything, lift up you eyebrows and throw you hands up in the air and say: "Oh Lord, who, *me?*"

He find himself quite around by the Queen's Park Savannah, walking and thinking. And he see a old woman selling orange. The woman as if she sleeping in the heat, she propping up she chin with one hand, and she head bend down. Few people passing; Razor Blade size up the situation in one glance.

He mad to bounce a orange from the tray, just to show that he could do it and get away. Just pass up near—don't even look down at the tray—and just lift one up easy as you walking, and put it in you pocket.

He wish One Foot was there to see how easy it was to do.

But he hardly put the orange in his pocket when the old woman jump up and start to make one set of noise, bawling out: "T'ief, t'ief! Look a man t'ief a orange from me! Help! Hold him! Don't let 'im get away!"

And is as if that bawling start the pliers working on him right away; he forget every thing he was thinking, and he start to make races across the savannah.

He look back and he see three fellars chasing him. And is just as if he can't feel nothing at all, as if he not running, as if he standing up in one spot. The only thing is the pliers going clip clip, and he gasping: Oh God! Oh God!

Enchanted Alley

Michael Anthony

Leaving for school early on mornings, I walked slowly through the busy parts of the town. The business places would all be opening then and smells of strange fragrance would fill the High Street. Inside the opening doors I would see clerks dusting, arranging, hanging things up, getting ready for the day's business. They looked cheerful and eager and they opened the doors very wide. Sometimes I stood up to watch them.

In places between the stores several little alleys ran off the High Street. Some were busy and some were not and there was one that was long and narrow and dark and very strange. Here, too, the shops would be opening as I passed and there would be bearded Indians in loincloths spreading rugs on the pavement. There would be Indian women also, with veils thrown over their shoulders, setting up their stalls and chatting in a strange sweet tongue. Often I stood, too, watching them, and taking in the fragrance of rugs and spices and onions and sweetmeats. And sometimes, suddenly remembering, I would hurry away for fear the school-bell had gone.

In class, long after I settled down, the thoughts of this alley would return to me. I would recall certain stalls and certain beards and certain flashing eyes, and even some of the rugs that had been rolled out. The Indian women, too, with bracelets around their ankles and around their sun-browned arms flashed to my mind.

I thought of them. I saw them again looking shyly at me from under the shadow of the stores, their veils half hiding their faces. In my mind I could almost picture them laughing together and talking in that strange sweet tongue. And mostly the day would be quite old before the spell of the alley wore off my mind.

One morning I was much too early for school. I passed street-sweepers at work on Harris' Promenade and when I came to the High Street only one or two shop doors were open. I walked slowly, looking at the quietness and noticing some of the alleys that ran away to the backs of fences and walls and distant streets. I looked at the names of these alleys. Some were very funny. And I walked on anxiously so I could look a little longer at the dark, funny street.

As I walked it struck me that I did not know the name of that street. I laughed at myself. Always I had stood there looking along it and I did not know the name of it. As I drew near I kept my eyes on the wall of the corner shop. There was no sign on the wall. On getting there I looked at the other wall. There was a sign-plate upon it but the dust had gathered thickly there and whatever the sign said was hidden behind the dust.

I was disappointed. I looked along the alley which was only now beginning to get alive, and as the shop doors opened the en-chantment of spice and onions and sweetmeats emerged. I looked at the wall again but there was nothing there to say what the street was called. Straining my eyes at the sign-plate I could make out a "c" and an "A" but farther along the dust had made one smooth surface of the plate and the wall.

"Stupes!" I said in disgust. I heard mild laughter, and as I looked before me I saw the man rolling out his rugs. There were two women beside him and they were talking together and they were laughing and I could see the women were pretending not to look at me. They were setting up a stall of sweetmeats and the man put down his rugs and took out something from a tray and put it into his mouth, looking back at me. Then they talked again in the strange tongue and laughed.

I stood there awhile. I knew they were talking about me. I was not afraid. I wanted to show them that I was not timid and that I would not run away. I moved a step or two nearer the wall. The smells rose up stronger now and they seemed to give the feelings of things splendored and far away. I pretended I was looking at the wall but I stole glances at the merchants from the corners of my eyes. I watched the men in their loincloths and the garments of the women were full and many-colored and very exciting. The women stole glances at me and smiled to each other and ate of the sweetmeats they sold. The rug merchant spread out his rugs wide on the pavement and he looked at the beauty of their colors and seemed very proud. He, too, looked slyly at me.

I drew a little nearer because I was not afraid of them. There were many more stalls now under the stores. Some of the people turned off the High Street and came into this little alley and they bought little things from the merchants. The merchants held up the bales of cloth and matched them on to the people's clothes and I could see they were saying it looked very nice. I smiled at this and the man with the rugs saw me and smiled.

That made me brave. I thought of the word I knew in the strange tongue and when I remembered it I drew nearer.

"Salaam," I said.

The rug merchant laughed aloud and the two women laughed aloud and I laughed, too. Then the merchant bowed low to me and replied, "Salaam!"

This was very amusing for the two women. They talked together so I couldn't understand and then the fat one spoke.

"Wot wrang wid de warl?"

I was puzzled for a moment and then I said, "Oh, it is the street sign. Dust cover it."

"Street sign?" one said, and they covered their laughter with their veils.

"I can't read what street it is," I said. "What street this is?"

The rug merchant spoke to the women in the strange tongue and the three of them giggled and one of the women said, "Every marning you stand up dey and you doe know what they carl here?"

"First time I come down here," I said.

"Yes," said the fat woman. Her face was big and friendly and she sat squat on the pavement. "First time you wark down here but every marning you stop dey and watch we."

I laughed.

"You see 'e laughing?" said the other. The rug merchant did not say anything but he was very much amused.

"What you call this street?" I said. I felt very brave because I knew they were friendly to me, and I looked at the stalls, and the smell of the sweetmeats was delicious. There was barah, too, and chutney and dry channa, and in the square tin there was the wet yellow channa, still hot, the steam curling up from it.

The man took time to put down his rugs and then he spoke to me. "This," he said, talking slowly and making actions with his arms, "From up dey to up dey is Calcatta Street." He was very pleased with his explanation. He had pointed from the High Street end of the alley to the other end that ran darkly into the distance. The whole street was very long and dusty, and in the concrete drain there was no water and the brown peel of onions blew about when there was a little wind. Sometimes there was the smell of cloves in the air and sometimes the smell of oilcloth, but where I stood the smell of the sweetmeats was strongest and most delicious.

He asked, "You like Calcatta Street?"

"Yes," I said.

The two women laughed coyly and looked from one to the other.

"I have to go," I said, "—school."

"O you gwine to school?" the man said. He put down his rugs again. His loincloth was very tight around him. "Well you could wark so," he said, pointing away from the High Street end of the alley, "and when you get up dey, turn so, and when you wark and wark, you'll meet the school."

"Oh!" I said, surprised. I didn't know there was a way to school along this alley.

"You see?" he said, very pleased with himself.

"Yes," I said.

The two women looked at him smiling and they seemed very proud the way he explained. I moved off to go, holding my books under my arm. The women looked at me and they smiled in a sad, friendly way. I looked at the chutney and barah and channa and suddenly something occurred to me. I felt in my pockets and then I opened my books and looked among the pages. I heard one of the women whisper—"Taking larning. . . ." The other said, "Aha. . . ." and I did not hear the rest of what she said. Desperately I turned the books down and shook them and the penny fell out rolling on the pavement. I grabbed it up and turned to the fat woman. For a moment I couldn't decide which, but the delicious smell of the yellow, wet channa softened my heart.

"A penny channa," I said, "wet."

The woman bent over with the big spoon, took out a small paper bag, flapped it open, then crammed two or three spoonfuls of channa into it. Then she took up the pepper bottle.

"Pepper?"

"Yes," I said, anxiously.

"Plenty?"

"Plenty."

The fat woman laughed, pouring the pepper sauce with two or three pieces of red pepper skin falling on the channa.

"Good!" I said, licking my lips.

"You see?" said the other woman. She grinned widely, her gold teeth glittering in her mouth. "You see 'e like plenty pepper?"

As I handed my penny I saw the long, brown fingers of the rug merchant stretching over my head. He handed a penny to the fat lady.

"Keep you penny in you pocket," he grinned at me, "an look out, you go reach to school late."

I was very grateful about the penny. I slipped it into my pocket.

"You could wark so," the man said, pointing up Calcutta Street, "and turn so, and you'll come down by the school."

"Yes," I said, hurrying off.

The street was alive with people now. There were many more merchants with rugs and many more stalls of sweetmeats and other things. I saw bales of bright cloth matched up to ladies' dresses and I heard the ladies laugh and say it was good. I walked fast through the crowd. There were women with sarees calling out "Ground-nuts! Parata!" and every here and there gramophones blared out Indian songs. I walked on with my heart full inside me. Sometimes I stood up to listen and then I walked on again. Then suddenly it came home to me it must be very late. The crowd was thick and the din spread right along Calcutta Street. I looked back to wave to my friends. They were far behind and the pavement was so crowded I could not see. I heard the car horns tooting and I knew that on the High Street it must be a jam session of traffic and people. It must be very late. I held my books in my hands, secured the paper bag of channa in my pocket, and with the warmth against my legs I ran pell-mell to school.

Black Sun

Emilio Díaz Valcárcel

Black Bernabé Quirindongo felt the blood boil in his veins whenever he heard his kind of music. Seated at the door of his wooden shack, surrounded by the other closely packed together huts of the tiny Negro colony of the town, he would spend hours and hours searching for meaning to the sounds. At the edge of the plot of land a dozen black faces crowded around, eyes burning, hands like knotted vines pounding against their knees, to help out Bernabé Quirindongo, whose fingers beat futilely against the flimsy wall partition, against the floor; not once was there a rich, full sound like the one ringing in his head. Luciana Quiles, leaning out from the window of her shack, had been watching the boy since he was very small; from the beginning she understood the rhythm which tortured him; the little black boy had been born a drummer.

Mama Romualda, sweltering over her little stove, fanning the flames with a greasy piece of cardboard, grew sad thinking about her black son's harmonic frustrations. She sold chitterlings which even the daintiest and blondest little girls of the town licked their lips over. In an old tin can she would drop the coins, one by one. Black Bernabé Quirindongo, black good-for-nothing to the people, wanted a hide on which to unload his rhythm; he pestered his mama demanding the marvelous skin of a bongo for his fingers.

Pa-coo-*pah,* moved his lips, pa-coo-*pah,* but the wooden wall, or the floorboards, or the garbage can produced only a disappointing noise under his miraculous fingertips. The black faces, huddled together at the edge of the lot, beat their palms together. Neighbor Luciana Quiles, seventy years old, granddaughter of slaves, caught up by a dizziness that shook her bony body, led the group with her cattle bell of a voice.

In the silent late afternoons the coconut groves atop the little rise turned into metallic shadows, the horizon burned red and Bernabé Quirindongo's soul was filled with a noisy peace, expressible only through the slow roll of the skins. In the mornings the sun ripened on the tips of the pines, nailing daggers of light within the shack and Bernabé Quirindongo (pa-coo-*pah,* his lips moved) would have described it all with a joyous drum roll. Thunder volleys burned the silence above the shack, scared away the peace of the whites, rolled on until quenched in the brambles on the other side of the river and Bernabé Quirindongo, better than anyone else, could have reproduced their sonorous mystery by vibrating his sausage-like fingers. But Bernabé Quirindongo, black good-for-nothing, who beat the air in search of a nonexistent bongo, had to pour out his soul through his lips.

"Pa-coo-*pah,*" he murmured.

When Bernabé Quirindongo was sent to the little town hospital because of a hernia, his mama Romualda Quirindongo got drunk and began to beg, her eyes swimming in tears. Of each dollar collected, she drank half. It was a sight that amused even the most refined whites. The black woman went up and down the streets, staggering along in her faded rags, and her enormous breasts wobbled as if they, too, were drunk; she pleaded, whined, begged. Later, alone, she counted the money.

Actually, it was never known whether or not the Negro was being cured of a hernia. The truth is that one morning, after all his mama's pleas and collecting, he appeared at the door of the shack with a new bongo. Luciana Quiles herself, who understood about such things, yanked off the price tag. Bernabé attacked the skins and his thick lips followed the cadence and emitted sounds of a bongo being beaten: "r-roc ko-*to,* ta-coo-*pah.*" His eyes, fixed in a faraway gaze, seemed to be aflame. His noise bothered no one: his mama's last husband, the red-skinned man who appeared one morning stretched out in the tall grass of the abandoned dairy farm, had left for the center of the island, cursing the coast.

Bernabé had never known his father. Luciana Quiles was suspicious of a Jamaican who landed, twenty years back, when the tiny colony had only half a dozen tumbledown hovels, to work on the bridges. For all purposes, Romualda was the boy's papa and mama. Last Three Kings' Day, while Bernabé was tuning his instrument and the admiring black faces began to crowd together outside the plot, Romualda gave him a nail clipper.

"This is so you don't break the skin," she told him. Old Luciana Quiles hugged her. Coc, ko-*ro*, pa-*coo* said the bongo on that memorable date.

Romualda had many arguments with the people. Her son was no idiot, he had simply turned out to be a musician; let them look around all over town for anyone—anyone, mind you!—who could match his harmony. The young boys gathered around him with *güiros* and maracas, trying to pick up a rhythm. Bernabé Quirindongo didn't even look at them, and his eyes, glowing, stared over their shoulders. When his fingers were drumming, not even his own mama nor the neighbor Luciana Quiles merited a glance. He was complete concentration. All ears. A casually shouted word was enough to set the skins to releasing their harmonies together with the murmuring lips. Ramón! R-roco-*to*-bem-*bon*. When lightning tore up the horizon above the guava bushes, he would wait motionless, ear ready, until the deafening roar of the thunder reached him. His fingers then came to life. The black faces ran through the rain to listen to the miracle. Bo-*roam boam,* and his eyes turned loose for a moment while his magical hearing registered the noisy cadence.

"Thass a black saint," neighbor Luciana Quiles would say. "He gonna die through the ears."

Romualda felt proud of her boy and encouraged him. She passed her greasy hand over her son's bent head. There was a somewhat ancestral vengeance in those drumbeats. Her black boy was redeeming her from something she couldn't understand. She felt light, agile; some indefinable weight dropped from her whenever she listened to the percussion in the doorway of her shack.

One morning, without Bernabé Quirindongo's seeing her, the lightest of the daughters arrived. She had silky hair and yellow eyes. Mariana brought a six-month-old mulatto in her arms and stated it very clearly, so all the neighborhood could hear: the baby, born in one of San Juan's slums, would not be taken away from her by anyone. She let them know his name: Milton, Milton Quirindongo, and she kept watching the people just in case anyone said something. She would raise him even though he had no father. For him, the best blankets in the world, the tenderest looks, the best bottles, the softest bed, the best scraps of food. Bernabé didn't even bother to look at his nephew, busy as he was. Black Romualda, enthused by the milky color of her grandson, changed the course of her affection. She felt her knees go soft when her grandson bawled. She sold her pork cracklings in a hurry, neglected the seasoning of her fried delicacies, forgot to give her customers the change. The memory of her husband disappeared like a mongoose into a bush. Nobody else existed for her.

And Bernabé Quirindongo, with his dauntless face, his eyes aflame, searched for the meaning to the sounds. The baby cried: gwa, pa coo-*pah*. "I've dropped the frying pan," his mama said. Tan, tan ta-*ran*, he answered, moving his lips, purple and cracked by silence. The black faces crowded about the plot, eyes and teeth white, hands restless, surrounding his cadence. Luciana Quiles quaked in a trance; an atavistic wriggling shook her parchment-like flesh. "Bernabé! . . ." Merecum-*bay*. The sounds leaped forth crazily. "Mariana!" Baram barambana.

Mariana worked in the afternoons. She went to wash dishes in the house of the richest man in town. From there she brought pieces of chicken, dainty tidbits wrapped in newspaper for her little mulatto. Romualda stayed in the kiosk, sweltering over the stove, blowing on the live coals. Her bloodshot eyes became tender when she looked at her grandson and now words no longer sounded in the house. There were no words in the house, but the bongo was new although grease had stained it almost blue.

One day Bernabé's little nephew woke up with a fever. Luciana Quiles and her half-dozen blacks came running: she brought a concoction of herbs. Then came a pale man, dressed in white and wearing a strange rubber necklace. The Negro, in

the door of the shack, waited with his fingers ready on the skins.
Only the indistinct murmur from the pale man and the women
in the bedroom.

"Doctor," begged a voice. "Doctor," Bernabé repeated, and for
the first time he felt helpless at not being able to translate the
word on his instrument.

"He won't die?" asked the same voice. Rrrrrr, sounded the
skins in vain, lifelessly. Suddenly he felt an indefinable anguish
descend upon him, covering him.

He spent some time trying to attract the neighbors, already
weary of his efforts. Luciana Quiles looked at him with a furrowed brow, a bad omen. Thunder made him fall into a sort of
trance: from that came his best music. But the sickness of the
baby had Mariana so worried that, in an outburst of hopeless
rage, she broke the skin of the bongo.

"While he's sick, don't make any noise in this house," she said
and pushed the sharp heel of her shoe through the skins, which,
upon breaking, produced a dissonant noise (pru-*oh*, pru-*ah*),
hurting the Negro's ears.

Without a bongo, Bernabé Quirindongo felt fenced in by the
silence. The afternoons became heavy and insufferable. The
black faces turned away, presenting only the disdainful backs of
their heads. His fingers beat unsuccessfully on the walls, the
stone that served as a doorstep, his knees, the stool. Romualda
didn't want to replace the skins. Everything she earned she spent
on her grandson, who was getting better as the days went by. The
neighbors all came to the shack, passing Bernabé by without even
looking at him, and peered tenderly at the color of the little mulatto. Bernabé spent his time hunting for new resonant surfaces
that could take the place of his instrument. His lips moved in desperation: ta ta ta. But it was not the same. He had already lost two
good thunder storms with long fiery lightning flashes, as well as a
large number of words for which he could have found rhythmic
synonyms. An inexpressible sensation of confusion began to
mount up in his head. He beat upon whatever came within
reach: a wash basin, the bare beams of the house; he would stand
on the stool and anxiously pummel the tin roofing, which only
gave forth a hopeless *toom toom*. The back of a chair offered him
an immense possibility; he went at it, but as he beat it with his

convulsive fingers he noted that the sound came out opaque, dissipated, from the termite-damaged wood. He had to content himself with an inferior quality, while a series of impulses in disordered flight made him move his fingers incessantly. At times he seemed to beat the skins of an invisible bongo, and his gaze remained fixed beyond the pines and the bamboo fences. Pa-coo-*pah*, he murmured; sweat streamed from his armpits.

A rumor swept the town: it began like a superstitious whisper in the Negro colony, broke out at last, and leapt from mouth to mouth through all the municipality, filling the eight streets.

"Bernabé Quirindongo isn't playing anymore."

"Bernabé Quirindongo, black good-for-nothing."

"Bernabé Quirindongo, crazy Negro beating the air."

"Bernabé Quirindongo, widower of a bongo."

Romualda was still blind and deaf to her son's need.

"Mustn't make no noise," she would say, putting her finger to her lips.

Mariana watched him, scowling.

So Bernabé Quirindongo lived isolated in an ominous territory of silence. An infinite number of noises, lost for lack of a skin, assaulted his memory.

One afternoon, looking at the roof in search of a board or something suitable to release his intolerable tension, he noticed that the sky had become stern. There were black clouds that for a moment seemed to split apart into two islands; a streak of lightning had lashed the air above the long necks of the pines. The sky was like an immense black skin. He tuned his ear, eagerly. The thunder rolled through the valley, full and round, magnificent. His fingers moved nervously. "Boo-*room boom*," his lips articulated. The rain scourged the earth abruptly, like an enormous ejection of spittle. Tic-tic-ticky vibrated the drops on the tin. The pines bent in slow reverence. Boom, ba-*room*, a thunder clap said to him petulantly. A sharp-pointed heel, gleaming, slashed the skin of the sky. Bernabé Quirindongo, good-for-nothing. "Bernabé!" shouted the voices brought by the rain. "Quirindongo," let loose a thunderbolt. "Bernabé Merecumbé!" cried a gust of wind as it swept across the wall.

Bernabé Quirindongo felt that the marvelous rhythm of nature was enclosing him in a monstrous bongo. His fingers beat frenetically upon the partition-wall. Mariana could not scold him: she was working in the town. Mama was taking care of the kiosk. Boom, the thunder mocked. Tic-tic-ticky, laughed the rain, which leaned against the wall. Toc-toc-toc, said a drop which hammered solemnly into a tin can. "Where's your skin, your bongo bo-rom-*bom*?" a furious voice asked him. Without a bongo, black Bernabé Quirindongo was lost. The voices harassed him in the little living room.

The window, opening abruptly, let out a roar of laughter. Toc-toc-*boom*-tic-ticky.

He threw himself against the floor and pounded on it until his fingertips hurt. But his fingers could not drag from the boards the world of unbelievable sounds that beat in his brain. *Boom*, ba-*room*, ticky-tic-toc, ko-*toh*. From the bedroom the baby's voice called him quietly.

"Waaaaaayyyyy, Bernabé."

His heavy lips trembled: "Waayyyy, merecoom-*bay*." Ba-*room*, challenged the sky. "Black Bernabé Cumbé Quirindongo Dongo doesn't have a rawskin bongo, borom-*bon*," they whispered in his ear. Toc-toc-ticky.

"Waaaayyyyyy!" his nephew called again.

The branch of a tree slapped against the back of the house: tac, tac, tac. The wind whistled its mockery of the powerless fingers.

"Waaayyyyy," the baby called for a third time.

Bernabé Quirindongo went to his nephew and looked at him seriously, thoughtfully. The baby twisted among the blankets, shaking his little fists. "Waaayyyy, merecum-*bay*. Where's your skin, good-for-nothing!" they said in his ear. Boom ba-*room*. The smooth forehead, the young skin . . .

Ta coo-*pah*, sounded the gifted fingers on the skin of the forehead.

Boom, ba-*room*, they beat on the chest.

The thunder challenged him, *boom*, ba-*room*. "*Ha!*" laughed the window.

Black Bernabé Quirindongo was sweating, drawing out rhythm from his new skin. The tension was fading: he had unloaded a great part of his rhythm and felt there was still much more to be expressed. While the thunder continued to roll, calling him, while sonorous words hummed in his ear, he would have marvelous sounds with which to parry them. Ta coo-*pah, boom.*

Until Mariana's fingernails seized him furiously and threw him to the floor. Goo-*whop!* creaked the floor without the slightest acoustics. Mariana's shouts were terrible: there was no resonant quality in them. The black faces squeezed about the entrance of the shack, with Luciana Quiles at the fore, shaking her fists in the midst of the flashing half-light, beneath the persistent rain; they wanted to kill Bernabé Quirindongo, black good-for-nothing, bereft of his bongo.

Mariana kicked him unrhythmically.

Romualda and a policeman arrived: tuc, tuc, beat the night stick on the Negro's head, with the fortunate timing of a pair of sticks in a dance band.

Mama Romualda was shouting very unpleasantly, way out of tune.

The policeman grabbed Bernabé and carried him off through the rain.

Pa-*coom,* ba-*room,* the sky shouted at him.

"Pa coo-*pah,* pa coo-*pah,*" he went off, saying.

Translated by C. Virginia Matters

At the Great Ecbo

Guillermo Cabrera Infante

It was raining. The rain came crashing down between the old, dilapidated pillars. They were both sitting down and the man was
staring at the white tablecloth.

The waiter came up to take the order in an unusually courte-
ous fashion. At least he's civil, the man thought: it must be because of her. He asked her what she wanted.

She looked up from the menu. The dark stiff paper cover bore
the inscription: "La Maravilla—Menu." Her eyes seemed lighter
now with the snow-white light coming in from the park and the
rain. "The timeless light of da Vinci," he thought. He heard her
talking to the waiter.

"And you sir?" The waiter was addressing him now. Well
then! He really means to be polite. The fellow's not at all bad-
mannered.

"Something simple. Have you any meat?"

"No, not today. It's Friday."

These Catholics. Obsessed with their rules and regulations. He
thought it over for a moment.

"No dispensation?" he asked.

"What did you say?" asked the waiter.

"Bring me lamb chops. Grilled. And mashed potatoes. Oh yes,
and a black beer."

"Would you like something to drink?"

I could bet on it. She said she would have a beer. Just like a woman.

While they were fetching the lunch he looked at her. She seemed to have become a different woman. She looked up from the tablecloth at him: You never give up, he thought. Why don't you look beaten today? You ought to.

"What are you thinking about?" she asked and her voice sounded strangely soft and calm.

If only you knew. He said:

"Nothing."

"Were you examining me?" she asked.

"No. I was looking at your eyes."

" 'Eyes of a Christian in a Jewish face,' " she quoted.

He smiled. He was slightly bored.

"When do you think it'll stop raining?" she asked.

"I don't know," he said. "In a year's time maybe. Perhaps in a minute or two. You never know in Cuba."

He always spoke like that: as if he'd just got back from a long trip abroad or had been brought up there, as if he were a tourist and just passing through. In fact he'd never been out of Cuba.

"Do you think we shall be able to go to Guanabacoa?"

"Yes, I do. Though I don't know if there'll be anything going on. It's raining pretty hard."

"Yes, it is."

They stopped talking. He was looking out at the park beyond the mutilated pillars, along the roadway there still with its cobbles and the old, creeper-choked church: at the park with its sprinkling of puny trees.

He realized she was looking at him.

"What are you thinking about? Remember we swore we would always tell each other the truth."

"I'd have told it you anyway."

She checked herself. First she bit her lips and then opened her mouth extremely wide as if to utter words larger than her mouth. She did this habitually. He had advised her not to, as it didn't suit an actress.

"I was thinking," he heard her and wondered if she had started to speak then or earlier, "I don't know why I love you. You're exactly the opposite of the sort of man I dreamed about, but all the same I can look at you and feel in love with you. And you're nice."

"Thank you," he said.

"Oh dear!" she said, upset. She looked again at the tablecloth, at her hands and unpainted nails. She was tall and slim and she looked beautiful in the dress she had on, with its broad, square décolletage. Her breasts were in fact small, but the prominent bone structure of her chest made her appear to have a large bust. She wore a long, ornate pearl necklace and had her hair done up in a high bun. Her lips were full and even and very pink. And she used no makeup, except perhaps for some mascara which made her eyes bigger and lighter. She was put out and didn't speak again before the end of the meal.

"It's not stopping."

"It isn't," he said.

"Anything else?" said the waiter.

He looked at her.

"No thank you," she said.

"I want some coffee and a cigar."

"Very good," said the waiter.

"Oh yes, and the bill please."

"Yes sir."

"Are you going to smoke?"

"Yes," he said. She loathed cigars.

"You do it on purpose."

"You know I don't. I do it because I like it."

"It's not good to do everything one likes."

"Sometimes it is."

"And sometimes it isn't."

He looked at her and smiled. She didn't smile.

"Now I wish it hadn't happened."

"Why?"

"What do you mean why? Because I do. Do you think everything is so easy?"

"No," he said. "On the contrary, everything is hard. I'm serious. Life is complicated and hard. Everything is hard."

"It's hard to go on living," she said. He could follow her train of thought. She was back on the old subject. At the beginning she had spoken only of death, all day, all the time. Then he had made her forget the idea of death. But yesterday, yesterday evening to be exact, she began talking about death again. Not that he found the topic unpleasant, but he was more interested in its literary aspects and although he thought a lot about death, he didn't like to talk about it. Especially with her.

"Dying presents no problems," she said finally. Now it had come out, he thought and looked out at the street. It was still raining. Just like *Rashomon,* he thought. All we need is an old Japanese to come on and say: I don't understand, I don't understand . . .

"I don't understand," he ended up saying out loud.

"What exactly?" she asked. "That I'm not afraid of death? I always told you I wasn't."

He smiled.

"You look like the Mona Lisa," she said. "Always smiling."

He looked at her eyes, her mouth, her décolletage—and remembered. He liked remembering. Nothing was better than remembering. Sometimes he believed that he found things interesting only in so far as he could go over them again later. Like this now: this moment exactly: her eyes, her long eyelashes, the yellow-olive color of her eyes, the light reflected from the tablecloth on to her face, her eyes, her lips: the words they pronounced, the tone and the quiet, caressing sound of her voice, her teeth, her tongue which at times reached the edge of her mouth and was quickly withdrawn: the murmuring rain, the tinkling glass and the rattling plates and cutlery, a remote, inscrutable music coming from nowhere: the cigar smoke: the damp, fresh air from the park: he was deeply moved by the idea of knowing what his exact recollection of this moment would be like.

"Let's go," he said.

"But it's still raining," she said.

"It's going to go on all afternoon and evening. It's three o'clock already. Besides, the car is just outside."

They ran to the car and got in. He felt that the atmosphere inside the small car was going to asphyxiate him. He settled himself carefully and started the engine.

They passed and left behind the narrow, winding streets of old Havana, the old beautiful houses, some of them mercilessly demolished and turned into blank, asphalt car parks, the intricately-worked iron balconies, the huge, solid and beautiful

customs building, the Muelle de Luz and the Alameda de Paula,
a faultless pastiche, and the church of Paula looking like a half-
built Roman temple and the stretches of city wall and the tree
growing on top and Tallapiedra and its stench of sulphur and pu-
trefaction and the Elevado and Atarés castle looming up through
the rain and the Paso Superior, dull and gray, and the crisscross
of railway lines down below and of electric cables and telephone
wires up above and at last the open highway.

"I should like to see the photographs again," she said in the end.

"Now?"

"Yes."

He brought out his wallet and passed it to her. She looked
at the photographs silently in the dim light inside the car. She
didn't say anything when she gave him the wallet back. Then,
when they left the highway and turned into a side road, she said:

"Why did you show them to me?"

"Because you asked to see them of course," he answered.

"I don't mean now," she said.

"I don't know. I suppose it was the sadist in me."

"No, it wasn't that. It was vanity. Vanity and something else.
You did it to get hold of me completely, to assure yourself that I
was yours above everything: above the act, desire and remorse.
Especially remorse."

"And now?"

"Now we're living in sin."

"Is that all?"

"Yes. Don't you find it enough?"

"And remorse?"

"Where you'll always find it."

"And pain?"

"Where you'll always find it."

"And pleasure?"

It was an old game. Now she was supposed to say where pleasure
was to be found exactly, but she didn't say anything. He repeated:

"And pleasure?"

"There's none to be had," she said. "We're living in sin."

He pushed the waterproof flap back a little and threw his cigar
away. Then he told her:

"Open the compartment in the dashboard."

She did so.

"There's a book in it: take it out."

She did so.

"Open it at the bookmark."

She did so.

"Read what it says."

She saw that it said in capital letters: "Neurosis and Guilt Feelings." And she closed the book and put it back in the compartment and closed it.

"I've no need to read anything to know how I feel."

"But," he said, "it's not supposed to tell you how you feel but why you feel the way you do."

"I know quite well why I feel like this and so do you."

He laughed.

"Of course I do."

The small car bounced and then turned off to the right.

"Look," he said.

Ahead of them, to the left, a small graveyard shone all white, damp and wild through the rain. Its sterilized symmetry belied thoughts of worms and foul corruption.

"Isn't it beautiful!" she said.

He slowed down.

"Why don't we get out and walk round it for a few minutes?"

He gave her a brief, half-taunting look.

"Do you know what time it is? It's four already. We're going to get there when the party's over."

"You're insufferable," she grumbled.

That was the other half of her personality: the little girl. She was a monster, half woman and half child. Borges should include her in his fantastic fauna, he thought. The infanti-female. Along with the catoblepas and the amphisbaena.

He saw the village and stopped the car at a fork in the road.

"Could you tell me where the baseball ground is please?" he asked a group of people and two or three of them described the way in such detail that he knew he would get lost. At the next crossing he asked a policeman who showed him the road.

"Aren't people obliging here," she said.

"They are. Man on foot and man on a horse. Serfs will always oblige a feudal lord. Nowadays a car is a horse."

"Why are you so arrogant?"

"Me?"

"Yes, you."

"I don't think I am quite. It's just that I know what people think and have the courage to say it."

"It's the only sort of courage you have . . ."

"Perhaps."

"Not even perhaps. You know yourself . . ."

"All right, I do. I warned you from the beginning, though."

She turned round and looked at him closely.

"I don't know how I can love such a coward," she said.

They had arrived.

They ran through the rain to the building. At first he thought there wasn't going to be anything on because he couldn't hear anything for the rain and—amongst some corporation buses and a few cars—saw nothing but a few boys dressed in baseball kit. When he went in he felt as if he had penetrated a magic world:

there were a hundred or two hundred Negroes dressed in white from head to toe: white shirts and white trousers and white socks and their heads covered with white caps which made them look like a conference of colored cooks and the women were also dressed in white and there were a few white-skinned women among them and they were dancing in a ring to the rhythm of the drums and in the middle a huge Negro who was already old but still powerful and wore dark glasses so that only his white teeth could be seen as another part of the ritual dress and who thumped on the floor with a long wooden stick that had a carved Negro's head with hu-man hair as a handle and this Negro with the dark glasses sang and the others answered he shouted olofi *and paused while the holy word re-sounded against the walls and the rain and he shouted* olofi *again and then sang* tendundu kipungulé *and waited and the chorus repeated* olofi olofi *and in that atmosphere so strange and turbulent yet cool and damply lit the Negro sang again* naní masongo silanbasa *and the chorus repeated* naní masongo silanbasa *and again his slightly gut-tural and now hoarse voice sang out* sese maddié silanbaka *and the chorus repeated* sese maddié silanbaka *and again*

She came up close to him and whispered in his ear:

"It's divine!"

Damned theater slang, he thought, but he smiled because he

felt her breath on the back of his neck and her chin resting on his shoulder.

the Negro sang olofi *and the chorus answered* olofi *and he said* tendundu kipungulé *and the chorus repeated* tendundu kipungulé *and all the time keeping the rhythm with their feet and going endlessly round in a circle in a close group knowing they were singing to the dead and praying that the dead might rest in eternal peace and that those still alive might be comforted and waiting for their leader to say* olofi *again so that they could say* olofi *and begin again with the invocation* sese maddié

"Olofi is God in their language," he explained to her.

"What does the rest of it mean?"

For me to have to explain what Olofi means is bad enough, he thought.

"They're hymns to the dead. They sing to the dead so that they may rest in peace."

Her eyes shone with curiosity and excitement. She clutched his arm. The dance went on, round and round, tirelessly. Young and old alike. One man wore a white shirt completely covered with white buttons in front.

"Look," she said into his ear. "He's got hundreds of buttons on his shirt."

"Sh!" he said, because the man had looked up.

silanbaka bica dioko bica ndiambe *and he thumped his stick rhythmically against the floor and great drops of sweat ran down his arms and face and made faintly dark patches on the immaculate whiteness of his shirt and the chorus said after him again* bica dioko bica ndiambe *and close to the man in the middle other leaders were dancing and repeating the chorus's response and when the Negro in dark glasses murmured* take it! *one of them chanted* olofi sese maddié sese maddié *and the chorus repeated* sese maddié ses maddié *while the Negro in dark glasses thumped his stick against the floor and wiped away the sweat with a handkerchief that was also white*

"Why do they dress in white?" she asked.

"They are worshipping Obbatalá, the god of the pure and un-blemished."

"Then I can't worship Obbatalá," she said as a joke.

But he looked at her criticizingly and said:

"Don't talk nonsense."

"It's true. It's not nonsense."

She looked at him and then turned her attention to the Negroes and said, ridding what she had said before of all insinuation:

"Besides, it wouldn't suit me. I'm much too pale for white dresses."

and at his side another Negro swayed in time to the music and something indeterminate which went against the rhythm and interrupted it with his fingers on his eyes and he opened his eyes extremely wide and pointed to them again and emphasized the sensual and somewhat disjointed and mechanical movements of his body which nevertheless seemed possessed by a superior power and now the chanting reverberated against the walls and olofi olofi sese maddié sese maddié *invaded the whole building and reached two Negro boys in baseball kit who listened and looked on as if unwilling to embrace something that was theirs and reached the other spectators and drowned the noise of the beer bottles and the glasses in the bar at the back and flowed down the steps of the stands and danced among the puddles in the baseball pitch and went on over the sodden fields and through the rain reached the aloof and distant palm trees and went on further into wild country and seemed to want to surmount the far off hills and scale them and crown their summits and go on higher still* olofi olofi bica dioko bica dioko ndiambe bica ndiambe ndiambe y olofi y olofi y olofi *but again* sese maddié *but again* sese maddié *but again* sese *but again* sese

"That man's being sent," he said, pointing to the mulatto who had his fingers in his huge ears.

"Is he really?" she asked.

"Of course. It's only the hypnotic effect of the music, but they don't realize it."

"Would I be affected by it, do you think?"

And before telling her that she would, that she could be intoxicated by that rhythm, he became afraid that she would rush off and dance with them and so he said:

"I don't think so. It's only for the benighted, not for people like you who have read Ibsen and Chekhov and know Tennessee Williams off by heart."

She felt slightly flattered but said:

"They don't seem benighted to me. Primitive I agree, but not benighted. They believe. They believe in something neither you nor I can believe in and they are guided by their belief and live according to its rules and die for it and afterwards they sing ritual songs to their dead. I think it's wonderful."

"Mere superstition," he said pedantically. "It's something barbaric and remote and alien, as alien as Africa, where it comes from. I prefer Roman Catholicism with all its hypocrisy."

"That's remote and alien too," she said.

"Yes, but there's the Bible and Saint Augustine and Saint Thomas and Saint Teresa and Saint John of the Cross and Bach's music . . ."

"Bach was a Protestant," she said.

"It doesn't matter. A Protestant is a Catholic who can't sleep at nights."

He felt easier now because he felt he was witty and capable of talking above the drums and the chanting and the dancing, and because he had overcome the fear he had felt when he came in.

and sese *but again* sese *and* olofi sese olofi maddié olofi maddié maddié olofi bica dioko bica ndiambe olofi olofi silanbaka bica dioko olofi olofi sese maddié maddié olofi sese sese *and* olofi *and* olofi *and* olofi olofi

The music and the singing and the dancing suddenly stopped, and they witnessed how two or three Negroes grabbed the mulatto with the frenzied eyes by the arms and prevented him from knocking his head against one of the pillars.

"He's gone," he said.

"You mean he's been sent?"

"Yes."

They all gathered round him and carried him to the end of the hall. He lit two cigarettes and offered one to her. When he had finished his cigarette he went over to the wall and threw the stub out on to the damp field, and then he saw the Negress coming up to them.

"If you'll allow me sir," she said.

"Of course," the man said, without knowing what it was he had to allow.

The old Negress said nothing. She could have been sixty or seventy. But you never know with Negroes, he thought. Her face was small and fine-boned; her skin was intricately wrinkled and glistened about the eyes and mouth, but was taut over her prominent cheekbones and pointed chin. Her eyes were keen and gay and wise.

"If you'll excuse me sir," she said.

"What is it?" he said and thought: I'm sure she wants some money off me.

"I should like to speak to the young lady," she said. And so she thinks she can touch her more easily. She's doing the right thing because I hate charity.

"But of course!" he said, standing back a little and wondering uneasily what the old woman really wanted.

He saw the girl listening carefully at first and then lowering her earnest gaze from the old Negress's face to the ground. When they had finished talking he came up again.

"Thank you very much sir," the old woman said.

He didn't know whether to proffer his hand or bow slightly or smile. He chose to say:

"Not at all. I must thank you."

He looked at her and noticed that something had changed.

"Let's go," she said.

"Why? It's not over yet. It goes on till six. They go on singing till sunset."

"Let's go," she said again.

"What's going on?"

"*Please,* let's go."

"All right, let's go. But first tell me what's going on. What's happened? What was that old nigger woman on to you about?"

She looked at him unkindly.

"That *nigger woman,* as you put it, is a great person. She has lived a lot and knows a lot and if you really want to know she has just taught me something."

"Really?"

"Really."

"And may one know what the schoolmistress had to say?"

"Nothing!"

She moved away toward the door, finding her way with her graceful courtesy through the groups of Faithful who had come to worship Obbatalá. He caught her up at the door.

"Wait a minute," he said, "I did bring you here."

She said nothing and let him take her arm. As he was unlocking the car a boy came up to him and said:

"Hey mister, can you settle an argument? What sort of car's that? German?"

"No, it's English."

"It's not a Renault, is it?"

"No, it's an MG."

"Just like I said," the boy said with a satisfied smile, and rejoined his friends.

Always the same thing, he thought. Never say thank you. And they're the ones who breed most.

It had stopped raining and the air was fresh and he drove carefully until he found the road out to the highway. She hadn't broken her silence and when he looked into the driving-mirror, he saw that she was crying.

"I'm going to stop and put the hood down," he said.

He pulled over to the side of the road and saw that he was stopping close to the little graveyard. As he lowered the hood and fastened it down behind her he wanted to kiss the nape of her neck, but he felt as if he was being repulsed as strongly as he had been attracted on other occasions.

"Were you crying?" he asked her.

She lifted up her face and showed him her eyes without looking at him. They were dry, but very bright and slightly red at the rim.

"I never cry, darling. Except at the theater."

He was hurt and said nothing.

"Where are we going?" he said.

"Home," she said.

"You're quite sure?"

"Surer than you might think," she said. Then she opened the compartment, took the book out and turned toward him.

"Here you are," she said shortly.

When he looked he saw she was handing him the two portraits—the one of the smiling, solemn-eyed woman and the one of the little boy, taken in a studio, with huge, solemn eyes and no smile on his lips—and realized that he was taking them automatically.

"I'd rather you kept them."

TRANSLATED BY J. G. BROTHERSTON

My Aunt Gold Teeth

V. S. Naipaul

I never knew her real name and it is quite likely that she did have one, though I never heard her called anything but Gold Teeth. She did, indeed, have gold teeth. She had sixteen of them. She had married early and she had married well, and shortly after her marriage she exchanged her perfectly sound teeth for gold ones, to announce to the world that her husband was a man of substance.

Even without her gold teeth my aunt would have been noticeable. She was short, scarcely five foot, and she was very fat. If you saw her in silhouette you would have found it difficult to know whether she was facing you or whether she was looking sideways.

She ate little and prayed much. Her family being Hindu, and her husband being a pundit, she, too, was an orthodox Hindu. Of Hinduism she knew little apart from the ceremonies and the taboos, and this was enough for her. Gold Teeth saw God as a Power, and religious ritual as a means of harnessing that Power for great practical good, her good.

I may have given the impression that Gold Teeth prayed because she wanted to be less fat. The fact was that Gold Teeth had no children and she was almost forty. It was her childlessness, not her fat, that oppressed her, and she prayed for the curse to be removed. She was willing to try any means—any ritual, any prayer—in order to trap and channel the supernatural Power.

And so it was that she began to indulge in surreptitious Christian practices.

She was living at the time in a country village called Cunupia, in County Caroni. Here the Canadian Mission had long waged war against the Indian heathen, and saved many. But Gold Teeth stood firm. The Minister of Cunupia expended his Presbyterian piety on her; so did the headmaster of the Mission school. But all in vain. At no time was Gold Teeth persuaded even to think about being converted. The idea horrified her. Her father had been in his day one of the best-known Hindu pundits, and even now her husband's fame as a pundit, as a man who could read and write Sanskrit, had spread far beyond Cunupia. She was in no doubt whatsoever that Hindus were the best people in the world, and that Hinduism was a superior religion. She was willing to select, modify and incorporate alien eccentricities into her worship; but to abjure her own faith—never!

Presbyterianism was not the only danger the good Hindu had to face in Cunupia. Besides, of course, the ever-present threat of open Muslim aggression, the Catholics were to be reckoned with. Their pamphlets were everywhere and it was hard to avoid them. In them Gold Teeth read of novenas and rosaries, of squads of saints and angels. These were things she understood and could even sympathize with, and they encouraged her to seek further. She read of the mysteries and the miracles, of penances and indulgences. Her scepticism sagged, and yielded to a quickening, if reluctant, enthusiasm.

One morning she took the train for the County town of Chaguanas, three miles, two stations and twenty minutes away. The Church of St. Philip and St. James in Chaguanas stands imposingly at the end of the Caroni Savannah Road, and although Gold Teeth knew Chaguanas well, all she knew of the church was that it had a clock, at which she had glanced on her way to the railway station nearby. She had hitherto been far more interested in the drab ochre-washed edifice opposite, which was the police station.

She carried herself into the churchyard, awed by her own temerity, feeling like an explorer in a land of cannibals. To her relief, the church was empty. It was not as terrifying as she had expected. In the gilt and images and the resplendent cloths she found much that reminded her of her Hindu temple. Her eyes caught a discreet sign: CANDLES TWO CENTS EACH. She undid the knot in the end of her veil, where she kept her money, took out three cents, popped them into the box, picked up a candle and muttered a prayer in Hindustani. A brief moment of elation gave way to a sense of guilt, and she was suddenly anxious to get away from the church as fast as her weight would let her.

She took a bus home, and hid the candle in her chest of drawers. She had half feared that her husband's Brahminical flair for clairvoyance would have uncovered the reason for her trip to Chaguanas. When after four days, which she spent in an ecstasy of prayer, her husband had mentioned nothing, Gold Teeth thought it safe to burn the candle. She burned it secretly at night, before her Hindu images, and sent up, as she thought, prayers of double efficacy.

Every day her religious schizophrenia grew, and presently she began wearing a crucifix. Neither her husband nor her neighbors knew she did so. The chain was lost in the billows of fat around her neck, and the crucifix was itself buried in the valley of her gargantuan breasts. Later she acquired two holy pictures, one of the Virgin Mary, the other of the crucifixion, and took care to conceal them from her husband. The prayers she offered to these Christian things filled her with new hope and buoyancy. She became an addict of Christianity.

Then her husband, Ramprasad, fell ill.

Ramprasad's sudden, unaccountable illness alarmed Gold Teeth. It was, she knew, no ordinary illness, and she knew, too, that her religious transgression was the cause. The District Medical Officer at Chaguanas said it was diabetes, but Gold Teeth knew better. To be on the safe side, though, she used the insulin he prescribed and, to be even safer, she consulted Ganesh Pundit, the masseur with mystic leanings, celebrated as a faith healer.

Ganesh came all the way from Fuente Grove to Cunupia. He came in great humility, anxious to serve Gold Teeth's husband, for Gold Teeth's husband was a Brahmin among Brahmins, a *Panday,* a man who knew all five Vedas; while he, Ganesh, was a mere *Chaubay* and knew only four.

With spotless white *koortah,* his dhoti cannily tied, and a tasselled green scarf as a concession to elegance, Ganesh exuded the confidence of the professional mystic. He looked at the sick

man, observed his pallor, sniffed the air. "This man," he said, "is
bewitched. Seven spirits are upon him."

He was telling Gold Teeth nothing she didn't know. She had
known from the first that there were spirits in the affair, but she
was glad that Ganesh had ascertained their number.

"But you mustn't worry," Ganesh added. "We will 'tie' the
house—in spiritual bonds—and no spirit will be able to come in."

Then, without being asked, Gold Teeth brought out a blanket,
folded it, placed it on the floor and invited Ganesh to sit on it.
Next she brought him a brass jar of fresh water, a mango leaf and
a plate full of burning charcoal.

"Bring me some ghee," Ganesh said, and after Gold Teeth had
done so, he set to work. Muttering continuously in Hindustani he
sprinkled the water from the brass jar around him with the
mango leaf. Then he melted the ghee in the fire and the charcoal hissed so sharply that Gold Teeth could not make out his
words. Presently he rose and said, "You must put some of the ash
of this fire on your husband's forehead, but if he doesn't want
you to do that, mix it with his food. You must keep the water in
this jar and place it every night before your front door."

Gold Teeth pulled her veil over her forehead.

Ganesh coughed. "That," he said, rearranging his scarf, "is all.
There is nothing more I can do. God will do the rest."

He refused payment for his services. It was enough honor, he
said, for a man as humble as he was to serve Pundit Ramprasad,
and she, Gold Teeth, had been singled out by fate to be the
spouse of such a worthy man. Gold Teeth received the impression that Ganesh spoke from a firsthand knowledge of fate and
its designs, and her heart, buried deep down under inches of
mortal, flabby flesh, sank a little.

"Baba," she said hesitantly, "revered Father, I have something
to say to you." But she couldn't say anything more and Ganesh,
seeing this, filled his eyes with charity and love.

"What is it, my child?"

"I have done a great wrong, Baba."

"What sort of wrong?" he asked, and his tone indicated that
Gold Teeth could do no wrong.

"I have prayed to Christian things."

And to Gold Teeth's surprise, Ganesh chuckled benevolently.

"And do you think God minds, daughter? There is only one God and different people pray to Him in different ways. It doesn't matter how you pray, but God is pleased if you pray at all."

"So it is not because of me that my husband has fallen ill?"

"No, to be sure, daughter."

In his professional capacity Ganesh was consulted by people of many faiths, and with the license of the mystic he had exploited the commodiousness of Hinduism, and made room for all beliefs. In this way he had many clients, as he called them, many satisfied clients.

Henceforward Gold Teeth not only pasted Ramprasad's pale forehead with the sacred ash Ganesh had prescribed, but mixed substantial amounts with his food. Ramprasad's appetite, enormous even in sickness, diminished; and he shortly entered into a visible and alarming decline that mystified his wife.

She fed him more ash than before, and when it was exhausted and Ramprasad perilously macerated, she fell back on the Hindu wife's last resort. She took her husband home to her mother. That venerable lady, my grandmother, lived with us in Port-of-Spain.

Ramprasad was tall and skeletal, and his face was grey. The virile voice that had expounded a thousand theological points and recited a hundred *puranas* was now a wavering whisper. We cooped him up in a room called, oddly, "the pantry." It had never been used as a pantry and one can only assume that the architect had so designated it some forty years before. It was a tiny room. If you wished to enter the pantry you were compelled, as soon as you opened the door, to climb on to the bed: it fitted the room to a miracle. The lower half of the walls were concrete, the upper close latticework; there were no windows.

My grandmother had her doubts about the suitability of the room for a sick man. She was worried about the lattice-work. It let in air and light, and Ramprasad was not going to die from these things if she could help it. With cardboard, oilcloth and canvas she made the latticework air-proof and lightproof.

And, sure enough, within a week Ramprasad's appetite returned, insatiable and insistent as before. My grandmother claimed all the credit for this, though Gold Teeth knew that the ash she had fed him had not been without effect. Then she realized with horror that she had ignored a very important thing. The

house in Cunupia had been tied and no spirits could enter, but
the house in the city had been given no such protection and any
spirit could come and go as it chose. The problem was pressing.

Ganesh was out of the question. By giving his services free he
had made it impossible for Gold Teeth to call him in again. But
thinking in this way of Ganesh, she remembered his words: "It
doesn't matter how you pray, but God is pleased if you pray at all."

Why not, then, bring Christianity into play again?

She didn't want to take any chances this time. She decided to
tell Ramprasad.

He was propped up in bed, and eating. When Gold Teeth
opened the door he stopped eating and blinked at the unwonted
light. Gold Teeth, stepping into the doorway and filling it, shad-
owed the room once more and he went on eating. She placed the
palms of her hands on the bed. It creaked.

"Man," she said.

Ramprasad continued to eat.

"Man," she said in English, "I thinking about going to the
church to pray. You never know, and it better to be on the safe
side. After all, the house ain't tied—"

"I don't want you to pray in no church," he whispered, in English too.

Gold Teeth did the only thing she could do. She began to cry.

Three days in succession she asked his permission to go to
church, and his opposition weakened in the face of her tears. He
was now, besides, too weak to oppose anything. Although his appetite had returned, he was still very ill and very weak, and every
day his condition became worse.

On the fourth day he said to Gold Teeth, "Well, pray to Jesus
and go to church, if it will put your mind at rest."

And Gold Teeth straight away set about putting her mind at
rest. Every morning she took the trolleybus to the Holy Rosary
Church, to offer worship in her private way. Then she was emboldened to bring a crucifix and pictures of the Virgin and the
Messiah into the house. We were all somewhat worried by this,
but Gold Teeth's religious nature was well known to us; her husband was a learned pundit and when all was said and done this
was an emergency, a matter of life and death. So we could do
nothing but look on. Incense and camphor and ghee burned

now before the likeness of Krishna and Shiva as well as Mary and Jesus. Gold Teeth revealed an appetite for prayer that equalled her husband's for food, and we marveled at both, if only because neither prayer nor food seemed to be of any use to Ramprasad.

One evening, shortly after bell and gong and conch-shell had announced that Gold Teeth's official devotions were almost over, a sudden chorus of lamentation burst over the house, and I was summoned to the room reserved for prayer. "Come quickly, something dreadful has happened to your aunt."

The prayer-room, still heavy with fumes of incense, presented an extraordinary sight. Before the Hindu shrine, flat on her face, Gold Teeth lay prostrate, rigid as a sack of flour. I had only seen Gold Teeth standing or sitting, and the aspect of Gold Teeth prostrate, so novel and so grotesque, was disturbing.

My grandmother, an alarmist by nature, bent down and put her ear to the upper half of the body on the floor. "I don't seem to hear her heart," she said.

We were all somewhat terrified. We tried to lift Gold Teeth but she seemed as heavy as lead. Then, slowly, the body quivered. The flesh beneath the clothes rippled, then billowed, and the children in the room sharpened their shrieks. Instinctively we all stood back from the body and waited to see what was going to happen. Gold Teeth's hand began to pound the floor and at the same time she began to gurgle.

My grandmother had grasped the situation. "She's got the spirit," she said.

At the word "spirit," the children shrieked louder, and my grandmother slapped them into silence.

The gurgling resolved itself into words pronounced with a lingering ghastly quaver. "Hail Mary, Hare Ram," Gold Teeth said, "the snakes are after me. Everywhere snakes. Seven snakes. Rama! Rama! Full of grace. Seven spirits leaving Cunupia by the four-o'clock train for Port-of-Spain."

My grandmother and my mother listened eagerly, their faces lit up with pride. I was rather ashamed at the exhibition, and annoyed with Gold Teeth for putting me into a fright. I moved toward the door.

"Who is that going away? Who is the young *caffar*, the unbeliever?" the voice asked abruptly.

"Come back quickly, boy," my grandmother whispered. "Come
back and ask her pardon."

I did as I was told.

"It is all right, son," Gold Teeth replied, "you don't know. You
are young."

Then the spirit appeared to leave her. She wrenched herself
up to a sitting position and wondered why we were all there. For
the rest of that evening she behaved as if nothing had happened,
and she pretended she didn't notice that everyone was looking at
her and treating her with unusual respect.

"I have always said it, and I will say it again," my grandmother
said, "that these Christians are very religious people. That is why I
encouraged Gold Teeth to pray to Christian things."

Ramprasad died early next morning and we had the an-
nouncement on the radio after the local news at one o'clock.
Ramprasad's death was the only one announced and so, although it came between commercials, it made some impression.
We buried him that afternoon in Mucurapo Cemetery.

As soon as we got back my grandmother said, "I have always
said it, and I will say it again: I don't like these Christian things.
Ramprasad would have got better if only you, Gold Teeth, had listened to me and not gone running after these Christian things."

Gold Teeth sobbed her assent; and her body squabbered and
shook as she confessed the whole story of her trafficking with Christianity. We listened in astonishment and shame. We didn't know
that a good Hindu, and a member of our family, could sink so low.
Gold Teeth beat her breast and pulled ineffectually at her long hair
and begged to be forgiven. "It is all my fault," she cried. "My own
fault, Ma. I fell in a moment of weakness. Then I just couldn't stop."

My grandmother's shame turned to pity. "It's all right, Gold
Teeth. Perhaps it was this you needed to bring you back to your
senses."

That evening Gold Teeth ritually destroyed every reminder of
Christianity in the house.

"You have only yourself to blame," my grandmother said, "if
you have no children now to look after you."

The Wharf Rats

Eric Walrond

I

Among the motley crew recruited to dig the Panama Canal were artisans from the four ends of the earth. Down in the Cut drifted hordes of Italians, Greeks, Chinese, Negroes—a hardy, sun-defying set of white, black and yellow men. But the bulk of the actual brawn for the work was supplied by the dusky peons of those coral isles in the Caribbean ruled by Britain, France and Holland.

At the Atlantic end of the Canal the blacks were herded in boxcar huts buried in the jungles of "Silver City;" in the murky tenements perilously poised on the narrow banks of Faulke's River; in the low, smelting cabins of Coco Té. The "Silver Quarters" harbored the inky ones, their wives and pickaninnies.

As it grew dark the hewers at the Ditch, exhausted, half-asleep, naked but for wormy singlets, would hum queer creole tunes, play on guitar or piccolo, and jig to the rhythm of the *coombia*. It was a *brujerial* chant, for *obeah*, a heritage of the French colonial, honeycombed the life of the Negro laboring camps. Over smoking pots, on black, death-black nights legends of the bloodiest were recited till they became the essence of a sort of Negro Koran. One refuted them at the price of one's breath. And to question the verity of the *obeah*, to dismiss or reject it as the ungodly rite of some lurid, crack-brained Islander was to be an accursed paleface, dog of a white. And the *obeah* man, in a fury of rage, would throw a machete at the heretic's head or—worse—burn on his doorstep at night a pyre of Maubé bark or green Ganja weed.

On the banks of a river beyond Cristobal, Coco Té sheltered a colony of Negroes enslaved to the *obeah*. Near a roundhouse, daubed with smoke and coal ash, a river serenely flowed away and into the guava region, at the eastern tip of Monkey Hill. Across the bay from it was a sand bank—a rising out of the sea— where ships stopped for coal.

In the first of the six chinky cabins making up the family quarters of Coco Té lived a stout, pot-bellied St. Lucian, black as the coal hills he mended, by the name of Jean Baptiste. Like a host of the native St. Lucian emigrants, Jean Baptiste forgot where the French in him ended and the English began. His speech was the petulant *patois* of the unlettered French black. Still, whenever he lapsed into His Majesty's English, it was with a thick Barbadian bias.

A coal passer at the Dry Dock, Jean Baptiste was a man of intense piety. After work, by the glow of a red, setting sun, he would discard his crusted overalls, get in starched *crocus bag,* aping the Yankee foreman on the other side of the track in the "Gold Quarters," and loll on his coffee-vined porch. There, dozing in a bamboo rocker, Celestin, his second wife, a becomingly stout brown beauty from Martinique, chanted gospel hymns to him.

Three sturdy sons Jean Baptiste's first wife had borne him— Philip, the eldest, a good-looking, black fellow; Ernest, shifty, cunning; and Sandel, aged eight. Another boy, said to be wayward and something of a ne'er-do-well, was sometimes spoken of. But Baptiste, a proud, disdainful man, never once referred to him in the presence of his children. No vagabond son of his could eat from his table or sit at his feet unless he went to "meeting." In brief, Jean Baptiste was a religious man. It was a thrust at the omnipresent *obeah*. He went to "meeting." He made the boys go, too. All hands went, not to the Catholic Church, where Celestin secretly worshiped, but to the English Plymouth Brethren in the Spanish city of Colon.

Stalking about like a ghost in Jean Baptiste's household was a girl, a black ominous Trinidad girl. Had Jean Baptiste been a man given to curiosity about the nature of women, he would have viewed skeptically Maffi's adoption by Celestin. But Jean Baptiste was a man of lofty unconcern, and so Maffi remained there, shadowy, obdurate.

And Maffi was such a hardworking *patois* girl. From the break of day she'd be at the sink, brightening the tinware. It was she who did the chores which Madame congenitally shirked. And toward sundown, when the labor trains had emptied, it was she who scoured the beach for cockles for Jean Baptiste's epicurean palate.

And as night fell, Maffi, a long, black figure, would disappear in the dark to dream on top of a canoe hauled up on the mooning beach. An eternity Maffi'd sprawl there, gazing at the frosting of the stars and the glitter of the black sea.

A cabin away lived a family of Tortola mulattoes by the name of Boyce. The father was also a man who piously went to "meeting"—gaunt and hollow-cheeked. The eldest boy, Esau, had been a journeyman tailor for ten years; the girl next him, Ora, was plump, dark, freckled; others came—a string of ulcered girls until finally a pretty, opaque one, Maura.

Of the Bantu tribe Maura would have been a person to turn and stare at. Crossing the line into Cristobal or Colon—a city of rarefied gaiety—she was often mistaken for a native *señorita* or an urbanized Cholo Indian girl. Her skin was the reddish yellow of old gold and in her eyes there lurked the glint of mother-of-pearl. Her hair, long as a jungle elf's was jettish, untethered. And her teeth were whiter than the full-blooded black Philip's.

Maura was brought up, like the children of Jean Baptiste, in the Plymouth Brethren. But the Plymouth Brethren was a harsh faith to bring hemmed-in peasant children up in, and Maura, besides, was of a gentle romantic nature. Going to the Yankee commissary at the bottom of Eleventh and Front Streets, she usually wore a leghorn hat. With flowers bedecking it, she'd look in it older, much older than she really was. Which was an impression quite flattering to her. For Maura, unknown to Philip, was in love—in love with San Tie, a Chinese half-breed, son of a wealthy canteen proprietor in Colon. But San Tie liked to go fishing and deer hunting up the Monkey Hill lagoon, and the object of his occasional visits to Coco Té was the eldest son of Jean Baptiste. And thus it was through Philip that Maura kept in touch with the young Chinese Maroon.

One afternoon Maura, at her wits' end flew to the shed roof to Jean Baptiste's kitchen.

"Maffi," she cried, the words smoky on her lips, "Maffi, when Philip come in tonight tell 'im I want fo' see 'im particular, yes?"

"Sacre gache! All de time Philip, Philip!" growled the Trinidad girl, as Maura, in heartaching preoccupation, sped towards the lawn. "Why she no le' 'im alone, yes?" And with a spatter she flecked the hunk of lard on Jean Baptiste's stewing okras.

As the others filed up front after dinner that evening Maffi said to Philip, pointing to the cabin across the way, "She—she want fo' see yo'."

Instantly Philip's eyes widened. Ah, he had good news for Maura! San Tie, after an absence of six days, was coming to Coco Té Saturday to hunt on the lagoon. And he'd relish the joy that'd flood Maura's face as she glimpsed the idol of her heart, the hero of her dreams! And Philip, a true son of Jean Baptiste, loved to see others happy, ecstatic.

But Maffi's curious rumination checked him. "All de time, Maura, Maura, me can't understand it, yes. But no mind, me go stop it, *oui,* me go stop it, so help me—"

He crept up to her, gently holding her by the shoulders.

"Le' me go, *sacre!*" She shook off his hands bitterly. "Le' me go—yo' go to yo' Maura." And she fled to her room, locking the door behind her.

Philip sighed. He was a generous, good-natured sort. But it was silly to try to enlighten Maffi. It wasn't any use. He could as well have spoken to the tattered torsos the lazy waves puffed up on the shores of Coco Té.

II

"Philip, come on, a ship is in—let's go." Ernest, the wharf rat, seized him by the arm.

"Come," he said, "let's go before it's too late. I want to get some money, yes."

Dashing out of the house the two boys made for the wharf. It was dusk. Already the Hindus in the bachelor quarters were mixing their *rotie* and the Negroes in their singlets were smoking and cooling off. Night was rapidly approaching. Sunset, an iridescent bit of molten gold, was enriching the stream with its last faint radiance.

The boys stole across the lawn and made their way to the pier.

"Careful," cried Philip, as Ernest slid between a prong of oyster-crusted piles to a raft below, "careful, these shells cut wussah'n a knife."

On the raft the boys untied a rowboat they kept stowed away under the dock, got into it and pushed off. The liner still had two hours to dock. Tourists crowded its decks. Veering away from the barnacled piles the boys eased out into the churning ocean.

It was dusk. Night would soon be upon them. Philip took the oars while Ernest stripped down to loin cloth.

"Come, Philip, let me paddle—" Ernest took the oars. Afar on the dusky sea a whistle echoed. It was the pilot's signal to the captain of port. The ship would soon dock.

The passengers on deck glimpsed the boys. It piqued their curiosity to see two black boys in a boat amid stream.

"All right, mistah," cried Ernest, "a penny, mistah."

He sprang at the guilder as it twisted and turned through a streak of silver dust to the bottom of the sea. Only the tips of his crimson toes—a sherbet-like foam—and up he came with the coin between his teeth.

Deep sea gamin, Philip off yonder, his mouth noisy with coppers, gargled, "This way, sah, as far as yo' like, mistah."

An old red-bearded Scot, in spats and mufti, presumably a lover of the exotic in sport, held aloft a sovereign. A sovereign! Already red, and sore by virtue of the leaps and plunges in the briny swirl, Philip's eyes bulged at its yellow gleam.

"Ovah yah, sah—"

Off in a whirlpool the man tossed it. And like a garfish Philip took after it, a falling arrow in the stream. His body, once in the water, tore ahead. For a spell the crowd on the ship held its breath. "Where is he?" "Where is the nigger swimmer gone to?" Even Ernest, driven to the boat by the race for such an ornate prize, cold, shivering, his teeth chattering—even he watched with trembling and anxiety. But Ernest's concern was of a deeper kind. For there, where Philip had leaped, was Deathpool—a spawning place for sharks, for barracudas!

But Philip rose—a brief gurgling sputter—a ripple on the sea—and the Negro's crinkled head was above the water.

"Hey!" shouted Ernest, "there, Philip! Down!"

And down Philip plunged. One—two—minutes. God, how long they seemed! And Ernest anxiously waited. But the bubble on the water boiled, kept on boiling—a sign that life still lasted! It comforted Ernest.

Suddenly Philip, panting, spitting, pawing, dashed through the water like a streak of lightning.

"Shark!" cried a voice aboard ship. "Shark! There he is, a great big one! Run, boy! Run for your life!"

From the edge of the boat Philip saw the monster as twice, thrice it circled the boat. Several times the shark made a dash for it endeavoring to strike it with its murderous tail.

The boys quietly made off. But the shark still followed the boat. It was a pale-green monster. In the glittering dusk it seemed black to Philip. Fattened on the swill of the abattoir nearby and the beef tossed from the decks of countless ships in port it had become used to the taste of flesh and the smell of blood.

"Yo' know, Ernest," said Philip, as he made the boat fast to a raft, "one time I thought he wuz rubbin' 'gainst me belly. He wuz such a big able one. But it wuz wuth it, Ernie, it wuz wuth it—"

In his palm there was a flicker of gold. Ernest emptied his loin cloth and together they counted the money, dressed and trudged back to the cabin.

On the lawn Philip met Maura. Ernest tipped his cap, left his brother, and went into the house. As he entered Maffi, pretending to be scouring a pan, was flushed and mute as a statue. And Ernest, starved, went in the dining room and for a long time stayed there. Unable to bear it any longer, Maffi sang out, "Ernest, whey Philip dey?"

"Outside—some whey—ah talk to Maura—"

"Yo' sure yo' no lie, Ernest?" she asked, suspended.

"Yes, up cose, I jes' lef' 'im 'tandin' out dey—why?"

"Nutton—"

He suspected nothing. He went on eating while Maffi tiptoed
to the shed roof. Yes, confound it, there he was, near the standpipe, talking to Maura!

"Go stop *ee, oui,*" she hissed impishly. "Go 'top ee, yes."

III

Low, shadowy, the sky painted Maura's face bronze. The sea,
noisy, enraged, sent a blob of wind about her black, wavy hair.
And with her back to the sea, her hair blew loosely about her
face.

"D'ye think, d'ye think he really likes me, Philip?"

"I'm positive he do, Maura," vowed the youth.

And an ageing faith shone in Maura's eyes. No longer was she
a silly, insipid girl. Something holy, reverent had touched her.
And in so doing it could not fail to leave an impress of beauty. It
was worshipful. And it mellowed, ripened her.

Weeks she had waited for word of San Tie. And the springs of
Maura's life took on a noble ecstasy. Late at night, after the others had retired, she'd sit up in bed, dreaming. Sometimes they
were dreams of envy. For Maura began to look with eyes of comparison upon the happiness of the Italian wife of the boss riveter
at the Dry Dock—the lady on the other side of the railroad tracks
in the "Gold Quarters" for whom she sewed—who got a fresh
baby every year and who danced in a world of silks and satins.
Yes, Maura had dreams, love dreams of San Tie, the flashy half-
breed, son of a Chinese beer seller and a Jamaica Maroon, who
had swept her off her feet by a playful wink of the eye.

"Tell me, Philip, does he work? Or does he play the lottery—
what does he do, tell me!"

"I dunno," Philip replied with mock lassitude, "I dunno myself—"

"But it doesn't matter, Philip. I don't want to be nosy, see? I'm
simply curious about everything that concerns him, see?"

Ah, but Philip wished to cherish Maura, to shield her, be kind
to her. And so he lied to her. He did not tell her he had first met
San Tie behind the counter of his father's saloon in the Colon
tenderloin, for he would have had to tell, besides, why he, Philip,
had gone there. And that would have led him, a youth of meager

guile, to Celestin Baptiste's mulish regard for anisette which he
procured her. He dared not tell her, well-meaning fellow that he
was, what San Tie, a fiery comet in the night life of the district,
had said to him the day before. "She sick in de head, yes," he had
said. "Ah, me no dat saht o' man—don't she know no bettah,
egh, Philip?" But Philip desired to be kindly, and hid it from
Maura.

"What is today?" she cogitated, aloud, "Tuesday. You say he's
comin' fo' hunt Saturday, Philip? Wednesday—four more days. I
can wait. I can wait. I'd wait a million years fo' 'im, Philip."

But Saturday came and Maura, very properly, was shy as a
duck. Other girls, like Hilda Long, a Jamaica brunette, the flower
of a bawdy cabin up by the abattoir, would have been less genteel. Hilda would have caught San Tie by the lapels of his coat
and in no time would have got him told.

But Maura was lowly, trepid, shy. To her he was a dream—a
luxury to be distantly enjoyed. He was not to be touched. And
she'd wait till he decided to come to her. And there was no fear,
either, of his ever failing to come. Philip had seen to that. Had
not he been the intermediary between them? And all Maura
needed now was to sit back, and wait till San Tie came to her.

And besides, who knows, brooded Maura, San Tie might be a
bashful fellow.

But when, after an exciting hunt, the Chinese mulatto returned from the lagoon, nodded stiffly to her, said good-bye to
Philip and kept on to the scarlet city, Maura was frantic.

"Maffi," she said, "tell Philip to come here quick—"

It was the same as touching a match to the *patois* girl's dynamite. "Yo' mek me sick," she said. "Go call he yo'self, yo' ole hag,
yo' ole fire hag yo'." But Maura, flighty in despair, had gone on
past the lawn.

"Ah go stop *ee, oui,*" she muttered diabolically. "Ah go stop it,
yes. This very night."

Soon as she got through lathering the dishes she tidied up and
came out on the front porch.

It was a humid dusk, and the glowering sky sent a species of
fly—bloody as a tick—buzzing about Jean Baptiste's porch.
There he sat, rotund, and sleepy-eyed, rocking and languidly
brushing the darting imps away.

"Wha' yo' gwine, Maffi?" asked Celestin Baptiste, fearing to wake the old man.

"Ovah to de Jahn Chinaman shop, mum," answered Maffi unheeding.

"Fi' what?"

"Fi' buy some wash blue, mum."

And she kept on down the road past the Hindu kiosk to the Negro mess house.

IV

"Oh, Philip," cried Maura, "I am so unhappy. Didn't he ask about me at all? Didn't he say he'd like to visit me—didn't he giv' yo' any message fo' me, Philip?"

The boy toyed with a blade of grass. His eyes were downcast. Sighing heavily he at last spoke. "No, Maura, he didn't ask about you."

"What, he didn't ask about me? Philip? I don't believe it! Oh, my God!"

She clung to Philip, mutely; her face, her breath coming warm and fast.

"I wish to God I'd never seen either of you," cried Philip.

"Ah, but wasn't he your friend, Philip? Didn't yo' tell me that?" And the boy bowed his head sadly.

"Answer me!" she screamed, shaking him. "Weren't you his friend?"

"Yes, Maura—"

"But you lied to me, Philip, you lied to me! You took messages from me—you brought back—lies!" Two *pearls,* large as pigeon's eggs, shone in Maura's burnished face.

"To think," she cried in a hollow sepulchral voice, "that I dreamed about a ghost, a man who didn't exist. Oh, God, why should I suffer like this? Why was I ever born? What did I do, what did my people do, to deserve such misery as this?"

She rose, leaving Philip with his head buried in his hands. She went into the night, tearing her hair, scratching her face, raving.

"Oh, how happy I was! I was a happy girl! I was so young and I had such merry dreams! And I wanted so little! I was carefree—"

Down to the shore of the sea she staggered, the wind behind her, the night obscuring her.

"Maura!" cried Philip, running after her. "Maura! come back!"

Great sheaves of clouds buried the moon, and the wind bearing up from the sea bowed the cypress and palm lining the beach.

"Maura—Maura—"

He bumped into some one, a girl, black, part of the dense pattern of the tropical night.

"Maffi," cried Philip, "Have you seen Maura down yondah?"

The girl quietly stared at him. Had Philip lost his mind?

"Talk, no!" he cried, exasperated.

And his quick tones sharpened Maffi's vocal anger. Thrusting him aside, she thundered, "Think I'm she keeper! Go'n look fo' she yo'self. I is not she keeper! Le' me pass, move!"

Towards the end of the track he found Maura heartrendingly weeping.

"Oh, don't cry, Maura! Never mind, Maura!"

He helped her to her feet, took her to the standpipe on the lawn, bathed her temples and sat soothingly, uninterruptingly, beside her.

V

At daybreak the next morning Ernest rose and woke Philip.

He yawned, put on the loin cloth, seized a "cracked licker" skillet and stole cautiously out of the house. Of late Jean Baptiste had put his foot down on his sons' copper-diving proclivities. And he kept at the head of his bed a greased cat-o'-nine-tails which he would use on Philip himself if the occasion warranted.

"Come on, Philip, let's go—"

Yawning and scratching Philip followed. The grass on the lawn was bright and icy with the dew. On the railroad tracks the six o'clock labor trains were coupling. A rosy mist flooded the dawn. Out in the stream the tug *Exotic* snorted in a heavy fog.

On the wharf Philip led the way to the rafters below.

"Look out fo' that *crapeau*, Ernest, don't step on him, he'll spit on you."

The frog splashed into the water. Prickle-backed crabs and oysters and myriad other shells spawned on the rotting piles. The boys paddled the boat. Out in the dawn ahead of them the tug puffed a path through the foggy mist. The water was chilly. Mist

glistened on top of it. Far out, beyond the buoys, Philip encountered a placid, untroubled sea. The liner, a German tourist boat,
was loaded to the bridge. The water was as still as a lake of ice.

"All right, Ernest, let's hurry—"

Philip drew in the oars. The *Kron Prinz Wilhelm* came near.
Huddled in thick European coats, the passengers viewed from
their lofty estate the spectacle of two naked Negro boys peeping
up at them from a wiggly *bateau*.

"Penny, mistah, penny, mistah!"

Somebody dropped a quarter. Ernest, like a shot, flew after it.
Half a foot down he caught it as it twisted and turned in the
gleaming sea. Vivified by the icy dip, Ernest was a raving wolf and
the folk aboard dealt a lavish hand.

"Ovah, yah, mistah," cried Philip, "ovah, yah."

For a Dutch guilder Philip gave an exhibition of "cork." Under
something of a ledge on the side of the boat he had stuck a piece
of cork. Now, after his and Ernest's mouths were full of coins, he
could afford to be extravagant and treat the Europeans to a game
of West Indian "cork."

Roughly ramming the cork down in the water, Philip, after the
fifteenth ram or so, let it go, and flew back, upwards, having thus
"lost" it. It was Ernest's turn now, as a sort of end-man, to scramble forward to the spot where Philip had dug it down and "find"
it; the first one to do so, having the prerogative, which he jeal-
ously guarded, of raining on the other a series of thundering leg
blows. As boys in the West Indies Philip and Ernest had played it.
Of a Sunday the Negro fishermen on the Barbadoes coast made a
pagan rite of it. Many a Bluetown dandy got his spine cracked in
a game of "cork."

With a passive interest the passengers viewed the proceedings.
In a game of "cork," the cork after a succession of "rammings" is
likely to drift many feet away whence it was first "lost." One had
to be an expert, quick, alert, to spy and promptly seize it as it
popped up on the rolling waves. Once Ernest got it and endeav-
ored to make much of the possession. But Philip, besides being
two feet taller than he, was slippery as an eel, and Ernest, despite
all the artful ingenuity at his command, was able to do no more
than ineffectively beat the water about him. Again and again he
tried, but to no purpose.

Becoming reckless, he let the cork drift too far away from him and Philip seized it.

He twirled it in the air like a crap shooter, and dug deep down in the water with it, "lost" it, then leaped back, briskly waiting for it to rise.

About them the water, due to the ramming and beating, grew restive. Billows sprang up; soaring, swelling waves sent the skiff nearer the shore. Anxiously Philip and Ernest watched for the cork to make its ascent.

It was all a bit vague to the whites on the deck, and an amused chuckle floated down to the boys.

And still the cork failed to come up.

"I'll go after it," said Philip at last, "I'll go and fetch it." And, from the edge of the boat he leaped, his body long and resplendent in the rising tropic sun.

It was a suction sea, and down in it Philip plunged. And it was lazy, too, and willful—the water. Ebony-black, it tugged and mocked. Old brass staves—junk dumped there by the retiring French—thick, yawping mud, barrel hoops, tons of obsolete brass, a wealth of slimy steel faced him. Did a "rammed" cork ever go that deep?

And the water, stirring, rising, drew a haze over Philip's eyes. Had a cuttlefish, an octopus, a nest of eels been routed? It seemed so to Philip, blindly diving, pawing. And the sea, the tide—touching the roots of Deathpool—tugged and tugged. His gathering hands stuck in mud. Iron staves bruised his shins. It was black down there. Impenetrable.

Suddenly, like a flash of lightning, a vision blew across Philip's brow. It was a soaring shark's belly. Drunk on the nectar of the deep, it soared above Philip—rolling, tumbling, rolling. It had followed the boy's scent with the accuracy of a diver's rope.

Scrambling to the surface, Philip struck out for the boat. But the sea, the depths of it wrested out of an aeon's slumber, had sent it a mile from his diving point. And now, as his strength ebbed, a shark was at his heels.

"Shark! Shark!" was the cry that went up from the ship.

Hewing a lane through the hostile sea Philip forgot the cunning of the doddering beast and swam noisier than he needed to. Faster grew his strokes. His line was a straight, dead one. Fancy

strokes and dives—giraffe leaps . . . he summoned into play. He
shot out recklessly. One time he suddenly paused—and floated
for a stretch. Another time he swam on his back, gazing at the
chalky sky. He dived for whole lengths.

But the shark, a bloaty, stone-colored mankiller, took a shorter
cut. Circumnavigating the swimmer it bore down upon him with
the speed of a hurricane. Within adequate reach it turned,
showed its gleaming belly, seizing its prey.

A fiendish gargle—the gnashing of bones—as the sea once
more closed its jaws on Philip.

Some one aboard ship screamed. Women fainted. There was
talk of a gun. Ernest, an oar upraised, capsized the boat as he
tried to inflict a blow on the coursing, chop-licking maneater.

And again the fish turned. It scraped the waters with its deadly fins.

At Coco Té, at the fledging of the dawn, Maffi, polishing the
tinware, hummed an *obeah* melody

> *Trinidad is a damn fine place*
> *But* obeah *down dey.* . . .

Peace had come to her at last.

The Cow on the Rooftop

Lino Novás Calvo

A Story of the Cuban Revolution

My More Than Forgotten Chucho Moquenque (wherever you may be):

Don't expect this letter to start off with a long complaint. Too late for that. Complaints, what for? What's done is done and the cow on the rooftop. The great Hurricane came and swept away the illustrious rubble, leaving the roots, some still embedded in the earth, others standing on end. Also some flowering but crushed branches, just like me, living on as though by a miracle. Because the Miracle exists in this Jungle, nobody can deny it. Or rather it is able to exist, which is the same thing.

I can't tell if your liking for tall tales has rubbed off on me without my knowing it. At least it tempts me now. So many things have rubbed off on me, Chucho Moquenque, even your inclination for changing bed partners. Remember the dances at Luyano? You were always a scoundrel, Chucho. Just like the sparrow hawk, always scampering off. Bite and run. So, as soon as you saw the conflagration come you took flight.

"You stay here for a little while, my love," you said, "while I set up the hideout over there."

People who know you told me about it; I can well imagine what that hideout is like. That sort of thing isn't for you. You're always on the go. Everything in the safe and the bank you took with you to sell to the highest bidder. You left me the almost worthless house and lot, my job at the Ministry of Communications that would soon end, and a little boy who began to grow up too fast. Before running off, you told me:

"Rita, it's time to escape: a few months longer and you won't be able to." How right you were, Chucho Moquenque! Three months later the year ended, as did so many other things, including Chucho Moquenque for me and naturally Rita Fernandez for him. Period. Curtain comes down. The end. And now to another point.

I want to speak to you about it in this letter. I have my reasons. Thirteen years ago today you fled. You always said that was a lucky number. I wish it were. I don't even know if I have any ill feeling toward you; if I had, it would be like the ill feeling a person harbors toward the one he has killed. We are what we are and with you the situation might have been even worse. When I realized I was alone, I was relieved. You had made up your mind; there was no reason to be upset; the die was cast. I felt like telling you: "So long, Chucho, that's the last I'll ever see you." And I went my own way.

I didn't hesitate, because it was the only road I could take. I quickly took up with the new *Jefe*. The woman you abandoned, Chucho, was beautiful. You yourself used to tell her: "Rita, how pretty, how really pretty you are!" You at least left me that asset. The new *Jefe* didn't last long, and neither did my job at the Ministry. Everything began to change so fast. I won't tire you with all that since everyone knows it. But what I must tell you is that three men entered my life since then, that is, by official count. There were others too. To die, there is always time to die; the worst thing is to suffer. One resists this. I think we all have a cork in our soul to prevent us from sinking, especially if we are Cuban. But even cork, like the Island, gets soaked. We've gone only backwards since then: backwards, backwards. You should see what that means!

But that's not what I want to talk to you about.

Your son—that's right, Chucho, he was yours, even though you doubted it—would be twenty now, if he were alive. He was seven when you fled. I noticed then he was looking more and more like you. Maybe for that reason I immediately gave him up to the *Juventudes,* if you know what that is. I doubt it, but it doesn't matter. I didn't see him again after that. A few messages, some letters (increasingly propagandistic) that became less and less frequent, and nothing else. I supposed they were educating him in their own special way out there in the countryside, from one military camp to another. In High School, he reached the top of the honor roll, or whatever they call it now. He had someone else tell me that. By then he was already a junior party leader. He seemed to be doing well, but things were going badly for me, as for everybody, if that's any consolation. When I saw him I was half frightened. In his uniform (a coarse, light-colored khaki) he looked just like you when at his age you would put your jacket on to go to the beach. Those same watery, half-closed eyes that hid the evil in them, the same thick hair that came down to form an arrow in front, that same mouth forever in movement, saying what's on your mind and then contradicting it. For a moment I didn't know whether to run to embrace him or run away from him. Or maybe to look for something to hit him on the head with.

You remember, Chucho, that you always called me a born actress, perhaps because during those first years at the University I took part in some plays. What impressed you most was my role as a madwoman in the work by Novás Calvo. You told me then: "But, Rita, I bet you're really crazy. Impossible to pretend so well." We both laughed. The Revista de Avance thought you were right. Some student troublemakers began to call me the Madwoman. It was around 1931 and both of us then dropped out of school.

You're probably wondering what the point of all this is. I'll tell you. I've always suspected that because you thought I was an actress you distrusted me, in or out of bed. I even think that it was the accumulation of your doubts that drove you from me like a rocket once you had a good pretext. It must not have even bothered you leaving me alone in the vortex with a child in that flimsy house of ours in the Kholy development. If you could, you might have taken the house with you too. At that time I didn't believe you capable of that much. Resigned at last, I consoled myself saying: "At least he left me our son." That's right, Chucho, he was really ours. Yours and mine, however much you distrusted the actress who didn't exist or who remained submerged.

With you gone and the boy under their control, the actress reappeared when she saw herself alone in the house. You will never know, Chucho, how I felt seeing myself alone in that storm. I don't love you, I know, but I want to save you the details, though to tell you would be like summing up the endless misfortunes of an infinite number of other people. You can't imagine it: right in the midst of the foulest winds of land or heaven. What else was there to do then except put my head down, or rather try to raise it above the sea waves? Dying itself would be glory. But I've already said that one resists dying. I never could imagine it was so difficult to die . . . and so easy to kill.

You may understand this better if I go back a bit in my story. As I told you, at first I went from lover to lover. I was still pretty and the reemerging actress in me helped a lot. Rehearsing before the wardrobe mirror—at least they never took that away from me—I was amazed at my own artistry. I also used the tape recorder you left me, the one you had used in your French classes at the Normal School. I coordinated gesture and voice just like a professional. The actress feigned being a partisan of the revolution, and very gracefully went from one bureau to the next, from one *Responsable* to another. It's good to talk to you a little about her, so what you will read won't be amiss.

You never really knew that actress, Chucho. She wasn't the one you had seen on stage, nor the one you later thought was feigning love for you offstage. She was those two plus a third, all in one. I myself was surprised that it turned out so well, so naturally. With so much pretending I might have come to identify myself with the lie. First, so I could keep the house, just as soon as you escaped and they took our boy away. They wanted the entire house. Like hungry beasts they swarmed around. They promised to leave me a little corner, maybe the back room or the room on the rooftop. After that—the tenants were now ex-maids with their children and husbands—they could give me the front half or the rear half. I pretended. I armed myself with words and anger. I became a revolutionary. I went to see this one and that one. I got in touch with Diaz Aztarain, with Dr. Cabral . . . Do you remember Dr. Cabral? He's the son of the alienist who treated my deranged mother, and he is an alienist too. He had gone to the Sierra in his last year of medicine and when he returned they put him in charge of the insane. I finally managed to keep them from taking the house away from me. It was the only thing they didn't take away.

But everything here was collapsing. You gone, and everything else beginning to go; clothes, shoes, food, even water. Ay, Chucho, even though I have no love for you, may you never know such deprivation! Everything disappeared as if by magic. For some time we—and I'm including now neighbors and friends—stretched out the little there was, until everything was all threadbare. The ration lines went three times around each block. No need to tell you about that. It certainly came out in all the newspapers of the world. But one thing is to read about it and another to suffer through it. I was thrown around from one place to another, from one office to another, and I had to give part of my ration to the woman or women who stood in line for me. I had to go to the bureau even though there was nothing for me to do, and when I got back I was happy to find an egg or a cup of rice. Sometimes I ambled along Obispo, Galiano, and San Rafael, secretly afraid not to find anything, but these lingering walks through once well-stocked streets just increased my anguish. First, the store mirrors, high, wide, square, in all sizes, relentlessly shiny, reflecting my wasted, tired-eyed, overly made-up image, like that of a madwoman I was playing. And then those empty storewindows, the endless vacant storewindows, open mouths of corpses. Said like that, it no doubt smacks of literature to you. You should see it through my eyes. That image of mine in the mirrors kept on burning in my mind. I saw myself another person, and indeed I was.

But there was still a third person, which I would have to create. And soon.

It wasn't even hunger itself. I hardly felt it any more. I was getting adjusted to it, just like I was to the repetition of phrases and watchwords. You have no idea, my dear dead husband (and you'll soon see, you were the dead one) how willingly one can become just a machine. A dilapidated little machine like those that still operate around here coughing out their agony. A dark fear then begins to envelop us, as if made of crocodile shadows or perhaps vulture shadows that may draw near to devour us. Fear of staying on to the very end, without the little bit we still have left so that some blood may still circulate through our veins.

That was what my situation became. No strength was left in me even for those futile walks in front of the sarcastic mirrors and the empty storewindows. I returned home motivated only by the desire to exchange what I had—a month's salary, some old article of clothing or footwear—for something more to eat. At times, with considerable risk, it could be done. As more and more people risked such illegal traffic, it became less dangerous.

It was on one of those afternoons when one of those hucksters came to offer me a milk cow. He kept her for himself in a small house in the Orfila district (do you remember Orfila, Chucho Moquenque?), and apparently it was his turn to leave the island on one of those flights reserved for antirevolutionaries. This man (good luck to him!) found out that I still kept the new suit you forgot to take out of the cleaner's in your haste to leave. He also asked me for any gold, silver, and platinum jewelry I might still have. I gave him all I could, and one night (I'll never know how) he brought me the cow, and the two of us (I'll never know how either) took her up to the rooftop and put her in your room. At least that cubicle where you would go at night to write your poisonous articles was to serve some purpose.

It was a gift from San Lazaro, or perhaps from the *Viejo Touleño* from whom I sought some consolation.

The cow was young, gentle, and good. My greatest joy was to go to the bushes to find the finest grass for her in payment for the spurts of milk she gave me each day. It was like a return to glory. I've had some men in my life. I once loved you dearly, Chucho Moquenque. But I never loved anyone like I loved that cow.

You yourself would sometimes sing mockingly that the good things and the glories of life never come or reach us too late. Drunk as I was with my new happiness and my new love for the cow, I got to forget Bebo (your son, you know), who had never before been absent from my thoughts. The entire world reduced to a milk cow.

I became an expert. I read and inquired as if for a thesis. I knew how to take care of her. All I had was my precious cow. Now that you are in that land of abundance, Chucho Moquenque (that is, if you're still alive), you will never, never understand this. Because in that sense you are indeed dead.

Don't think this is just an image. You are really dead. Dead from a shot in the head, which is where it should be, because all evil comes to us from the head. Your ex–Rita Fernandez is the one who is telling you and she should know.

Because it was you, Chucho, who suddenly came one night to take the cow away from me. You, in the form of your son (or vice-versa) at the age of twenty-one. On seeing him come in, I walked forward three steps to throw my arms around his neck, but his face (those slanting eyes, that shined menacingly, that twisted grimace) stopped me. I embraced him just as I used to embrace you even when I knew that you repelled me and that therefore deep down I repelled you.

Later I was to remember one of those many sardonic quotations you cited just like a typical pompous literature teacher: "You're not the one who deceives me; it's my dream that deceives me." That's right, Chucho, vile Chucho, because you were my dream, although you never believed it.

Our son returned, your Raulin (Bebo), and at once I began to shudder. Raulin was Chucho grown up. He was a man now, with a peach fuzz beard, rat-like eyes, and a twisted mouth. The first thing he did was to walk around the house and take a look at the backyard. He came back to the dining room (where I remained motionless) with a cruel smile and these words:

"Well, Mom, you've gotten along pretty well. There's room for more people here."

Without waiting for my answer, he leaped up the stairs. Halfway up he turned around to look back at me over his shoulder and again I saw those sharp murderous teeth, like those of a biting dog. I must have become transfigured, because that's how I felt inside. A minute later he would feel that way too looking at the cow. A whirlwind of thoughts passed through my head as I looked at the top of the stairs to see him reappear. He took quite a while. He must have been looking the cow over, feeling her as a buyer would. He reappeared and stopped at the top. I couldn't begin to describe his face to you. It was that of a young Satan I had seen on a religious engraving. His smile showed all his teeth now and his eyes told me first what his mouth—your mouth—would tell me seconds later halfway down the stairs.

"Mom, it's wrong what you're doing. It's against the law. That cow has to be turned over to the people."

Hand and heart and thought moved in unison. He had left his FN rifle (that's what they call it) on the table. I quickly grabbed it. I don't think he even had time to notice. He was just putting his foot down on the first step when I pulled the trigger. He fell flat.

I will need a sea of words to tell you what happened after that. Words like waves. Your son raised up his arms, opened his mouth, and hit his forehead against the tile floor. I don't think the neighbors heard anything; only one shot, short and abrupt like the breaking of a dry twig. Your twig, Chucho, your little twig, now under the earth.

But the neighbors answered my shouts. No, the shouts weren't mine any more, they belonged to the other me, the actress, who now took my place for good. Because the one who was your Rita ceased to exist right there, and it was the other one who replaced her.

Within an hour the news was on the radio. The actress went fluttering around the house like a wounded bird. At times she sang, at times she laughed. She sank into long silences and then spoke with those no longer there. When the militia came she was doing ballet steps around her dead son, your murdered son, you yourself.

No, don't think I really became insane. At least, not completely, but just enough to provide the actress with the stimulus and the naturalness to make her performance convincing. Even the radio announced (the set was turned on and I could hear it very well) that the criminal had lost her mind, for she had killed her son and had a cow on the rooftop.

I went to jail just like in a performance. I left my house singing the 26th of July hymn and speaking of incongruous matters to strangers, as if I knew them. I called one militiaman Chucho and reminded him of how much we loved each other in Puentes Grandes; and I called a militiawoman Mamita. Acting crazy was so natural for me.

The news soon spread and reached the ears of Dr. Cabral. I don't know if I told you that Dr. Cabral had an affair with me when he came down from the Sierra and before they put him in charge of the insane—both male and female. After that, on the way to Havana he would come by to spend a few hours with me. At that time I was an accomplished romantic actress and Dr. Cabral was thrilled with my performance. He went around saying:

"But, my angel, how luscious you are!"

The news of my crime must have intrigued him and he asked to examine me. Permission was probably rather easy to get. After a few days, I don't know how many, I was under his care, in the new sanitarium. There was no trial, as far as I knew. I didn't see Raulin's funeral either.

Since then I've been a celebrated figure among the patients. They let me move around freely, telling the crazy women lies they believe and truths they doubt. The more farfetched the lies, the easier they are believed. I also teach them how to sing and dance, which Dr. Cabral tells me has great therapeutic value. I am the star of this permanent theatre of the absurd.

Time has not dimmed my talents as an actress. I think the role of a madwoman has become so much a part of me that even if I wanted to I could no longer act sane. Foreign doctors have often come here, and Dr. Cabral has explained my case to them and allowed them to examine me. They have subjected me to a lot of tests, from reflex actions to the most insidious questions. I have learned how to put on a good act. Not one of them appeared to have left with any doubts about me; they all think I'm a highly intelligent woman, but insane just the same.

The doubt is within me, and so I'm writing you this letter, which I'll send to Dr. Cabral—maybe if he wants to he can forward it to you. I'm well treated here, I have privileges, I keep entertained with the roles I play. To take me out of here, to send me away to pick tomatoes, would be like taking away my cow the second time. Dr. Cabral frequently has me brought to his office to examine me—a splendid place, with wide, soft sofas. We then make love as we did before. The woman is different, but our lovemaking is the same.

My doubt, Chucho, is this: Does Dr. Cabral really think I'm crazy? A thousand times I ask myself this question.

TRANSLATED BY MYRON I. LICHTBLAU

Caribbean Siren

Fanny Buitrago

In a remote, diffuse period of his life—before true childhood and memories—Leandro Palma acquired his first obsession. The impassioned, nostalgic desire to possess a piece of land. A desire inculcated by ancient lullabies, ballads from a nanny torn from the fresh grass of her native country, from trembling wheat fields, from the pungent smell of fresh manure under her fingernails. Yearnings of a stooped, arthritic grandmother, yoked to a crepitant city, who in her dreams spoke of a vigorous husband, a wild colt, a cow, the mantilla of the Sunday mass, and the frostbitten winter fields of her youth.

One might assume that he did not become possessed but that Leandro Palma was imbued with the ancient ghost of ownership, inherited through the blood, with or without lullabies.

These anterior wanderings were the creation of an idle people. Later on. When the idea of the obsession came to light and Palma was overwhelmed by many disillusionments, his blond hair flecked with gray, a prisoner of his desires in the vicinity of Summer Point. A place where finally he tread on land of his own.

His second obsession. A violent and uncontrollable passion for the Caribbean Sea was the fault of Diógenes Santana—who doesn't remember him?—known as the crazed painter of the islands. In his lifetime he portrayed the devouring evil that afflicts all kinds of people, beings scattered in the strangest places on this planet, without the slightest linkage. All of them enslaved to one of the oldest demons of creation: the sea.

Leandro Palma, son of a Colombian diplomat and a French beauty. Born in Bogota, D.E.—educated in Paris—settled on the island. He first confronted the tortuous and irresistible image of his primary and most desperate love in a drugstore in Cali or Popayán during the course of a tedious trip. Cupid awaited him on the shelf for glycerine, hydrogen peroxide, and senna bags, balanced on a nickel-plated postcard stand. It was the painting of a siren-mother, sold by the painter's lover during a period of hunger (Santana was always down on his luck), and reproduced by the thousands by an astute, asexual, and implacable photographer from Antioquia. The jade-haired, glaucous-eyed siren with her ice-encrusted, old, gold-colored tail nursing her offspring on the sizzling sand of Johnny Key. Amongst empty beer bottles, Coca-Cola caps, plastic cups, rusty cans, and starving dogs.

His acquisition of the postcard ordained the path the boy would follow. The same disdained path of the legendary Ulysses. But, before setting out, Leandro Palma completed several attempts to fit into daily reality. He obtained a degree in philosophy. He took a course in sculpture and carving. He worked in experimental theater groups. He wrote two successful novels. He married a pianist from Cali, bought a grand piano, and had a stillborn son. He didn't often think of the siren. Although in his dreams he sensed her singing and would awaken, startled.

The dead child became the pretext to justify an absurd, untiring wandering around different Caribbean islands and coastal regions. Thus, Leandro Palma dragged his wife, staggering from here to there, searching for the place where the woman-fish of the postcard had been painted. The postcard became ragged cardboard, faded from constant handling, its letters long ago erased.

He found the island when Carolina Palma, docile companion, complained of worry and exhaustion, and he had begun to despair of ever finding the universe, a universe he understood perfectly, created by Santana's ill-fated brush.

To obtain the desired land facing Johnny Key, in the exact spot where the painter—submerged in turbulent delirium—had seen the female of a cursed species, cost him months of wandering and humiliating mishaps. The inhabitants of the island were already aware of the value of the land and of the terrible and impractical transactions made by their ancestors and contemporaries. New housing developments and tourist hotels had increased the market value in an alarming fashion. Few owners wished to sell, rent, or form a joint venture. They didn't trust foreigners, especially one like Leandro Palma, with his gringo looks, French accent, and Latin name. They were suspicious of his refined elegance, his arrogant wife, the grand piano packed away in a warehouse—a strange, excessive piece of furniture, barely conceivable in a church choir or the salon of a casino. They considered shady his intentions of staying in a place so far from the continent.

These intentions were explained in an advertisement in *El Centinela* requesting: "A small piece of land, in an area far away from the city, looking out to the sea and in a direction parallel to Johnny Key." The offers were few and at astronomical prices because people instantly thought in terms of contraband merchandise, cocaine, or other equally sinister businesses.

Juliana Campos read unwillingly and rarely, but the ad came at just the right time. She needed money urgently to satisfy the pressing needs of her five sons and to cancel many debts. She owned enough land facing the sea so that she could easily dispose of a tiny piece in Summer Point. A place distant from the center of town, the hotel area, and the old neighborhoods. At that time investors had no interest in that area, and Juliana Campos was anxious to get out of a difficult situation.

"Stupid gringo!" she mocked, when she related to her friends the details of the transaction. "I snatched his soul and he remained grateful. The idiot bought a wasteland and he can't complain to anybody! That's what he gets for being such a chump!"

The land was one of the harshest in Summer Point. Where a breeze was rarely felt. It was part of the spoils obtained by Juliana Campos in an eventful case against her husband, who, in turn, had inherited it from his first wife (a certain Dolores Cheng or Ana Robinson), who, according to gossip, he killed by dint of annoyances and blows. Useless death, by the way. Sebastian Campos's dark destiny caused him to fall in love with the authoritarian Juliana Payares, from whom he miraculously escaped, a ruined man, without so much as a good-bye.

The purchase of "The Siren," as the Palmas property was baptized, was a terrible deal. But no one had enough courage to warn the foreigners or to bring upon themselves the wrath of Juliana . . . Why bother the new proprietor? . . . What did it matter? . . . That fellow Palma wasn't a man in his first youth; he could afford his whims.

Leandro Palma had inherited an annuity and he had a small amount of money from the sale of his books, but this was barely enough to meet the high construction costs. It took him two years to dig a well and build a one-story wooden house, advised throughout by an architect more interested in brandy and women than in grand projects. He designed the tables, chairs, the railing of the porch, some of the furniture, and built them from boards and boxes he bought at the huge imports warehouse. Around the house he planted plum trees, icaco plums, bougainvillea, and *matarratones,* which died in a fortnight from the heat and were replanted under an auspicious moon. Palma was stubborn: he was a client beloved by the one and only fertilizer and manure dealer in the city. Each day he patiently worked the harsh backyard soil where nettles, garden balsam, and rickety weeds began sprouting. The land wasn't barren, but no one had taken care of it for generations. On the other hand, the foreigner, stubborn *pañaman,* obviously loved it. And the land was willing to yield.

After five years of residing on the island, the pianist gave birth to a girl and bought a parakeet. Palma cultivated a tiny rosebush with bright red roses, the choicest specimen in that wasteland he proudly signaled as his fruit garden. He didn't write anymore. Perhaps because of the heat, or the drowsy atmosphere people breathe in the Caribbean for months at a time. When he wasn't busy with his rosebushes and vegetables, he remained for hours on the porch of the house. Hypnotized, he would contemplate the sea or carve a piece of wood into the shape of a siren. His wife, Carolina, devoted herself to daily chores, to the child, to cleaning, to the kitchen, and to the parakeet and after dusk coaxed from the piano incomprehensible melodies—overwhelming or choleric—that forced tourists to stop whenever they passed Summer Point or were carried to the center of the city by the echo and murmur of breaking waves.

The couple was pleasing to the eyes. They had kind words, agreeable manners, and a house with open doors. Although it was never known that they visited anyone. She, tall, harmonious and dark-skinned, with the face of an Egyptian statue, pale, olive skin, and undulating hair combed into a garland that she liked to decorate with a single bougainvillea; she was graying prematurely, had varicose veins on her legs, but walked like a queen. By contrast, Palma's hair resembled flax and his white skin was reddish from the sun. Yet he belonged to that class of men accustomed to arousing admiring exclamations in the street. And in the first years after his arrival he provoked a commotion whenever he went downtown on a motorcycle, wearing canvas shoes, tweed pants, and a tight-fitting shirt. Later on, only female tourists paid any attention to him, enraptured by such an athletic specimen, such refined movements, so closely resembling those British actors in fashion magazines.

"Good heavens . . . !" they exclaimed. "What a man!"

As she grew, the child didn't look like either parent. She had clear brown eyes, copper-colored hair, and the pale, white skin of a redhead, hidden behind a cloud of freckles. The Palma family, not at all interested in joining a social club or standing out in the community, formed a separate nucleus, apart from existing social and gossip circles. They had few neighbors, due to the location of Summer Point, and they were happy—in this way—although they got along fairly well with the few they had.

Half a kilometer from their house, in a lonely and modern two-story house, lived an old man, Longino Fernandez, who grumbled about the ingratitude of his children and grandchildren. A kilometer away, the boisterous Orozco family, where laughter, hurried journeys, and brawls proliferated. Further on, the Francises, an old married couple, a pair of Protestants, pious, tidy, eager to help without being annoying.

In time Juliana Campos became their closest neighbor. One day, in a rush, without first digging a well, she had the adjacent land cleared and built a house using secondhand wood. Her financial situation forced her to rent the house in San Luis and move to the unattractive Summer Point.

In spite of the Palmas' deliberate isolation, those staying on the island—both nationals and foreigners—who only rarely so-

cialized with island families, developed the custom of showing
their guests the beautiful house known as "The Siren." Especially
on Sundays they would drive around the island as the culmina-
tion to a sunny morning on the beach and an arduous workweek,
and everybody would eat lunch in the restaurants along the way,
Miss Angie, El Hoyo Soplador or Bahía Marina.

After admiring the airy house, the siren carved by Palma, resting embedded in one of the pillars of the porch railing, the plum
trees, and the *matarratones*—already bushy and in bloom—and
maybe tasting a very cold sherbet, the visitors would pass through
the living room, then on to the vegetable garden in the back—
that garden, which no one believed in at first, the subject of many
nasty jokes. The same one that, when the child celebrated her
tenth birthday, was as real as that the sea is the fountain of life.
They left delighted. They related what they had seen in their narrow offices, stores, clubs, and favorite bars. And on any given day
they asked for a bunch of fresh mint, a handful of peas, or a
freshly cut rose.

For years the counterfeit vegetable garden of Leandro Palma
enabled Juliana Campos to laugh heartily at his expense. "Stupid
gringo . . . !" she'd say. "Not even stones can grow there!"

Suddenly, she stopped laughing. She needed to bother her
neighbors to get water from their well until her sons finished digging her own. It was embarrassing; it called for composure. A
skinny woman with tense flesh and lapidary voice, she looked at
the world with small, phosphorescent eyes and infinite contempt
from behind frail, costume-jewelry eyeglasses—a world she accused of having perverted, obsessed, and dragged her husband
into a den of iniquity. Juliana had complaints, diatribes, and impressive recriminations, which she applied to ninety percent of
the adult inhabitants of the island. What, with his buddies and
binges, his serenades and brawls, and messing with the tourists
and the women, and the roosters, and the horse races, and his
illegitimate children, and the dollar, and the aviation, and on
and on and on. Leandro Palma and his wife were not part of all
that, having appeared on the island after Campos's escape. They
didn't know the ingrate. To them, Juliana's rancor was completely unfounded.

For a few years following the sale, sustained by the money

from the sale, Juliana had even felt gratitude. The land in Summer Point had only produced taxes. It was not an honorable place to live, lacking coconut groves nearby to supply water and daily food, so far from La Loma, from San Luis, from Bahía Sonora, from her relatives, from church, and from gossip . . . How life had changed! Not even in her worst nightmare had she considered abandoning San Luis, and even less had she imagined ending in that disgraceful Summer Point, almost like a beggar. The rent from the other house enabled her to get by, to buy groceries for the week and extras for her five sons (none of whom had a steady job). Of course, no more luxuries. Good-bye to canned goods, American silks, and French perfume. And there was no hope for improvement. Because of the distance to town, the Campos family managed to get a Jeep. The little money her sons earned disappeared on women and gasoline.

The roof that sheltered them clattered at night with the slightest breeze or a passing car. The wooden walls were full of termites. There were rats, slugs, ant nests, and filthy roaches. Not so much as the shadow of the well her sons were digging existed; they were so busy trying to earn a living . . . "Poor boys! It was bad enough dealing with their father's abandonment." She didn't have the strength to clear the land around the house. Or to dig the well. Thanks to the clothes from the good old days, people did not give her alms . . . and to be forced to breathe the same air as the Palma family! Lately she had been getting water at night, hiding from peering eyes, without giving thanks or degrading herself as if she were a starving nobody.

Occasionally. She couldn't resist the impulse to go to the neighbors. She would ask them for the time, a newspaper, or a cold glass of water, not going beyond the railing, determined not to accept their invitation to enter the house. She didn't go with the pretext of being a guest. She didn't want to give Carolina Palma any satisfaction . . . She would return to her home confused, with the furniture from their terrace still striking her retinas, the polished tiles burning her feet, a flow of opposing smells assaulting her nose: aroma of fresh leaves, damp soil, ripe lemons, mulberries in season. And the fluttering of hummingbirds feeding on the bougainvillea.

In her filthy kitchen, with the foul smell of kerosene and lard,

Juliana Campos pondered her arid land, devoid of water, a complete wasteland. A place without future possibility or redemption. She found it unjust that other people enjoyed what by all rights belonged to her children. She easily found reasons for her anger. Reasons for hatred. Reasons and more reasons. She cursed her husband, the island, the rotten luck of defenseless women.

What she forgave her neighbors for the least was their shameless display of a siren nursing a dolphin—embedded in their railing—a carving that ignored modesty, an affront to the religious feeling of the rest of the community. She sensed in the mute figure the ghost of a woman who had been loved a thousand times, loved like she was never loved. This feeling was enough to make her furious . . . ! She wasn't a true believer, but she felt like a champion of decency, and she began to see the fetid presence of sin in the wooden siren, not so much because of her nakedness, but because she had been created by Diógenes Santana. As a young woman, she had seen the painting. They couldn't deceive her. Even dead and buried, the painter remained synonymous with all human flaws, death, blasphemy, corruption . . . and Leandro Palma entertained his leisure time carving sin? And he did it on island soil. On her land. On the property of her ancestors. While she washed and cooked like a beast of burden, and her children worked as waiters, baggage handlers or clerks in a warehouse. Yes, yes, yes, yes, yes. She remembered. Santana had been murdered!

Day after day Juliana Campos distilled the liquor of hatred in her heart. When she heard the piano she found even the color of the sea revolting. Horrible music, without a religious refrain, incomprehensible, pagan, obviously rejected by the Lord. And she snorted like a lion, her fists tightly clenched.

"That fake gringo will find out. He'll find out who Juliana Campos is."

Her crepitant rancor, pampered and fermented, was filtered into her sons' food. The five young men, good-for-nothings, incited by irritating, long, tiresome speeches, began to take the affronts seriously, regaling them to everyone in the shops and canteens. They went along with their mother's game, and she set about on a campaign of visits and gossip: the story of her misfortune came to light, and the sale of the land became a fraud perpetrated in the tender days of her youth, when she needed a man most, a helping hand.

"The sale is invalid!" she would say in an even tone, very even, to anyone who would listen to her. "That gringo, exploiter, con man, he deceived me completely . . . cheat, bully!" her voice cried, "to take advantage of a poor woman, without a husband, loaded down with children . . ."

People would stimulate her caustic tongue, adding more pepper to the pot. The so-called Palma was indifferent to them and, aside from gossiping, what other daily entertainment is there on a Caribbean island?

Leandro Palma descended from the gentle and private world he had forged for himself and his family when Carolina began to prepare for her annual trip to the mainland. She was traveling earlier that year because the child needed to go to a dentist and she needed a change of air.

As a good neighbor, Juliana Campos offered her services. She could keep an eye on the house when Palma had to go into town, wash the dishes, take care of the weekly cleaning, water the vegetable garden. It was the first time she acted so obligingly, and there was no apparent motive to suspect her. And even though Palma led a sort of primitive life, he had not acquired the slightest reflexive reaction to danger. His talent with earthly matters didn't go beyond the earth he cultivated. In general, his behavior continued to be that of a city dweller. Otherwise, instead of remaining enslaved to the sea, he would have made it a friend, an accomplice, the oasis of an amateur fisherman. Also, his roots in the island were completely superficial. He never concerned himself with forging attachments or making friends, whether real friends or true attachments. No one was there to warn him!

Alone in the house of "The Siren." Facing the prospect of boring weeks ahead of him, Palma allowed Juliana Campos to prepare the Sunday meal. From month to month the visitors increased. There was a lot to be done. To be vigilant that the fragrant lemons were not mishandled or bruised, the rosebushes stepped on, or cigarettes crushed against the trees by the entrance. Juliana was a help.

She prepared a porgy in sauce. A small, red one, from a recipe with secret ingredients—or that was what she said.

"It's so good, you'll lick your fingers!" she boasted when she served it, surrounded by white rice, tomato slices, and crackling onion rings.

Leandro Palma ate half of the porgy, which was not as delicious as it looked, and discreetly threw the rest in the garbage. His life was saved thanks to curious visitors. A doctor, a tourist, took him to the emergency room of the hospital, where he was given an emetic and told to see a specialist. The same night he managed to get a plane ticket to Miami, where, in a private clinic, they found the ravages caused by the poison and made him undergo a rigorous treatment to restore the burnt flora of his stomach.

Incredulously, Palma believed it was all an accident. His error, perhaps. In this way he guarded against hurting Juliana Campos's feelings and he ignored the matter of the poisoned fish. Nevertheless, despite himself, he let down his guard and he listened to the remarks of the talkative Mrs. Orozco, his other neighbor, a woman given to gin and gossip. No. No. Impossible! He didn't believe it. He showed himself offended at the tenebrous insinuations. He was sure of Mrs. Campos's kindness. He wouldn't hurt her by listening to bubbling slander.

"If something happens to you, mister," the Orozco woman said to him, "remember that I warned you, and you're asking for it . . . Now you know what she is!"

"She's a good woman," Palma said. "She doesn't have any reason to wish me wrong."

"I warned you! . . ." the Orozco woman insisted.

Words thrown to the wind.

One morning, a few days later, Palma found his bushy plum trees frightfully mutilated and the *matarratones* chopped to their roots. He remained quiet! He didn't have any proof against the Campos family, and he was limited by his city dweller's caution. That is, until the parakeet, domesticated with so much love by Carolina, was stoned to death.

This time Palma went to the Chief of Police and denounced the assaults on his property. He didn't give any names; he wasn't sure of anything. He believed he was acting honestly. But, at dusk, he removed the siren housed in the railing. That would be the next target of those wily, evil-minded enemies, who were willing to crucify him if they could. He was sure.

However, the barbaric incident of his sickness, the devastation of the trees, and the death of the parakeet only reached their exact dimension of terror when Carolina Palma returned.

"Let's get out of here," she blew up hysterically. "I beg you, I beg you, for your daughter's sake . . ."

Let's get out of here!

He refused to leave. He was trapped in a web of a thousand passions. He was no longer his own master. The adventurous spirit also deserted him. He had little interest in knowing other places or in changing the routine of his life. He wanted to work his land, contemplate the sea and the Johnny Key, marry off his daughter, grow old beside his wife. He wasn't willing to abandon the island carrying a piece of wood in the shape of a siren and a fistful of shattered dreams.

His defenses against the Campos family were the useless, absurd choices of a man from a different environment. Instead of soliciting the good offices of a well-known sorcerer, or hiring a group of thugs (the Campos family was famous for their cowardice in the face of stronger foes), he decided to start a friendly dialogue with his neighbors. Words like *friendship, collaboration, mutual help* were heard between the two families. Although there was no way of reasoning with Juliana Campos. Offers by Palma to help her build a new house, to teach her the secrets of the soil, or to dig a well fell on deaf ears.

"He comes to ask me for cocoa . . ." she related. "The nerve of him, the miserable *paña* . . . He's not even a gringo!"

Leandro Palma bought a dog for his daughter and paid one of the Orozco boys, Efraím, to keep an eye on the house when he was absent, with the excuse of working in the garden . . . silly precautions, bah! In those days he found the tires of his motorcycle slashed; the vehicle never functioned well again because they had also put sugar in the fuel tank. They threw garbage in the well. Late at night, invisible musicians sang obscene songs nearby. Not even the child's favorite doll was safe; it was found cut open, hanging from the highest branch of a tree.

It was not long before the pants and shirts that had flattered him danced on his body. His face was stained with a film of dark amber, while an uncontrollable fear appeared in his beautiful, now evasive, brown eyes. But he refused to leave.

Juliana Campos behaved brazenly in front of him. Emboldened to a state of put-on airs and pretensions.

"You'll remember me, miserable gringo . . . !" she yelled, spitting every time she walked by the house of the siren. Embedded in her skin was a zeal for dispute, the longing for the land, the poisonous virus of envy. She was always sending written requests to the National Quartermaster General, to the President of the Republic, to the Director of Planning, and making accusations against her neighbors at Police headquarters. She cherished the idea of starting a court action and went from moneylender to moneylender, exploring the possibility of selling her rights and guaranteeing total victory. All of a sudden the land in Summer Point had been taken from her by force . . . and by force she intended to recover it!

"I don't have sons under my roof," she'd threaten. "I have five wild cubs that sooner or later will devour that old gringo."

A hot morning in July. At the height of the tourist season. The Campos family chased Leandro Palma down the long street, assailing him with boisterous laughter and curses, riding in their noisy, mud-stained Jeep. The scene seemed copied from one of those cheap, serialized movies that come with the seal "Special for Latin America," productions in which gringos and Italians are brought together to gratify bad taste and violence.

The people—residents and tourists—who filled the sweltering marketplace could barely scatter. Palma running crazily, zigzagging in front of the Jeep, his voice hoarse from screaming for help, moving even the foundations of the buildings. Behind the wheel, the oldest of the Camposes charged ahead, terrorizing the pedestrians; the street turned into an ocean of screams, insults, moans, vulgarities . . . ! Simon Castillo, owner of the store Fantasia, fired five shots into the air, scaring the scoundrels and sending them in a frenzy toward La Loma Road. They laughed with a deafening roar, like schoolchildren saved from a misdeed, spewing forth disgusting jokes and double entendres as their vehicle sped by.

Simon Castillo, a well-to-do islander, tried to calm the persecuted. He made him drink two shots of liquor.

"Leave the island, mister," he told him. "This isn't good for you anymore; think about your daughter. The Camposes are bad people, capable of any outrage. Leave, mister."

Palma, drinking a glass of water, thanked him out loud for the advice, although he didn't intend to follow it.

At daybreak he left for the beach, carrying the small siren wrapped in a piece of rubber and tied tightly with a piece of nylon string. He rented a motorboat and headed out to sea, rocked by the foamy dawn surf, to throw her into the outskirts of Johnny Key: thus he abandoned his first love, a desperate and irreversible love since the age of thirteen, acquired as a second skin in a dusty drugstore in Cali or Popayán. He had decided to send his wife and daughter to the mainland, removing them from the impending horror. He believed, in good faith, that the fight was just beginning.

Juliana Campos, who saw him leave, stood at attention like a sentry at a bend in the road to Summer Point. Around seven o'clock in the morning, Efraím Orozco showed up exhibiting a tired pace, sleepy eyes, and a smile of rotting teeth.

"Hello, Mrs."

She, cajoling, joined the boy. Cunningly. She had known him since he was a kid, so there was nothing unusual in her coming over to talk a little bit. They chatted about this and that, about girls and guys, including the accursed Palma family. Abruptly, without any explanation, she offered him seven hundred pesos to kill the gringo. Orozco's brain was obtuse and slow to comprehend, although not as slow as Juliana Campos thought.

"To kill is a sin," the boy said. "I'll have to confess to the priest and that'll make it worse. Also, the blond pays me and gives me food, lots of food. To kill is a bad thing, Mrs. But if you order it, I'll ask my mother for permission."

"Kid, what are you thinking? . . . I was kidding! . . . Come, let's go home and have a taste of coffee to tone up the body."

Efraím accepted docilely. Juliana was an expert in matters of spells, curses, love potions, ointments, and prayers. She experimented with all of them on her dissolute husband! *Something* was in the coffee. Stupefied, Orozco allowed himself to be locked in the only room of the house with a door and lock. Juliana's bedroom.

A short while later, Efraím Orozco roared like a beast in heat, while Juliana hummed to him in a persuasive tone through the cracks in the door.

"The gringo must be killed . . . the gringo is bad . . . the gringo must be killed," and with covetous zeal, "kill the gringo, kill the gringo, kill the gringo . . ."

Leandro Palma returned at the stroke of twelve. He found Juliana's five sons on his property destroying with blows of their machetes a home built on the foundation of an obsession. The glass of the windows of "The Siren" was destroyed, the banisters cut up like firewood, the shining floor tiles cracked with a pick. Inside, Carolina pounded on the piano without managing to attract attention. It was a workday, not a single car could be seen at Summer Point. Over the furious sound of the piano could be heard the frightened crying of the child, and the barking of the dog, injured in one leg.

When Riqui Campos took out the gun, all the anguish contained within Leandro Palma surfaced. His voice became a single, terrifying scream, because he had never fully believed that he faced death . . . "Don't kill me! Don't kill me . . . ! I'll give you whatever you want, but don't kill me!" At that moment, in the house next door, Juliana Campos released Efraím Orozco, transformed into a crazed monster.

She howled:

"Kill him . . . ! Kill him . . . ! Kill him . . . !"

The gun ended up in the hands of Efraím Orozco.

Juliana screamed:

"Shoot him . . . !"

Palma didn't even get a chance to run. Efraím Orozco emptied the six bullets from the chamber. He didn't hesitate. And right away, Riqui and Toni Campos finished him off on the floor, with machetes, just in case.

In a while Eligio Bermúdez, an importer from the street of the suppliers, arrived in a pickup truck. He stopped when he saw Palma in a trail of blood and Carolina, the child, and the dog next to him. Without saying a word, the three of them placed the body in the pickup truck and set out for the hospital. The dog ran and ran behind the truck and at a crossing managed to jump in. He accommodated himself on Leandro Palma's chest, dirty from the soil, while the inflamed crowd rushed into the street demanding justice from the National Superintendent.

"Leandro Palma was killed!"

"Leandro Palma was killed!"

"The Campos boys killed Leandro Palma!"

"They killed him!"

By nightfall, when the event had already gone from mouth to mouth and from house to house, Efraím Orozco showed up on the terrace of the Sonora Hotel. The usual domino players, who for many years had been gathering in the same place, barely paid any attention to him. He passed by, without looking or saying hello, and squatted under a table. He was crying.

His godmother, the obese Madame Corinne, interrupted her game and approached him solicitously.

"What's the matter, my dear child, my son? What's the matter?"

"I killed the gringo, Godmother. I didn't want to kill him and I killed him. And he hadn't done anything to me!"

And dissolving in tears, fear, and a pain that threatened to trepan his mind, he collapsed on the round, full chest of Madame Corinne. The other domino players were attentive.

"Why, my dear child, my son, why?"

"I don't know, I don't know . . . ! I didn't want to kill him, Godmother."

Madame Corinne took charge of the situation.

"You're not going to pay for what the low, mean Campos boys did . . . ! You didn't do anything on purpose and you've got to shut up . . . ! Forget this business or you'll lose your godmother . . . !" Then she planted herself with arms crossed and said to her coplayers: "You haven't seen anything, be careful!"

To find a quiet place to play dominoes—away from annoying women and captious spectators—is not an easy task on an island of industrious people, practically all of whom make their living from tourism. Madame Corinne had her doll shop next to the Sonora Hotel. Not for all the money in the world did the tireless players want to lose Madame, their tranquillity, and less so, their privileges. They remained quiet. They had nothing in common with Leandro Palma. They couldn't care less about Juliana Campos.

For several days the islanders showed their anger at the despicable murder of Leandro Palma. They threatened a general strike. They went en masse to his funeral. They wrote a lengthy denunciation in *El Centinela*. But the matter stopped there. Juliana Campos spent four days in the jail at La Loma and then was released for lack of evidence. No one dared link her boys to the murder.

Carolina Palma departed for the mainland with her daughter, her dog, and her grand piano. She left the property in the hands of a real estate agent. Shortly afterward she married the third violinist of the National Symphony Orchestra. She never returned to the island, in spite of all the local legends ... "Anyone who drinks water from the Rock Hall well will return for all eternity to the island."

Perhaps businesses in this remote region of the country have seen better days. Perhaps no one wants to buy the house of the siren. It could be the fault of the heat at Summer Point or because of the proximity of the Campos family, who also don't dare occupy it. That family grows rapidly, due to marriages and mistresses, but at their core they remain the same, growing old in the midst of disputes and sporadic jobs. Condemned to live in the muck of misery.

It's possible that potential buyers dread becoming victims of a devastating, misguided passion or tremble with fear at the voice of the siren, who can be heard crying in Summer Point whenever a storm is imminent.

TRANSLATED BY CARMEN C. ESTEVES

Red Hot Peppers

Patrick Chamoiseau

When she arrived from the hilly region of Martinique's Morne-aux-Gueules, Anastasia made Mom Gaul's spirits soar. The old woman dropped her basket of weariness and pulled laughs and smiles from a forgotten place in her head. Feeling as soft as the heart of a coconut, she hugged Anastasia every day and murmured to her: My child, *ichewe mwen*, this is where you belong . . .

At that time Mom Gaul was selling potato curls fried in rape oil to support herself. The old woman spent her days tending four oil-filled cauldrons while Anastasia peeled the potatoes. At night they put on fresh clothes. Mom Gaul wore a long-sleeved blouse and a starched skirt that had been ironed so often it was shiny. Each of them carried a bucket of fries as they followed the set course that Anastasia made through the center of town. Mom Gaul knew in advance where to sell her fries, and before refilling any orders, she made sure she collected a deposit from every single bar in town.

The purple sky was alive with fireflies when they walked through the park. Couples were relaxing in the fresh air under the tamarind trees. Children darted between the carts of the peanut vendors, delighting in their newfound freedom on the noisy paths. Mom Gaul and Anastasia walked slowly along the boardwalk, inhaling deeply and breathing in the salt spray from the nearby sea. They sold their fries to young girls lingering around the bandstand, their heads filled with dreams of passion, their hearts open.

So life wove itself without too much sparkle or misery through the days of the two women, around the nasal voice of Ching the Chinaman who dispensed sacks of potatoes and a ready smile for faithful clients. Anastasia forgot Morne-aux-Gueules, her friends Fefee, Ti-Choute, and the others. With the earnestness of a single woman, she became completely absorbed in her new life selling fries. It wasn't long before she developed into a full-breasted, beautiful young girl, with just enough quiver and excitement under her skin that love, always on hand, merely waited to deal her its cards of joy and pain.

Mom Gaul suffered with her back. Sometimes it got so bad Anastasia would have to go to the market by herself. She took on Mom Gaul's rhythm and her short, heavy steps, her rollicking Barbadian saunter, and even, to some extent, her silhouette, which curved like a coconut palm in the wind. Completely baffled by this pretty flower who walked just like an old sorceress, the young men never talked to her of love, dances, or strolls, and never noticed the sway in her hips. This pattern was broken one evening. Zozor Alcide-Victor, a clear-skinned mulatto with curly, impeccably groomed hair, had limpid eyes that missed nothing, and on rainy days, they reflected the dark green color of dame-jeanne bottles of rum.

Ladies and gentlemen, Zozor Alcide-Victor was the product of a clandestine love affair between a Syrian and his servant. When the Syrian community heard that someone in their group was having conjugal relations with a Negress, they put him on solemn notice during one of their gatherings around a huge radio transmitting programs in Arabic. They threatened the expectant father with a boycott that would force him to sell off his stock and close his store. Terrified, the father of Zozor Alcide-Victor rushed to the woman whose ears he had been filling with promises of undying love, giving her instead the usual excuse. "No, the child can't bear my name, but I won't neglect him, you can be sure of that. I'm his father, and may Allah punish me if I ever forget him."

After a lonely year, sustained by bitterness and the public dole, and taking full measure of Allah's indifference, Zozor Alcide-

Victor's mother had to rely on a bottle of acid and a pair of scissors to recall the worthless father to his promises if not his responsibilities. The Syrian community saw the damage to their obedient brother and put their heads together around the mighty radio. They found a solution to the problem that risked drawing the spotlight of unwelcome attention to their comfortable and prosperous existence.

So despite the absence of his father, from his infancy Zozor Alcide-Victor had a fabric store located near the marketplace, between China's Place and Ching the Chinaman. This windfall allowed him to spend his obligatory school years snoring beside his inkwell, beyond the reach of the marvels of French culture. Without this boon, he would have had to beg bread from the dogs. With the revenue from his store placed in trust, he set about his noisy, even licentious life, the cause of sentimental suffering for women of every hue. He counted 1,807 Negresses, 650 mulattoes, 400 chabines, numerous quadroons, albinos, and half-blooded Indians, two Chinese, and an entire regiment of octoroons among his conquests. He was already notorious when he emerged from under the shadows of the bandstand, where he loitered in the fresh air, to make his advance toward Anastasia and her studied way of walking.

Zozor Alcide-Victor bought her whole bucket of fries in one stroke and then with a lordly hand gave them all away to the children. He said two words to her, maybe four, and kept her company for about five hundred yards. Then he bowed graciously, expressing his distress about having to leave so quickly but assuring her they would see each other again very soon. All this was accomplished with such ease, aplomb, smiles, and modulated tones, such tentative brushings with the tips of the fingers, such liquid looks capturing glints of moonlight, and a volley of such precise French that Anastasia felt queasy right down to the tips of her toenails for the next few days. That evening, when she realized he wasn't waiting for her near the bandstand, an intense and inexpressible bitterness overwhelmed her. (Oh, you young girls all dewy with anticipation, you sweet and innocent blossoms of morning, yes, you tender shoots eager to grow: your harvest is not an arching toward the sky, but a thrust of the knife. Beware, beware of love!)

Anastasia lost her taste for life. The cauldrons no longer
amused her. The glistening fries nauseated her. Mom Gaul's ban-
ter bored her. So she wrapped herself in a sweet and dreamy
melancholy. Understanding nothing, the old woman thought
she was in the clutches of some spell, and took pains to fortify her
blood. She sought recourse in a suitable countercharm after she
saw Zozor Alcide-Victor headed straight for them one evening in
the park. He offered a conquering hand to Anastasia, whose
sturdy legs crumbled under her in an excess of emotion. Mom
Gaul understood immediately! Zozor Alcide-Victor held the
young girl up as he questioned the old woman who was looking
at him pointedly: Was she in pain . . . ? The evidence was plain.
The seducer was sure of his victory, but Mom Gaul's hostility
forced him to make the purchase of two bags of fries, a show of
hasty homage before he disappeared quickly into the shadow of
the bandstand.

His reappearance sent Anastasia even deeper into melancholy.
The old woman ministered to her loss of appetite and weight and
faded complexion, resistant to cup after cup of lemon balm tea.
All to no avail. Whenever she went to sell, Mom Gaul avoided the
park. But her back began to bother her again, and she had to re-
sign herself to sending Anastasia to the market alone. With the
same wisdom that denies rivers the power to carry away what fate
holds, she said without illusion or conviction: Don't go near the
park.

The young girl stayed away the first two nights. On the third
night, annoyance numbed her defenses and drew her steps to
the forbidden place. Zozor Alcide-Victor, handsome, smiling,
and available, found her there, just as in the worst Italian novels.
Seeing her alone and trembling, he pulled out his repertory of
great stories, his tales of heroism during the state of emergency
and the hours of alarm, which permitted him one, two, three, to
lure the love-blind girl under the tamarind tree where he regularly carried out his impromptu seductions. He thrilled her with
unsuspected joys and strange pangs and sent her soaring to un-
precedented heights, adding his tribute of moans and impossible
tears to the pleasure.

Later, Mom Gaul saw her on the doorstep looking like a bird
disoriented by the rain, her eyes misty and her body limp, and

she knew that the inevitable had happened. She inveighed against her with bitter words, comparing her to Saint Peter's women, good-time girls for sailors temporarily in port. Anastasia said nothing. For days, she said nothing. Shut like a shell around the happiness she had discovered, she paid no attention to the old woman's distress. When the market day ended, Anastasia headed straight for the park, passing half the night there, and then she returned home looking more foggy than a road in the Red Hills. One night, Mom Gaul followed her and surprised Zozor Alcide-Victor, who already had his arms open to his new conquest.

"You no-good dirty pig of a monkey dog, why don't you leave my little girl alone?"

No stranger to this kind of aggression, the seducer calmly faced Mom Gaul and let loose a tirade of incomprehensible French that froze her on the spot. Then he left quietly, Anastasia hanging on his arm, heading for the aphrodisiac shade of his usual tamarind tree.

This episode widened the gap between the two women. They didn't even look at each other any more. Anastasia stopped fixing the potatoes altogether. Mom Gaul lost her smile, her wrinkles reappeared, and she resumed her habit of selling alone. The little shack began to resemble a hole containing two male crabs. This marred the new happiness of Anastasia to such an extent that Zozor Alcide-Victor noticed and solved the problem. It wasn't really a problem, he said, it's only a matter of getting a new place to stay. I'll find one for you . . .

That's how Anastasia left Mom Gaul. She paid the rent on her shack by selling a rainbow of desserts at the end of her street. During recess at the Perrinon school she set her tray before the gates, and the kids danced around her. In time, Mom Gaul forgot her bitterness. She paid frequent visits to the former light of her life. At first she brought casseroles, knives, sheets. Then she came just to talk, for friendship, and stayed, dreading the return to her newly dull shack. She also avoided Zozor Alcide-Victor, who came often, apparently devoted to his new conquest . . .

Pepi also loved Anastasia and wasn't at all discouraged by the news of a love affair between these two beautiful people. He held on tight to his first crazy hope. Smelling of cologne, he called on

Anastasia regularly, on Sunday and during the week, at night and at noon. He brought litchi nuts, mangos, and other delicacies. When he showed up on her better days, he managed to get one or two smiles from her. But in the marketplace, Pepi seemed as cloudy as a mountain top. His eyes never rested anywhere. He often remained immobile, victimized by his dreams. Mom Eli, his mother, teased him: "What's her name, son?" His visits began to bore Anastasia. She no longer smiled and refused his fruits, finally suggesting gently that he shouldn't come any more. What would the neighbors think, and what if Zozor . . . ?

Pepi's dreams faded for the second time. He started to drink alone, at any hour, without the slightest thirst, and he began to stagger in the alleys, singing profane songs about Saint Peter that upset Mom Eli and offended some of the female vendors who were Christian. Neglecting his duties at work, he unfurled a stream of nonsense words, and ended his days sprawled out on the widest sidewalks. We thought it was all over for him when he stopped changing his overalls, darkly stained with vomit and the filth of the gutters. In the worst moments of his delirium, he camped under Anastasia's window, singing love couplets at the top of his voice to the girl who eluded and afflicted him.

One day she came out, took him by the hand, and, bracing him, led him into her house. She cleaned his face with a cloth dipped in cologne and hot water, smoothed his hair which had grown to twice its usual length, and refreshed his body. She wrapped him in a clean sheet and then washed his clothes. He was in ecstasy, letting Anastasia take charge of him while he followed her movements with a dazzled gaze. She spoke to him gently, and ironed his shirt and pants dry. Pepi bent his head, hypnotized. She dispelled his alcoholic fog with salted coffee; then suddenly he fell asleep across the chair. She had to wait for Mom Gaul to come in order to get him into bed. Instead of the usual aimless talk during their evenings together, the two women now took hold of the lover sleeping off his rum. They woke him up for a bowl of thick soup and two dried sardines.

Mom Gaul left, and Pepi and Anastasia remained face to face, eyeing each other from behind the steam rising out of their bowls. He might have embraced then and there the one who consumed his soul. Her gestures were full of gentleness, and her look compassionate. But destiny was pitiless, and the old hall began to creak with Victor's dancing step. When her seducer opened the door, Anastasia was already shooing Pepi out with both hands. In his perpetual rum fog, Pepi walked right into ruin, explaining incomprehensible things to the angels. It wounded us to see him mumbling to himself when things were slow at the cash register.

He was wrenched from passion's abyss when Mom Gaul died suddenly. The old woman's lifeless body was found sitting up very straight behind her buckets, drawing everyone into a net of sadness. Her skin had the gray ashiness of volcanic debris. Pepi came to his senses. He took her in his arms and carried her to her shack across town. He was busy at the side of Anastasia, Bidjoule, and Mom Eli, taking papers to town hall, finding a coffin. At the wake, his eyes never rested on Anastasia, praying silently. Two days after the funeral, taking up his wheelbarrow again and returning to work, he climbed to the top of the fountain, compelling the market to silence while he cried out:

"Mom Gaul, despite the misery you suffered, your eyes never lost the radiance that comes with appreciation and an understanding of life and all growing things . . ."

Hearing this homage, we all began to flood the earth with our tears—Bidjoule alone had dry eyes.

Even today, despite the pain and trouble that these memories excite, we still see the good times we enjoyed after the war, and a nostalgic wave washes over us. That was a damn good market season! We took pride in our work and we were the best, Didon, Sirop, Pin-Pon, Lapochode, and Sifilon, and despite our graying hair we all thought we were indestructible. Bidjoule had so much vigor and so did Pepi, this great laborer with whom we identified. Seeing him overcome the fatality of his monstrous father and that impossible love for Anastasia proved he was solidly planted in life, hard and resistant as barwood. True, there was some bitterness in his look, one or two wrinkles in his forehead, but at noon in the market, he displayed his astonishing energy in the midst of the peasant women and in the furor of work—he was royal. We did not yet know that suffocation was pressing down on him, and on us too.

* * *

Something terrible happened to remind us of the wages and the wonders of time: Mom Eli was reading the newspaper, and began to moan, "Oh my God, Oh my God!" Fearing some awful news about Pepi, we rushed in screaming: BLASTIT! . . . the only worthwhile exorcism we had against destiny.

"Anastasia is in jail!" cried our queen, powerless.

We had only suspected Anastasia's agony, but we saw it all very clearly when Mom Eli spelled out each word in the article. We knew that Zozor Alcide-Victor had given her quite a bit of attention at first. Then he had made himself as scarce as a piece of meat in wartime. Patiently, the faithful woman would wait for him, her shoulder pressed against a corner of the window, softly kneading a wad of sweet dough. Driven by nagging desires, her seducer would appear only to spread her flat against the kitchen table, between bits of eggshell and dustings of flour. Then he promptly disappeared without saying where he was going or when he would return. Weeks would then pass. The old hallway no longer reverberated with the tiptap of his nimble foot.

Because of her constant heartache, Anastasia began to resemble a dull, dry coconut, something that stunned us all. Fighting apathy, she lost herself as she made the cakes and numbed her mind with the nonstop motion required to fix her desserts. Preserving the green papayas didn't take as much concentration as she focused on the process, but it was only by exerting herself regularly and meticulously over the pots that she staved off her distress. The days began to repeat themselves: anxious waiting by the window, selling at the school gates, and the staccato appearances of Zozor Alcide-Victor, who grabbed her without saying anything. On Thursday night, she would slip into red shoes splashed with white flowers and go sniff the park's night air. She would forget herself in the sharp odor of the fallen tamarinds and prowl around the tree where the man who had crushed her heart conducted his sacrifices.

Soon she started living like a recluse without even the desire or courage to appear in the sunlight. Her shutters stayed closed. Her hair came out in clumps. Her beautiful plum-skinned complexion grew as dull as avocados picked in the rain. She no longer chased the dust from her hut but made her desserts mechanically, watching them pile up in the corners of her two rooms, smelling of rancid sugar and attracting ants and flies. From then on, her life transpired completely in her head, where she had Zozor all to herself. She imagined him always present and extremely attentive. That's why she spoke in such a soft voice, and smiled so often as if in the throes of a private joy.

The wretched woman's decline didn't at all affect Zozor Alcide-Victor, recent devotee to strange pleasures, who smoked *ganja* from Guyana and indulged himself in the peculiar pleasures of sodomites. Anastasia was now turned on her stomach under his assaults and this filled her with shame. Consumed by this new craving, the man who dominated her heart pushed her face against the kitchen table sticky with sugar or into the corrupted sheets on the straw mattress, depriving her of the sight of his beautiful face, radiant with the sacred pleasure she gave him. That was the worst. That was the one frustration that sealed the destiny of the Syrian bastard, proving that one can trifle with a monkey but can only go just so far.

One day, at the end of one of Victor's long absences when her inner sun had eclipsed under the incessant rain, Anastasia slid a kitchen knife into her blouse as soon as the bastard's step resounded in the hall. As usual, he burst into the room like a gust of wind, then, after pushing her over on her stomach, penetrated his love slave. He came quickly, reciting an Arabic poem during his orgasm. Sitting on the bed while Anastasia cleaned herself up, he sanctimoniously smoked a cigarette which gave him time to gather his strength for a second go-round. He was enjoying the languor of his muscles, and didn't notice Anastasia's fixed stare or her robotic way of walking as she approached him. She had almost touched him when he pushed her away with his hand, thinking she was already begging for another ride: Come on, Anastasia, you can wait a minute, can't you? . . . At the first blow, the knife sank behind his left clavicle. The second grazed some ribs and pierced his lung. The third severed his carotid artery. When the fourth blow disemboweled him, he was dead. At least that's what the medical expert said later in the report presented before the court.

She was imprisoned in the women's section of the main penitentiary. The police had discovered her lovingly curled around the bastard's body, singing softly in his ear the same Creole lullabies that old women croon to sick children. Anastasia was put into solitary confinement and watched over by a female guard dressed in white. The guard knitted doilies that she sold to her friends to tide her over the difficult times at the end of the month. The prisoner learned how to make Caribbean baskets, a now forgotten art. The empty little section surrounded by deserted cells added an unreal echo to their voices. The woman on night duty came at seven. The two women ate together by the light of the bulb in the little dining area. Anastasia might just as well be there as somewhere else, what did it matter? When Mom Eli got permission to visit and found her serene, she understood that the former slave of love was finally at peace. That was the first and last time that news about Anastasia made our lips curl in a smile.

(Farewell, Anastasia, cinders remain in hearts that flame.)

TRANSLATED BY BARBARA LEWIS

Etc.

Luis Rafael Sánchez

Here it goes: a tale that's no tale because it just happened yesterday at the corner of bus stop 17. I'm not saying it right, stop 17
has four corners. The corner of Franklin's Department Store.
The Franklin store that advertises a closeout sale every Tuesday.
Come to think of it, yesterday was Tuesday. It's not important
that yesterday was Tuesday. What's important is that today is
Wednesday. And this story is today, Wednesday, a day old. And,
being a day old, it's much too new.

Yesterday, Tuesday, I was hanging out at Franklin's corner
like every morning for the past few months. I'm not telling it
right. Every morning comes out as meaning from Monday to
Sunday, when what I'm saying is from Monday to Saturday. On
Sunday you don't see me hanging around stop 17. Sundays I stay
in bed until the laziness of it tires me. Afterward, I listen to what
there is to be listened to: the Baptist radio program with a good
measure of rhythm and invectives against male bestiality. The
sermon that announces my dark and terrible death gets added
to the sermon that announces my also dark and terrible life. 'Cause
my wife airs her dammits on a Sunday and uses me as laundry
post. My wife is a lunatic, first cousin to a fishwife, a declared en-
emy of anything that's polite. My wife doesn't think twice about
calling me a sweet talker, a minor-league trickster, a honey-
tongued bullshit artist, and other endearments that I won't re-

close to one another. But everything has another side to it: the frights one has, the hassles that go with the territory of this devotion to humanity. The dirty-minded people who embrace the filthy idea that you're trying to goose them. Pardon the expression. The people who pull it in, hide their backsides, just so as not to give a fellow a chance. Like just the other day a guy, who saw himself as a heavy dude, insulted me, 'cause he said that I was willfully and with premeditation rubbing a lady that happened to be his wife. I swear the bastard was lying, but I thought it better to get off the bus than to lay him flat with three punches. Let's get on with the tale.

Yesterday, Tuesday morning, I was hanging out at Franklin's corner like every other morning for the past few months, watching without interest what was in my range of vision, just a cheek-wiggling ass on a special-sale spree; cheeks that fluttered in a flowered print between the passersby: crazy, delicious, wild. I want to make it perfectly clear that my eyes in no way tried to make contact with the cheeks. I was born a decent man, decent to the point of not looking at my wife's nakedness unless it's through a peephole. I repeat, then, that in no way did my eyes roam over the flowered cheeks, it's just that they bunched up right in front of me. Now you can understand the hold that this blessed bus stop has on me. You just have to lean on one of Franklin's columns and say to the eyes: *"Don't even blink that the feast is laid out."* Careful! Don't misunderstand me. You tell that to your eyes. The mouth has nothing to do with it. First of all, prudeness. To pick up the thread of my story, the eyes, my eyes, could barely hold their own, so moved were they with the delicious cheeks that now were peeling merrily away toward the Sanrío Men's Store and Thom McAn. Like if all of a sudden they'd discovered that the slips, brassieres, and skirts in Franklin's were nothing to brag about. It wasn't until the juicy cheeks were some distance away from me that I started to follow them. Nobody was aware of my chase. I'm not telling it right. Chase comes out meaning stalking when what I'm saying is that I started walking down Ponce de León Avenue with the utmost discretion. Discretion. That quality is of my own invention, like it or not. And to it, add the other: prudeness. I'm not vulgar. I'm not going to be disrespectful to myself with a slur. I don't scratch my parts as a silent

peat out of politeness. Still and all, I give her all my Sundays
she can do with them and me whatever she fancies. So let it
understood that I'm on stop 17 only from Monday through Sa
urday. OK.

Yesterday, Tuesday morning, I was hanging out at Franklin's co
ner like every morning for the past few months. Heavy thing, the
last few months. Make a note of it. February the eighteenth p
April the twentieth add up to a man hanging by his balls. The f
tory closed on the eighteenth. The nineteenth we were all out
the streets, all two hundred of us. You have no idea of how ma
bellies get fed by just two hundred salaries. Take my case: the
mine and there's my wife's. There's also my wife's aunt's: a si
lady, an antiquated lady, a pain-in-the-ass lady. There's also
wife's cousin's: a wino, a hustler, and an I'll-take-what's-not-m
guy. No, they don't live with us, but they live off us. I'll continue

Yesterday, Tuesday morning, I was hanging out at Frankl
corner like every morning for the past few months, watching
pleasure what there was to watch: nothing more than the h
with which people crossed the street trying to beat the short
allowed by the traffic lights or the hurry with which people w
cover the sidewalks. Make a note of this: the two sidewalks
take you from Roberto H. Todd Avenue toward the Condado
tion and toward the Alto Del Cabro slum are almost deserted
the ones that take you from Roberto H. Todd Avenue dow
ward stop 18 and the one that takes you on Ponce de Leó
enue toward Telesforo Men's Store are constantly filled
women on their market day, secretaries on their coffee b
ladies with nothing to do, housewives, students from the
School or the Central High School. A real beehive. I shal
make known my love for the masses. Where there's a crowd
right at home. Stop 17, political demonstrations, Hiram Bi
Stadium, funerals, religious processions—oh, the human
it!—the airport, the Río Piedras bus terminal, the sho
malls. You'll understand my thing if I tell you that, on some
noons, I'll get to where I don't have to go, just so I c
squeezed tight on a bus. Take the Loíza route, the Villa Pa
route, the Puerto Nuevo route. If only Sundays were Mon
love the crush. I trip on it, wow! I tell myself that Judgme
won't be that terrible if it's true that we sinners will be

come-on. Yes, I scratch myself, I hungrily rub myself, I massage it from side to side. But all this from the underground safety of my pocket. To continue.

Yesterday, Tuesday morning, I was hanging out at Franklin's corner like every other morning for the last months. I was on what you might call a secret lookout for a butterfly ass. I was hoping that somewhere, a crowd would gather, a throng of bodies: a dozen women bewitched by a knickknack, the kind that usually bewitches a dozen women, I don't know, pots to make stew, a cut of fabric, embroidered blouses. In plain language I was waiting for a gathering of womanflesh, with the possibility of starting a, let's say, silent and passive communication, I swear passive, between my desire and the wild fluttering of cheeks that now, all of a sudden, stopped in front of a showy window display. I started to look at the clock of the Bank of San Juan that, come to think of it, had stopped at nine o'clock. See the kind of guy I am, looking at a clock so there's no way I could be called insolent. The Bank of San Juan's clock has two black hands and is round as they come. So while my right eye was glued to the idiotic clock, the corner of my left eye was sending the information it could gather by teletype. The charming little ass was undecided for less than an instant, because it immediately turned back. I have two eyes, a left one and a right one, and both stared reverently at the Bank of San Juan's clock. My eyes were on the stupid clock but that wind down my back was the result of a pair of charming cheeks. No, I didn't have to see them to know. They were at Franklin's window display again. In a flash, as if trained by James Bond, I ran for cover to the other side of the display, the side that because it has a column, I don't visit frequently. I stationed myself behind the column. What was wrong with this strategy was that the owner of the cheeks was now standing facing me. A very common type seen this way. Short and horribly common. No way to it, her best side was her backside. One of Franklin's salesladies, also known in my file as the round-as-a-hat-butt lady, carried out of the store a tray of quality hosiery, or so she hollered, at closeout prices, or so she hollered. The answer to my prayers! If the wild bunch got interested . . . if those delicious cheeks and seven other ladies were interested, maybe then I could . . . it could be the best morning ever! Then the laughter descended upon the scene. Now you'll understand.

Yesterday, Tuesday morning, I was hanging out at Franklin's corner like every other morning for the last months, when the outburst of laughter dropped from hell. To be exact, it came from the side of the store window display that formed a ninety-degree angle with my hiding place. The laughter had a magnetic quality, contagious, it was impossible not to be . . . yes, fascinated. Because of the column I couldn't see the owners of the laugh, but I could think them: a you-wouldn't-believe-how-fat lady and a miserly thin lady, both overflowing with grossness, of no backside value whatsoever. Since things are the way they are, I have to say that even me, a serious-minded person, smiled at hearing them celebrate what must have been a big joke. They were gasping. Laughing was tiring them. They were giving howls of tiredness, a thoroughly enjoyed and desired tiredness. All of a sudden, one of them, I swear it was the fat one, said: "Listen to this part." And started a long whispering to which my ears tuned in. "The hus-band was sacked from the factory for being fast. He tells everyone the factory was closed down. But that's not true. Sacked, period. No, it wasn't for stealing or embezzling. A gooser and no relation to the nursery rhymes. He goosed right and left. Smart aleck! A sweet talker, but always on the lookout for a good you-know-what." The laughter came out like a right hook. "Every time I come to stop 17 I watch my you-know-what because this is his ter-ritory." I was fascinated by the story, I laughed with the story. "But the incredible thing is that the pervert has a very attractive wife who's having an affair with a man she tells everyone is her cousin!" They laughed, as if there was no stopping them, laughed without the restraint one should keep when in a public place. They laughed. From laughing they started trembling, from trem-bling to choking, from choking to coughing. They coughed. A cough soaked with tears. I heard them blow their noses. I thought about that man loose on stop 17 while his wife cheated on him. I kept thinking that there are careless men. I mean, to leave themselves open, so wide open. To let their tricks be known just like that. Whoever has a weakness has a right to it, without publicity, or microphones, or accompanying music. No, he had to be a Sad Sack, a poor man with nothing to fall back on. A . . . a . . . a . . .

What anger! What frustration! The cheeks weren't there. But

just a moment ago . . . ! The Franklin's saleslady closed her tray of quality hosiery on sale. Among the people that crossed the street trying to beat the short time allowed by the green light, the crazy, delicious wild cheeks had disappeared. Lost them! I started walking toward Telesforo Men's Store. I looked without interest at women's backs. And, once in a while, at the men's faces. And in the men's faces for the one who could be the protagonist of the tale that was no tale. Maybe, without trying, without looking for him, I would find the man who was giving us a bad name. Fool, jerk, schmuck, cuckold, turkey, dupe, etc.

TRANSLATED BY CARMEN LILIANNE MARIN

A Walk to the Jetty

Jamaica Kincaid

"My name is Annie John." These were the first words that came into my mind as I woke up on the morning of the last day I spent in Antigua, and they stayed there, lined up one behind the other, marching up and down, for I don't know how long. At noon on that day, a ship on which I was to be a passenger would sail to Barbados, and there I would board another ship, which would sail to England, where I would study to become a nurse. My name was the last thing I saw the night before, just as I was falling asleep; it was written in big, black letters all over my trunk, sometimes followed by my address in Antigua, sometimes followed by my address as it would be in England. I did not want to go to England, I did not want to be a nurse, but I would have chosen going off to live in a cavern and keeping house for seven unruly men rather than go on with my life as it stood. I never wanted to lie in this bed again, my legs hanging out way past the foot of it, tossing and turning on my mattress, with its cotton stuffing all lumped just where it wasn't a good place to be lumped. I never wanted to lie in my bed again and hear Mr. Ephraim driving his sheep to pasture—a signal to my mother that she should get up to prepare my father's and my bath and breakfast. I never wanted to lie in my bed and hear her get dressed, washing her face, brushing her teeth, and gargling. I especially never wanted to lie in my bed and hear my mother gargling again.

Lying there in the half-dark of my room, I could see my shelf, with my books—some of them prizes I had won in school, some of them gifts from my mother—and with photographs of people I was supposed to love forever no matter what, and with my old thermos, which was given to me for my eighth birthday, and some shells I had gathered at different times I spent at the sea. In one corner stood my washstand and its beautiful basin of white enamel with blooming red hibiscus painted at the bottom and an urn that matched. In another corner were my old school shoes and my Sunday shoes. In still another corner, a bureau held my old clothes. I knew everything in this room, inside out and outside in. I had lived in this room for thirteen of my seventeen years. I could see in my mind's eye even the day my father was adding it onto the rest of the house. Everywhere I looked stood something that had meant a lot to me, that had given me pleasure at some point, or could remind me of a time that was a happy time. But as I was lying there my heart could have burst open with joy at the thought of never having to see any of it again.

If someone had asked me for a little summing up of my life at that moment as I lay in bed, I would have said, "My name is Annie John. I was born on the fifteenth of September, seventeen years ago, at Holberton Hospital, at five o'clock in the morning. At the time I was born, the moon was going down at one end of the sky and the sun was coming up at the other. My mother's name is Annie also; I am named after her, and that is why my parents call me Little Miss. My father's name is Alexander, and he is thirty-five years older than my mother. Two of his children are four and six years older than she is. Looking at how sickly he has become and looking at the way my mother now has to run up and down for him, gathering the herbs and barks that he boils in water, which he drinks instead of the medicine the doctor has ordered for him, I plan not only never to marry an old man but certainly never to marry at all. The house we live in my father built with his own hands. The bed I am lying in my father built with his own hands. If I get up and sit on a chair, it is a chair my father built with his own hands. When my mother uses a large wooden spoon to stir the porridge we sometimes eat as part of our breakfast, it will be a spoon that my father has carved with his own hands. The sheets on my bed my mother made with her own hands. The curtains hanging at my window my mother made with her own hands. The nightie I am wearing, with scalloped neck and hem and sleeves, my mother made with her own hands. When I look at things in a certain way, I suppose I should say that the two of them made me with their own hands. For most of my life, when the three of us went anywhere together I stood between the two of them or sat between the two of them. But then I got too big, and there I was, shoulder to shoulder with them more or less, and it became not very comfortable to walk down the street together. And so now there they are together and here I am apart. I don't see them now the way I used to, and I don't love them now the way I used to. The bitter thing about it is that they are just the same and it is I who have changed, so all the things I used to be and all the things I used to feel are as false as the teeth in my father's head. Why, I wonder, didn't I see the hypocrite in my mother when, over the years, she said that she loved me and could hardly live without me, while at the same time proposing and arranging separation after separation, including this one, which, unbeknownst to her, *I* have arranged to be permanent? So now I, too, have hypocrisy, and breasts (small ones), and hair growing in the appropriate places, and sharp eyes, and I have made a vow never to be fooled again.

Lying in my bed for the last time, I thought, This is what I add up to. At that, I felt as if someone had placed me in a hole and was forcing me first down and then up against the pressure of gravity. I shook myself and prepared to get up. I said to myself, "I am getting up out of this bed for the last time." Everything I would do that morning until I got on the ship that would take me to England I would be doing for the last time, for I had made up my mind that, come what might, the road for me now went only in one direction: away from my home, away from my mother, away from my father, away from the everlasting blue sky, away from the everlasting hot sun, away from people who said to me, "This happened during the time your mother was carrying you." If I had been asked to put into words why I felt this way, if I had been given years to reflect and come up with the words of why I felt this way, I would not have been able to come up with so much as the letter "A." I only knew that I felt the way I did, and that this feeling was the strongest thing in my life.

The Anglican church bell struck seven. My father had already bathed and dressed and was in his workshop puttering around. As if the day of my leaving were something to celebrate, they were treating it as a holiday, and as if nothing usual would take place. My father would not go to work at all. When I got up, my mother greeted me with a big, bright "Good morning"—so big and bright that I shrank before it. I bathed quickly in some warm bark water that my mother had prepared for me. I put on my underclothes— all of them white and all of them smelling funny. Along with my earrings, my neck chain, and my bracelets, all made of gold from British Guiana, my underclothes had been sent to my mother's obeah woman, and whatever she had done to my jewelry and underclothes would help protect me from evil spirits and every kind of misfortune. The things I never wanted to see or hear or do again now made up at least three weeks' worth of grocery lists. I placed a mark against obeah women, jewelry, and white underclothes. Over my underclothes, I put on an around-the-yard dress of my mother's. The clothes I would wear for my voyage were a dark-blue pleated skirt and a blue-and-white checked blouse (the blue in the blouse matched exactly the blue of my skirt) with a large sailor collar and with a tie made from the same material as the skirt—a blouse that came down a long way past my waist, over my skirt. They were lying on a chair, freshly ironed by my mother. Putting on my clothes was the last thing I would do just before leaving the house. Miss Cornelia came and pressed my hair and then shaped it into what felt like a hundred corkscrews, all lying flat against my head so that my hat would fit properly.

At breakfast, I was seated in my usual spot, with my mother at one end of the table, my father at the other, and me in the middle, so that as they talked to me or to each other I would shift my head to the left or to the right and get a good look at them. We were having a Sunday breakfast, a breakfast as if we had just come back from Sunday-morning services: salt fish and antroba and souse and hard-boiled eggs, and even special Sunday bread from Mr. Daniel, our baker. On Sundays, we ate this big breakfast at eleven o'clock, and then we didn't eat again until four o'clock, when we had our big Sunday dinner. It was the best breakfast we ate, and the only breakfast better than that was the one we ate on Christmas morning. My parents were in a festive mood, saying what a wonderful time I would have in my new life, what a wonderful opportunity this was for me, and what a lucky person I was. They were eating away as they talked, my father's false teeth making a *clop-clop* sound like a horse on a walk as he talked, my mother's mouth going up and down like a horse eating hay as she chewed each mouthful thirty-two times. (I had long ago counted, because it was something she made me do also, and I was trying to see if this was just one of her rules that applied only to me.) I was looking at them with a smile on my face but disgust in my heart when my mother said, "Of course, you are a young lady now, and we won't be surprised if in due time you write to say that one day soon you are to be married."

Without thinking, I said, with bad feeling that I didn't hide very well, "How absurd!"

My parents immediately stopped eating and looked at me as if they had not seen me before. My father was the first to go back to his food. My mother continued to look. I don't know what went through her mind, but I could see her using her tongue to dislodge food stuck in the far corners of her mouth.

Many of my mother's friends now came by to say goodbye to me, and to wish me God's blessings. I thanked them and showed the proper amount of joy at the glorious things they pointed out to me that my future held and showed the proper amount of sorrow at how much my parents and everyone else who loved me would miss me. My body ached a little at all this false going back and forth, at all this taking in of people gazing at me with heads tilted, love and pity on their smiling faces. I could have left without saying any good-byes to them and I wouldn't have missed it. There was only one person I felt I should say goodbye to, and that was my former friend Gwen. We had long ago drifted apart, and when I saw her now my heart nearly split in two with embarrassment at the feelings I used to have for her and things I had shared with her. She had now degenerated into complete silliness, hardly able to complete a sentence without putting in a few giggles. Along with the giggles, she had developed some other schoolgirl traits that she did not have when she was actually a schoolgirl, so beneath her were such things then. When we were saying our goodbyes, it was all I could do not to say cruelly, "Why are you behaving like such a monkey?" Instead, I put everything into a friendly, plain wishing her well and the best in the future. It was then that she told me that she was more or less engaged to a boy she had known while growing up early on in Nevis, and that soon, in a year or so, they would be married. My reply to her was "Good luck," and she thought I meant her well, so she grabbed me and said, "Thank you. I knew you would be happy about it." But to me it was as if she had shown me a high point from which she was going to jump and hoped to land in one piece on her feet. We parted, and when I turned away I didn't look back.

My mother had arranged with a stevedore to take my trunk to the jetty ahead of me. At ten o'clock on the dot, I was dressed, and we set off for the jetty. An hour after that, I would board a launch that would take me out to sea, where I then would board the ship. Starting out, as if for old time's sake and without giving it a thought, we lined up in the old way: I walking between my mother and my father. I loomed way above my father and could see the top of his head. I wasn't so much taller than my mother that it could bring me any satisfaction. We must have made a strange sight: a grown girl all dressed up in the middle of a morning, in the middle of the week, walking in step in the middle between her two parents, for people we didn't know stared at us. It was all of half an hour's walk from our house to the jetty, but I was passing through most of the years of my life. We passed by the house where Miss Lois, the seamstress that I had been apprenticed to for a few years, lived, and just as I was passing by a wave of bad feeling for her came over me, because I suddenly remembered that the first year I spent with her all she had me do was sweep the floor, which was always full of threads and pins and needles, and I never seemed to sweep it clean enough to please her. Then she would send me to the store to buy buttons or thread, though I was only allowed to do this if I was given a sample of the button or thread, and then she would find fault even though they were an exact match of the samples she had given me. And all the while she said

to me, "You'll never sew, you know." At the time, I don't suppose I
minded it, because it was customary to treat the first-year appren-
tice with such scorn, but now I placed on the dustheap of my life
Miss Lois and everything that I had had to do with her.

We were soon on the road that I had taken to school, to
church, to Sunday school, to choir practice, to Brownie meetings, to Girl Guide meetings, to meet a friend. I was five years old
when I first walked on this road unaccompanied by someone to
hold my hand. My mother had placed three pennies in my little
basket, which was a duplicate of her bigger basket, and sent me
to the chemist's shop to buy a pennyworth of senna, a pennyworth of eucalyptus leaves, and a pennyworth of camphor. She
then instructed me on what side of the road to walk, where to
make a turn, where to cross, and to look carefully before I
crossed, and if I met anyone that I knew to politely pass greetings
and keep on my way. I was wearing a freshly ironed yellow dress
that had printed on it scenes of acrobats flying through the air
and swinging on a trapeze. I had just had a bath, and after it, instead of powdering me with my baby-smelling talcum powder, my
mother had, as a special favor, let me use her own talcum powder, which smelled quite perfumy and came in a can that had
painted on it people going out to dinner in nineteenth-century
London and was called Mazie. How it pleased me to walk out the
door and bend my head down to sniff at myself and see that I
smelled just like my mother. I went to the chemist's shop, and he
had to come from behind the counter and bend down to hear
what it was that I wanted to buy, my voice was so little and timid
then. I went back just the way I had come, and when I walked
into the yard and presented my basket with its three packages to
my mother her eyes filled with tears and she swooped me up and
held me high in the air and said that I was wonderful and good
and that there would never be anybody better. If I had just conquered Persia, she couldn't have been more proud of me.

We passed by our church—the church in which I had been
christened and received and had sung in the junior choir. We
passed by a house in which a girl I used to like and was sure I
couldn't live without had lived. Once, when she had mumps,
I went to visit her against my mother's wishes, and we sat on her
bed and ate the cure of roasted, buttered sweet potatoes that had

been placed on her swollen jaws, held there by a piece of white cloth. I don't know how, but my mother found out about it, and I don't know how, but she put an end to our friendship. Shortly after, the girl moved with her family across the sea to somewhere else. We passed the doll store where I would go with my mother when I was little and point out the doll I wanted that year for Christmas. We passed the store where I bought the much-fought-over shoes I wore to church to be received in. We passed the bank. On my sixth birthday, I was given, among other things, the present of a sixpence. My mother and I then went to this bank, and with the sixpence I opened my own savings account. I was given a little gray book with my name in big letters on it, and in the balance column it said "6d." Every Saturday morning after that, I was given a sixpence—later, a shilling, and later a two-and-sixpence piece—and I would take it to the bank for deposit. I had never been allowed to withdraw even a farthing from my bank account until just a few weeks before I was to leave; then the whole account was closed out, and I received from the bank the sum of six pounds, ten shillings, and two and a half pence.

We passed the office of the doctor who told my mother three times that I did not need glasses, that if my eyes were feeling weak a glass of carrot juice a day would make them strong again. This happened when I was eight. And so every day at recess I would run to my school gate and meet my mother, who was waiting for me with a glass of juice from carrots she had just grated and then squeezed, and I would drink it and then run back to meet my chums. I knew there was nothing at all wrong with my eyes, but I had recently read a story in "A Girl's Own Annual" in which the heroine, a girl a few years older than I was then, cut such a figure to my mind with the way she was always adjusting her small, round horn-rimmed glasses that I felt I must have a pair exactly like them. When it became clear that I didn't need glasses, I began to complain about the glare of the sun being too much for my eyes, and I walked around with my hands shielding them—especially in my mother's presence. My mother then bought for me a pair of sunglasses with the exact horn-rimmed frames I wanted, and how I enjoyed the gestures of blowing on the lenses, wiping them with the hem of my uniform, adjusting the glasses when they slipped down my nose, and just removing them from their case and putting them on. In three weeks, I grew tired of them and they found a nice resting place in a drawer, along with some other things that at one time or another I couldn't live without. We passed the store that sold only grooming aids, all imported from England. This store had in it a large porcelain dog—white, with black spots all over and a red ribbon of satin tied around its neck. The dog sat in front of a white porcelain bowl that was always filled with fresh water, and it sat in such a way that it looked as if it had just taken a long drink. When I was a small child, I would ask my mother, if ever we were near this store, to please take me to see the dog, and I would stand in front of it, bent over slightly, my hands resting on my knees, and stare at it and stare at it. I thought this dog more beautiful and more real than any dog I had ever seen or any dog I would ever see. I must have outgrown my interest in the dog, for when it disappeared I never asked what became of it. We passed the library, and if there was anything on this walk that I might have wept over leaving this most surely would have been the thing. My mother had been a member of the library long before I was born. And since she took me everywhere with her when I was quite little, when she went to the library she took me along here, too. I would sit in her lap very quietly as she read books that she did not want to take home with her. I could not read the words yet, but just the way they looked on the page was interesting to me. Once, a book she was reading had a large picture of a man in it, and when I asked her who he was she told me that he was Louis Pasteur and that the book was about his life. It stuck in my mind, because she said it was because of him that she boiled my milk to purify it before I was allowed to drink it, that it was his idea, and that that was why the process was called pasteurization. One of the things I had put away in my mother's old trunk in which she kept all my childhood things was my library card. At that moment, I owed sevenpence in overdue fees.

As I passed by all these places, it was as if I were in a dream, for I didn't notice the people coming and going in and out of them, I didn't feel my feet touch ground, I didn't even feel my own body—I just saw these places as if they were hanging in the air, not having top or bottom, and as if I had gone in and out of them all in the same moment. The sun was bright; the sky was blue and just above my head. We then arrived at the jetty.

* * *

My heart now beat fast, and no matter how hard I tried I couldn't keep my mouth from falling open and my nostrils from spreading to the ends of my face. My old fear of slipping between the boards of the jetty and falling into the dark-green water where the dark-green eels lived came over me. When my father's stomach started to go bad, the doctor had recommended a walk every evening right after he ate his dinner. Sometimes he would take me with him. When he took me with him, we usually went to the jetty, and there he would sit and talk to the night watchman about cricket or some other thing that didn't interest me, because it was not personal; they didn't talk about their wives, or their children, or their parents, or about any of their likes and dislikes. They talked about things in such a strange way, and I didn't see what they found funny, but sometimes they made each other laugh so much that their guffaws would bound out to sea and send back an echo. I was always sorry when we got to the jetty and saw that the night watchman on duty was the one he enjoyed speaking to; it was like being locked up in a book filled with numbers and diagrams and what-ifs. For the thing about not being able to understand and enjoy what they were saying was I had nothing to take my mind off my fear of slipping in between the boards of the jetty.

Now, too, I had nothing to take my mind off what was happening to me. My mother and my father—I was leaving them forever. My home on an island—I was leaving it forever. What to make of everything? I felt a familiar hollow space inside. I felt I was being held down against my will. I felt I was burning up from head to toe. I felt that someone was tearing me up into little pieces and soon I would be able to see all the little pieces as they floated out into nothing in the deep blue sea. I didn't know whether to laugh or cry. I could see that it would be better not to think too clearly about any one thing. The launch was being made ready to take me, along with some other passengers, out to the ship that was anchored in the sea. My father paid our fares, and we joined a line of people waiting to board. My mother checked my bag to make sure that I had my passport, the money she had given me, and a sheet of paper placed between some pages in my Bible on which were written the names of the relatives—people I had not known

existed—with whom I would live in England. Across from the jetty
was a wharf, and some stevedores were loading and unloading
barges. I don't know why seeing that struck me so, but suddenly a
wave of strong feeling came over me, and my heart swelled with a
great gladness as the words "I shall never see this again" spilled
out inside me. But then, just as quickly, my heart shrivelled up
and the words "I shall never see this again" stabbed at me. I don't
know what stopped me from falling in a heap at my parents' feet.

When we were all on board, the launch headed out to sea.
Away from the jetty, the water became the customary blue, and
the launch left a wide path in it that looked like a road. I passed
by sounds and smells that were so familiar that I had long ago
stopped paying any attention to them. But now here they were,
and the ever-present "I shall never see this again" bobbed up and
down inside me. There was the sound of the seagull diving down
into the water and coming up with something silverish in its
mouth. There was the smell of the sea and the sight of small
pieces of rubbish floating around in it. There were boats filled
with fishermen coming in early. There was the sound of their
voices as they shouted greetings to each other. There was the hot
sun, there was the blue sea, there was the blue sky. Not very far
away, there was the white sand of the shore, with the run-down
houses all crowded in next to each other, for in some places only
poor people lived near the shore. I was seated in the launch between my parents, and when I realized that I was gripping their
hands tightly I glanced quickly to see if they were looking at me
with scorn, for I felt sure that they must have known of my never-
see-this-again feelings. But instead my father kissed me on the
forehead and my mother kissed me on the mouth, and they both
gave over their hands to me, so that I could grip them as much as
I wanted. I was on the verge of feeling that it had all been a mis-
take, but I remembered that I wasn't a child anymore, and that
now when I made up my mind about something I had to see it
through. At that moment, we came to the ship, and that was that.

The goodbyes had to be quick, the captain said. My mother introduced herself to him and then introduced me. She told him
to keep an eye on me, for I had never gone this far away from

home on my own. She gave him a letter to pass on to the captain
of the next ship that I would board in Barbados. They walked me
to my cabin, a small space that I would share with someone else—
a woman I did not know. I had never before slept in a room with
someone I did not know. My father kissed me goodbye and told
me to be good and to write home often. After he said this, he
looked at me, then looked at the floor and swung his left foot,
then looked at me again. I could see that he wanted to say something else, something that he had never said to me before, but
then he just turned and walked away. My mother said, "Well," and
then she threw her arms around me. Big tears streamed down
her face, and it must have been that—for I could not bear to see
my mother cry—which started me crying, too. She then tight-
ened her arms around me and held me to her close, so that I felt
that I couldn't breathe. With that, my tears dried up, and I was
suddenly on my guard. "What does she want now?" I said to myself. Still holding me close to her, she said, in a voice that raked
across my skin, "It doesn't matter what you do or where you go,
I'll always be your mother and this will always be your home."

I dragged myself away from her and backed off a little, and then
I shook myself, as if to wake myself out of a stupor. We looked at
each other for a long time with smiles on our faces, but I know the
opposite of that was in my heart. As if responding to some invisible
cue, we both said, at the very same moment, "Well." Then my
mother turned around and walked out the cabin door. I stood
there for I don't know how long, and then I remembered that it
was customary to stand on deck and wave to your relatives who
were returning to shore. From the deck, I could not see my father,
but I could see my mother facing the ship, her eyes searching to
pick me out. I removed from my bag a red cotton handkerchief
that she had earlier given me for just this purpose, and I waved it
wildly in the air. Recognizing me immediately, she waved back just
as wildly, and we continued to do this until she became just a dot
in the matchbox-size launch swallowed up in the big blue sea.

I went back to my cabin and lay down on my berth. Everything
trembled as if it had a spring at its very center. I could hear the
small waves lap-lapping around the ship. They made an unexpected sound, as if a vessel filled with liquid had been placed on
its side and now was slowly emptying out.

From the Ocean Floor

Edwidge Danticat

They say *dèyè mown, gin pi gro mown.* Behind the mountains are
more mountains. Now I know it's true. I also know there are
timeless waters, endless seas, and lots of people in this world with
no name. I look up at the sky and I see you there. I see you crying
like a crushed snail, the way you cried when I helped you pull out
your first loose tooth. Yes, I did love you then. Somehow when I
looked at you, I thought of red ants. I wanted you to dig your little whiskers in me and drain out all my blood.

I don't know how long we'll be at sea. There are thirty-six
other deserting souls on this little boat with me. A white sheet
with bright red spots floats as our sail. When I just got on board I
could still smell the semen and the innocence lost to it. I look up
there and I think of you and all those times you resisted. Sometimes I felt like you wanted to, but I knew you wanted me to respect you. You thought I was testing you, but all I wanted was to
be close to you. Maybe it's like you've always said—I imagine too
much. I am afraid I am going to start having nightmares once we
get deep at sea. I really hate having the sun in my face all day
long. If you see me again, I'll be so dark.

Your father will probably marry you off now, since I am gone.
Whatever you do, please don't marry a soldier. They're not human.

* * *

haiti est comme tu l'as laissé. bullets day and night. same merde. same bullshit. i'm tired of the whole mess. i get so edgy. i pass the time by chasing roaches around the house. i pound my heel on their heads. they make me so mad. everything makes me mad. i am cramped inside all day. they've closed the schools since the army took over. no one is mentioning aristide's name. papa burnt all his campaign posters and all his lavalas buttons. no one comes out of their house. not a single person. papa wants me to throw out those tapes of your radio shows. i destroyed some music tapes, but i still have your voice. i thank god you got the hell out when you did. all the other "yfd" members have disappeared. no one has heard from them. i think lucien might be in prison. or maybe he's dead. you can't ask any questions. papa worries a little about you. he doesn't hate you as much as you think. the other day i heard him asking maman, do you think the boy is dead. maman said she didn't know. i think he regrets being so mean to you. i'll write more later. i can't sketch anymore because i don't even like seeing the sun. we have our whole lives ahead of us. you used to say that. remember? but then again things were different then.

There is a pregnant girl on board. She looks like she might be our age. Nineteen or twenty. She looks like a dark banana, curved like one at least. Most of these people are much older than I am. I've heard that a lot of these ships have young children on board. I'm glad this one doesn't. I think it would break my heart watching some little boys and girls, looking into their empty little faces, day in and day out. It's hard enough with the adults.

I used to read a lot about America before I had to study so hard for the Rheto. Miami is sunny—it doesn't snow there like it does in other parts of America. I can't tell exactly how far we are from Miami. I can't even tell if we're about to drop off the face of the earth. Maybe the world is flat and we're going to find out. As you know, I'm not very religious. Still I pray every night that we won't hit a storm. When I do manage to sleep, I dream that we're caught in one hurricane after another.

I am more comfortable now with the idea of dying. Not that I've accepted it, but I know it might happen. It's part of my thinking these days. Am I making any sense at all? You always could understand me, even when I was just rambling on.

I really don't want to be a martyr. I know I'm no good to any-body dead, but if that's what's coming, I know I can't just scream at it and tell it to go away. I just don't want to die in a storm. Rain or bullets. If Aristide goes back to Haiti and the coup is reversed, I hope another group of young people can do *Jeunesse Parlée*. It was nice to have a show like that for a while, where we could talk about what we wanted from government.

There are a lot of Jesus people—Protestants—on this boat. A lot of them see themselves as Jobs or Children of Israel. I think some of them are hoping something will plunge down from the sky and part the sea for us. They say the Lord gives and the Lord takes away. I've never been given much. What was there to take away?

if i knew some good wanga i'd wipe their asses off the face of the earth. a group of students got shot in front of fort dimanche. they were demon-strating for the bodies of the radio six. that's what they're calling you all. the radio six. you have a name. you have a reputation. a lot of people think you are dead like the others. they want the bodies turned over to the families. this afternoon, the army finally did give some bodies back. they told the families to go get them at the indigent room at the morgue. madan roger came home with noster's head and not much else. honest to god, it was just his con de tete. they say a car ran over him and took the head off his body. when madan roger went to the morgue they gave her the head. by the time we saw her, she'd been carrying it all over port-au-prince. just to show what's been done to her son. the macoutes by the house were laughing at her. they asked her if that was her dinner. it took ten people to hold her back from jumping on them. they would have killed her, les chiens. i will never go outside again. not even on the porch to breathe the air. they are always watching you. like vultures, like bastards. at night i can't sleep. i count the bullets in the dark. i keep wondering if it's true. did you really get out? i wish there was some way i could be sure that you really went away. yes i will. i'll keep writing. i hate it, but i'll keep writing. you keep writing too o.k.? and when we see each other again, it will seem like we lost no time.

Aside from singing and telling stories, most of the time we watch the sea. If there's anything nice about this whole thing, it's the stars at night. They look so huge and so close. At times I feel like I can just reach out and pull one down. Like a breadfruit or soursop.

We're already out of songs to sing. When we sing *Haiti Chérie*, some of the women start crying as soon as we get to the part that says "I didn't know how great Haiti was until I left it." At times, I just want to stop in the middle of the song and cry myself. I keep acting like I'm just getting another attack of nausea, from the sea smell.

You probably don't know much about this, because you've always been so closely watched by that father of yours. In that gingerbread house, with your quiet genteel mother. No I'm not making fun. If anything, I'm a bit jealous. If I was a girl, maybe I would have been at home and not out politicking and getting myself into something like this.

Anyway, once you've been at sea for a couple of days it smells like every fish you've ever eaten, every crab you've ever caught, every jelly fish that's bit your leg. I am so tired of the smell. I am also tired of the way the people on this boat are beginning to smell. I don't know how the pregnant girl, Célianne, takes it. She stares into space all the time, and rubs her stomach.

I think she's running out of food. I can't help feeling like she'll have this child as soon as she gets hungry enough. She woke up screaming the other night. I thought she had a stomach ache. Some water started coming into the boat in the spot where she was sleeping. There's a crack at the bottom that looks as though it will split the boat in two, if it gets any bigger. The captain cleared everyone aside and used some tar to clog up the hole. Everyone started asking him if it was O.K., if they were going to be O.K. He said he hoped the Coast Guard would find us soon.

You can't really go to sleep after that. So we all stared at the tar by the lamplight. We did this until dawn. I can't help but wonder how long this tar will hold out.

papa found your tapes. he started yelling at me, asking if i was crazy keeping them. he is just waiting for the gasoline ban to be lifted so we can get out of the city. he's always on my back these days because he can't go

out driving his van. all the american factories are closed. even the ones
where we hoped to get some work next year. he kept yelling at me about the
tapes. he called me selfish and he asked if i hadn't seen or heard what was
happening to little bouzins like me. i shouted that i wasn't a whore. he
had no business calling me a malprope. he pushed me against the wall for
disrespecting him. he spat on my face. i wish those macoutes would kill
him. i wish he would catch a bullet in a finger or a toe so he could really
show how scared he is. he said to me, "i didn't send your stupid bastard
away." yes, you did. you stupid payzan. i don't know why i said that. he
slapped me and kept slapping me really hard until maman came and
grabbed me away from him. i wish one of those bullets would hit me.

The tar is holding up so far. Two days and no more leaks. Yes, I
am finally an African. I am even darker than your father. I wanted
to buy a straw hat from one of the ladies, but she wouldn't sell it to
me for the last two gourdes I have left in change. Do you think
your money is worth anything to me here, she asked me. Sometimes, I forget where I am. If I keep daydreaming like I've been
doing, I will walk off the boat to go for a walk.

The other night I dreamt that I died and went to heaven. This
heaven was nothing like I expected. It was at the bottom of the
sea. There were mermaids and dolphins all around me. They
were dancing and singing in Latin like they do in mass. You were
there too. You were with your family, off to the side. Your father
was acting like he was better than everyone else—as usual. I tried
to talk to you but every time I opened my mouth, water bubbles
came out, but no sounds.

they have this thing now that they do. if they come into a house and
there's a son and mother there, they hold a gun to their heads. they
make the son rape his mother. if it's a daughter and father, they do the
same thing. some nights papa sleeps at tonton pressoir's house. tonton
pressoir sleeps at our house. just in case. still no gasoline to buy. otherwise
we'd be in gressier already. papa has a friend who is going to get him
some gasoline from a soldier. as soon as we get some, we're going to drive
quick and fast until we find civilization. that's how he puts it. they say
things aren't as bad in the provinces. i'm still not talking to him. i don't

think i ever will. maman says it's not his fault. he's trying to protect us. he can't. the soldiers can come and do with us what they want. that makes papa feel weak, she says. he gets angry when he feels weak. why should he be angry with me? i'm not one of the cochons with the machine guns. she asked me what really happened to you. she said she saw your parents. they didn't want to tell her anything. i told her you took a canter when you heard that they were coming to raid the radio station. she said, he was a good boy, smart—because you took the rheto two years ahead of everyone else. she said papa didn't want you for me because you didn't look like you were going to do better for me than he and maman could. he wants me to find some mulatto man who'll do me good. it's always the same story. you're pretty enough even if we're not well connected. the kind of man he wants for me would never have anything to do with a pov malérèz like me. we're not exactly with the pétion-ville milieu. yes, she said, but you're educated. what she counts for educated isn't much to anyone but us anyway. they should be announcing rheto results next week. i'll listen for your name.

We spent most of yesterday telling stories. "Crick? Crack!" Sometimes it feels like we've been at sea so long. The sun comes up and goes down. That's how you know it's been a day. I feel like we're sailing for Africa. Maybe we'll go to Dahomey and ask for our land back. (Laugh, will you?) They would probably turn us away too. Someone has a transistor and sometimes we listen to radio from the Bahamas. I said that maybe there was another Haiti somewhere else because even though they talk different, their music sounds just like ours. Do you want to know how people go to the bathroom on the boat? They set aside a little corner for that. When I have to pee, I just pull it, lean over the rail and do it very quickly. When I have to do the other thing, I rip a piece of something, squat down and do it and throw the waste in the sea. I am always embarrassed by the smell. It's so demeaning having to squat in front of so many people in the first place. People turn away, but not always.

At times I wonder if there is really land on the other side of the sea. Maybe the sea is endless. Like my love for you.

*   *   *

last night they came to madan roger's house. papa and tonton pressoir hurried home as soon as madan roger's screaming started. the soldiers were looking for noster. madan roger was screaming. you killed him already. you can't kill him deux fois. they were shouting at her. do you belong to "yfd"? are you a member of youth for democracy? she was yelling: do i look young to you? papa had us tiptoe out of the house into the latrine out back. we could hear it all from there. i thought i was going to choke on the smell of rotting kaka. they kept shouting at madan roger. did your son belong to youth for democracy? wasn't he on the radio saying that military power had to go? didn't he write slogans? she cursed their mothers' cunts. you know she was just shouting it out. you killed him once already. you want to kill me too. go ahead. i don't care. i'm dead already. you've killed my soul. they kept at it. was your son a traitor? tell me who his traitor friends were. madan roger finally shouts, yes he was one. he hated you like i hate you criminals. you killed him. they start pounding her. we can hear it. it sounds like they're cracking some bones. maybe on her head. my mother is whispering to my father. you can't just let them kill her. go and give them some money like you gave them for your daughter. papa says the only money i have left is to get us the hell out of here tomorrow. maman whispers, we can't just stay here and let them kill her. maman starts moving like she's going to go out the door. papa grabs her and pins her to the wall. tomorrow we're going to gressier, he says, woman i'll make you stay. my mother buries her face in the shitty wall. she starts to cry. we can hear madan roger screaming. they're beating her, pounding on her until we don't hear anything else. maman tells papa you can't let them kill somebody just because you're scared. papa says oh oui, you can and that is just what you are going to do.

Célianne spent the night groaning. She looks like she's been ready for a while, but maybe the child was being stubborn. She just screamed that she's bleeding. There's an older woman there who looks like she's had a couple of children herself. She says Célianne's not bleeding at all. Her water broke.

The only babies I've ever seen right after birth are baby mice. Their skin looks veil thin. You can see all the blood vessels and all their organs. I've always wanted to poke them to see if my finger will go all the way through their skin.

I've moved to the other side of the boat so I won't have to look *inside* her. There is a crowd of people, just watching. The captain is asking the midwife woman to keep the girl steady so she won't rock any more holes into the boat. Now we have about three cracks being covered with tar. I am scared to think of what would happen if we each had to choose over one another. We'd probably all turn into vultures—all of us including me.

The sun will set soon. Someone jokes that this child will be just another pair of hungry lips. At least it will have its mother's tits, says an old man. We completely ran out of food yesterday.

there's a rumor that aristide is coming back. papa says we're not going to stay in port-au-prince to find out. they're selling gasoline again. the carnival groups have taken to the streets. there is a whole bunch of people going to the airport to meet him. we're heading the other way, to gressier. gressier is a big hole, but maybe i'll be able to sleep at night. it's not going to turn out well with aristide's second coming, maman says, people are just too hopeful. they'll believe anything. maman told papa that you took the canter. he told me before we left this morning that he was sorry. i don't know why parents have to be such strangers. i know he doesn't hate me. why can't he stop acting like he does? on our way to gressier, we saw all these dogs licking these dead people's faces. some of the bodies were young. maybe twenty. your age. i saw a soldier shoving a woman out of a hut, calling her a lougarou. papa didn't want to go in madan roger's house and check on her body before we left. he thought the soldiers might be sleeping there. he drove real fast all the way to gressier. i thought he was going to kill us. we stopped in a market in carrefour feuilles and maman got us some black pieces of cloth. we've wrapped them around our heads to mourn madan roger. in gressier, you don't see that many soldiers. when i'm used to the place, i'll sketch you something nice. i hope you are keeping your notebook, like you said before you left.

Célianne had a girl. The midwife woman is holding her to the moon and whispering prayers. The Protestants are praying in the name of Jesus. Some other folks are calling Erzulie and Papa Legba. We all threw our extra things into the sea, an offering for the new life. The boat needs to be lighter. My two dollars in *mon-*

naie had to go. I am afraid that soon they may ask me to throw out this notebook.

Célianne's child is a beautiful child. They are calling her Swiss, because the word "Swiss" was written on the knife they used to cut her umbilical cord. If she was my daughter, I would call her Soleil, Moon, or Star, after the elements. There is all kind of gossip about how Célianne became pregnant. Some people are saying that she had an affair with a married man and her parents threw her out. Gossip spreads here like everywhere else.

Do you remember our silly dreams? Passing the Rheto. Working ourselves through the *faculté* by getting jobs at the Italian factories. I know your father might never approve of me. I was going to try to win him over. He would have to cut out my heart to keep me from loving you. I hope you are writing like you promised. Jésus, Marie, Joseph! Everyone smells so bad. They get in these arguments about it's only misery that's lumped me with dirt like you. Can you imagine? They're fighting about being superior when we all might drown like straw.

There's an old toothless man leaning over to see what I'm writing. He is sucking on the end of an old wooden pipe. He looks like a painting. You could paint a museum with the sights you see here. I still feel like such a coward for running away. Have you heard anything about my parents? Last time I saw them on the beach, my mother had a *crise*. She just fainted on the sand. I saw her coming to as we started sailing away, but of course I don't know if she's doing all right. I am so glad they got out of Port-au-Prince when they did.

The water is really piling into the boat. We take turns pouring bowls of it out. I don't know what's keeping the boat from splitting in two. Swiss isn't crying. They keep slapping her derrière, but she's not crying.

of course aristide didn't come. they arrested a lot of people at the airport. shot a whole bunch of them down. i heard it on the radio. before we went to sleep last night, i told papa that i love you. i don't know if it'll make a difference. i just want him to know that i've loved somebody in my life. i know you understand. you're the one for big gestures. papa looked me straight in the eye and said nothing to me. i love you until my hair shivers at the thought of anything happening to you. papa just turned his face away like he was just rejecting my very birth. i am writing you from a high rock with my feet in this stream. the stream is too shallow for me to drown myself. i don't care. i've gotten so used to sleeping with maman. now i'm scared to sleep alone. she told me in the garden today that sometimes you have to choose between your father and the man you love. i just want him to know that i was capable of loving somebody. maman told me that her whole family didn't want her marrying him because he was a field hand and her family was from la lue and some of them had even gone to university. she whispered everything under a tree in the yard so not to hurt papa's feelings. i saw him looking at us hard. i heard him clearing his throat like he heard us anyway. like we hurt him somehow.

Célianne is lying with her head against the back side of the boat. The baby still won't cry. They both look very peaceful in all this chaos. Célianne is holding her baby real tight against her chest. She just can't seem to let herself throw it in the ocean. I asked her about the baby's father. She keeps repeating the story now like a prayer. She was walking home from school when some *Tonton Macoutes* came by in an army truck and grabbed her. They took her back in the *casernes* and about ten of them took turns raping her. She never told her family when she got home. She cut her knees with a razor and told them she fell and got blood on her clothes. A couple of weeks after her rape, she started throwing up and getting rashes. Next thing she knew she was getting big. She tried to hide it best she could until her family saw her bathing. Her parents threw her out when they found out she was pregnant. She found out about the canter and got on. She is fifteen.

the bastards were coming to get me for knowing you, but he gave them some money. all the money he had. our house in port-au-prince and all the land his father had left him. that's why he was so mad. somehow i can't bring myself to say thank you. i feel like he is more than my father— now he is also my savior. i owe him my life. they read the list of names of people who passed the rheto on the radio this morning. you passed.

* * *

We got some relief from the water. The captain used the last of his tar and it's staying for a while. A couple of people have volunteered to throw Célianne's baby overboard for her. She won't let them. They are waiting for her to go to sleep so they can do it, but she won't sleep. I never knew dead children looked purple. Purple like the sea after the sun goes down and before the moon comes up. The lips are the most purple. Célianne is slowly drifting off to sleep. She is very tired from the labor. I don't want to touch the child. If anybody's going to throw it in the ocean, I think it should be her. She smells like raw pigs' guts. Both of them. I keep thinking, they've thrown the placenta in the water, now they're going to throw the baby in. Won't these things attract sharks? Célianne's fingernails are buried deep in the child's naked back. The old man with the pipe just asked, "*Compère,* what are you writing?" I told him, "my will."

gressier's growing on me. at least there are no bullets. there are butterflies. tons of butterflies. there is a stream near the house. you can't bathe in the morning or at night because the water is freezing cold. the only time it feels just right is at noon and then there are eyes who might see you naked. i solved that by getting a bucket of water in the morning and leaving it in the sun and then bathing myself once at night. what scares me most here are the lizards that stick their tongues out at you before they run into the bushes. i see mountains. so many mountains. coffee mountains, tree mountains, mountains that are bare like rocks. i feel like i'm getting further and further away from you. here, we can't even see the sea. maybe we'll never see each other again. my hair shivers.

She threw it overboard. I watched her face tie up like a thread and then she let go. It fell in a splash, floated for a while, and then sank. They say I have to throw my notebook out. The water is rising up again and they are scooping it out. I know you will probably never see this, but it was nice imagining that I had you here to talk to. I hope my parents are all right. I asked the old man to tell them what happened to me, if he makes it. He just asked me to write his name in "my book." I asked him for his full name. It is Eliab Miracin André Nozius Joseph Frank Osnac Max-

imilien. He says it all with such an air that you would think him a
king. Someone saw a Coast Guard ship coming. I'm looking
where he's pointing. I see nothing. They are rushing me to throw
the notebook out. Always save a piece of sky in your heart for me.
If we never see each other again, we'll meet there.

*i sketched you two more butterflies today. there is a school house here
that hasn't been open for a while. it looks like schools in port-au-prince
will stay closed so we started one here. it's just this big church where all
these children come barefoot and in rags. they are so hungry to learn.
papa and i are starting to say more than hello every day. when he sees me
listening to the radio, he moves over a bit close and says, "anything?"
i'm not sure what he's hoping the news will be. all i hear from the radio
is more killing in port-au-prince. the cochons are refusing to let up. i
don't know what's going to happen, but i can't see staying here forever. i
am writing you with my foot in the stream again. yell sometime from the
sea. maybe i'll hear the echoes. i heard last night that another boat sunk,
off the coast of the bahamas. my hair shivers. i can't think about you being in there, in the waves. dèyè mown, gin pi gro mown. i will write
again soon.*

Hallelujah for a Woman-Garden

René Depestre

Et le cri que, la bouche tordue, cet être, en vain?
vut faire entendre est un immense allélulia perdu dans
le silence sans fin.

—Georges Bataille

First Canto

One Friday evening, Aunt Zaza came to our house for dinner.
She was put out that no one in the family could come with
her on holiday that week. Her annoyance only enhanced her
charms, which had suddenly transformed our humble supper
into a princely banquet: the glasses were finely etched Bac-
carat; the plates Sèvres; the cutlery was made of sparkling
silver. The cloth had been embroidered by Aubusson's very
hands. The tap water tasted like champagne; the bread savored
of carefully aged cheese. The aroma of the steaming fish could
have issued from the finest of kitchens. The very room was
brightened not by any lamp but rather by the gold-flecked
green eyes of Zaza—although my attention lighted immediately on her breasts.

"Why doesn't Oliver come to the farm with me?" she asked.

"Oh, Zaza, you know full well," said my mother, "that Oliver
has schoolwork to do. Besides, he's too careless in the ocean. He

insists on swimming out farther than anyone else. The gulf is shark-infested; the whole situation is dangerous."

"You're exaggerating, Agnes," my father objected. "Oliver knows how to handle himself now. And nothing's going to happen to him if Zaza is around."

"Fine," said my mother resignedly, "if he has an accident, be it on your head."

"The mountain air would do him good. The boy's always shut up with his books. Oliver, you won't swim out too far, give me your word on it," said my aunt.

I had no voice to answer; I nodded mutely.

"It would be best," Isabelle went on, "if you spent the night with me. Then we could be mounted and riding before dawn."

"A fine idea," my mother said, while my father did nothing to hide his pride—maybe even his envy—at seeing me leave alone with the woman who had become a legend in our family.

She was barely thirteen years old when they began to speak of her beauty in Jacmel. Three years later they came from Port-au-Prince to seek her out as the queen of their carnival. Up and down the parade route, the men and women of the capital fell into frenzies of admiration. Everything about Isabelle Ramonet demanded attention; her very flesh cried out to one and all: Take a good look; perhaps only once in a century will you see a creature whose being promises dazzling adventure!

As Isabelle's chariot passed, the transports of the crowd began to take on a mystical edge: after having exchanged a smile with the queen, a young man climbed a coconut tree on the avenue all at one go, mewling like a wounded animal. A middle-aged peasant cried out in a strangled voice: "I will give you a hand if you throw me a kiss!" At once, from her high throne, Isabelle blew a kiss at the unknown man. He honored his promise by pulling a butcher's knife out of his pocket and bringing it down on his left wrist in one tremendously violent blow. Then, seizing hold of his severed hand, he threw it at the feet of Aunt Isa, splashing the hem of her royal robes with blood. Someone discreetly removed the madman, and the festivities continued at an even more furious pace.

Once the carnival was over, hundreds of suitors begged for the young girl's hand in marriage. She turned them down gracefully, and went straight back to Jacmel. A triumphal arch greeted her at the gate of the little village in southwest Haiti. "Her homecoming was comparable to the coronation of a princess in the *Thousand and One Nights*," the local paper announced the next morning. A year later, she married the son of a coffee exporter who died shortly afterward in a motorcycle accident.

A rumor went round that Daniel Locroy had died from a mysterious malady he had contracted in his wife's arms: he had watched, as he kissed Isabelle, his genitals shrink like Balzac's magic *peau de chagrin*. When one morning he awoke to find his penis had disappeared and all that remained to him was half of one testicle, he put a bullet through his brain. A doctor put an end to this nonsense: he had seen Locroy's shattered body at the foot of a tree on Meyer Road, surrounded by the wreckage of his bike.

Fresh admirers took their place beneath the young widow's windows. She made it clear to the eager crowd that she had no intention of remarrying. By dint of evading the parties given in her honor, the horseback rides, the acrostics, poems, and love letters addressed to her, the spells known as *wangas,* and the hot-blooded provincial intrigues, she became the cabalistic focus of the village. She integrated herself into the countryside as completely as the ancient trees in the Army Plaza, the gulf waters that flowed over the rusty hull of the *Albano,* or the La Gosseline river.

And so, when Isabelle Ramonet left Jacmel for a few months' stay in Europe, only her relatives suffered from her absence. Her return would have provoked a reaction similar to the one that followed the carnival, had not an article in the *Nouvelliste* revealed that

The ever-ravishing Isabelle Ramonet, the unforgettable
Queen of the 1937 Carnival, was invited to star in a movie by
a European director, and politely declined his offer. Instead,
she chose to return to the village she had been born in,
deep in the southwest. One evening when the province's te-
dium weighs on her more heavily than usual, she will bitterly
regret turning her back on such an opportunity. We would
even go so far as to say that Isabelle has irrevocably lost the
only chance she had to imbue her little island with the

glamor of a new Greta Garbo. A faint hope, which we cannot in the least justify, still leads us to believe that it is not yet too late for her to reverse this unfortunate decision. For that is the outcome her thousands of admirers have expressed a wish for, at least to this publication.

Aunt Zaza received such idle chatter with calm disdain. She paid no more attention to the slanders that greeted her return. Indifferent to both praise and ridicule, thanks to the legacy that had been placed at her disposal by Locroy's demise, she built the first movie theater in Jacmel. On its screen I saw *Fanfan la Tulipe, Mathias Sandorf,* the stories of Charlotte, and many other silent movies.

Later, a rumor went round Jacmel that she had invested her money in the movie theater as a memorial to a famous actor who had been her lover in Paris and who had finally thrown her over for a Scandinavian star. It was added that this man had a taste for taking chances, for if he had persisted in his passion he too would have died in an accident on some European road. Such a great beauty could only inspire great tragedies. It was equally bruited about that the money that had paid for the construction of the cinema had its roots in the occult. It rose from pits that Isabelle's mother, the widow of General Cesar Ramonet, had dug in her garden several years before. She had then, in an atmosphere fraught with scandal, brought jars brimming with *louis d'or* and precious silverware out into the light of day.

Her frequent stays in the country once again made Aunt Zaza the subject of scandal in Jacmel. She owned a farm in the place known as the Magic Mountain, on a cliff that overlooked the sea. There she spent the majority of her weekends. She never went there alone for fear of being accused of having lovers drawn from the same shafts of gold that had purportedly given rise to the movie theater. She made sure she was always chaperoned by a friend or her mother.

In our family the myth of Isa did not derive solely from her physical charms: we never ceased praising her delicacy, her kindness, her simplicity, her generosity toward the poor. She was always ready to do a good deed, to oblige someone with a favor, without asking anything in return. She was unacquainted

with the mood swings, the whims, the fits of vanity, the simper-
ing, and the extravagances that often mar women's beauty.
She was no sacred cow, rather "an infinitely delicate shaft to the
heart," as she had been referred to one day by a friend of my
father's.

Aunt Zaza was to me, her favorite nephew, one with the screen
that had beguiled my adolescent nights. She was the source of
beautiful images. Often she came into the little auditorium to sit
by my side, and her very presence widened the horizons of the
films I watched. For a long time I allowed myself to believe that
the beams of light that wove stories I later dreamed about rose di-
rectly from her. But at the start of my fifteenth year, I began to
admire Zaza for what she was in the flesh.

Seated in the darkness by her side, I reached the point where
my attention drifted away from the tales on the screen and
turned instead to a cinema that disordered my spirit in quite a
different way. Isa ran a hand innocently through my hair, along
the nape of my neck, across my bare legs, without knowing her at-
tentions seared me from head to toe, and I reacted to her wom-
anly presence with the same uneasiness that some animals display
at the approach of a great storm or earthquake.

Second Canto

That night I slept in a soft bed in a room next to my aunt's.
"You must go to bed early," she told me, placing a chaste kiss on
my forehead. I had trouble getting to sleep: foreboding swelled
within me until I swore my very veins would burst.

When we left town, it was still pitch dark. I was a young king
who, in the company of his cousin, a foreign princess, passed
through his peacefully sleeping realm. We galloped for nearly
two hours, our two mounts in effortless rhythm. Zaza rode a
horse well. She laughed, her hair flowing in the wind, her body
poised for flight. I envied her her horse, a chestnut thorough-
bred, who seemed to know he was carrying the star of the city on
his back. Once we arrived at the mountain, our horses were given
in keeping to the peasant who saw to the farm.

"I didn't expect you this early," said Laudrun.

"We rode all out," my aunt apologized.

"Oliver has become quite some rider," Laudrun said affection-ately.

"He'll have to be more cautious in the sea," said my aunt. "Should we start out right away?" she then proposed eagerly.

A few minutes later we were all on the goat path that mean-dered across fields of corn and sweet potatoes only to open sud-denly onto a precipitous fall of rocks, whose vaulted ridges reverberated with the snores of sleeping lizards, drawn forth by the echoes of the mountain itself. Some two hundred meters be-yond this avalanche of living rubble, the path evened out without any warning into a beach of white, smooth sand. On our way down, Isabelle leaned on my shoulder to keep her balance. I didn't dare look at her in her bathing suit. Once we were on the beach, she ran on ahead of me, toward the sea. And then pic-tures began to drift through my mind, images that eddied and tore like leaves from a banana tree during a hurricane. I was made to pulse with the vital rhythm of the woman who raced in front of me. Her contours unwound in an incandescent harmony of fibers, tissue, nerves, muscles—flesh rounded into an irre-sistibly lyrical lushness. I began to run after her. When I reached the first breakers, she was already swimming strongly. I threw myself into her wake. When I had pulled myself to within a meter of her, she turned sharply and screamed as a joke, "A shark, Oliver, a shark!" We both began to swim hard for the shore. The surf tossed us up onto the sand, and there we stretched ourselves, out of breath. We looked at each other, laughing, unable to say a word.

"The water's wonderful, don't you think?"

"Wonderful," I said.

"You're glad you came?"

"Very glad, Aunt Isa."

"It's incredible how you've grown. You're already taller than I."

"I don't think so."

"Oh, yes, my dear. What would you want to bet?"

We leapt to our feet to compare height. She was scarcely taller than I. She was then thirty-two years old. I was exactly half her age.

"How quickly time passes, Oliver. I remember the day you were born as clearly as if it were last Thursday. You were born feet first, with a caul. Not five minutes into this world, and already you were laughing. I was the first to dandle you and discover you had eyes as green as mine. You didn't stop laughing and kicking and waving, just as if you were gaily greeting the world you just entered. 'Let's call him Oliver,' I said to Agnes."

"Why Oliver?"

"Because once upon a time it was a name that stood for wisdom and glory."

"I'm neither wise nor glorious."

"You're very wise for your age, and one day you will be glorious."

"And Isabelle? That's a name that stands for what?"

"It's a shade of café au lait, like me. One refers to an *isabelle* dress, an *isabelle* horse."

"It's also the name of a very famous queen."

"There's a wonderful story about that: once there was an Austrian archduchess. Her husband laid siege to a Belgian city. She vowed not to change her petticoat until the city fell. The siege lasted three years. And so they gave the princess's name to the color of her petticoat when at last her hopes were realized."

The sun shone extravagantly. We sighted some fishing boats on the horizon. The sky and sea played madly at being the sea and the sky. We regaled each other with anecdotes liberally salted with laughter. Over and over again, we threw ourselves into the waves. Toward eleven, we took the footpath back to the farm. When we got there, we were sweaty, our lips salt-rimmed, our eyes red and burning. We went straight down the path that led to the spring of fresh water. Fatigue lent Isa's gait a languor that took my breath away.

The small of her back arched gracefully; her buttocks were round and rich; her thighs and ankles seemed molded of some flawless metal. The spring's chill cooled my ardor, and we went back to the house. Home was a thatched cottage bathed in thirst-quenching shade. It was comprised of two rooms surrounded by a wide veranda. The front room was the living room; the other, the bedroom. My attention was drawn first to the lone bed, of another time and grand proportions. Then I saw Isa, who was taking off her swimsuit, oblivious to my presence. My body began to tremble; my teeth chattered. I suffered a sort of spasm that left me hardly able to breathe. Abruptly, I left the room. She caught up with me a moment later; she wore white shorts and a flowered shirt. She glowed.

I went back into the bedroom to change. I found no folding bed there, only that bridal couch in the center of the room. So I was going to sleep in the bed of an Austrian archduchess. Perhaps it had a trundle bed? No, there was only the one mattress. I climbed onto the bed and threw myself back into its softness. I had to bite the pillow in order to bear the rush of blood that jolted the pit of my stomach.

Eventually I joined Zaza under the arbor, where she was fixing lunch. The heady scent of cod, fricasseed in olive oil, rose from the charcoal stove. My aunt dug the seeds out of red peppers before tossing them into the sizzling frying pan.

"You must be hungry, my dear. Lunch will be ready soon. Our menu this afternoon is: salted cod with red peppers, bananas fried with mulberries, and slices of avocado and eggplant. To drink, the house punch. And Laudrun has promised to bring us fruit for dessert."

We were seated at the table, indulging our appetites, when Laudrun made his entrance bearing a platter with oranges, *pommes-cajous,* grapefruit, *cirouelles,* and bunches of *quenepes.*

"Oh, Laudrun, you're spoiling us," Isa said.

"I don't know what's wrong with the coconut trees this year," he grumbled. "They just won't bear fruit. And I know how much you love coconut."

"Thank you, Laudrun. By the way, I have a present for you."

My aunt left the table and returned shortly with a red scarf in her hand.

"A hundred thanks, old friend. I particularly need a red scarf to wrap General Ironsides up when I take him to the fights this Sunday. You've read my mind."

"Is your fighting cock as formidable as ever?"

"Oh, he's a brave lad!"

"A true warrior-cock," my aunt said, laughing, and we drank three toasts to the honor of General Ironsides.

We spent the rest of the day in the old man's company, touring the farm. We scarcely took two steps without stopping to hear about the various crops Laudrun was growing, the animals he had raised. The sharecropper also complained of the numerous abuses that the rural police and the local landowners continually inflicted upon the peasants in the region.

At the end of the afternoon, we went back to the beach. The water was still warm. We swam only a few strokes before returning to the beach. The spring had grown chilly with the dusk. Evening was upon us. A Haitian Saturday night raised a clamor in the hills: the harmonies of *tam-tams* surrounded us; birds chattered high in the trees, preparing themselves for sleep. We lit a hurricane lamp and made a dinner of some fruit. Afterward we settled in a pair of *dodines* on the veranda. My aunt asked after my studies. I told her that after I received my baccalaureate, I hoped to study medicine. She told me that she had always regretted not having been able to go to college. Then she told me about her trip to Europe. There she had found a world completely different from our own. People lived in the twentieth century. When one came from Haiti, one couldn't help but stare wide-eyed at Paris or London. But the lights of these metropolises were not as innocent as they seemed. Just then Laudrun's arrival interrupted our conversation.

Laudrun was a short, broad-shouldered man; his conversation was full of zest and riddled with surprises. He was hard-featured, but his laughing eyes mocked the rest of his face, especially when he set himself to tell a tale. He had scarcely settled himself on the veranda when he said, "Cric . . ."

"Crac," Aunt Isa and I chorused.

"Once upon a time there was," said Laudrun, "a young girl who had fallen in love with a fish from the river. She loved him so much that she spent her life at the edge of the water where her beloved swam. Naturally her favorite chore was doing the washing. When she had no laundry to wash, she stayed sitting on the river bank, as if she were eternally bleaching the precious cloth of her passion. Now and again, Zin Thezin flipped his dazzling fins above the water as a sign to his Lovena.

"But the pair lived on more than fresh water and tenderness. Oftimes, Lovena threw off her clothes and dove into the river to join her black buck, and Zin Thezin drew his bow in the darkness and played upon the body of his Lovena.

"One day, the young girl's father, highly disturbed by her long absences from home, hid himself in a copse near the river and lost no time in getting to the bottom of the matter. He took care not to say anything about it to Lovena, managing instead to send her as often as possible to do the marketing many miles away in order to keep her away from the farm.

"One morning, as soon as Lovena had left, he went to the river. He had learned the words Lovena used to signal her prince that he might show himself safely. Imitating Lovena's voice, her father felt a passionate hatred for the shameless fish and rejoiced at the idea of destroying him. After a moment, Zin, brisk with desire, leapt almost a meter above the river's surface. It had been several days since he had last lost himself in his mistress's warm flesh. Lovena's father cudgeled him hard on the head. Zin Thezin sank and drowned.

"Zin Thezin had once told Lovena that if misfortune ever befell him, wherever she was, she would know of it by blood dripping from her left breast. The moment Zin Thezin had been struck down to his death at the bottom of the river, Lovena discovered—in the middle of the market—that her left breast was bleeding freely. She staggered like a madwoman toward the river. When she got there, a broad scarlet stain marked the place where Zin had been overcome. She said not a word. She dragged herself home and found her father on the doorstep.

" 'Father,' she said. 'Did you kill my beloved?'

" 'Aren't you ashamed, you little slut, to have given yourself to an animal?'

" 'Father,' she interrupted him hotly, 'I didn't come here to discuss right and wrong with you. All I want you to tell me, yes or no—did you kill Zin Thezin?'

" 'Yes,' her father said, 'with a single blow from my cudgel, I sent your scum of a fish to his place at the bottom—'

"He never had time to finish his words. He was cut off by a machete plunged straight into his throat. Lovena hurled away the weapon stained by parricide and took off at a run down the path to the river. She sat on the sun-drenched grass of the bank, and began to sing.

"Zin Thezin, my crazy fish, Zin!
Zin Thezin, my crazy fish, Zin!

Captain of the waters
My crazy fish, Zin!
Lord of my thighs
My crazy fish, Zin!
King of my pain
My crazy fish, Zin!
My only season
My crazy fish, Zin!
Law of my blood
My crazy fish, Zin!
My poor love
My crazy fish, Zin!
Zin Thezin, my crazy fish, Zin!
Zin Thezin, my crazy fish, Zin!"

"Lovena's family, crouched in the copse, watched the scene, dumbfounded. The young girl's voice was so melodiously desperate, no one could move or say a word. They were all there, her mother, brothers, uncles, aunts, grandmother, dazed, less alive than the shrubs they hid behind. Lovena sang like a madwoman of the treachery done to her lover, her eyes fixed on the river that reflected the uncaring skies. Then, without interrupting her farewell lament, she let herself softly slide into the current. Even after she disappeared, her voice soared above the water. There are people who have the gift of hearing it on certain nights. Those are the same people who believe, rightly or wrongly, that there is a living thread that inextricably binds together stones, trees, fishes, humans . . ."

Laudrun spun other tales from the old Haitian romancers, but it was Zin and Lovena's love affair that moved us the most. When we were sated with stories, Aunt Isabelle said to Laudrun, "It's quite late. It's time to go to bed. Thank you, Laudrun, for your lovely tales."

"Goodnight all," he said.

"Goodnight, you old gossip."

Third Canto

Isa preceded me into the bedroom. When I came in, she was already in her nightdress. I took off my clothes slowly, as a four-

teenth-century soldier might have removed his armor. When my
aunt passed in front of the lamp on her way to the bed, the silhouette of her body, clearly visible, took my breath away. I stood
for a moment in my pajamas in a corner of the room, waiting for
I didn't know what.

"Open the window, put out the light, and come to bed," she
said.

I did as she said. The sheets were crisp and smelled good. I was
sweating, barely able to breathe.

"Goodnight, my dear."

"Goodnight, Aunt Isa."

She fell asleep quickly, but I couldn't. Little by little, my eyes
grew accustomed to the darkness in the room. The contours of
each object stood out sharply. Outside the window, I could see
shivering trees and a corner of the starry sky. How cruel it was not
to have been born a star, a tree, a fish—anything but the animal
transfixed by fear that I became when faced with the body of my
princess! Little by little, I felt her presence invade my very body.
By some fabulous transfusion, her blood emptied itself into my
veins and began to pump there. Thus drugged by her, I lapsed
into a deep sleep, only to be awakened by the early morning chill
that blew in from the ocean. I rolled over to warm myself.

"You're cold too?" Zaza asked.

"I'll go close the window," I said.

"No. The room will get stuffy. Just come closer to me."

I was in her arms. I was lost in her arms. I was still alive in
Zaza's wide-awake arms.

"We're warm now, aren't we?" she said, a moment later.

I didn't say anything. I didn't think about the way I held her,
or the way I drew her closer to me, or about anything else other
than the madness of having gone to bed with Zaza Ramonet!

"Have you forgotten that I'm your aunt? . . . Have you ever had
a woman?"

"Yes."

"Who?"

"Nadia."

"Nadi! That's absurd! Where? When?"

"Last year, at Meyer, when we were on holiday."

"Did you have her often?"

"Every day, all summer long." (I wasn't lying about that.)

"And I thought my niece was a virgin and took you for a little boy. When did you start to want me?"

"At the beach this morning; at my parents' house last night; for as long as I can remember, honestly—maybe since I was born. You chose my name for me."

A joyous self-assurance began to grow in me. I was lying with Zaza, flesh pressed against flesh, our hands clutching one another's, as if they were separate beings intent on crushing each other.

"And I thought you were so intelligent . . . You're my big, crazy fish."

"And your father's going to kill me with one blow from his cudgel."

"This is no fairy tale, you know."

"I know."

"Oh God, you're strong. You're . . . no, wait until I take off my nightgown . . . oh, yes . . . my whole body says yes."

My sixteen years devoured her mouth. At first her tongue and teeth clenched against my kisses. And so, with my lips half open, I kissed her gently and warmly, on her eyes, her ears, the nape of her neck, her temples, the crook of her elbow, the tips of her fingers—I nibbled those too—before once again taking her mouth. In the meantime, my splayed hands traversed her belly and thighs like tame spiders.

The more I caressed her the more wonderfully I sensed her. She too began to graze my shoulders with her half-parted lips, then moved on to my chest, my stomach—my entire body, my manhood included. When my turn came, I teased her feet, her calves, her knees, her thighs and her sumptuous *mons veneris*. Then I lingered on her round, firm, full buttocks, which revolved like a beacon on the twin hearths of my caresses. At my touch, each of her breasts opened the fabulous universe that was Zaza. A sudden thirst overtook me; I wanted to taste her fresh juices at the very source, mad as I was to sample Zaza. And my tongue ripened at the thought of measuring the incandescent eternity that was her vagina. Her sex had a supple, vibrant clitoris and a wide-open vulva; it was comestible, richly fruited, swollen with passion. I sank into her magnificence, which opened itself to my delectation like some prodigal fruit that, with its raw silkiness, its deep and humid gaze, its velvet teeth, the modeling of its beautiful, strong lips, and its high cheekbones, was a second face that danced, played, and bore ecstatic witness to the flavor, the beauty, the joy, and the indefatigable grace of the species. Having slaked my thirst there, I brought my mouth back to her consenting one, and our sexes, hungrily grafting into one another, flamed toward goodness, the one riding the other, the one sailing the other, the one turning to jelly and joyously living as the other in an orgasm that sent us dazzled to the dizzying limits of our very selves over and over again that night.

When the dawn soared skyward with the cocks in the neighboring trees, we were overcome with the urge to run naked to the beach. We reached the foot of the cliffs to feel our blood roiling once again. We rolled through the cool sand until the first waves touched us; there, washed by the tide, we once again claimed from life its spice, its plankton, its riptides, millstones, and all its secrets. This aquatic copulation bent us to an anonymous, manifold tempo. Before the legend of Adam and the crucifixion of Christ, Zaza and I existed as a single cosmic breath that joyously panted itself out in the early morning chill.

We returned to the farm in triumph. Our weariness tumbled into laughter. We were glad of what we had done—glad to be alive on this Sunday in the name of the Lord who tenderly opened his handsome Haitian arms to us. We slept until midday. We woke cheerfully and with a ferocious appetite. A little while later, we found ourselves seated before a lunch that Laudrun in his goodness had prepared for us: chicken grilled with red peppers, bananas and mulberries, fish *beignets,* grilled potatoes, eggplant and tomato salad, rice with red beans, coconut milk, and salt beef, slabs of pineapple and watermelon. We drank a mountain punch worthy of our recent ecstasies.

The table had been laid on the veranda. A warm breeze blew in off the gulf, and Zaza's white skirt freshened the afternoon. We ate in silence, lost in wordless delight. When I raised my eyes from my plate, I once again discovered the night's marvels in my lover's eyes, stitched with golden iridescence. After lunch, I helped Isa wash the dishes. Then we went for a walk.

The sea spun out its miles of lace in front of us; in places, a buried wave, purely for the sport of it, blew forth a giant flower of foam. Zaza went down the path ahead of me. As I watched the sensuous sway of her, I was overcome with murderous rage at anyone who had ever denigrated the flesh of women. Where had they buried those prophets—maddened by premature ejaculation—who had created the myth that women's charms led one into error and unhappiness? I longed to light a stick of dynamite on the tombs of those barbarous, vindictive pimps who throughout the ages have sought to wrench the cadences of a woman's body from those of the seasons, the trees, the wind, the rain, and the sea. Watching Zaza walk, her waves rolling underneath the sun, her flesh as ripe as fruit, her buttocks rounded like earth furrowed for a farmer, I thought of the terror and disgust of women's genitalia that religion had evoked.

Don't most languages refer to women's sexuality in the lewdest of terms? Everywhere the same coarse words defame the vagina and load it with abuse: *con, cunt, coc, pussy, bohio, porra, coño, twat,* and so forth. You've heard people say: He's a dirty son of a bitch; *por el coño de su madre; kolanguette manman'ou; lambi bounda mammam'ou.* As Isa walked in the afternoon, I banished those funereal, repulsive myths that had darkened and humiliated women by presenting their sensuality as the degraded extremities of human interaction.

We had reached the edge of the cliff, where a coconut grove grew. We looked down on the gulf of Jacmel as it stretched in front of us.

"Maybe we should sit here," said Zaza, indicating the trunk of a tree.

We sat down side by side. Not a ripple disturbed the afternoon: it was as sleek as the sky or the sea or Zaza's life. Far away, the fishing boats seemed motionless. Flocks of birds flew in perfect order, the only motion between the sky and the water. Remembrance seized its place within us as securely as certain gulls in their night nests, and opened our joy to the gulf's vast influence. Our silence trembled with all we had done and all we expected to do.

Little by little, the sea faded, washing away in its shadow the boats, the sand, the cliff faces, the sky, the coconut trees, and us. A star appeared, followed by thousands of others. We started

back toward the bungalow. We drank goat's milk and ate fruit
salad quickly. And then we threw ourselves on the bed without
lowering the lamp. I told Isa, as naked as the light, everything
that had passed through my mind as I had followed her down the
path. Without any shame, with a majestic simplicity, she opened
her thighs so I could celebrate in the newfound words of my sixteen years the glory of her sex.

Hallelujah, oh, pulse of life!

Hallelujah, your joyous musky patience during the long, dark
night of woman! I salute you, and I hold you up for the world's
admiration. For the love of you I am prepared to cross deserts
and wilderness, to defy hangmen and electric chairs, gas cham-
bers, and torture cells. I seed the street corners with your revolution in order to turn those who would find only a plane of
shadows in your radiance.

You are neither a reliquary nor a cesspool nor a source of
gloom and damnation. I am neither your prophet, nor your
slave, nor your conqueror, but simply a spellbound boy who
swears after having experienced you that your pulse belongs to
those laws that make the wind blow, the sun rise at break of day,
and the moon, the stars, the rain and snow keep their promises
to the earth's sweet harvest.

Only from you comes the unity and solidarity of life that continues to exist despite the senseless confusion in which humans
flounder.

Last Canto

Our affair lasted two beautiful years. We managed to meet in
the mountains each weekend. My grades, instead of suffering,
took wing in a way that set my parents' minds at rest. On the
days my grandmother came with us, I slept on the veranda, in a
folding bed. Grandmother had a half-paralyzed leg as a result of
an accident, and could not venture down the path that led to
the beach. And so Zaza and I, when we didn't make love right
there in the ocean, coupled in the windings of the rocks. Our
long absences bothered Cesar (Grandmother Cecilia had borne
this masculine name ever since the death of Isabelle's father and
my grandfather, General Cesar Ramonet, who had been shot

during an uprising in the hills of Jacmel). Cesar cast suspicious glances our way as she watched us return from the beach, our eyes sparkling, our movements unsteady, silently transformed the way some trees are after a storm. But her suspicions went no farther than a few mutterings that spilled from her fearful tongue, which we accepted as a matter of course. When she was present, we avoided any glance, word, or gesture that could have given us away. I was the well-brought-up nephew who kept my pearl among aunts' company.

Eventually, we were no longer content with our weekly encounters at the mountain. Often, toward the end of an afternoon after school had let out, I popped round her house before going home. She lived at the foot of town, in a villa lost in greenery. About two hundred meters before you actually reached the house, you had to walk down a narrow path of steps that was one of the vaunted charms of Jacmel. Since then, each time I have walked down a similar street in a foreign city, I have always—even in the plain light of day—been enveloped by the cool shadow where Zaza, gloriously naked, waits for me. We bowed before the same heaven. We called our rendezvous my second philosophy class, and at this edge-of-night school neither of us knew which was the teacher and which was the student, as we strove to exceed each other in fantasy and imagination.

One windswept October night, as I was studying my Greek, a rumor crept into my parents' house on gremlins' feet: the Parisiana cinema was in flames. All of Jacmel raced down to the disaster. When I reached the movie theater, it was nothing but coals glowing joyously in the Gulf wind. No one had seen Isa. Where had she gone? Had she stayed home? Her name flew through the crowd. The village idiot said he had seen her a few minutes earlier, running into the theater through an emergency exit because she said she heard someone screaming in the auditorium. When the fire had been brought under control, an unknown body was pulled from the inferno, charred, wearing a bracelet that identified it as the remains of Zaza Ramonet.

The following afternoon, the village followed her to the cemetery. As the huge cortège proceeded on its way, the twisted mouths of those who had loved her used such words as *queen, heroine, miracle* to describe her. I saw the haunted eyes of those who had coveted, defamed, and lampooned her, and who, faced with her death, were unable to beg forgiveness from the bundle of calcified bones that she had now become beneath her mountain of roses.

The religious service then took place: old Father Naelo, surrounded by his deacons, his tapers, and the accoutrements of a regal burial, gave a brief eulogy. I listened, hardly believing what I heard. He revealed that Isabelle Ramonet had been the parish's most generous benefactress, and that her soul's beauty so equalled her body's that Saints Philip and Jacques, the twin patrons of Jacmel, hadn't been the same since they saw and heard her in their church. He said that her horrible end was only the device by which God had chosen to remove her from the world, and that in her new Kingdom she had already recovered the radiance, more beautiful than ever, that endured to refresh the swollen hands and feet of our Savior.

When the cortège set out on its journey across Jacmel, I was struck by the silly spectacle of so many men helping to carry a coffin that weighed less than an empty nest. Abruptly it was the earth that swallowed her, in a single gulp beneath her flowers.

There was the trip back in the darkness that had fallen so early upon the living and dead alike. It was the town's first night without its pole star. In every household, over dinner people spoke only of Zaza: of the life she had led, her beauty, her bounteousness, her refinement, and the wind, fire, and ashes to which she had been reduced because she wanted to disappear with her cinema.

Caged behind the glass wall of my grief, I could not prevent my woman-garden from becoming, in the thousands of heads that bowed over their evening meal, a memory already receding into legend, into myth, into a tale that sparkled with cries of disbelief.

TRANSLATED BY ERICA OBEY

The Beautiful Soul
of Don Damián

Juan Bosch

Don Damián, with a temperature of almost 104, passed into a
coma. His soul felt extremely uncomfortable, almost as if it were
being roasted alive; therefore it began to withdraw, gathering itself into his heart. The soul had an infinite number of tentacles,
like an octopus with innumerable feet, some of them in the veins
and others, very thin, in the smaller blood vessels. Little by little it
pulled out those feet, with the result that Don Damián turned
cold and pallid. His hands grew cold first, then his arms and legs,
while his face became so deathly white that the change was observed by the people who stood around his bed. The nurse,
alarmed, said it was time to send for the doctor. The soul heard
her, and thought: "I'll have to hurry, or the doctor will make me
stay in here till I burn to a crisp."

It was dawn. A faint trickle of light came in through the
window to announce the birth of a new day. The soul, peering
out of Don Damián's mouth, which was partly open to let in a
little air, noticed the light and told itself that if it hoped to escape
it would have to act promptly, because in a few minutes somebody would see it and prevent it from leaving its master's body.
The soul of Don Damián was quite ignorant about certain matters: for instance, it had no idea that once free it would be completely invisible.

There was a rustling of skirts around the patient's luxurious bed, and a murmur of voices which the soul had to ignore, occupied as it was in escaping from its prison. The nurse came back into the room with a hypodermic syringe in her hand.

"Dear God, dear God," the old housemaid cried, "don't let it be too late!"

It was too late. At the precise moment that the needle punctured Don Damián's forearm, the soul drew its last tentacles out of his mouth, reflecting as it did so that the injection would be a waste of money. An instant later there were cries and running footsteps, and as somebody—no doubt the housemaid, since it could hardly have been Don Damián's wife or mother-in-law—began to wail at the bedside, the soul leaped into the air, straight up to the Bohemian glass lamp that hung in the middle of the ceiling. There it collected its wits and looked down: Don Damián's corpse was now a spoiled yellow, with features almost as hard and transparent as the Bohemian glass; the bones of his face seemed to have grown, and his skin had taken on a ghastly sheen. His wife, his mother-in-law, and the nurse fluttered around him, while the housemaid sobbed with her gray head buried in the covers. The soul knew exactly what each one of them was thinking and feeling, but it did not want to waste time observing them. The light was growing brighter every moment, and it was afraid it would be noticed up there on its perch. Suddenly the mother-in-law took her daughter by the arm and led her out into the hall, to talk to her in a low voice. The soul heard her say, "Don't behave so shamelessly. You've got to show some grief."

"When people start coming, Mama," the daughter whispered.

"No. Right now. Don't forget the nurse—she'll tell everybody everything that happens."

The new widow ran to the bed as if mad with grief. "Oh Damián, Damián!" she cried. "Damián, my dearest, how can I live without you?"

A different, less worldly soul would have been astounded, but Don Damián's merely admired the way she was playing the part. Don Damián himself had done some skillful acting on occasion, especially when it was necessary to act—as he put it—"in defense of my interests." His wife was now "defending her interests." She was still young and attractive, whereas Don Damián was well past sixty. She had had a lover when he first knew her, and his soul had suffered some very disagreeable moments because of its late master's jealousy. The soul recalled an episode of a few months earlier, when the wife had declared, "You can't stop me from seeing him. You know perfectly well I married you for your money."

To which Don Damián had replied that with his money he had purchased the right not to be made ridiculous. It was a thoroughly unpleasant scene—the mother-in-law had interfered, as usual, and there were threats of a divorce—but it was made even more unpleasant by the fact that the discussion had to be cut short when some important guests arrived. Both husband and wife greeted the company with charming smiles and exquisite manners, which only the soul could appreciate at their true value.

The soul was still up there on the lamp, recalling these events, when the priest arrived almost at a run. Nobody could imagine why he should appear at that hour, because the sun was scarcely up and anyhow he had visited the sick man during the night. He attempted to explain.

"I had a premonition. I was afraid Don Damián would pass away without confessing."

The mother-in-law was suspicious. "But, Father, didn't he confess last night?"

She was referring to the fact that the priest had been alone with Don Damián, behind a closed door, for nearly an hour. Everybody assumed that the sick man had confessed, but that was not what took place. The soul knew it was not, of course; it also knew why the priest had arrived at such a strange time. The theme of that long conference had been rather arid, spiritually: the priest wanted Don Damián to leave a large sum of money toward the new church being built in the city, while Don Damián wanted to leave an even larger sum than that which the priest was seeking—but to a hospital. They could not agree, the priest left, and when he returned to his room he discovered that his watch was missing.

The soul was overwhelmed by its new power; now it was free, to know things that had taken place in its absence, and to divine what people were thinking or were about to do. It was aware that the priest had said to himself: "I remember I took out my watch

at Don Damián's house, to see what time it was. I must have left it
there." Hence it was also aware that his return visit had nothing
to do with the Kingdom of Heaven.

"No, he didn't confess," the priest said, looking straight at the
mother-in-law. "We didn't get around to a confession last night,
so we decided I would come back the first thing in the morning,
to hear confession and perhaps"—his voice grew solemn—"to ad-
minister the last rites. Unfortunately, I've come too late." He
glanced toward the gilt tables on either side of the bed in hopes
of seeing his watch on one or the other.

The old housemaid, who had served Don Damián for more
than forty years, looked up with streaming eyes.

"It doesn't make any difference," she said, "God forgive me
for saying so. He had such a beautiful soul he didn't need to
confess." She nodded her head. "Don Damián had a very beautiful soul."

Hell, now, that was something! The soul had never even dreamed
that it was beautiful. Its master had done some rather rare things
in his day, of course, and since he had always been a fine example
of a well-to-do gentleman, perfectly dressed and exceedingly
shrewd in his dealings with the bank, his soul had not had time to
think about its beauty or its possible ugliness. It remembered, for
instance, how its master had commanded it to feel at ease after
he and his lawyer found a way to take possession of a debtor's house,
although the debtor had nowhere else to live; or when, with the
help of jewels and hard cash (this last for her education, or her sick
mother), he persuaded a lovely young girl from the poorer section
to visit him in the sumptuous apartment he maintained. But was
it beautiful, or was it ugly?

The soul was quite sure that only a few moments had passed
since it withdrew from its master's veins; and probably even less
time had passed than it imagined, because everything had happened so quickly and in so much confusion. The doctor had said
as he left, well before midnight: "The fever is likely to rise toward
morning. If it does, watch him carefully, and send for me if anything happens."

Was the soul to let itself be roasted to death? Its vital center, if
that is the proper term, had been located close to Don Damián's
intestines, which were radiating fire, and if it had stayed in his

body it would have perished like a broiled chicken. But actually how much time had passed since it left? Very little, certainly, for it still felt hot, in spite of the faint coolness in the dawn air. The soul decided that the change in climate between the innards of its late master and the Bohemian glass of the lamp had been very slight. But change or no change, what about that statement by the old housemaid? "Beautiful," she said . . . and she was a truthful woman who loved her master because she loved him, not because he was rich or generous or important. The soul found rather less sincerity in the remarks that followed.

"Why, of course he had a beautiful soul," the priest said.

" 'Beautiful' doesn't begin to describe it," the mother-in-law asserted.

The soul turned to look at her and saw that as she spoke she was signaling to her daughter with her eyes. They contained both a command and a scolding, as if to say: "Start crying again, you idiot. Do you want the priest to say you were happy your husband died?" The daughter understood the signal, and broke out into tearful wailing.

"Nobody ever had such a beautiful soul! Damián, how much I loved you!"

The soul could not stand any more: it wanted to know for certain, without losing another moment, whether or not it was truly beautiful, and it wanted to get away from those hypocrites. It leaped in the direction of the bathroom, where there was a full-length mirror, calculating the distance so as to fall noiselessly on the rug. It did not know it was weightless as well as invisible. It was delighted to find that nobody noticed it, and ran quickly to look at itself in front of the mirror.

But good God, what had happened? In the first place, it had been accustomed, during more than sixty years, to look out through the eyes of Don Damián, and those eyes were over five feet from the ground; also, it was accustomed to seeing his lively face, his clear eyes, his shining gray hair, the arrogance that puffed out his chest and lifted his head, the expensive clothes in which he dressed. What it saw now was nothing at all like that, but a strange figure hardly a foot tall, pale, cloud-gray, with no definite form. Where it should have had two legs and two feet like the body of Don Damián, it was a hideous cluster of tentacles like those of an octopus, but irregular, some shorter than others, some thinner, and all of them seemingly made of dirty smoke, of some impalpable mud that looked transparent but was not; they were limp and drooping and powerless, and stupendously ugly. The soul of Don Damián felt lost. Nevertheless, it got up the courage to look higher. It had no waist. In fact, it had no body, no neck, nothing: where the tentacles joined there was merely a sort of ear sticking out on one side, looking like a bit of rotten apple peel, and a clump of rough hairs on the other side, some twisted, some straight. But that was not the worst, and neither was the strange grayish-yellow light it gave off: the worst was the fact that its mouth was a shapeless cavity like a hole poked in a rotten fruit, a horrible and sickening thing . . . and in the depths of this hole an eye shone, its only eye, staring out of the shadows with an expression of terror and treachery! Yet the women and the priest in the next room, around the bed in which Don Damián's corpse lay, had said he had a beautiful soul!

"How can I go out in the street looking like this?" it asked itself, groping in a black tunnel of confusion.

What should it do? The doorbell rang. Then the nurse said: "It's the doctor, ma'am. I'll let him in."

Don Damián's wife promptly began to wail again, invoking her dead husband and lamenting the cruel solitude in which he had left her.

The soul, paralyzed in front of its true image, knew it was lost. It had been used to hiding in its refuge in the tall body of Don Damián; it had been used to everything, including the obnoxious smell of the intestines, the heat of the stomach, the annoyance of chills and fevers. Then it heard the doctor's greeting and the mother-in-law's voice crying: "Oh, Doctor, what a tragedy it is!"

"Come, now, let's get a grip on ourselves."

The soul peeped into the dead man's room. The women were gathered around the bed, and the priest was praying at its foot. The soul measured the distance and jumped, with a facility it had not known it had, landing on the pillow like a thing of air or like a strange animal that could move noiselessly and invisibly. Don Damián's mouth was still partly open. It was cold as ice, but that was not important. The soul tumbled inside and began to thrust its tentacles into place. It was still settling in when it heard the doctor say to the mother-in-law: "Just one moment, please."

The soul could still see the doctor, though not clearly. He approached the body of Don Damián, took his wrist, seemed to grow excited, put his ear to his chest and left it there a moment. Then he opened his bag and took out a stethoscope. With great deliberation he fitted the knobs into his ears and placed the button on the spot where Don Damián's heart was. He grew even more excited, put away the stethoscope, and took out a hypodermic syringe. He told the nurse to fill it, while he himself fastened a small rubber tube around Don Damián's arm above the elbow, working with the air of a magician who is about to perform a sensational trick. Apparently these preparations alarmed the old housemaid.

"But why are you doing all that if the poor thing is dead?"

The doctor stared at her loftily, and what he said was intended not only for her but for everybody.

"Science is science, and my obligation is to do whatever I can to bring Don Damián back to life. You don't find souls as beautiful as his just anywhere, and I can't let him die until we've tried absolutely everything."

This brief speech, spoken so calmly and grandly, upset the wife. It was not difficult to note a cold glitter in her eyes and a certain quaver in her voice.

"But . . . but isn't he dead?"

The soul was almost back in its body again, and only three tentacles still groped for the old veins they had inhabited for so many years. The attention with which it directed these tentacles into their right places did not prevent it from hearing that worried question.

The doctor did not answer. He took Don Damián's forearm and began to chafe it with his hand. The soul felt the warmth of life surrounding it, penetrating it, filling the veins it had abandoned to escape from burning up. At the same moment, the doctor jabbed the needle into a vein in the arm, untied the ligature above the elbow, and began to push the plunger. Little by little, in soft surges, the warmth of life rose to Don Damián's skin.

"A miracle," the priest murmured. Suddenly he turned pale and let his imagination run wild. The contribution to the new church would now be a sure thing. He would point out to Don Damián, during his convalescence, how he had returned from the dead because of the prayers he had said for him. He would tell him, "The Lord heard me, Don Damián, and gave you back to us." How could he deny the contribution after that?

The wife, just as suddenly, felt that her brain had gone blank. She looked nervously at her husband's face and turned toward her mother. They were both stunned mute, almost terrified.

"He's saved, he's saved," the old housemaid cried, "thanks to God and you." She was weeping and clutching the doctor's hands. "He's saved, he's alive again. Don Damián can never pay you for what you've done."

The doctor was thinking that Don Damián had more than enough money to pay him, but that is not what he said. What he said was: "I'd have done the same thing even if he didn't have a penny. It was my duty, my duty to society, to save a soul as beautiful as his."

He was speaking to the housemaid, but again his words were intended for the others, in the hope they would repeat them to the sick man as soon as he was well enough to act on them.

The soul of Don Damián, tired of so many lies, decided to sleep. A moment later, Don Damián sighed weakly and moved his head on the pillow.

"He'll sleep for hours now," the doctor said. "He must have absolute quiet."

And to set a good example, he tiptoed out of the room.

TRANSLATED BY LYSANDER KEMP

The Sign of Winter

Magali García Ramis

Written and recorded testimonials about
Professor Antón Orlandi's Life

He is searching for the secret of how to carve it in wood, a hundred times in a row, without cracking the wood. He is trying to
fashion an embroidery in the wood with the web of his sign, as his
father used to make with flowers and geometrical designs in the
first decades of the century. He, who has the hands of an angel,
who has never worked with anything other than pen or pencil, all
of a sudden wants the wood to speak between his hands. He does
not want to carve stalks of wheat, he does not want elongated lo-
tus flowers, nor tulips; he does not want waves of water or decora-
tive lines of late Art Deco; he does not want the sign of the
plumed serpent that he drew so many times for his students
when, with magic gestures and love in his voice, he initiated them
in the study of the symbols of the New World; he wants only the
sign of winter, the primeval and medieval, taken from the book
of signs of Rudolf Koch; the sign of winter, for him a sign of
refuge, and we followed him at a distance, being his shadows, trying to protect him from those who sometimes make fun of him,
because Antón Orlandi is dying.

*(From an unpublished narrative text written by Juan A. Rivera, a stu-
dent of Professor Orlandi, at the request of his classmates)*

* * *

I am dying/I know it. They look at me with pity or with surprise, they are so young that these feelings are juxtaposed and confused in them. They were never able to see me as a teacher. They know that I was only one more professor. I was not hard with them, nor too soft either, I did not have much faith in them because I have not had it in myself for a long time. I came to Puerto Rico to discover my father's work and I stayed. I came without having roots here, because what roots can one have if he leaves a place at the age of eight? I barely remember . . .

(Tape recording found in the study of Professor Orlandi, transcribed by his friend Dr. Gustavo Ramírez)

He began to carve it in the cracks and on the orange doors of the Humanities Building. Sometimes he drew it on walls. Some afternoons we saw him walking through the deserted hallways and all of a sudden going into a classroom to trace it on a wooden desk, as if he were going to paint graffiti. It was, undoubtedly, the sign of winter, signalling that, in spite of his apparent strength, he had arrived at the twilight of his life and he wanted to protect himself.

Three reasons are generally given for his decision to hasten the flow of the signs even though he was still relatively young. At fifty-five, one doesn't yet have to make the sign of winter. The three reasons have to do with his professional life, his family, and his romantic life, but we do not know exactly what happened to him. Following are some facts that may contribute to his biography.

He came to Puerto Rico about twenty years ago to try to find his father's work. Although we do not have specific details about his upbringing, his life, according to the stories he told his colleagues and students, began when he returned to Puerto Rico, hired a *carro público* and began to dream inwardly, in spite of the heat, the cherry-scented deodorant, and the rush. When he arrived at Cabo Rojo, stopped in San Germán, when he jumped out of the car in Rincón and hours later forced the driver to return South once more, when looking at his father's map he identified, as the car drove by, facades of the houses that Jacob Orlandi had decorated, Antón began to live.

(Fragment from "Inventory," a narrative portrait of Professor Orlandi written by his student María Rosa Martínez)

. . . It was almost twenty years ago, I remember because my baby daughter was turning three that day and I said to him, "Look, mister, if you want to go all the way there, I'll take you, but we must return today to Mayagüez because it's the baby's birthday, OK?" He said yes to everything and he hired my car. I had been driving a *carro público* for around seven years and I had seen a lot of strange people, but no one like that teacher. He insisted on going straight to Cabo Rojo, and on the way there we stopped at every old house he felt like looking at. He carried a bunch of papers and maps, and he kept telling me where to go. Sometimes we would follow dirt roads that led nowhere or we would reach houses that didn't exist anymore because there was nothing left of them, and he would get out to look on the ground for pieces of wood, bits of banisters or decorations like the ones that houses used to have in the old days. We spent almost the entire day in Cabo Rojo, and when I told him that we had to leave, he offered me a wad of money to stay with him for a few more days. I told him that we couldn't, that it was my daughter's birthday, but he insisted. I called my wife and I explained. He was a quiet man, like the gringos, calm, although he was not a gringo; he was, he told me, Puerto Rican and he spoke like us. He was ruddy and redheaded, a *colorao* and he told me that he had gone North, to New York, as a child and now he had come back. We stayed that night in the house of the godfather of one of my kids. The next day we went on to San Germán. There he took notes and marked some things on his maps; he stared at every house, spellbound. He told me that many of those wooden decorations had been made by his pa. I almost laughed to his face because I thought that he was a little loony. But years later, when my daughter got a scholarship and went to study at the University of Río Piedras, she took classes with him. I used to go pick her up on weekends, and one day she pointed him out to me and I realized that it was true, that he was an art teacher or something like that, a teacher of design or something like that, as my daughter used to say. And that his father had truly been a craftsman who made many of the decorations on the old houses in this area.

(Testimonial by Mr. Natividad Pérez, carro público driver from Mayagüez, as part of several interviews taped by Rosario Pinto, one of Professor Orlandi's students)

It is known that his father arrived on the Island from Europe while still very young, on the ship *Bohème,* a ship on which for forty years many islanders and adopted islanders would arrive and depart, especially the rebels, the cowards, and the weak of spirit. Jacobo may have been a rebel, or perhaps one of the spiritually weak, but he knew too little Spanish to be able to understand the mockery he was the subject of when, having married a year after his arrival, he obeyed his wife in everything and drew exquisite lace patterns that she would then weave and sell from house to house. Jacobo was a professional carpenter, and when Matilde Orlandi heard businessman Mr. Antonio Wiscovich say that he needed a craftsman to decorate the balcony of his house with wooden carvings, she persuaded him to hire Jacobo. The success of that first incursion into banister carving made him famous all over that region.

Jacobo then became the master of the laces. He travelled throughout the towns of the southwest, decorating balconies, galleries, verandas, *mediopuntos* dining rooms, young ladies' bedrooms, libraries, studies, and even private chapels.

But when Matilde caught a chill in the cool night air and died, he lost interest in carved woods, in lace, which reminded him too much of his wife, and his life collapsed. So he took his son, Antón, by the hand, and he boarded the *Bohème* for New York. There he found a job in a furniture factory and he dedicated his life to his work and to his son. He was able to take advantage of the opportunities that a big city like New York can offer bright kids, as Antón Orlandi Catinchi undoubtedly was. Jacobo pushed him to study and he received a scholarship from a Catholic school. On Sundays, after mass, Jacobo used to take him to museums, to walk the streets of the city's boroughs, lined with stately homes, and to admire the buildings, and especially their decorations. "They are signs," he used to say. "They are signs of the time, of the ones who made the buildings, or of the ones who live in them." When Jacobo died Antón was already a man, and well on his way toward a profession, teaching.

(From Armando Vega Catinchi, Some Puerto Rican-Corsicans and Their Contributions to the Cultural Development of the Southwest, p. 511 [work in progress]. Mr. Vega Catinchi is a lawyer, poet, and notary public.)

From what I can remember, I think that Antón Orlandi returned to the Island and he devoted himself to cataloging the woodworks made by his father; at the same time he started to develop the first courses about images and signs in Puerto Rico. He was interested in visual signs, religious signs, governmental, medical symbols—in short the entire iconographic language, and we are talking about a period when the majority of the intellectuals and academics on the Island did not know these areas of study, weren't inclined to analyze them.

Now, I know, through conversations with common friends, that what supported him, I mean the axis of his life, so to speak, consisted of some adjacent supports, not any interior force like the wise and the old have. He was a pleasant colleague but with a very low opinion of himself. When people talk, as you may have heard, of the three reasons that pushed him to unrest, maybe to madness and eventually to his death, I always think that the most important was when he realized that, in spite of his studies and classes and conferences, in spite of the fact that several times there were reviews in the newspapers about his activities, let us say that in spite of the fact he left traces of his passage through life, he considered himself mediocre, especially after they denied him the sabbatical.

And the other two reasons?

Well, the second was discovering the meanness of the one we believed to be our most just and irreproachable colleague. Antón was never able to recover from that crisis. You see, one chooses one's friends. So, when one has made the wrong choice and one finds oneself intimately tied to someone who turns out to be a swine, the blow is very deep inside, and it is directed at oneself, at the failure in the choice one has made.

Did you also suffer from that failure?

We all suffered, but, of course, for obvious reasons I can't say anything else about that.

The third reason was a woman.

Yes, and it is well known that that woman in particular left him and it affected him profoundly. She is a woman with whom he was seen for more or less two years. She wasn't the first in his life, nor the last, nor the most beautiful, nor in any way the least attractive, but in short, a woman . . .

(Notes from a conversation between Professor Thomas Goodwin, friend of Professor Antón Orlandi, and the journalist Elsa Aponte just after Professor Orlandi's death. Miss Aponte had been a student of both teachers, and she talked to Goodwin in order to obtain information about Antón Orlandi's life, explicitly agreeing beforehand that she would not reveal any facts about the private life of the deceased professor.)

I visited her on a Sunday afternoon. She lived in the neighborhood of Santurce, a short distance from where Antón had lived. She recognized me immediately, although we hadn't spoken in more than ten years. I used to see her often walking toward her job in a government office in Old San Juan. She was a little heavier than when she was going out with Antón, but just as serene, her hair intensely brown, her dark eyes with green eye shadow, always green eye shadow, her body extremely sensual, even under the austere, long-sleeved dresses and earth-brown colors she used to wear.

Come in, sit down, she said without surprise or displeasure.

I have come, after such a long time, because we are writing a book about his life.

You knew him better than I. What could I add? she said, beginning to talk immediately about Antón, who was the only link between us.

But he lived in love with you for almost three years. You were fundamental in his life. (I wanted to add: you were fatal in his life, but I restrained myself.)

Fundamental? No one is fundamental in anyone's life. Do you want something to drink? She went to her tiny kitchen. The apartment was a humid place with lots of green, full of plants, especially ferns. She gave me whiskey; she knew I drank whiskey. She remembered it from the times the three of us stayed up till dawn talking and drinking in the bars by the seashore.

You were not in love with him, were you?

I don't have to answer you; you want information about Antón, not about me.

Do you have pictures of him? Or something he gave you, any detail, anything? Do you know any fact about his life that he told only you and that could be published? I won't use your name, no one knows that I came to see you. You know that I am up front, that if I say to you no one, it means no one.

I know you, Gustavo, I know that he was your friend, I know that you are sincere, and I also know that you are extremely weak, that to please everyone, to avoid being rejected, you can be honorable, proper, and even an asshole, if necessary.

I did not come here to speak about me but of Antón—I cut her short quickly.

She didn't make any gesture. She left without saying a word and entered her bedroom. In a short while, she returned with a folder full of photos, newspaper clippings, boxes of matches from restaurants, napkins from bars, and a wooden lighter carved with the sign of winter. I felt I was on the edge of a revelation; I tried to concentrate as much as possible so as to place that object on the long list of detailed information that I had about Antón's life. Then I heard music.

She had turned on the radio to a station that played American instrumental music, Muzak almost. Outside, the afternoon light shone intensely. Time was about to stop as it does on Sundays at three o'clock in Santurce.

When did he give you this? I asked her.

He sent it by mail about six months before his death, with a note that I tore up. It said something about the end of hopes or about a new beginning. I don't know. He asked me to use that lighter always and forever. But I threw it in that envelope with other mementos of him.

Why didn't you use it?

She stood still, and with a voice barely audible she said, *I was seeing someone; he would have found that uncommon lighter strange.*

She turned around and stared at me. *Real all you want,* she added, *take notes, if you wish, but do not take the letters with you. If you need any photo, take it, make a copy, and return it to me, but by mail. And, please, don't come back here. Shut the door when you leave.*

She went to her bedroom, to cry, I knew right away. I tried to concentrate on what I was reading but I couldn't avoid thinking about her. I got up; I opened her bedroom door and went to her. I sat down next to her; she let me run my fingers through her hair, so brown and so soft. She let me embrace her. I felt like a swine for taking advantage of her weakness, but I did. I began to ask her all that I could. Why did you leave him? He could have struggled with life if you had been at his side.

He wasn't capable of loving anything or anyone for a long time. We lasted two years; that was all he could last with someone. After that, he'd turn neglectful, he would become cynical about life and about people; he did not love himself and he couldn't love anyone else.

But you loved him.

Yes, she said, and we didn't speak anymore because I began to caress her face, to embrace her, and spent the afternoon with her. We made love desperately slow, she because I reminded her of Antón in some way, I because she was his and I wanted to be like him. I had never admired anyone more than I admired him. I felt part of his life because I was loving the woman he loved most, because I was under her sheets, looking at her nakedness, feeling her hard mouth against mine. When night fell, I got dressed without speaking. Naked, she leaned back on the bed's headboard.

Now you have something else to detail his life, Gustavo, she said, but without rancor, as if she had been freed of something she had kept inside for years and truly wanted to appear in the biography.

Now I do not know if I wish to finish the book, I said and left.

(From Dr. Gustavo Ramírez's personal diary, dated August 14, 1982)

I dare tell you this because I know that it won't leave this room. Really, it was a very hard blow for all of us. I, myself, felt ashamed to have discovered Marcos Plá's secret. And even more to have discussed it with Antón. Sometimes it's better not to mention those things. Marcos was our guru—don't you remember having seen all of us, Antón, Gustavo, Thomas, and Marcos, heading toward La Torre Restaurant for coffee? You see, we shared a lot. He was a tall and slim man, talkative with acquaintances, quiet with strangers. He lived in a small apartment right in the middle of Río Piedras, between old buildings and rambling student boardinghouses. When we were fed up with life, when we wanted good company to go to the movies, when we wanted to have a few beers after some conference, the ideal companion was Marcos. We used to consider him the most upright man, the most knowledgeable Humanities professor, and certainly he was the most articulate of us. He spoke with such fluency and had such an exquisite vocabulary that it was a pleasure to talk with him. We used to think that his solitude was creative, and we did not have reason to suspect otherwise.

I do not have the gift of prophesy or anything like that; I do not have a trace of extrasensory powers. What I had that day was a vision, I swear to you, like the ones the prophets describe in the Bible. I saw something that I was not really seeing. I saw René de Jesús, a good-looking young athlete, leaving Marcos's apartment at 11:00 at night. A week before, I had also seen Jimmy Robles, the one that stutters, the weakling, leaving Marcos's house late at night, coming down the back stair by the garage as if in a daze. I don't know why I connected both images. But right then I remembered that the previous night Marcos had said to Antón that René had problems, that he was very intelligent but because of sports had neglected his classes, and that if he did not get an A in Antón's class he would lose his scholarship. At that time I did not pay any attention to the comment, but later I did. A few days later, I heard Marcos saying the same thing about Jimmy Robles to Dr. Palacios. And, although it was common for us professors to be interested in the students and even to allow them to visit us in our houses, because at that time, at the end of the decade of the sixties and beginning of the seventies, there was an open, a more informal, and healthy relationship between teachers and students, still, something stuck in my mind from seeing those young men and listening to Marcos intercede for them.

I started to spy, to ask questions here and there, and suddenly, everywhere, I began to see the signs of Marcos's corruption. He exchanged favors for favors, he was able to obtain high grades for his students with his sly pleas in return for a few hours with the young men who dropped by his place. Somehow he coaxed them, and, if it was necessary, he threatened them. One from the ROTC, I was told, had wanted to ambush and kill him because Marcos had blackmailed his brother.

One day I couldn't hold all this in anymore, and I stopped Antón in a corner of the square in front of the theater.

I do not know how to begin to tell you all that I have inside about Marcos, I began.

What is going on? What are you talking about?

About Marcos, Antón, about Marcos Plá. He has been getting several young men in trouble, he invites them to his house, and in exchange . . .

Since when are you a moralist? Gustavo has gone to bed with several of his prettiest students, and you, didn't you seduce the niece of the Dean of Business last term?

This is different, Antón. I am not speaking about voluntary relations between adults, I am not talking about going to bed or not, but about blackmail, getting them to go to bed with him in exchange for favors, or if not he rats on them as happened with the brother of the ROTC cadet.

Antón remained pensive for a moment. Something was hurting a lot; I was able to notice it on his face. He thought before speaking.

I always suspected something, but I tried to erase it immediately. I did not want to face this truth. Everything that he offers to us is good, positive, creative, and the rest, up to now, I was able to forgive. As long as we had not spoken about it, do you understand? he emphasized, mumbling. *As long as things aren't said, aren't shared, aren't communicated, one does not have to confront them. Only at the moment when one says, "This one is a swine," or, "That one is mediocre," only then does that reality become evident, only then must it be accepted. I would have preferred that you had never talked to me about Marcos, that we had never shared this, that the perfect harmony of our group of friends had never been broken . . .*

(Declarations from Professor Américo González, Assistant to the Dean of Studies, to his journalist friend Elsa Aponte de Goodwin. Both agreed beforehand that everything said by González would be off the record. That is why this information was never used in Mrs. Aponte's series "Professors We Remember from the U.P.R.")

*   *   *

At his house located near Loíza Street, where students and scholars used to gather to talk in the evenings at a time when there were lovers of architecture but no School of Architecture at the University of Puerto Rico, at that house, full of wooden decorations rescued from houses on the verge of collapse, now arrive the solicitous women from the University administration to urge Antón to defend his rights, to force him to eat, to look after his personal grooming. The rest of us have deserted him because nothing can be done now. They are the queens around a dying King Arthur.

Professor, you must sign these triplicates in order to receive the pension on time if you are already thinking about retiring. Master Orlandi, if you would only send a tiny outline, of one page, signed by you, for the course that you promised to give next semester, I am sure that the Dean will approve it. But you have to make an effort.

Mr. Orlandi, try to follow the recommendations of the department's chair, apply for help from the University, fill out the papers and I'll type them.

But Antón pays no heed and goes on carving. After visiting him, the mortuary queens leave. He continues his carvings of signs and recites his biography with the passion of one who knows he has no time left.

(From Dr. Ramírez's diary, dated March 2, 1972)

My life began when I returned to Puerto Rico to study my father's work. Later I saw other works/other signs condemned to meet the same fate as many of Jacobo Orlandi's creations. The Gauthier mansion is abandoned, eaten by termites, waiting to be destroyed. Someone has stolen all its wooden decorations/now it looks like a toothless house. What value can a house like that have? Those details/fragile ornaments, those perishable details, are the only things that sustain houses like that between life and death; if they are removed, what is left? There are houses with tiny mosaics encrusted around the doors, or in the columns at the entrance. There are those with a simple wooden banister; once it is removed it takes away the house's reason for being. I also was fatally wounded when I lost my decorations. The simple ones. I was never able to dwell deeply in anyone's life, but they sustained me, they gave me time, and now it is ending.

(Part of the tape found in Professor Orlandi's house; this segment transcribed by Professor T. Goodwin)

I denied him permission for a sabbatical because I believed that he didn't have the necessary background to write a text about the symbols used in wood carvings and decorations on the houses in the southwestern region of the Island. He was an amateur, that's for sure, and in love with the subject because his father had been a craftsman. And certainly, he could have prepared a good documentation, such as an oral history of the craftsmen that still live in that region. But a text with the scholarly rigor that it demands, no, Professor Orlandi did not have the necessary academic tools for that. In twenty-five or so years that he was at this campus he didn't publish a single book, and all of a sudden, too late, that became his craze. There were other professors with higher rank and more experience and with more right to a sabbatical than he. The two sabbaticals he took before were for traveling, but he didn't produce anything. I know that he was very disappointed with that decision, and maybe that accelerated—but did not cause, please listen to me carefully, accelerated—the crisis he suffered later and that led to his regrettable death.

(Unpublished interview with the Emeritus Dean of the Humanities Faculty, Dr. Ramón Hoyos Labra, made by Prof. Ascencio Martínez of the Provost's Office, as part of the materials that he is collecting for the purpose of writing an oral history of the University, as his current sabbatical project)

We believe that he finished carving the sign of winter in that enormous wooden frieze he was making on a Monday afternoon. The next day, Tuesday, we visited him and found him more or less better; his voice was very soft. We began to speak with him about the studies he wanted to make of ornamental details in wood. His interest had expanded to include decorations on mo-

saics and glass. Since he didn't have a car it was difficult for him
to go to other towns, especially to those that had examples of his
father's work, so he began to take an interest in the houses of
Santurce. Juan A., María Rosa, and I offered to take pictures of
the ornaments he wanted to study, in order to get him excited
and to continue his work. Because by that time he did not have
any friends; only the students were with him till the end. He listened to us, apparently with a lot of interest, but he continued to
scribble the sign of winter, which is one from Koch's text. It is not
a negative sign; on the contrary, it illustrates the shelter a person
or a house receives from the snow and the cold. Rudolf Koch was
an eminent scholar of graphic arts who gained fame in his native
Germany and in all Europe, a calligrapher, designer of typogra-
phy, and bookbinder. The first English edition of his book was
printed in London in 1930. Professor Orlandi received it as a
present from his father at the age of twelve and always treasured
it. The book is a collection of ancient symbols from diverse European religions and cultures. Prof. Orlandi used to say that he particularly liked the sign of winter because it made him feel secure.
He told us that his father died in winter and he always associated
that sign with the security and strength that his father offered
him.

Four days after we made this visit, *Doña* Monsita, the cleaning
woman, found him very sick and called an ambulance. They took
him to the Auxilio Mutuo Hospital, and there he died of a heart
attack, they said.

*(Statements made to the press by the students Rosario Pinto, Juan A.
Rivera, and María Rosa Martínez immediately after Professor Orlandi's
death)*

October 27, 1973

San Juan Town Hall
Office of Community Relations

Dear Mr. Rivera, Miss Martínez, and Miss Pinto:
    We wish to inform you that, after consulting with our
lawyers and with the public officials in charge of mainte-
nance of the graves in the Old San Juan Cemetery, we have

found that it is impossible to allow people who are not relatives of a deceased to change the tombstone that marks a grave.

We understand your interest in and love for the late Professor Antón Orlandi, but the gravestone, paid for by the members of the Humanities Faculty from the Río Piedras Campus, has a cross because Professor Orlandi was Catholic, and we are not empowered to allow you to erect another over his grave that contains what you call the sign of winter. Frankly, this is not allowed . . .

(Fragment of a letter received by Juan A., María Rosa, and Rosario from San Juan Town Hall and torn up right away, so it would not turn out to be the beginning of a cycle of deception, so it would not mark their lives, so it would not be a sign)

TRANSLATED BY CARMEN C. ESTEVES

In Foreign Parts

Thea Doelwijt

They were in a foreign, sunny country, but the people there spoke the same language as they did, so it did not strike anyone how strange they were. People did look at Alena, but, after all, she has beautiful long brown hair and when she walks, m-mmm, when she walks you want to go to bed with her. Alena, however, doesn't want to go to bed with anyone—only with Orlo.

They were living in a strange house with lots of rooms in it where Alena played lots of roles, with Orlo as her sole audience. She made strange clothes, which she showed off to him like a fashion model; she prepared strange dishes, which she served up to him like a servant-girl. Orlo never saw Alena—he didn't want that—as a charwoman, a washerwoman, a gardener-woman.

Both of them liked her role as a lover best of all, yet Orlo saw her less and less in bed. For many nights now Orlo had been meditating. Tonight too. He clapped his hands together but did not see the mosquito that had been circling round for some time fall to the ground. They won't get the better of me, the mosquito thought, grimly. He dived under the table and landed on Orlo's big toe. God, what a thirst I had, he thought in between two sips.

Orlo wrinkled his nose. He thought of rats which sometimes die a sudden death, in a gutter or in the middle of some back-yard. The stench they carry about with them their whole life long rises up in all its triumph after they die screaming with laughter at the people who scurry past, retching—forbidding them to think for one moment: poor, dead rat.

Rats, Orlo thought, look at you with eyes full of hate and loathing, just as you want to look at them. Strange. In the twilight this evening a rat had been sitting in the pouring rain in the middle of the road and Orlo had braked for him. Orlo didn't understand a bit of it.

Oh, how glad I am, the rat thought, when it finally began to rain.

He had been waiting for it from five o'clock on. He jumped up and scurried out of the gutter. He hadn't been sitting in the rain for two minutes when he saw the light coming at him. For a moment he thought of going on quietly sitting there, but he knew he ought not to kid himself; he knew he had to be off.

"Mi Gado, mi Jesus, mi Masra, mi T'ta," he cursed as he raced away. "One can't even have a quiet bath nowadays." Orlo lifted his leg and scratched his big toe. Mosquitoes were the very devil, mosquitoes were the first creatures he had learned to kill. You get like that in a strange country; even though you feel quite at home, you act differently all the same, until you no longer know who you were and who you are. What then?

"You must decide," Alena said. "It was you who wanted to come here."

"Yes, but you can say something too, can't you?"

"You never do what I want anyway."

"That's not true. If you say you want to leave, then we will."

Alena smiled. "Darling," she said, "it's your problem. If you want to stay here, I'll stay too. If you want to go away, I'll go with you. You'd go alone otherwise."

Shbap! A beetle in the ashtray. I smoke too much, thought Orlo, looking at the beetle, which kept colliding with a cigarette stub.

I mustn't panic, thought the beetle, but I must get out of here, in a hurry. Seen from the air, it had looked like a nice quiet little spot, with a few white hills; now he was here he was almost choking to death. I don't understand a thing about it, he thought, and I don't want to understand a thing about it either. Ow! he biffed his head against a bauxite wall.

"Stupid," said Orlo, and he held out a matchstick towards him.

My God, the beetle thought. This is the end. He pulled in his legs and went rigid with mortal fear.

"Come on, get a hold on it and then I'll pull you out."

Orlo gave the beetle a little push with the matchstick, which rolled him over on to his back. The beetle screamed blue murder, but Orlo didn't hear. "Sorry."

Orlo pushed the beetle back on to his feet with the matchstick. Now! the beetle thought, and made a run for it. Ow! Another wall.

"Calm down now, you'll never get out that way!" Nothing for it then.

Orlo got hold of the beetle by his back between thumb and forefinger and put him on the table.

The beetle had lost all sense of direction. Instead of flying away he crept under some papers where he began to feel so stifled that he could not hold back a shriek of alarm. Orlo lifted up a sheet of paper.

Where am I now? What's going on now? the beetle wondered, at his wit's end. He crept into a newspaper. Do as you like then, Orlo thought and forgot his existence.

He sat suddenly silent and tensed, listening intently. He would do that on an evening, several times. He was trying to identify the exotic sounds of this country. If he didn't succeed, he grew afraid, although he didn't, of course, know why. He didn't care what might become of him, but nothing must happen to Alena, though he didn't know how Alena would manage, if anything happened to him.

All the houses in the neighborhood are dark after ten o'clock. Friends don't usually come along after ten o'clock.

After ten o'clock the night beasts gather together to whistle *tori* to each other, the whole night through. Orlo had never seen them, the beasts of the night. They probably don't even exist; they probably only have to whistle to show how quiet the night is. And perhaps, too, they only have to whistle and whisper to camouflage the strangest and most menacing noises.

Whatever is the matter with me? Orlo wondered. He wished he didn't keep seeing the dog's corpse before him all the time. He had good eyes for discovering corpses along the road (chunks of bloody, stinking flesh) and quickly looking the other

way. That *was* a dog, his eyes saw, and that a cat, and these are in-
sides, intestines, and actually, actually we haven't seen anything
at all, his eyes said.

But yesterday they really had seen something and that's why
now Orlo didn't merely see the trees, staring like inquisitive
women neighbors at the man at the open window, not merely
the drawing of the clown on the wall, who didn't respond to his
feelings of solidarity, not merely all the things which made
him feel at home in this room. Now he saw as well the legs of the
dead dog, pointing up to the sky, its bloated body, the black gash
in its throat where it had bled to death, the dead eyes at the side
of the road.

A cockroach glided across the wall. Orlo jumped up, his slip-
per in his hand. He hated the idea of them sometimes invading
his room, even if Alena did keep the house so beautifully clean—
that he knew. He struck out. What lousy luck, thought the cockroach, as it fell to the ground.

Orlo struck again, too hard. The cockroach's stomach split
open and a dirty-white, sticky mess poured out of it. He didn't
want to see it. "Alena, come and sweep something up!"

"What is it?"

"Sweep that up!"

"Why don't you do it yourself?"

Orlo didn't reply. He went and sat down at his table again, his
head between his hands. He listened to Alena. That was that.
Don't think about it.

"I'm going to bed. I'm tired. Are you going to sit here much
longer?"

Orlo stood up and flung his arm round Alena.

"I'll take you to bed and come along later."

In the bedroom Orlo saw that a moth had hanged itself.

"What a shame," Alena said. "He's worn himself out flying
around."

"Not at all. Look, there's the little bench he's kicked away.
He's committed suicide."

For two days and one whole night I've tried to live, the moth
thought. And now I've had enough. He looked about him and
suddenly caught sight of the thread the spider had left dangling.
Is that an omen? He flew up to it but swerved aside at the last mo-

ment to the top of the mirror. Now I can still go in any direction
I choose. I can go to the left and to the right, upwards and down-
wards. I can even still fly out of the window, if I want to. But to
the left and the right, as the moth knew, are walls on which
they'll shortly be spraying a deadly poison. Up there the light
drives me frantic and down there there'll be some silly dog that'll
snap at me without meaning or wanting to. That'd be a senseless
sort of death. And if I fly out of the window, I shall immediately
dash into another room where light is burning, shriek with enthusiasm, shout for joy that I've found the answer at last . . . only
afterwards, pretty soon afterwards, to start thinking and doing
the same things all over again. I'm not all keen on things any
longer, thought the moth. He picked up a small bench and flew
towards the spider's thread, and making a loop in it, put his head
inside. Then he kicked the bench away.

"Dodo!" Orlo cried. "Come to bed!"

The dog crept under the bed.

"Shall I use the Flit spray?"

"Oh, leave it," said Alena.

"Sleep well then." Orlo kissed Alena on her eyes, her nose and
then lightly on her lips.

"Don't be too late."

Orlo did not reply, turned off the light, and peered into the
dark hall (the light had gone again) stretching out as though it
were God. He pulled the bedroom door to behind him and whispered angrily to the hall:

"Act naturally, why can't you? You're nothing very special.
Agreed, you're long and lofty, but you belong to me and so you
will remain. Without me you're powerless."

The hall stared gloomily ahead as Orlo entered the kitchen
and went up to the ice-box. Now, I have to take the beer bottle
out first and then get hold of the cola bottle. He ran his fingers
through his hair in irritation: it takes too much time, we haven't
got all night. He tugged the bottle of cola clumsily over the top of
the beer bottle and crossed to the sink.

Plop! said a couple of frogs. They've grown smaller still, Orlo
thought. But I can't prove it.

He went to his room, picked up a magnifying glass and followed the frogs with it as they leaped away from him, up against

the kitchen walls and into dark hiding places. Orlo removed his glasses and laid them on his left arm.

"Just look," he said softly (Alena didn't have to hear it). "Even you will see that there's nothing to be seen . . ."

He made the glasses grow bigger and smaller with the magnifying glass. Suddenly he shivered. I'm an intermediate station. How nasty and hot that was, the frog thought, jumping into a cup.

Rum in the glass, the tray of ice cubes at last wrested loose and under the tap, ice cubes in the glass, a dash of cola.

God, what a thirst I had, Orlo thought in between two sips. He lifted an ice-cube out of the glass and wiped it across his clammy forehead. A feeling of cramp shot across his belly. I'll have to go to the lavatory when I should be studying frogs. Strange, that they should be getting smaller. Where have I left that magnifying glass? Where are my glasses? Oh, leave it—lavatory first. Seated on the pot, he stared down at the floor where a number of ants were busy with the job of living. Orlo narrowed his eyes a little and looked down at his bare feet (he would always kick off his slippers when on the lavatory) which formed part of the ants' landscape. They haven't any notion that they're crawling over the feet of a lifesize human being. To them I am enormous, to them I am immense, infinite; to them, Orlo thought, I am God. He nodded at them. I am your God, he whispered. No reaction. The ants went on crawling about as though He didn't exist. They did not know Him, they did not see Him, they did not recognize Him, they did not even recognize His little toe.

Orlo lifted up his feet and dangled them above their heads like a threatening thundercloud. After this, he had to devote all his attention to his own needs for a while, and he forgot the ants and plumped his feet down on the floor without thinking. He looked upwards and listened to the bats as they led a life all unknown to him under the roof. Why were they chasing about like that now?

When he looked down again the ants had disappeared. There was just a small black spot moving across the floor. Again he narrowed his eyes—I'm a shortsighted God—and then discovered that he was looking at the corpse of a small, shriveled-up fly which was being pushed along by a small black ant. He's sweating like a navvy out in the midday sun. It's too crazy for words.

"You'll never manage that on your own. Hey!"

Suddenly Orlo saw another ant a little further off. That's all absolutely wrong too—that's not the way things should be in My Kingdom.

"Go and give your comrade a hand," He commanded. "Can't you see him struggling away there?"

The ant looked the other way. Oho! We're having none of that! Orlo leaned over and intervened with a Divine finger. He gave the ant a push and all but crushed him to death. "Sorry."

Then of one of His fingers He made a wall over which no ant could climb. The ant swerved aside, still didn't want to go to his colleague's aid. Orlo didn't give up. He placed His finger in front of, at the side of, behind the ant, showing him in this way where a job of work was awaiting him. It mustn't go on for too long, Orlo thought.

"Get a move on!"

The ant, however, had other ideas in mind, other things to do and tried, with an angry expression on his face, to go his own way.

"Goddammit!" Orlo picked up the ant carefully—yes, carefully—between His thumb and forefinger and put him down next to his sweating comrade.

"Cooperation," Orlo whispered, "makes things so much easier."

Something cracked, something got broken, something was crushed fine. The ant with the dead fly looked up, vexed.

"Mi Gado," he sighed, "that on top of everything else! Now I've got a casualty to look after too!"

"Just let me lie here," groaned the injured ant.

"Are you crazy? Of course, I'll help you. Can you stand on your feet? What happened actually?"

"I've no idea," said the injured ant. "No idea."

I'm the Benevolent God, Orlo thought as he pulled the chain. Suddenly everything is clear. It is finished. In bed he drew Alena close to him. "I love you."

"What's the matter?" Alena asked sleepily.

Orlo laughed. He felt good. "We could easily go home for a while, you know," he said.

"What?"

"Shall we go home?"

* * *

They were in their own country, but it was a strange, cloudy land. They spoke their own language, yet people noticed how strange they were.

People often looked at Alena, but, after all, she has beautiful long brown hair and when she walks, m-mmm, when she walks you want to go to bed with her. Alena, however, doesn't want to go to bed with anyone—only with Orlo.

They were living in a strange hotel with lots of rooms in it where people lived whom you never saw. The few you encountered in the corridors or on the terrace could only whisper. Alena lay in bed the whole day long under blankets of orange wool. Orlo still thought them endearing blankets, because under them during the first nights she had acted her role as a lover so well—better even than usual.

Their friends from former days had come to visit them only during the first days. They laughed, because Orlo and Alena felt cold while the sun was shining. Now the sun was not shining anymore.

In those first days they had gone into the wood. Arms round each other, Orlo and Alena had said how beautiful the brown leaves were and how strange it was that here you didn't need to be afraid of anything.

They spread out a coat on the moss and lay close to each other. But Orlo had not felt at home, he didn't recognize the sounds anymore, the leaves spoke a different language, the wind in the trees sounded strange. He sat up.

"Do come and lie down," Alena said.

"I can hear something."

Alena laughed.

"I have to protect you, don't I?" said Orlo. He picked up a twig and broke open the soil with it.

"What are you doing?" Alena asked sleepily.

"I'm looking for ants."

"Be glad there aren't any here."

"Here too there are ants, I'm sure. Before they were here too."

"We've picked a nice spot," Alena said. "Do come and lie down again."

Orlo remained sitting up.

"What's wrong now?"

"I want ants!" Orlo snapped at her.

Alena sat up too and flung her arms round Orlo's neck. "Aren't you pleased we're here? Do you want to go back?"

"I don't know," Orlo said. "I don't know."

"We've got to get used to it," Alena said. "We've got to get used to this country again, to the people, to everything. After a while everything won't seem so strange anymore. After a while we'll have friends again, after a while we'll live normally again."

But it had grown colder and colder and Alena had stayed in bed longer and longer. She did not play roles anymore.

Orlo always wore a thick coat and a woollen scarf. Dressed like this, he would sit meditating, days and nights at his desk in the hotel room, staring at strange walls. He ordered strange drinks, listened to strange sounds. He was never really afraid anymore.

Animals he no longer saw, not live ones, not dead ones.

Never once did he know he was God. Many a night a strange mist hung in the air, and the trees were unrecognizable.

TRANSLATED BY JAMES BROCKWAY

Little Ants

J. M. Sanz Lajara

The Colonel was a methodical man and a brave man. He got up every day at the same time, at the very moment when the sun appeared above the palm trees, drank the same glass of water, did the same setting-up exercises, shaved, washed, dressed, and proceeded to make the same minute inspection of the barracks and of the troops. The Colonel had the most brilliant service record imaginable and had received all the decorations. Undoubtedly, he was an exceptional soldier.

The town was clean and orderly, a small group of houses on the edge of the ocean, surrounded by palms and coconut trees. Almost all the little houses were white, and almost all the residents within were black. The sky was blue most of the time, although once in a while it became gray or even bright red. The sea was also blue, although one morning it was chocolate-colored, but that was during a hurricane.

No one in the town was important. On the outskirts, nevertheless, there was a green house with a zinc balcony, and that house was different, for it was where the Colonel's sweetheart lived. She was a terrific and very beautiful mulatto, but the Colonel was the only one who knew this, for he was very jealous and did not allow anyone to talk to her. Their love was something private, full of kisses and sighs and promises and even arguments, but always in private, behind closed doors. The Colonel's sweetheart could not mix with the townspeople.

The townspeople feared but respected the Colonel. All recognized in him a true hero, although, truth to tell, he spoke so little that his real character was a mystery. And the people stopped worrying about the Colonel's character, lest it annoy him. It was very important to get on well with him.

Along the road that led out of town, flirted with the sea, and lazily disappeared into the belly of a very ugly mountain, there lived an idiot. He was a poor man with a childish face. He had never talked, and he was always drooling as if he were cutting teeth, although he already had his teeth. He did not comb his hair or shave, and someone had to dress him every day, because otherwise he might well have gone out naked, and that would have displeased the Colonel.

The idiot did absolutely nothing of importance. Every afternoon they let him sit at the edge of the road, and there he would take some dirt in his hands and set it down somewhere else or, with a stick, trace furrows that no one took any notice of. Undoubtedly, he was the least important man in town.

Every afternoon, when the Colonel rode in his Chevrolet from the barracks to his sweetheart's house, he had to pass by the house of the idiot, but since he was so preoccupied with keeping the town clean and the inhabitants from plotting a revolution, he never noticed him.

But one time the Chevrolet broke down. It coughed urgently, and came to a halt in front of the idiot's house. The Colonel, now in a bad humor, had to get out of the car, and he was much vexed because he wanted to kiss the sultry lips of his mulatto sweetheart.

"What's your name?" he asked the idiot, who, not knowing how to talk, laughed. It was the first time anyone had laughed at the Colonel.

A very disheveled woman came out of the hut and said to the Colonel, most respectfully to be sure, "Colonel, please excuse my grandson, because the poor boy has been an idiot from birth."

"Aha!" the Colonel exclaimed. "And what is he doing with that stick? Don't you see he is sitting on an anthill? Those ants sting."

Sure enough, the idiot was sitting on an anthill, but, despite the Colonel's fears, he appeared to be playing with the ants. Anyway, if the ants stung him, how could he complain, not knowing how to speak?

"Colonel," the old woman said then, "he plays with the little ants. They are his only toys."

The Colonel scratched his head and turned his back on the old woman. Undoubtedly, he had never known anyone who played with ants, and he began to watch the idiot with interest.

There were many, a great many, columns of ants. They were coming out of the grass, from the trunks of the palm trees, from the mounds of sand. They were real armies, the Colonel thought, surprised, that moved in orderly fashion, worked in orderly fashion, and surrounded the idiot on all sides, also in good order. The Colonel was never mistaken, and he decided that they were very foolish ants to waste their time amusing an idiot.

When the Chevrolet's engine had stopped coughing, the Colonel proceeded to his sweetheart's house, and the idiot went on playing with the little ants. The grandmother breathed easily, for it would certainly have been unpleasant if the Colonel had been annoyed by her grandson and the ants.

The Colonel continued to catch sight of the idiot every afternoon from his Chevrolet, but paid him no heed. One day during his siesta, however, the Colonel, who never had nightmares, awoke all excited because he had dreamed of the idiot. It was a very strange dream, in which he was playing with ants and the idiot had the insolence to pass by dressed as a colonel riding in the Chevrolet. The Colonel could not go back to sleep but began to pace about, naturally frightening the sentries, who were not accustomed to receiving orders at siesta time.

The Colonel went on with his business, paying no further attention to the matter. But he had the same dream some nights later, and then on other nights as well. The fifth or the sixth time, the Colonel decided that these nightmares were very annoying and he would have to do something about them. He went to see the idiot.

"Even though you don't know how to talk, idiot, you must respect the orders I have issued. Madam," he said, calling the old woman, "you must wash him, comb his hair, and not let him sit here playing with ants."

The old woman assented with many obeisances, and the Colonel would have left satisfied, if the idiot had not laughed. The Colonel thought that punishing the idiot would be unworthy of an officer like himself, and went on in his Chevrolet to his sweetheart's house. They made love, but she said she found him very preoccupied and not himself today. The Colonel laughed happily, because that was nonsense, like everything sweethearts say under such circumstances.

One day the Colonel had to punish a soldier, and he ordered him to prison. When they brought in the prisoner, looking very sad, the Colonel countermanded his order and pardoned him. "After all," he said to himself, "the offense is not a serious one."

The soldiers were very much surprised, because it was the first time the Colonel had shown weakness. But since soldiers do not like to think, they went about their duties and quickly forgot that the Colonel had pardoned one of them.

One day the Colonel thought about the idiot when he was not dreaming, and he decided that this was too much and went to see him immediately.

When he asked the old woman about him, he learned that the idiot, following his orders, was playing with the little ants behind the house instead of out in front as before.

"Do you mean to tell me," the Colonel asked, "that the idiot has taken the ants around there?"

"No, no, Colonel. The little ants followed him."

"Aha!" exclaimed the Colonel. "This I must see!"

And so he went to the patio behind the house and there, indeed, he saw the idiot sitting on the ground, holding his stick and directing the columns of ants.

"Incredible," he said to himself. "Incredible."

He scratched his head. He was about to scratch it again when it occurred to him that the order shown by the idiot's ants was like that he had established in the town. And he smiled. The idiot, his head raised like a broken broom, imitated the Colonel's smile. And from that day on they were friends.

It is difficult to describe or explain the friendship of a colonel and an idiot, but that is how it was. Every day, on the way to his sweetheart's house, the Colonel stopped his Chevrolet, waited for the Sergeant to open the car door, and got out in front of the idiot's house. Then he went to the patio and stood very quietly behind the idiot. No one ever knew what he was thinking.

He would spend at least an hour there. He was fascinated by the little ants running here and there, carrying dead insects or parts of insects, building dams and tunnels, touching noses or whatever, even making love. The idiot's omnipotent stick alone presided over all that activity. And the Colonel scratched and scratched his head so much that he began to grow bald. He came to have practically a football field on top of his skull.

All the Negroes in the white houses began to whisper about the Colonel's visits to the idiot. No, no, it was not possible that such a brilliant soldier could take pleasure in ants and an idiot. Moreover, how could such a methodical person as the Colonel leave his sweetheart, the mulatto, to visit an idiot?

And while the people were whispering, some began to take advantage of the situation. The soldiers arrived late at their barracks or went around drinking rum on the beach, the fishermen stopped fishing, and a big lad with a thin face like a chewed caramel spoke in a low voice of insubordination.

"It's impossible!" he repeated in the little plaza or in the streets. "This Colonel is a fool."

One day a telegram arrived for the Colonel. His face turned red when he read it, and he took the Chevrolet, this time without the chauffeur, and drove to the capital.

The Minister of War received him and said: "Colonel, this is inexcusable. A model officer like you disregards his obligations, neglects his troops, and lets the very men by whom he should be respected criticize him," and he pounded a pile of unsigned letters on his desk. "Either you take some action or I will break you to captain and make you my aide!"

"Minister—" the Colonel began.

"I don't want to listen. Shoot this idiot and the matter is done with!"

As the Colonel was a very obedient officer and did not want to lose his decorations, he clicked his heels, gave a military salute, about-faced, and marched off to return to the town.

"Bring the idiot to me!" he ordered the Sergeant of the Guard.

And they brought him, with his stick in his hand. The Colonel said, without a tremor in his voice: "For causing unrest, for vagrancy, because order must reign in this town, and because no one—no one, do you hear me?—can go around organizing ants, I order you to be shot. Let him be executed tomorrow morning at seven!"

The idiot, since he could not talk, laughed. And the soldiers, grave and obedient, took him to a cell, where he spent the night unable to sleep, vainly looking for his ants.

As for the Colonel, he did not close his eyes that night and he even spoke some rather ugly words, too ugly to be repeated, even if they were a colonel's words.

At six-thirty in the morning they took the idiot out to the patio and asked him what his last wish was. Once more he laughed, so the Sergeant decided that anyone so stupid might very well be shot.

At six-forty-five the squad fell in, and they stood the idiot against a wall that was painted white. At six-fifty the Colonel came down from his quarters, with his face rather furrowed but with his shoes very well polished, his blouse impeccable, the insignia on his cap shining like a little star invented by some poet for a romantic sonnet.

"Everything in order?" he asked.

"Everything in order," the Sergeant repeated.

"Absolutely everything," the Captain decided to add, for he wanted a promotion.

"Let us see," the Colonel said then. And, followed by the Captain and the Sergeant, he approached the idiot and stood looking at him.

Although he knew very well that the idiot could not speak, being a very methodical man and officer he asked him: "Are you resigned to your fate? Have you anything to say before you are executed?"

The idiot did not reply. The Colonel grabbed him by the hair and jerked his head up. You wouldn't believe it, but in the idiot's eyes there were two big tears, so big that they ran down his cheeks and joined the drivel from his mouth.

The Colonel did not care for those tears, and said to him, in the stentorian voice he had used when he was a lieutenant, "Why do you cry? You have to die sometime. You must die like a man, without tears, on your feet."

Undoubtedly, the Colonel was a flawless officer.

The idiot, whose face was still looking up, as the Colonel's hands had left it, half-opened his moist lips and, to the amazement of the firing squad, the Sergeant, the Captain, and even the Colonel, heavily pronounced the first words of his life: "Little ants . . . little ants. . . ."

The Colonel remained very stiff and took off his cap. Then he gave the idiot a gentle look, like that of a wave falling on the beach, and drew his pistol.

"That's fine," the Sergeant said to himself, "he is going to execute him himself, as an example to the troops."

But it did not work out that way. Precisely at seven o'clock, the Colonel put the pistol to his head and shot himself. A clean and perfect shot, as if it had been fired by a great officer and a better marksman. And the Colonel fell to the ground dead, with his eyes wide open and surprised, but infinitely illuminated.

They led the idiot back to his cell, smiling because he had discovered he could say "little ants."

They would execute him later. Now they had to bury the Colonel, because they could not leave the body of such a methodical and brilliant officer as the Colonel was in life to lie on the ground in the barracks patio.

Sketches in Transit . . . Going Home

Dionne Brand

He had fucked one hundred women, he'd counted them, he was
secure, no man could question his balls. His reputation was un-
questionable among men and women alike. A real bull of a man,
a man with his share of adventures. The scars from these shone
from his body in between the bright skin. He took every opportunity to be amusing and dangerous. Now he swung his hips imitating the stewardess's gait. Ten minutes earlier he had said, within
her earshot and that of the other men, that she was fat in the
ankles but at the same time passable. He offered to buy everyone's Canadian money if they wanted Trinidad dollars. He had
ten thousand dollars' worth, he said.

"I have plenty money in Alberta," he said.

He had a paunch that women loved, he said. They couldn't
get enough of him. The stewardess, he said, really wanted him,
she was asking for it, look how she was leaning over him asking
him if he wanted a drink, he had exactly what she wanted. A man
with a good wood—twelve inches standing up. They didn't call
him "Iron" for nothing.

"I hear Fitzroy in Vancouver now!"

"Oh yes," she said, leaning across the aisle to the woman who
said she knew her from home. She didn't want this conversation.
Fitzroy, the son of a bitch, was probably doing damn good. It
would wreck her holiday to think about him. He'd left her after

getting his "landed." Thank god she hadn't been stupid enough
to get pregnant for him, though it was close. Two summers ago
he had come to Toronto for Caribana, but that was the last time
she saw him. He was still looking well. He hadn't changed a day
since the old days. Jasmine got up and smiled at the woman
across the aisle who was beginning to say something else about
Fitzroy. She escaped to the bathroom. She was going for Carnival. In the plane, now up above the office buildings she had
cleaned for the last twenty years, she was going home. Like the
rest on the plane, she'd saved for the trek every five years. Home!
To be rich for two weeks and then back to the endless dirty floors
at night and the white security guard trying to feel her breasts as
she left the building. But for now, track-suited, tennis-shoed,
photo-gray sunglasses perched on her well-coiffed hair, she flew
the three thousand miles to the hot town, Port-of-Spain, with talk
in the streets about oil dollars.

"I can't stand the heat now, you know. I just break out in a
rash; that is why I can only spend a week or two in Trinidad."

This she said to herself, rehearsing her excuses for running
out of time and money at the end of two weeks. She'd head back
to Toronto, to starvation for the next six months and her back
bending over a mop, burning against the naked fluorescent
lights as payday crawled toward her.

They loved these new idiosyncrasies of theirs. Living "away,"
they adopted them like children, eager to forget their past. They
commented on them at every social gathering, rivalling each
other for outrageousness.

"I can't eat my bread white any more."

"I would miss the winter if I ever go back."

"Life is much better here, yes."

"Alberta better, it don't have a set of Black people. That is why
I like it there."

It was a sign of prosperity to lose the taste for homemade
bread and to feel like fainting in the heat.

"Everybody's prospering over here, things so cheap it's no
wonder."

It was a sign of improved class to live in a neighborhood without Black people.

The plane was full. Most, going home. For Carnival. They had

arrived at the airport with their entourages to see them off. Suit-
cases piled high, stuffed with bluejeans, pots, microwaves, bicy-
cles, toys, whiskey, electric saws, toasters. All the things which
were the reason for emigrating in the first place, piled up, ready
to go back. They had stood in line hardly looking at each other;
jostling to reach the baggage check. The line stretched for one
hundred meters, swelled by well-wishers, cousins with parcels for
home, letters for mothers, strangers who'd come to the airport
speculating that someone going home would take a suitcase for
them. Here in the baggage line they were half here and half
there, half reserved and half jubilant.

They hesitated before smiling with each other. They had
learned hesitancy here. They had learned caution. It wasn't
proper to yell each other's names across a street here. It wasn't
right to blare music out of windows for neighbors to hear.
Heaven knows enough policemen had come knocking on their
doors for that faux pas. Here, all that was courtesy became insult;
all that was human turned to signs of backwardness. They had
traded bold-facedness for high-rise apartments. Going home,
they sized up each other's clothing and hairstyles. Did they look
good enough to have lived here, did they look good enough to
return and not have someone notice that life here wasn't all that
rosy. Did they look good enough to inspire envy. They waited for
the doors of the plane to close behind them. They sensed their
ordinary cheerfulness rising to be released. They knew it would
be embarrassing to let go in the airport. Behind the doors they
would breathe out the relief of leaving Toronto, that uncomfortable name of a city, where their lives were tight and deceptive.
What a joy it would be to talk and have people answer, to settle
into gregariousness and frown on reserve.

Ayo, noticing them in the baggage line and now sitting among
them, was going home too. Not like them, she was really going
home. They were going back as tourists for Carnival. Ayo was going back for good, but not to Trinidad. She watched them half
with derision and half wanting to be one of them, to get caught
up in the Carnival spirit. She, like them, had been grown for export, like sugar cane and arrowroot, to go away, to have distaste
for staying. She had been taught that there was nothing worthwhile about staying: you should "go away and make something of

yourself," her family had said. It was everyone's dream to leave. Leaving was supposed to change class and station. "You could be something," they'd said. This something was based on the exceptions who had returned, M.D.s or LL.B.s in hand, and had been elevated to brown-skin status: not like the rest of them "nigger people." To be something meant that, no matter what else. The majority of those who had gone away worked hard all their lives, without letters behind their names, without changes in the texture and color of their skins, and had not returned, but had sent messages in letters and parcels and money, enriching the myth of easiness and prosperity in the metropole. On the other occasions, on which Ayo had returned, she had found the myth alive and kicking and had made enemies trying to dispel it. No one back home believed that things were not better out here and no one could be convinced of it. People home would look rather nastily and accuse her of liking good things for herself and not for others.

Shanti Narine, gold bracelets from the Orinico blazing on her arms, spat food into her napkin. It made her ill, thick and gluey. It was what white people ate and she wanted to get the taste for it, but it made her ill. It was the kind that they put on airplanes to confound immigrants and third world people. She was afraid to ask what it was. "Quiche," she heard someone in back say. It looked green to her, *bhaji*, spinach.

Ayo, sitting across the aisle, smiled toward her in sympathy, then looked away to allow her privacy. They never let up, did they! If you thought you had their lingo down, they gave you spinach quiche to remind you that you didn't know anything. Then they threw in something with whipped cream on it so you couldn't tell whether to eat it or shave your armpits with it. And so in the middle of the plane you would make a fool of yourself and they would be able to identify you and take away your passport when you arrived or give you a curt nod off the plane, when they kicked you out.

Shanti Narine toyed with her food, put whitener in her tea, gave up on the quiche. She was one-quarter of the way to Bermuda anyway and, as delicately as she could, she spat skin and pit of a grape into her hands, fat, bejewelled, yellow gold of the interior. She said that one day she was sitting in her father's shop in

Georgetown and that she noticed the Queen's face on the Canadian dollar. It was a face like a behind she said. Her sister Vidya had sent it, and looking at it she remembered her sister. Her sister had got the chance to go. Not she, because she was older and promised to a man in Berbice. She had only seen the man once, before their marriage. He was a fat little man with a giggle, like a young boy. She was disappointed by his look. She was expecting someone at least thinner. He saw the pout on her lips and said to her rudely, "Well, you not no door prize either!" and then to his own father, "Pa, I tell you the girl wouldn't like me." He stomped into the yard trampling on the zinnias which were hers, and the next time she saw him was on her wedding day.

Her little sister refused the little man's cousin and got away with it just because she was the baby. Her sister got everything that she wanted by behaving childishly. It never worked with Shanti. If she came whining to her father he always told her, "Girl, behave like a woman, eh!" But that's how Vidya got to Canada. She left to study and hoping to marry a white man. Both of which she had done. She had said that Guyana people weren't good enough for her, and her father agreed. But he had agreed to nothing for Shanti and stuck her in Berbice with a little fat man who raised goats and told her that she was lucky to get him because look how ugly she was. She'd run away from him countless times, except that her father would drag her back after a beating, saying that his days for minding big snake was over.

It wasn't that the little fat man was rotten to her, as much as he was boring. He said nothing, he did nothing, he just remained there like a lump which was plain, yet revolting. He was a sick yellow-green, somehow blending into the walls and the dirt. It would have been easy to ignore him, except that he was drab and she dreaded the odd night when he would roll over next to her, placing his clammy hands on her breasts. She lived with his drabness for fifteen years, bearing his five drab little children, until it was too much.

Now the flight attendant had her passport and everybody on the plane, she figured, must be in her business. Vidya had had to put up a bond for her to stay three weeks. Now she was being deported for staying a year. She should have gone to New York. Hell with Toronto! Who wanted to stay in their pissing tail place!

Leather-jacketed Tony Beard was going home until September to come back and continue at Wiilfred-Laurier doing business. He didn't like math, though who could, he always asked. But business was good to do, things were opening up, if you can't do business you're nothing in the Caribbean, for sure. He hugged his mother in the baggage line telling her that when he returned there'd be no problems, for sure. He'd cool his head and be more mature. She was proud of this light-brown child she'd made, thanked the lord that he had the good sense to go into business and love his mother at nineteen. In her prayers she beseeched that he marry a white girl, or better still marry into one of the French Creole families in Port-of-Spain. She'd denied herself and taken years of shit at the hospital. If anyone at home knew half the hell she had seen in Toronto since she left Piarco airport waving a white-gloved finger.

Her boy read a Toronto tabloid all the way to Antigua, lingering over the sunshine girl across from an article on the inferiority of Blacks. He agreed with the article, he thought. It didn't mean Blacks like him. It meant those "nigger people" his mother always referred to, whom he should "never, never have nothing to do with . . . all they do is drag you down," because he was light-skinned and educated and different. His eyes hovered on the sunshine girl again. His lips pouted and opened, sucking in air.

The Canadians on the plane were pleasant, Ayo had noticed, since the baggage line. They looked people in the face and smiled, much harder than the faked skin-teeth smile they usually wrung from their lips. It had been the hardest thing for her to get used to or to learn. That meaningless jerking of the mouth into a smile which did not spread to the eyes and was gone in a second. But now they were smiling broadly, trying to catch someone's attention. They had suddenly become interested in Black babies, patting and cooing at every last one on the plane. Their eyes became uncertain, a little frightened perhaps, yet condescending. Ayo noted their Robinson Crusoe eyes.

He was confiding stories about how many women he had fucked and how many more he could fuck to a friend whom he met on the plane. His breath wheezing between his teeth. He was anticipating the fêting and the drinking and the bacchanal. His cock was like a weapon, he said, like a hungry animal. As he stood in the aisle he patted it and stroked it, made sure that it was there by feeling for it every five minutes. He introduced it to women with a movement of his hand lifting it and smiling. It would get a good workout for Carnival. He would press up against them in the bands of revellers. He could rub up against at least seventy-five in one day during Carnival. This was how skillful Iron was.

The plane had been an hour in the air. It was midnight. This was the Tuesday overnight to Port-of-Spain. They'd get to Antigua at 4:00 a.m.; Barbados at 6:00; Port-of-Spain at 7:30. Ayo was exhausted just thinking about the long ride. She would pass the time watching, reading, ignoring the blasts of calypso coming from somebody's ghetto blaster. She hoped that the stewardess would tell whoever it was, to shut it off. Calypso music and clinking glasses raised such a din in the aircraft that Ayo felt more claustrophobic than usual. The honeyed, high, singing-talk of Trinidadian women spread through the huge cabin, aeolian in the artificial wind and counterpointed by the calypso. The men, voices staccato, emphasizing some spurious point about a Carnival past. The truth was that all of them were too tired to last the four days of drinking, fucking, dancing, and not sleeping that Carnival required; too old, not from age, but from living in another way, to remember their last Carnival in other than exaggerated phrases. The truth was that their living away so long had dulled their taste and criticalness about a good Carnival; had made the words a little stale and bitter in their mouths, dated in their delivery.

Fitzroy my ass! She was getting tight and sweet, downing a rum from the three little bottles of Bacardi she'd asked the stewardess for. It wasn't so much Fitzroy as it was how plain the thing was from the beginning. After this long, she was still vexed with herself for not seeing what was right in front of her face. Fitzroy was a rip-off artist plain and simple. No love or screw or anything good like that. A rip-off artist. He used to call her "Jazz! Jazz baby!" She hoped nobody home asked her about Fitzroy. She was going home to have a good time, not to remember fucking-Fitzroy. Fitzroy was an asshole and that is what got her vexed. Imagine, she getting messed up by an asshole. It wasn't good to be kind to people. Jasmine downed the second bottle of Bacardi and pushed her seat back, tapping her foot to the cabin full of calypso.

Ayo was going home. Not home to Trinidad, home to Grenada. Trinidad was actually home, but right this minute she could not identify with the affected happiness on the plane. She thought it was affected. She was a humorless woman, short and severe-looking. Too humorless to appreciate the fêting mood and the good cheer which enveloped the cabin, too humorless to join in. They were fooling themselves, what were they so happy about, she thought. Stretching her legs up the aisle, she had discovered a friend, Diana, also going home. Diana had exclaimed in that long melodic woman-talk way, asking her if she was crazy not to be going to Trinidad for Carnival, when it was so close to Grenada. She'd smiled in a superior way, saying that she didn't know what Trinidadians had to be happy about. She couldn't keep it up, she said. Diana agreed weakly saying, "But, you know how it is girl." They didn't talk about why she was going to Grenada. Ayo skirted the issue, expecting the usual disapproval about the revolution. She didn't want to fight about politics. In this Carnival atmosphere it would be ridiculous to explain history. And besides, they were too big island/small island conscious to appreciate what a little place like Grenada could do. She'd be damned if she'd explain herself to this backward set of people anyway. They didn't say anything when Gairy the dictator was there, but all of a sudden now they were up in arms. All they could think about was what this and that cost. Well it had made her sick living in Toronto. All people ever thought about was how much more they could get and take. With people dying all over the world, it was just sick, sick, sick. And don't talk about the rip-offs! How could she explain to these people that they were a bunch of idiots. They were so grateful for living away, when it was their sweat! . . . as if they didn't work! . . . as if the whole damn world wasn't built on slavery! Well if they were too damn stupid to see that, let them go right ahead. What the hell did they have to be so happy about? She wasn't no Trinidadian with them. She had decided and they had decided. She was going to Grenada and they were going to Trinidad. That was it. She begged off, walking back to her seat next to Shanti, and sat down, pouring more gin into her glass, wishing that they would get to Barbados fast so that the Trinidadians would leave.

They were becoming more and more uninhibited, the music

louder, the laughter more infectious and elongated. Canadian anonymity was giving way to Trinidadian familiarity. The "oh jesus" and the "oh Gord darlings" were leaking out, spreading over the plane, restored to their eclectic meanings—"hell, I haven't seen you in a long time," "it's good to see you," "I love you," "you must be joking," "forgive me," "don't do that," and at least one hundred others. Now, over Bermuda, faces slackened by alcohol and distance from Canada, they relaxed into easiness. The accents returned, minding to keep that hint of "away" to impress friends at home. The Canadians on the plane were forgotten. They were too nervous to complain about the noise anyway. Not the revelers. Going home, they became more and more belligerent. They felt that they owned the airspace, the skies going south. Coming north maybe, the Canadians could tell them what to do, but not going home. They blared the music even louder and danced in the aisles. Even as the lights dimmed for sleep the two hours before Antigua, a sizeable, hard-core group carried the party on.

The small airport at Antigua lit up as they trooped off the plane. The tri-star, Trinidadians called it. They sailed on it as if it were not an ordinary plane and they boasted about it as if no one else ever sat in one. The boasting had become boisterous by Canadian standards. The entire group going home, more confident and assured.

Unsuspecting Antiguans slept through the invasion of huge tape recorders, walkmans, jheri curls, crepe soles (now called running shoes), digital watches, male sacks, pot bellies, Carnival, kaiso, intent arguments about american commodity items, who had what and what was more expensive than what, how much money who had, how much scotch cost and who didn't drink rum anymore, grand charges about the coming parties at the public service association and, lastly, insults at how small the Antigua airport was compared to Piarco and Toronto.

4:00 A.M. The rush of excitement came and left Antigua like a lone Carnival band in Princess Town.

The first gust of hot sea air had washed their faces of nostalgia. All the years of talking about going home, promising not to live in Canada forever, swearing that they couldn't possibly die there, hating the cold and cussing the winter days, vanished. All the years of reminiscing about the food and the smells and the hang-outs and the streets and the warmth of people, all the "only five years more," "only until I get a diploma," "only until I save a little money," all the "I could never live in this place," faded. They were struck instead by ambiguity as they stepped off the plane at Piarco. Love which was not love because it could not center itself on a shape, a piece of land. Love which only recollected gesture and not movement, event and not time. They glimpsed, half-understood, half-seen, themselves. Wrapped in the gauze of hot sea air, they were silent momentarily. Useless as cash crop. Then, waving like sugar cane stalks in a breeze, they remembered, Carnival.

At 5:00 A.M. Ayo had left them thankfully, in Barbados, kissing Diana good-bye.

In the airport, waiting the three-hour wait to St. Vincent, she'd met a Guyanese man, Phillip Arno, and they talked about Burn-ham and capitalism. The man said that he was now a capitalist but had been a socialist once and she would soon find out about these islands. He said that he had been to Tanzania and Somalia and it was the very Burnham government that had sent him and, in every case, it was greed that fucked up the place. He had worked and worked and then they had him watched and threat-ened him and they turned the Guyanese national service, that he'd helped to set up, into a brothel. The ujaama villages never worked in Tanzania.

"Mental manual division of labor," she threw back in her best new marxist voice.

"Mental manual what? Greed!" he returned.

He was going to St. Lucia, anyway. His import-export business took him island-hopping. His neck was stiff from boarding houses. She was very interesting. He wished that he was going the same way.

"What was your name again?" he asked.

Ayo wondered why Caribbean men talked so incessantly and, getting a little carried away, suspected that he was an agent pumping her for information. After all, he used to be in the Guyanese army and had helped to set up the national service. She took his card. Asked him who he knew in Guyana.

He said that he wished the revolution well.

She doubted it.

He had made so much money in Brazil, importing and exporting, he was getting fat, he said. He'd look her up when he came.

She hoped not.

Ayo continued her journey to Grenada. She was going to a new home. Home had already begun, even though she didn't like Barbados. In the three-hour wait for the sun and the plane to St. Vincent, then Grenada, a short drizzle broke out in purple breaths of rain over Bridgetown. The sun coming up between the rain convinced her that she was home.

She'd always thought that it was stupid to die. She knew that the moment it happened, it would be like a shrug of the shoulder. Now it was confirmed. Flying over the Caribbean sea, in the LIAT, at eight in the morning, she saw a tiny sailboat below and the ocean purple all around it. If you just jumped out, you could remain alive for quite a while. Enough time to shrug, to find out how awkward and stupid the idea was.

A Brazilian woman, tall, slender, and brown, walking with a cane, smoked Marlboros, and a German man next to her read *The Advocate*. There was wealth in the woman's movements, in the man's heavy stomach. And all of it could plop next to the boat in the purple ocean. Ayo noticed tiny cockroaches in the fifteen-seater, and fifteen passengers. He moved again, the German bush jacket who got on board with the Brazilian woman, he was making her dizzy. The plane was small and treacherous enough without him moving around. This was the face, though. Distinct, proprietary. Yes, this was the real face of things. The bursting stomach, cheeks and bush jacket and the rich-looking Brazilian woman. It took years in the Indies to do this, Ayo imagined, to fill out his body so that it looked as greedy as he was. His mouth came to resemble a gesture of discontent at these people. It was right there, so that he didn't have to summon up the feeling anymore, just use his face as it was. Turn it toward the offending one or simply walk down a street. Everyone would get the message. Sometimes the whole damn island would get it, when his face appeared in the commerce section of the local newspaper or on the front page, a caption reading, "The executive manager of Geest has said that the banana industry in St. Vincent is in crisis, unless farmers produce a better quality product." Spread out on the plane, he waited to get there, to show them his face.

Ayo's stomach heaved on the take-off from St. Vincent. Would they never get to Grenada, she wondered. She asked the stewardess for a cup of coffee instead of the orange juice, thinking that it would help. The Trinidadians had kept her awake until Barbados. The morning sky, the purple ocean, had buoyed her into thinking that she was not tired or airsick. Besides, the work ahead of her would never tolerate feebleness. She was going home to own some place, before she died. She was determined to end the ambiguity. What had she said for years. When the revolution comes, I'm going to be there.

The coffee made her stomach worse. She had to go to the toilet. She got up, asked the man beside her to move, and went toward the rear of the little plane. The door to the toilet would not close, and when she turned in the little space there was an exit door which made up one of the walls of the rusty little plane. She jerked back in dismay. One slip of the hand while trying not to sit on the seat of the commode and you'd be out of the airplane, somewhere between the sky and the Grenadines. Back in her seat again, through the window, there was one of the islands that she was going to. She wished that they would land. It was the end of the rainy season but everything was still a dark green, except the sea which was aqua in some places and navy blue in others.

Through the window she saw the island. She could see a few houses dotted between the bush. It looked like a quiet place. There. Now customs, an hour's drive, and a small room to sleep.

The Parade Ends

Reinaldo Arenas

For Lázaro Gómez, witness

Now she's escaping me. She's losing me again in this sea of legs
so tightly packed that they join together, in this jumble of rags
and compressed bodies, over puddles of piss, of shit, of mud, between bare feet that sink in that flattened paste of excrement.
I'm looking for her, I keep looking for her as if she were (as in
fact she is) my only salvation. But, the bitch, she's slipping away
again. There she goes, miraculously making her way, sliding between muddy shoes, between bodies that can't even fall over,
though they're fainting (they're jammed so tightly against one
another), through the crying, the piss, getting away from me with
each wriggle, while avoiding at the same time, thanks to I don't
know what incredible intuition, the fatal footfall. My life depends
on you, my life depends on you, I say to her, crawling along too,
like her. And I pursue her, I keep pursuing her in the shit and
the mud, laboriously and mechanically pushing aside bellies,
asses, feet, arms, thighs, a whole amalgam of stinking flesh and
bones, a whole arsenal of vociferating lumps that move, that
want, like me, to walk around, change places, turn, and that only
cause contractions, wiggling, stretching, convulsions which don't
manage to cut the knot, take a step, break into a run, to show
some real movement, something that really gets going, advances,
leaving everyone trapped in one big spiderweb which stretches

out on one side, contracts here, rises over there, but doesn't manage to break loose anywhere. So they draw back and push forward, back and forth, kneeing and kicking, now raising their arms, their heads, their noses, everything to the sky in order to breathe, to see something other than the compression of their own stinking bodies. But I'm following, I haven't lost sight of her yet and I'm following, pushing these bodies aside, crawling, kicked and cursed, but without giving up, pursuing her. For there (for with her), I say to myself, goes my life . . . Life, above all, life in spite of everything, life however it is, even without anything, even without you (and in spite of you) amid the din that rises now, amid the shrieks and the songs, for they're singing, singing again, and no less than the national anthem. Life, now, while I pursue you over the excrement to the sound of the notes (or shouts) of the national anthem, holding you as justification and refuge, as an immediate solution, as sustenance, the rest (what is the rest?) we'll see about later. Now only that lizard matters to me, that damned lizard that's hiding from me again, sly and covered with excrement, between the thousands and thousands of feet which are also sinking in the shit. *Life* . . . I was, again, like so many years ago already, at that extreme where life is not so much as a useless and humiliating repetition, but only the incessant memory of that repetition, which, in the beginning, was also a repetition, I was at that point, at that final place, at that extreme, where the act of being doesn't even matter, or rather it isn't really certain that it's true. So, standing, or better yet, bent over, since the garret didn't allow him to straighten out completely, he contemplated inside that old room of ancient hotel come to ruin and hence inhabited by people like him or even worse—vociferating creatures with no other concept nor principle nor dream but to be able, at all costs, and in spite of everything, to survive, that is to say, not to die of hunger right away—, he was contemplating, staring in that position, without moving, not at the past nor the future, both not only dark but illusory, he was staring, in short, at the impoverished piece of improvised stairway that led "on high," that is to say to the narrow dormer where he had to walk not bent over, but on all fours so as not to smash his head against the ceiling. That's how he was, between the front wall that faced the hallway and the other wall that faced the other wall of the other building. Now he advanced a little more and his eyes met flush with his eyes, with his figure reflected in the mirror incrusted (screwed) right in the exit door of the hall, which was always being kept temporarily closed. He wasn't that one then, now he was this one. He wasn't running through the savannahs or grasslands anymore. He was running, sometimes, through the hysterical tumult, trying to catch a crowded bus or to get in line for bread or yogurt. So, making an effort, he separated himself from his image—this one for now—, recrossed the cubicle, his kingdom, in two steps, sat down on a seat, also improvised thanks to a combination of poverty and necessity, a kind of bench with a parody of a pillow or cushion covering it. Then, before even thinking about a solution, before he could even think about how to think of a solution, the roar of a wave crashed violently, the scream, the howl of a boy (it had to be called something), the inordinate noise of a television, some radios, and, besides, of someone knocking at the closed door of the elevator, and another who, from a window, was calling in endlessly repeated shouts to somebody who obviously isn't there, or who's deaf, or doesn't want to answer, or died, finally his neighbors, people just like him, made him forget that which, like a puff of air, had crossed his imagination, had attempted to conceive—what was it, what was it—. And, hearing that kind of incessant paraphernalia, an enormous sensation of calm invaded him, a unanimous sensation of renunciation, of impotence, overwhelmed him, as always, since years ago, in a sort of stupor, of inertia, of absolute abandon, of mortal (hope?) grief, a sensation of feeling beyond all resistance, all competition, all vital possibility, a security (a rest, a weariness) of absolute death, of death definitive and complete, yes, if it weren't that in spite of everything he had a friend, and, therefore, he was still breathing ... But with difficulty, with quite a bit of difficulty, raising and spreading out his hands, only in that way was he able to take in a little of that contaminated and absolutely stinking air and to continue, that is to dive again into the furor and the sweating bodies, crawling once again through the dirt, pushing aside legs, humps, feet, in order to reach where he was, because he was certain that he was there, naturally, in that tumult, someplace in that tumult forming a part of the tumult; that's why he was pushing, raising

his head, breathing, searching, and continuing to brush aside
bodies, bundles, without excusing himself, who was going to say
"excuse me" in such a place?, and he continued, calling out to
him sometimes, trying to make himself heard in the midst of that
din. And the terrible thing was that with each moment it was becoming more difficult to go on. More were coming, more people
kept arriving, more people who were jumping the fence (the
gate had already been closed) and entering; they were entering
however they could, punching, kicking. What an uproar, what an
uproar. In the middle of the clamor and the dust and the shooting they kept advancing, climbing up the fence and jumping; old
people, pregnant women, babies, kids; especially kids, all of them
wanting to reach the wire fence, while the group of soldiers was
getting thicker. And they kept arriving, police, militia, men in
uniform or in disguise, disguised as civilians, preventing the others—the crowd—from approaching the fence. It was no longer a
cordon, but a triple cordon, heavily armed. Bursts from machine
guns were heard now and shouts of "Stop right there, you son of
a bitch!" and again the clamor and the howling of those who,
right there before their very eyes, were being ripped open by machine-gun fire, without having been able to jump the fence, without even having been able to touch it, without having been able
to make it. Immediately, numerous men (military and civilian)
hurriedly getting out of their Alfa Romeos, were dragging the
corpses to their vehicles and departing hastily down Fifth Avenue. But now, not only were they running a risk out there, the
inflamed mob, who at all costs wanted to get past the cordon (the
cordons) and enter, but those inside too were being machine-
gunned. Somebody, one of the top brass, a *mayimbe*, a *pincho*,
pulled up abruptly before the fence, and, beside himself, began
shooting at them. In the midst of an infernal roar, the mass re-
treated without being able to retreat, they pressed even more
tightly together, they hid their heads behind each other, they
backed up as if trying to climb inside themselves, and whoever
fell, having been hit by a shot, or simply having slipped, couldn't
catch himself anymore, his last sight would be the thousands and
thousands of feet in a circular stampede, stepping on him and
returning to step on him again. "The anthem, the anthem,"
someone shouted. And suddenly, only a single unanimous and

thundering voice came out of the immense, besieged multitude,
a single song, loud, coughed up, out of tune, extraordinary, crossing the fence and filling the night. Ridiculous, ridiculous, he was
saying to himself, but for a moment he interrupted his search, he
stopped, ridiculous, ridiculous, he was saying to himself, that anthem again, ridiculous, ridiculous, but he was crying . . . Horrible, horrible, because everything was horrible, terrifying,
anew, again, always; but worse, but worse now, because now he
couldn't give himself the luxury, as then, of wasting time, his
time. So, bent over in his low and narrow hole, he was reviewing,
again reviewing all the time lived, all the time lost, and he was
stopping there once again, at the improvised and urgent stairway, beneath the roof, also improvised and urgent, by the urgent
and improvised table (the cover of a tank over a barrel), improvised, improvised, improvised, everything improvised, and,
what's more, he himself, everyone always improvising and accepting. Hearing the improvised and endless speeches; living in an
improvised poverty where even the terror that he was suffering
today, tomorrow, provisionally, would be substituted by another,
reinforced, renovated, augmented, and so on, by improvisation.
Provisionally suffering improvised laws that suddenly fomented
crimes instead of reducing them; suffering improvised rages
which naturally assailed him and those who were living like him,
on the margins, in a cloud, in another world, that is in this improvised 3' × 4' room over an improvised garret, alone . . . To
leave for the street, to go down the garbage-strewn stairs (the elevator never worked), to reach the street, what for? . . . To leave
was to declare (one more time) that there was no exit. To leave was
to know that it was impossible to go anywhere. To leave was to
risk that they would ask him for identification, information, and,
in spite of carrying on him (as he always carried) all the calami-
ties of the system: identity card, union card, worker's card, obligatory military service card, CDR card, in short, in spite of going
like a noble and tame beast, well branded, with all of the marks
with which his owner obligatorily stamped him, in spite of everything, to leave was to run the risk of "falling," of "shining" badly
in the eyes of a cop, who could designate him (out of moral conviction) as a *suspicious character, unclear, unstable, untrustworthy,*
and without further legal procedure, to end up in a cell, as had

happened to him already on several occasions. Besides, he knew
what that meant. On the other hand, what a spectacle he was going to see if he went out, if not the anatomy of his own sadness,
the overwhelming spectacle of a city in collapse, the taciturn figures, timid or aggressive, hungry and desperate, and, of course,
hunted. Figures, besides, now alien to dialogue, to intimacy, to
any possibility of communication, ready, simply (vitally), to
snatch his wallet, tear off his watch, tear the glasses right off his
face, in the event that he committed the imprudence of going
out to the street with them on, and that's all, to run off through
the deteriorating panorama. Besides, he, and here was his triumph, his means of escape, his hope, was not completely certain
that he would be (that he would feel) absolutely alone ... And
with that hope, with that good fortune, he remained, just as he
was: one foot on the improvised stairway, his face fading already
before the broken-down mirror, his head bent so as not to bump
into the ceiling of the garret, serene, still, waiting, since he was
sure that, from one moment to the next, like every morning, yes,
it had to be so, his friend would arrive. Finally, he took a step
through the improvised room and sat down in the improvised
seat. But where had he gone, where was he, where can he be, but
you have to go on, you have to keep advancing, you have to find
him somewhere, up on the roofs, up a tree, he can't have vanished, he has to be in this chaos, in this immense mob which is
getting thicker now, more hysterical, grabbing hold of somebody, at last, throwing him in the air and catching him again only
to keep throwing him, it's a police infiltrator, they say, who was
trying to take the Peruvian flag down from the flag pole. And
now thousands of arms, of closed fists, of desperate people,
pounce on him, swinging him around. "Lynch him, execute him,
tear him to pieces," they shout, and the man disappears and ap-
pears and disappears again, swallowed by that desperate sea until
he's hurled outside the fence, where the shooting continues,
now at the trees, in the air, at the cars, which, from a considerable distance and at great speeds, try to break through the barriers and get in. I go up to where the furor is most intense, I
scrutinize, I push, I keep looking around among the desperate
faces, among those who sleep standing up ... But nothing, but
nothing, I don't see you, although I know, I know very well that

you're someplace nearby, here, not far from me, looking for me, too. We are here, we are here, although we haven't been able to find each other yet, amid the danger and the shooting, amid the stench that keeps getting more intolerable, and the rioting, and the punches, and the quarreling, the fights which desperation and hunger and this overcrowding provoke, but at least able then, now, right now, to scream, to scream ... To get out, to get out, that was the question. Before it had been to join up, to liberate, to rise up, to hide, to emancipate ourselves, to gain independence, but now none of that was possible anymore, not because it had succeeded or it wasn't necessary, but rather because now it wasn't even possible to conceive of those ideas out loud, nor even in a whisper, it was pressing, and so we two keep talking, while we walk fearfully along the Malecón, all but deserted, although it isn't even 10 o'clock at night yet. The problem isn't to say "we've got to get out," I know that as well as you, the other one, his friend, was saying to him. The problem, the question, is how to leave here. Yes, we were saying, how to leave. On one or two inner tubes from a truck, you say, with a canvas on top and a pair of oars. To launch ourselves to sea. There's no other escape. It's true, it's true, I was saying. There's no other solution. I, you say, can get the inner tubes and the canvas. You have to keep them in your room. My family mustn't find out anything. But that's not the hardest part, you were saying. There's the other. The surveillance. There's surveillance everywhere, you know, one can't even approach the beach at night. The most difficult thing is, precisely, to reach the coast with two tubes, and food and some bottles of water. Yes, I was saying. That's right. First we have to go over the terrain, to study it, to go without anything, to see which is the best spot. I've heard it's Pinar del Río, you were saying. At least the current is strongest there, it can carry us, bring us way out. Some boat will pick us up. They have to pick us up, once at sea somebody will spot us, and pick us up. But listen, I say, it's possible that a Russian ship, or Chinese or Cuban could pick us up and we'll return again, not here, to the Malecón, to the streets, but to jail ... They're giving five years now for what they call illegal exits, you say. And where are the legal ones? I was asking. Could we go if we wanted to, could we do it in peace, like others do it anywhere else in the world, or almost anywhere? Of

course not, you were saying. But them, they're the ones who
make the laws here and the ones who put us in jail. That's true, I
said. Not only is there the problem of making it to the sea but
also to the other side of the sea. To make it, you say, to make it
somehow. Without their finding out that we're planning to leave.
Them, them, I was saying. But for all that they keep watch, they
can't keep track of everything; they can't, even if they live only
for that, to watch over us, to check us at every moment, incessantly. Maybe you're right, you said. And as we were returning (it
was best not to talk about it in the room) we finished rounding
out the plan, the escape, the possibility, the attempt, but now
that clever one has disappeared again, she's slipped away, sliding
beneath the mud and excrement. Changing color, she's escaped
me again. A shriek is heard in the crowd. A woman jumps hysterically as she puts her hands on her thighs. "An animal, an animal," she says, "an animal's gotten in here." And she keeps
jumping up and down. Until she jumps out of her skirt. There
she goes, fleeing again, changing color and trying to hide herself, the bitch, among the muddy shoes, bare feet, climbing up a
thigh, leaping to a back, now sliding between stacks of sweaty
necks, over a mob which falls back, forming a single mass on the
ground. I pass over them too, I step on the face of somebody (a
woman, a child, an old man, I don't know) without strength left
to complain, and I follow, now crouched down, on all fours,
sometimes raising an immense clamor of protests, kicked and
shoved in turn, but watching her, following her, without losing
sight, now up close . . . But they, in effect, yes, they were control-
ling everything, they did keep watch over everything, they did
hear everything. They had foreseen everything. That's why they
arrived so early. I came down from the garret hastily, thinking it
was you. It was they. In that moment everything happened, happens, as if it had already happened. I had thought about it so
many times (I had expected it), had calculated what could happen, so that now, when they enter, while they say to me, "Don't
move. You're under arrest," and begin to search, I don't know,
really, I don't know if everything is taking place in this instant or
if it already took place, or if it's always taking place. Since it's
such a miniature space, they don't have to spend much time
searching. Two of them turn everything over up above in the gar-

ret, one stays with me, guarding me; the others feel around under the cushions, above the false roof, in the improvised closet.
There they are, of course, the tires, the canvas, and something
that I didn't even know you'd been able to get hold of (and now,
worst of all), a compass. Quickly and minutely the search is concluded, in my presence, but without taking me into account. Papers, letters, books, the inner tubes, the canvas, and, of course,
the compass, which I didn't even know that you had hidden in
the closet, everything in these moments is an object, motive,
body of the crime, cause for suspicion, for guilt. A photograph, a
foreign sweater, arguments, for them convincing, too, parts of
the same crime. Finally, they order me to take off my shoes, they
take my footprint, they command me to get dressed completely
again. "Let's go," one of them says to me, while he puts a hand at
the back of my neck. So we leave. The hall is completely deserted
now, although I know that they're all there, behind doors
opened a crack, fearful, watching . . . A woman who had her eye
knocked out by a stone, a man whose arm was crippled by a bullet, another with his swollen legs bursting, another woman who is
squeezing her belly, shouting that she doesn't want to have a
baby, because if she does, they'll take her out of here, another
man who crawls along blindly because he lost his contact lenses.
"Quiet, quiet, let's see if we can get the 'Voice of America.' "
Shouts and more shouts calling for silence, but nobody keeps
quiet, everybody has something to say, something to suggest,
some solution, some complaint, some urgent business. "Let the
Ambassador speak, let the Ambassador speak." But nobody is listening, everyone wants to be heard. "We're going to die of
hunger, we're going to die of hunger. These sons of bitches want
to starve us to death." Shouts and more shouts, me, too, shouting, yelling for you, pushing aside people more furious every moment, punching and moving forward, through the excrement,
the urine, the crippled bodies and the uproar (outside, the
shooting, again the shooting), looking for you . . . Nighttime, can
it be night? Who can tell if it's night or day now . . . Nighttime,
nighttime, it's nighttime. Now it's always nighttime. In the middle of this medieval tunnel and with an enormous light bulb,
which is never turned off, above my head, of course it must be
night all the time. Everyone reduced to the same uniform, the

same shaved head, the same shout for the count-off three times a day. A day? Or a night? At least, if I could reach the window with its three sets of bars, I would know what it really is now, night, day, but in order to get near there you have to belong to the "leadership," to be one of the "pretty boys." Little by little they pass the time, it passes, or we pass, I am passing. It's not that I'm getting used to it, nor getting adapted, nor accepting it, but I go on surviving. Luckily, in the last visit you managed to bring in some books. Light is not lacking here. Silence, silence, yes, that's something that I almost can't remember. But the problem, you tell me, consists of bearing it, of surviving, of waiting. Luckily they didn't grab me in the room. At least I can bring you a few things. Here are some corn meal cakes, cookies, sugar, and more books. Time passes, time passes, you say. Time, I say, it passes? . . . It passes knowing that outside there are streets, trees, people with colorful clothing, and the sea. The visit ends. We say good-bye. To enter. Here's the worst moment. When in a blue line, scalped and escorted, we enter the tunnel, a long, thin stone vault which brings us, once again, to the circular cave that endlessly oozes bugs, mold, urine, those fumes, those fumes of accumulating, overflowing excrement, and that din, that constant shouting of the prisoners, that beating on the bunks and walls, that impotence, that caged up violence which has to get out somehow, to manifest itself, to explode. If, at least, I think, barricaded in the last bunk, they would kill each other in silence. But that din, that deafening and monotonous stamping, that cackling, that jargon which you have to pick up whether you want to or not, pick it up or perish. Ah, if somebody were interested in my soul, if somebody loved it forever, maybe, in exchange for it . . . But it's absolutely impossible to continue thinking, with that uproar, with that uproar which rises now and attacks . . . As if tormented by a strange plague, the trees have suddenly lost all their leaves, one at a time, like lightning, they've been torn off and devoured. Now, with their fingernails, with pieces of wire, kicking with their heels, everyone begins to tear the bark from the trunks; the roots, the grass, too, disappear. "Whoever has a piece of bread hidden away is risking his life," I hear somebody say. That's why I follow you, that's why, and even more than that. You are my goal, my salvation, my hope, my incentive, my love, my great, my only

real true love. And now, once again you provoke an immense
clamor when you climb into somebody's pants who had been
sleeping on his feet, propped up by the crowd. "A buggering
lizard," they shout, since in spite of everything, or because of
everything, they keep a sense of humor. "No, it's queer," retorted
someone else, "I scared it off just when it was coming up to my
fly." "Maybe it's a real man," a woman is saying now, "since it
went up my dress." "Grab it, grab it, it's fresh meat." And at the
shout of that password, everybody springs at you. Letting out a
howl, I cross over their heads. I won't let them, I won't let them, I
won't let the others get you, even if they kill me (for now I see
their hungry, delirious, crazy faces looking at me furiously), I
keep on pushing them, making my way, pursuing you. "Food,
food." The voice of alarm sounds. Screaming. Now everyone, forgetting about you, is trying to reach the fence where they, the police, so they say, are beginning to put little cardboard boxes with
food rations along the fence. The chaos increases by the instant,
for all that some people try to impose order. We hear that they're
only passing out eight hundred little boxes for the ten thousand
or so of us who are here. Punches, rioting again, shouting, for
the first time they've saved me, they've saved us, you and me, so
that now, with greater zeal, having an open field, I pursue you. I
reach, at last I reach the place again that I hate so much, and yet
long for: the improvised room. Now it all looks so dazzling. The
deteriorating and unpainted walls shine; the wall of the other
building seems like marble to me. I touch these improvised seats,
this improvised stairway; all the rustic and scarce furnishings that
surround me are, for me, something new that I look at, touch, I
could say with a certain love. Five years in that cave, you say to
me. Of course everything must seem to shine like new to you.
And you also tell me what you suffered: investigations, persecu-
tions, who knows what, but now we've got to forget everything
and go on, you say. Now we'll be watched even more carefully, I
say. That's why, you say, the best thing is to forget about escaping
for a while. Pretend that you're adapting and don't say anything
to anybody. Whenever you've got to get something off your chest,
talk only to me. To the rest, not a word. All of this happened to
us for not being cautious. Yes, I say, although I never spoke to
anybody about the plan. But they're very cunning, you say, more

than you can imagine. They may not have developed the production of shoes, food, or transportation, but as for persecution, they're first class. Don't forget it . . . I don't forget it, I don't forget it, how am I going to forget it . . . They're out there, some in uniform, others in civilian clothes, all armed, beating, running down, assassinating, those who, crouched in the trees, on the water tanks, on the empty houses, are trying to get closer, to make it to where we are. And now they, out there, put the boxes of food (a hard-boiled egg, a handful of rice) at their feet, on the other side of the fence. They're calm, looking at us here inside. When one of us stretches out an arm to take a box, they lift their feet and squash his hand, or they give him a smart kick in the chest. If somebody screams, then their laughter is louder, much louder than the screams. Others, more sadistic, or more refined, wait for one of us to take a box and when he's already bringing it inside, they beat him until his arm breaks. And fresh laughter is heard again. But you're neither among those who, pushing and kicking, have reached the fence, nor among those who now pull back their crushed and empty hands. Maybe you're up above, on top of the roof of the building, or inside, right in the building, with the Ambassador himself, tending the gravely wounded or the women with newborns, or the old. Yes, sure, that's where I should have gone first, that's why, because you're with the sick, or, sure, sick yourself, gravely ill, that's the reason why I haven't been able to find you. If not for that, you, sooner than I, would have found me. Back, back, to go back, to return through the shoving and kicking, to get back, to enter the building no matter how, back, back . . . I had reached it, I had reached that moment in which life not only lacks any meaning, but, moreover, we don't even ask ourselves if it ever had one, I say, referring to myself, of course. In a tone no less tragic for its grandiloquence, and in the middle of this dilapidated room. And I go on: because it's not even possible to be sad anymore. Even sadness itself is abolished by the noise, by the constant eruption of the cockroaches, the siren of the patrol cars, by the what will I eat today, what will I eat tomorrow. Yes, even sadness requires its space, at least, a little silence, a place where it can be kept, exhibited, taken out for an airing. In hell it isn't even possible to be sad. You simply live (you die) day by day, I say, I said. And you answered me: write, write all of this down, begin to write everything that you're suffering, starting right now, and you'll feel better. Really, I was thinking of doing that for a long time already, but what for? For you, for yourself, for the two of us, you say. And that's just how it is. Deliriously, angrily, constantly and in minute detail, I go on giving vent to my fear, my fury, my resentment, my hatred, my failure, our failure, our impotence, all the humiliations, swindles, tricks, and finally, simply, the punches, kicks, the constant harassment. Everything, everything. All the terror: on paper, on the white sheet, once filled, carefully hidden above the false roof of the garret, in the dictionaries, or behind the window: my revenge, my revenge. My triumph. *Jail to rot, jail to be shipwrecked and never to be able to float away, jail to give up, forgetting, not even conceiving that the sea existed, and, much less, the possibility of crossing it* . . . My triumph, my triumph, my revenge. Walks down streets that burst, since the pipes can't hold any more, between buildings you have to avoid so that they won't come down on top of you, between frowning faces that scrutinize and sentence us, between closed businesses, closed markets, closed theaters, closed parks, closed cafés, sometimes displaying signs (justifications) already dusty. CLOSED FOR RENOVATION, CLOSED FOR REPAIRS. What kind of repairs? When will the so-called repairs, the so-called renovation, be finished? When, at least, will they begin? Closed, closed, closed. Everything closed . . . I arrive, I open the innumerable padlocks, I go running up the improvised stairway. Here she is, waiting for me. I uncover her, pulling back the canvas, and I contemplate her dusty and cold dimensions. I wipe off the dust and run my hand over her again. With light strokes of the hand I clean her back, her base, her sides. I sit down, desperate, happy, at her side, before her, I move my hands over her keyboard, and, quickly, everything is set in motion. The ta ta, the ringing, the music begins, little by little, then more quickly, now at full speed. Walls, trees, streets, cathedrals, faces and beaches, cells, minicells, large cells, starry night, bare feet, pines, clouds, hundreds, thousands, a million parakeets, stools and a climbing vine, everything approaches, everything arrives, all are coming. The walls expand, the roof disappears, and, naturally, you are floating, floating, floating, torn up, dragged along, elevated, carried, transported, memorialized, saved, on altars, and, by that minus-

cule and constant cadence, by that music, by that incessant ta
ta ... My revenge, my revenge. My triumph ... Bodies armored
in excrement, children sinking in excrement, hands that search in
shit, turning it over and over. Hands and more hands, round,
thin, plump, bony, face up, face down, joined, spread out, clos-
ing into fists, scratching heads, testicles, arms, backs, clapping,
rising up, crawling, falling faint, black, yellow, brown, white,
transparent, tightly clenched and pale from days and days of
hunger, swollen, mangled, mutilated by the beating when they
tried to get hold of a little box of rations on the other side of the
fence, where the patrol cars are now circling constantly, carrying
loudspeakers that don't stop blaring menacingly for an instant.
"Anyone who wishes to take refuge with the Cuban authorities
may do so and return to his home." And day and night, day and
night, the shooting, the thirst, the threats, the hunger, the beat-
ings. And now, suddenly, the rainstorm, the torrent of rain, paci-
fying the dust, fusing trees, automobiles, country homes, and
military units, soldiers stationed, barricaded, in a state of alert all
around us ... The typical spring shower, unexpected, torrential.
Some people try to protect themselves with their hands; others,
lowering their heads, huddle up, wanting to crouch down, to
take shelter inside themselves. Many who sleep, continue sleeping, while the water runs over their foreheads, their faces, their
closed eyes, without managing to wake them up. Others attempt
to bend down, to protect themselves underneath the rest, causing an avalanche of protest, of remonstrances, and some kick or
other shot out at random. I take advantage of the confusion, the
state of near calm, of immobile stacking which the shower is causing in order to make my way, scrutinizing the drenched faces, the
contracted and drenched bodies, shaken by contractions and
trembling, and I go on, I go on examining them, looking at
them, deciphering the streaming faces, searching for you. I know
that you're around here somewhere, one step away from me, perhaps, that you must be here. "They want to break us through
hunger, illness, terror, this storm is surely their doing too, one of
their tricks," says a woman, gone mad in the downpour, as she
makes signs, crosses in the air and strange gestures ... And I return, full of fuel, arguments, fear. I run, I go up the sordid stairway, I open the innumerable padlocks. Burning, I climb up to

the improvised garret. My treasure, my treasure. I look for my treasure which I'm going to enlarge right now, my revenge, my triumph which has gone on growing thicker, and now it's not one, not ten, nor a hundred pages, but hundreds. Hundreds of sheets stolen from sleep, from terror, from rest, from fear, slugged out in the heat, in the noise of the streets, of the neighbors; won, striking out against the mosquitos, against the pestilential vapor (vapors) that rises, that falls, that arrives from every floor, from everywhere. Thousands of sheets won from the shrieks of sinister infants who seem to have settled a tacit accord to erupt in their demonical uproar whenever I sit down before the keyboard. Pages and more pages conquered with furious blows of the fist, the feet, the head, struggling furiously against television, record players, portable radios, cars without mufflers, shrieks, leaps, the scraping of pots, inopportune visits, figures, bodies, almost unavoidable, constant blackouts . . . Tapping, tapping in the darkness, quickly, quickly, each moment more quickly, tapping, tapping, before they return, quickly, quickly, triumphantly, triumphantly, in the darkness . . . And new disturbances, lights, bulbs, signal flares, that break out now on all sides, illuminating Fifth Avenue, the whole area, in such a way that it's as if it were high noon. Somebody, the driver of a rented Chevy has managed to break through the barriers, the three cordons, and has just smashed into the Ambassador's own car, which had been standing parked at the entrance, at an extraordinary speed. At last the man gets out of the wrecked car; he begins to crawl, injured, toward the fence, where all of us are watching him; slowly, grabbing onto the grass, he continues creeping. Then the official cars move in, focusing on him, the soldiers, lanterns in hand, are also encircling him, as they shine their lights on him, members of the three cordons, soldiers, judo experts, police, making a circle around him, allowing him to continue crawling. The driver almost reaches the fence now, where everyone, including me, stares at him. Finally, when his hands are already touching the wire fence, they, tightening the circle of lights, advance slowly, aiming at him. Two of them bend down and, taking him by the belt and the shirt, they lift him in the air and carry him away. He, looking at us, opens and closes his mouth, but says nothing, nothing is heard, although there is total silence in these moments . . . Nothing, nothing, there's nothing, not one sheet, not the smallest trace of a sheet, not even the last one, the one that was still unfinished in the typewriter. I turn over the drawers, the mattress, the drapes, the improvised seats, I tear down the false roof, the covering of the improvised stairway; with methodical dread the books are examined, shaken out. But nothing. Of the hundreds and hundreds of scribbled pages, not a clue remains, not a hint as to how they disappeared . . . Them, them, of course, them, you tell me, while I, giving up, stop turning over the junk. Of course they're the ones, you continue. Then they'll come to arrest me, I say. Maybe yes, maybe no, you tell me, as worried as I am, although trying to hide it, trying, even without arguments, to cheer me up, to console me. Maybe they won't come, you say. Everything was in order, I say, they didn't knock anything over. How could they have gotten in? Don't be naïve, what can't they do? They run the country, they run all of us, they know every move you make, what we say, and, maybe, even what we think. Don't you get it? That's what they've done it for: so that you'll know that they know. Don't you realize that precisely what they want is for you to realize it? for us to understand that we're in their hands, that we've got no escape? that just the way they took those papers, without anybody (not even you) finding out, they can simply eliminate you? And you'll appear strangled, hung, a suicide or dead of natural causes—a heart attack, a collapse, who knows, however they want—and the door and the room and everything will be intact, perfectly neat, in order. And maybe even a letter will appear, drawn up in your handwriting, signed by your hand, your farewell . . . He stops talking. For a moment the two of us remain stooped over the heap of overturned books. Now he takes a blank piece of paper, a random sheet, and he slowly lifts it to his lips, chewing it as if it were a blade of grass. Then you tell me, now in a very low voice: I don't think they'll come looking for you, for us. This was only a demonstration, a subtle bluff. In short, a proof of their cunning, their power, their control . . . And now, what are we going to do? I say. To play the game, you say, even lower. Listen up: to play the game or perish. Let's turn ourselves around, you say to me now in a whisper. Later, between the two of us we'll arrange everything . . . And we leave . . . That's how it was, at that point, as it had been for years, at that place, at that extreme, his hand lying on the improvised stairway, his eyes contemplating the narrow panorama, the four improvised seats, the embedded mirror (in that moment the noise of the nearest radio became intolerable), but he stayed that way, at that extreme, at that border, at that point, in that sort of unending recollection of a repetition, cautiously stooped over, looking at the panorama which stopped abruptly only two paces away: the deteriorating wall of the building alongside and the old closed door which faced the hallway where now somebody, or a group, is clamoring noisily for the elevator that never goes up. They shout and pound. But what a way of pounding on the old artifact, the skeleton, the cage, which, of course, doesn't move. Elevator! Elevator! And the pounding follows, just the same. Again, again, elevator! And the cackling, the uproar continue, everything gives signs of noise, but nothing gives signs of life . . . So, thinking, commenting in a low voice, protesting, ironizing, sometimes, very cautiously, certifying his existence only when he was outside of the room, in an open and desolated space, the Malecón, an empty street, a field, and looking, the two of them, cautiously, in all directions. Because now as his friend, his only friend, had told him, it wasn't only a matter of suffering, but of praising out loud all that was suffered, of shouting support of all the horror, not writing against it, or on the margins, but in favor, unconditionally, and to leave the sheets, as if carelessly, on the improvised table, in an evident but discreet place, in case they came in. And the two of them, in the evenings, in a natural, normal voice, not very loud, so that they weren't going to think that they were doing it facetiously (they're very clever, very clever, the other used to say), they discussed the "advantages," the "successes," the "nobility" of the system, the constant "progress." The newspaper, *Granma*, was read out loud. But not so loud, please, that they can think that we're fooling around. The premier of the latest Soviet film, *The Great Patriotic War*! (was it that one?), *A Man of Truth*! (could it be that?), *Moscow, You Are My Love*! (that?): how marvelous, how many positive aspects, a true gem . . . But no, not so loud, please, that they can suspect, that they can realize that we're fooling. *We Are Soviet Men*! Lower, lower. *They Fought for the Fatherland*! . . . Quiet, keep quiet. *The Ballad of the Russian Soldier*! Sssh. And to applaud. At the auditorium, on the corner, in the square, while we watch how they watch us with that gaze of disdain and distrust, or

with the ironic faces of braggarts, for never, never are they going
to admit to being satisfied, even when from so much pretending
you forget your true face, who you are, your role ... But now, in
this moment, when you had just gotten out of bed a few minutes
ago and were descending half-dressed down the improvised, verti-
cal stairway headed toward the improvised plumbing of that improvised hole, standing thus, hunched between the garret and the
ground floor, now, thus, suddenly, he was struck by the certainty
(once more, yes, but always renewed) that he could not make it to
the bathroom anymore (that box), nor take another step
(through that trash), rather he couldn't even move a hand from
one step to another (since whether going down or up the improvised stairway it was necessary to support oneself with one's hands,
too). So, unmoving, in that position, he was looking, not at the
past, nor the future (what was that?), he was looking at the rotting
planks, some stain (could it be humidity?) on the wall, and, at last,
suddenly, although now without being surprised, at his own face
reflected in the mirror. And an infinite inertia invaded him to the
sound of that pot (could it be the people upstairs? could it be the
people downstairs? could it be those from in front?) being
scraped furiously. And in that noise, completely undone and im-
potent, he felt that he was finally dissolving, becoming paralyzed,
disappearing, no longer feigning a defeat in order to pull himself
together later, to gain time, to go on, but rather he was simply defeated, liquidated. It was then—in this moment—that they
knocked at the door. It was he, his friend who was knocking, as he
always did and who was entering then, since naturally he had the
keys to all the padlocks. Shutting the door, he came closer to him
until he put his lips to his ear. You haven't heard yet? he said to
him. About what? People are entering the Peruvian Embassy.
They withdrew the guards since yesterday. They say the place is already full. I'm going over there. Let's go, I told him. No, you said.
Wait. They've got too much on you. I'll go first to see what's going
on. And if it's true that there's no surveillance, I'll come and get
you. Wait for me here. And he left. But he didn't remain standing
any longer on the improvised stairway. He had to do something:
to get dressed, to wait. And I waited the whole day, from noon until nearly dusk. People were running through the hall, sneaking,
trying not to make noise, something they had never tried to avoid,

even the radios were turned off. I open the door, I go down the stairway. Nobody is talking on the street, but somehow everyone seems to communicate with each other. I hurry to catch a bus headed toward the Embassy. The bus is more crowded than ever, which is difficult to imagine. Almost all of them are young. Some of them even discuss their plans openly: to enter the Embassy quickly. Before they close it. They're sure to close it any minute, says somebody beside me. The problem is to get there, the other replies. And not to leave, because not only are they making a file on anyone who leaves, but they also start kicking him and take him away to prison. And they keep talking. Now I know why you didn't return. I've been an idiot. I should have realized before that if you didn't come it was because it was impossible. And you must have thought that if you didn't return, I wasn't going to be such a shithead that I would stay in the room. Quickly, now the problem is to enter quickly. And to find you, to meet you quickly before it occurs to you to leave to look for me and they take you prisoner, if they haven't already. And everything is my fault, idiot, idiot. Quickly, quickly, since I'm sure you're waiting for me, that it hasn't occurred to you to leave, that you've thought, logically, that when you couldn't return, I would come to see what was happening . . . In droves, through the shower of rocks, the dust, and the shooting, they're entering, we're entering. All kinds of people. Some I know or at least have seen before, but now we greet each other euphorically, in a communion of mutual sincerity, never manifested before, as if we were old and dear friends. People and more people, from Santo Suarez, from Old Havana, from El Vedado, from every neighborhood, people and more people, especially young people, hopping the fence, dodging or receiving blows, running amidst the shooting and the din of the loudspeakers and the sirens of the patrol cars, entering, jumping now in a terrified parade, between kicks in the ass, shots, bodies that roll over and fall, a woman who drags a child by the arms, an old man who tries to open a path for himself with his cane. Everyone in an incredible throng, jumping over the railings, the gate, filling the gardens, the trees, even the roof of the Embassy building. So, in the immense dust cloud, between hands that push and shove, amid shrieks, threats, explosions, forming a single almost impenetrable mass, we manage still to get past the security which becomes stronger every minute, and we jump, we enter, we fall into the crowd that can hardly move, here, on the other side of the fence, surrounded already by a circle of official vehicles, and patrol cars which keeps getting thicker, Alfa Romeos, Yuguly, Volgas, the whole administrative class, the high civilian and military officials have arrived in their shiny new cars to see, to contain, to repress, to try by any means to suppress this spectacle. And, as if that weren't enough, they just blocked up the entrances of the streets that lead to the Embassy with cars and barriers, and they've dispersed, everyone knows it, thousands and thousands of soldiers in civilian clothing throughout the area to keep anyone else from reaching here. Now a motorcycle cop is braking violently in front of the military cordon surrounding the Embassy. "Sons of bitches!" he shouts at us. And he takes out his pistol. Here we all retreat as much as we can, trying to move away from the fence. The cop, pistol in hand, comes up to it. He takes a leap and falls to the other side, next to us. With great speed he takes off his uniform, wraps his pistol in it and throws the whole bundle over the fence, to the other side, where they are. Here, inside, applause is heard, shouts of "*Viva!*" The cordon that surrounds us is tripled. It begins to get dark. Here the uproar we're making reaches such dimensions that even the din and the shooting from outside can't be heard at times. "They're going to machine-gun us, they're going to machine-gun us," a woman shouts suddenly. And the mass, we, attempt to retreat anew. The trees disappear, the roof of the building disappears. Everything is no more than a moving anthill, people who clamber, people who cling, who cling even tighter to one another. Screaming. Some who fall wounded. Now there is a general panic, because somebody really is firing at us here, inside. But that's not what I continue watching or dodging. I make my way, I go back, because I have to find you; I have to locate you, to reach you, wherever you are. In the middle of this terrorized crowd, hardly able to move, and now almost completely night, I must find you, so that you'll see that I came, too, that I had the courage to make it, that I didn't stay behind, that they couldn't annihilate me—annihilate us—completely, and that here I am, here we are, trying again, anew. The two of us. *Alive*, still *alive* . . . That's why it doesn't bother me now to step on this human mass which seems to be sleeping now, here, in the very entrance of the

residence, maybe, surely, you're inside. This is the last place to
check, and here you must be, without a doubt, ill. The commission for maintaining order attempts to stop me, but I push them
aside and go on. People stretched out on the floor, old people,
women in labor, new-born babies, the sick, in short those who
need to be here, under a roof. And I go on, I go on looking for
you, opening rooms, cubicles, pavillions, or whatever the hell this
place is called. "Hey," a half-naked woman says to me now, "get
lost, the Ambassador will be furious, they've eaten up everything
including his parrot" . . . But I keep on searching all the little
compartments. I push that door where two bodies are rolling
around incredibly. I go up to them, I separate them mechanically
and look at their faces, which stare at me disconcertedly. And I
leave. "It's unbelievable," says an old man with his legs bandaged
provisionally in some rags, "to feel like screwing when we've spent
two weeks without anything to eat" . . . I leave, again I cross the sea
of people, people who are collapsing already, or who can hardly
hold themselves up, staggering, propping each other up and after
all that, when they finally pass out, they don't reach the ground,
because the ground doesn't exist. Covering the earth, the shit, the
piss, are the feet, everybody's feet, feet standing on other feet
sometimes, a single foot sometimes supporting the whole body.
So, through that immense jungle of feet that are trying to crawl
along, I crawl along. I go on, pursuing you. You're not going to escape me. You're not going to escape me. Don't think, you bitch,
that you're going to escape me. Now, less than ever. Now that nobody even pays attention to you since they can hardly look at anything, yes, now you won't escape me, and I follow, I follow behind
her, who (the clever one) is now running toward the fence, toward the outside. But I continue, day and night, scrutinizing the
faces. You could be one of them. Is it you? Will you be one of
them? Hunger makes faces change. Hunger can make our own
brothers unrecognizable. Maybe you're looking for me and you
don't recognize me. God knows how many times we may have
met, looking for one another without recognizing each other. Really, will we still be able to recognize each other? Quickly, quickly,
for with each passing moment, we'll be more disfigured, we'll be
less able to find, to discover, to recognize each other. That's why
it's best to shout. Loud. Really loud. Above those damned loud-

speakers. As loud as possible. Calling you. But how, then, if I
shout, am I going to hear when you call me? I shout, I keep quiet
for a moment, waiting for your answer and I shout again. Even
though we may not recognize one another, we have to hear each
other. To hear our names, our calls. And, finally, to identify each
other . . . So I keep advancing and shouting in the tumult which
now convulses once again. "Food, food, they're handing out
food," they shout. And again the crowd, finding energy from I
don't know where, advances toward the fence. The same rite, the
same kicking. "They're going to knock down the fence," somebody shouts. "If they knock it down we won't be on Peruvian territory anymore." But the tumult is really uncontainable. Who can
get through in the middle of that chaos? But I make an attempt, I,
too, push and hurl myself through the punches, slaps, kicks. Pushing faces and bodies which roll aside, I continue toward the far
end. Now I'm sure that I'll be able to find you, yes, you must be
there, alongside the fence, as an intelligent person like you would
logically be, ready to grab the first thing they hand out, to hear
the first thing they say, to retreat before the first danger. I should
have thought of it. Of course you have to be there. So, pushing,
kicking, biting, crawling through the web of bodies which are
crawling too, I make it to the fence, I grab onto the wire. There's
nobody who's gonna tear me away from here, shit, nobody's
gonna get me off o' here, I shout, and I begin to look at the faces
of all those who manage to reach there. But you're not among
them either, those who, risking their lives, like me, are climbing
up the wire fence. I look again and again at those desperate faces,
but none of them, I know, is yours. Bleeding hands that don't
want to let go of the wire, but they aren't yours. Defeated, I stop
looking at the fence, and I look through it, toward the outside,
where they are, fed, bathed, armed, in uniforms or plain clothes,
now preparing to "serve" us the food. And I discover you, finally I
discover you. There you are, with them, outside, uniformed and
armed. Talking, making gestures, laughing and conversing with
someone, also young, also uniformed and armed. I turn to contemplate you again while they begin, you begin, to pass out the little boxes of food. Now they (you) approach from all sides, all
along the fence. The gun in one hand, the little box in the other.
The distribution begins. The clamoring and the pushing of those

who are next to me are worse than ever. They crush me, they want to crush me, they want to stand on me to get one of those filthy boxes that they're passing out. Idiot, idiot, I say to myself while they trample me, climbing up over my body, using me as a trampoline, as an elevation, as a promontory, to raise themselves up a little and desperately stretch their hands over the fence. Idiot, idiot, I say to myself; and while they are all walking over me, standing on top of me, jumping over me, I begin to laugh wildly, as if all those feet, all those hooves covered with shit and filth were tickling me ... "This guy's gone crazy," somebody says. "Leave him alone, he could be dangerous," says another. And they start moving away getting down off my body. Outside, laughing also, they methodically distribute the boxes of food all along the fence. They stand next to it and wait for somebody to stick out his hand to stomp on it with their feet ... I could, right now, stretch out my arm and get that box. Anyway, even if I get stomped on or kicked in the chest, I won't die of hunger. But don't let them think that I'm going to give them that pleasure. Don't think I'm going to make you happy, don't let them believe, don't you believe, that I'm going to eat that shit, that filth, that swill. And much less let you step on my hand in exchange for a hard-boiled egg. For that reason, just so they won't have the pleasure, I stay this way without moving, triumphant, looking at them (at you), outside there, carting that filth back and forth. I'm looking at them this way and laughing, while desperate arms are waving over my head. Then I discover you, I see you for the first time, there, also outside, fleeing from a shiny boot, running, crawling stealthily along the asphalt, and entering, what a coincidence, here, in the riot, where we are. Here she comes, here she comes, there she goes, almost drowsy now, with hardly any energy left to keep fleeing, but still moving, beneath the bodies, over the hands and faces which barely blink when she crosses over them. She's had it now. She can't go on anymore after so many hours of trying to escape me. And now, she stops as if stunned, with her mouth open on top of somebody's shoulder, who's lying face down on the ground, trying desperately to leap somewhere ... At last I've got you, bitch, yes, now, though you're covered with filth, you've got no escape.

TRANSLATED BY ANDREW BUSH

BIOGRAPHICAL NOTES

Michael Anthony (b. 1932) was born in Mayaro, Trinidad. He is a novelist, short-story writer, and historian. His best-known works include *The Year in San Fernando* (1965), *Cricket in the Road and Other Stories* (1973), and *Sandra Street and Other Stories* (1973). In 1993 he published *The Chieftain's Carnival and Other Stories,* a collection in which all of the stories are based on significant events in Trinidad's history. Although he lived for many years in London, he returned to Trinidad to settle in 1970.

Reinaldo Arenas (1943–1990) was born in Aguas Claras, Cuba. Arenas wrote movingly of his childhood and persecution by the Cuban authorities in his memoir, *Before Night Falls* (1993). He gained international fame with his novel *El Mundo Halucinante* (1969; *Hallucinations,* 1971). His novella *Old Rosa* (1989) bears special mention. Arenas came to the United States with the Mariel boat lift of 1980. Suffering from AIDS, he committed suicide in New York City in 1990. *The Assault* (1994), a novel, was published posthumously.

Juan Bosch (b. 1909) was born in La Vega, Dominican Republic, and is the nation's best-known writer. His short-story collections include *Camino Real* (1933), *Ocho Cuentos* (1947), *Cuentos Escritos en el Exilio y Apuntes Sobre el Arte de Escribir Cuentos* (1962), and *Mas Cuentos Escritos en el Exilio* (1964). His two novels are *La Mañosa* (1936) and *El Oro y La Paz* (1964). He has also written essays, biographies, and historical works. He was elected president of the Dominican Republic in 1963 but was ousted in a military coup seven months later.

Dionne Brand (b. 1953) was born in Guayaguayare, Trinidad, and moved to Toronto in 1970. She is a poet and short-story writer; her works include *Winter Epigrams & Epigrams to Ernesto Cardenal in Defense of Claudia* (1983), *Chronicle of the Hostile Sun* (1984), and *Sans Souci and Other Stories* (1988).

Fanny Buitrago (b. 1946) was born in Barranquilla, Colombia. She published her first novel, *El Hostigante Verano de Los Dioses* (1963), at the age of 17. Other novels include *Cola de Zorro* (1970), *Los Pañamanes* (1979), *Los Amores de Afrodita* (1983), and *Señora de la Miel* (1993). An imaginary Caribbean island is the setting for her short-story collection, *Bahía Sonora, Relatos de la Isla* (1976).

Lydia Cabrera (1900–1991) was born in Havana, Cuba. Her most important works are the stories collected in *Cuentos Negros de Cuba* (1940), first published in French in 1936, and *¿Por que? Cuentos Negros de Cuba* (1948), and her seminal work on Santeria, *El Monte* (1954). Other ethnological works include *Vocabulario Congo* (1984), a dictionary of the Bantu languages spoken in Cuba, and *La Lengua Sagrada de los Ñañigos* (1988), a dictionary of the languages used in the rituals of the Abakua society. She translated Aimé Césaire's *Cahier d'un Retour au Pays Natal* into Spanish. She maintained a lifelong partnership with the Venezuelan writer Teresa de la Parra and lived for many years in Miami.

Guillermo Cabrera Infante (b. 1922) was born in Gibara, Cuba. His best-known work is the alliterative and pun-filled *Tres Tristes Tigres* (1967; *Three Trapped Tigers,* 1971). Other works include *La Habana Para un Infante Difunto* (1979), *Holy Smoke* (1986), *Writes of Passage* (1993), and *Mea Cuba* (1994). He makes his home in London.

Patrick Chamoiseau (b. 1953) was born in Martinique and is the author of *Chronique des Sept Misères* (1986), *Solibo Magnifique*

(1988), *Antan D'Enfance* (1990), and *Texaco* (1992), winner of France's prestigious Prix Goncourt and soon to be published in English by Pantheon.

Edwidge Danticat (b. 1969) was born in Haiti and came to the United States in 1981. A graduate of Barnard College and Brown University, she has published many short stories and is the recipient of numerous fiction awards. *Breath, Eyes, Memory* (1994), her first novel, has been published by Soho Press.

René Depestre (b. 1926) was born in Jacmel, Haiti, and is best known for his poetry. He was an important figure in the radical arm of the Negritude movement. As a result of his disaffection with the Duvalier regime, he spent most of his life in Cuba and was one of the founding forces behind the Cuban publishing house Casa de las Américas. Depestre's best-known works include *Un Arc-En-Ciel Pour L'Occident Chretien* (1967; *A Rainbow for the Christian West*, 1972), the novel *El Palo Ensebado* (1975; *Festival of the Greasy Pole*, 1990), and the collection of short stories *Alleluia Pour une Femme-Jardin* (1981). Depestre lives in France.

Emilio Díaz Valcárcel (b. 1929) was born in Trujillo Alto, Puerto Rico. He is a novelist and short-story writer whose works include *El Asedio y Otros Cuentos* (1958), *El Hombre que Trabajo el Lunes* (1966), *Figuraciones en el Mes de Marzo* (1972; *Schemes in the Month of March,* 1979), and *Harlem Todos los Dias* (1978). He lives in Río Piedras, Puerto Rico.

Thea Doelwijt (b. 1938) was born in Den Helder, The Netherlands, of a Surinamese father and a Dutch mother. She went to Dutch Guiana (later Suriname) in 1961 to work and remained there until 1984, when a deteriorating political situation under the military regime forced her to return to The Netherlands. She is the author of the novel *Wajono* and the plays *Land te koop* and *Ba Uzi* and is the editor of the anthology *Kri, Kra.*

Magali García Ramis (b. 1946) was born in Santurce, Puerto Rico. She worked as a journalist for *El Mundo* and *El Imparcial.* Her first story, "Todos los Domingos," won first prize in the prestigious contest of the Ateneo Puertorriqueño. She has published the short-story collection *La Familia de Todos Nosotros* (1976) and the novel *Felices Días, tio Sergio* (1986). *La Ciudad que me Habita* (1993) is a collection of essays.

Jamaica Kincaid (b. 1949) was born in St. John's, Antigua. She is a short-story writer and novelist. Many of her stories were first published in *The New Yorker*. Important works include *At the Bottom of the River* (1983), *Annie John* (1985), and *Lucy* (1990). She occasionally writes a column on horticulture for *The New Yorker*.

Claude McKay (1890–1948) was born in Sunnyville, Jamaica, and left the island in 1912. A poet, novelist and short-story writer, he is frequently linked to the Harlem Renaissance. His best known works include the novels *Home to Harlem* (1928) and *Banana Bottom* (1933), considered a West Indian classic, the short-story collection *Gingertown* (1932), and *Selected Poems* (1953).

Marcelin Brothers. Philippe Thoby-Marcelin (1904–1975), and Pierre Marcelin (b. 1908) were born in Port-au-Prince, Haiti. They collaborated on several novels, including *Canape-Vert* (1944), one of the first Haitian works of fiction to be translated into English. The English translations of the novels *Le Crayon de Dieu* (1951; *The Pencil of God,* 1952) and *Tous les Hommes sont Fous* (1970; *All Men are Mad,* 1970) contain introductions by Edmund Wilson. Their *Contes et Legendes d'Haiti* (1967; *The Singing Turtle, and Other Tales from Haiti,* 1971) are stories based on Haitian folklore and ethnology.

Seepersad Naipaul (d. 1953) was born in Trinidad. He was the father of V. S. and Shiva Naipaul. For most of his life he was a journalist with the *Trinidad Guardian*. His collection of short stories, *Gurudeva and Other Indian Tales,* was published in 1943.

V. S. Naipaul (Vidiadhar Surajprasad) (b. 1932) was born in Chaguanas, Trinidad. Naipaul emigrated to England and graduated from Oxford University in 1954. Important works include *The Mystic Masseur* (1957), *Miguel Street* (1959), *A House for Mr. Biswas* (1961), *The Mimic Men* (1967), *Guerillas* (1975), *A Bend in* *the River* (1979), *The Enigma of Arrival* (1987), and *A Way in the World: A Sequence* (1994). The often-quoted "History is built around achievement and creation, and nothing was created in the West Indies" is from Naipaul's *The Middle Passage* (1962).

Lino Novás Calvo (1905–1983) was born in Galicia, Spain, and was seven years old when his mother sent him to Cuba to live with an uncle. He was one of Cuba's most important short-story writers when he left the island in 1961 to seek asylum in the United States. Among his works are *La Luna Nona y Otros Cuentos* (1942), which includes the three stories he published in *Revista de Occidente* in 1932, and *Maneras de Contar* (1970), published in exile. He taught at Syracuse University in the sixties. His short story "La noche de Ramón Yendía," translated as "That Night," is his most widely anthologized piece.

Jean Rhys (1894–1979) was born in Roseau, Dominica. The novelist and short-story writer came to England in 1907. Her works include *The Left Bank and Other Stories* (1927), published with the help of Ford Maddox Ford; the novels *After Leaving Mr. Mackenzie* (1931), *Voyage in the Dark* (1934), *Good Morning, Midnight* (1939), and *Wide Sargasso Sea* (1966), the short-story collection *Tigers are Better-Looking* (1968), and *Smile, Please: An Unfinished Autobiography* (1979).

Luis Rafael Sánchez (b. 1936) was born in Humacao, Puerto Rico, and is best known for his novel *La Guaracha del Macho Camacho* (1976; *Macho Camacho's Beat*, 1988). Other works include the novel *La Importancia de Llamarse Daniel Santos* (1989), the short-story collection *En Cuerpo de Camisa* (1961), and the plays *O Casi el Alma* (1965) and *La Pasión Según Antígona Perez* (1968). *La Guagua Aérea* (1994) is a collection of essays.

J. M. Sanz Lajara (Jose Maria) (1917–1967) was born in the Dominican Republic. Sanz Lajara served as Dominican ambassador to Argentina in the fifties. He is the author of the short-story collection *El Candado* (1959). Other works include *Cotopaxi* (1949), *Caones* (1950), *Aconcagua* (1951), *Viv* (1961), and *Los rompidos* (1963).

Samuel Selvon (1923–1994) was born in South Trinidad and grew up in San Fernando, Trinidad. He emigrated to England in 1950 and was part of the first significant wave of Caribbean writers to seek their literary fortunes abroad. His novels include *A Brighter Sun* (1952), *The Lonely Londoners* (1956), *Moses Ascending* (1975), and *Moses Migrating* (1983). His stories are collected in *Ways of Sunlight* (1957) and *Foreday Morning: Selected Prose 1946–1986* (1989).

Ana Lydia Vega (b. 1946) was born in Santurce, Puerto Rico. Vega collaborated with Carmen Lugo Fillipi on her first published work, the stories in *Vírgenes y Mártires* (1981). *Encancaranublado y Otros Cuentos de Naufragio* (1982) won the Casa de las Américas award.

Eric Walrond (1898–1966) was born in Georgetown, British Guiana (now Guyana). His youth was spent in the Panama Canal Zone, where he learned to speak Spanish fluently. He and Claude McKay are the West Indian writers linked to the Harlem Renaissance. His most important work is the short-story collection *Tropic Death* (1926).